Critical Praise for Matthew Stokoe

High Life

"Stokoe's in-your-face prose and raw, unnerving scenes give way go a skill-
fully plotted tale that will keep readers glued to the page."
Publishers Weekly

"One of the most unstinting, imaginative, brutal and original contemporary
novels ever written about the punishments that come with the prioritization
of fame..."
Dennis Cooper

"Soaked in such graphic detail that the pages smell, Matthew Stokoe's *High
Life* is the sickest revision of the California crime novel, ever."
Paper Magazine

"...an unholy hybrid of Raymond Chandler's best work and Bret Easton
Ellis's *American Psycho.*"
Henry Flesh, Lambda Literary Award-winning author of *Massage*

Empty Mile

"Beautifully written and deeply gripping, *Empty Mile* is a great read. I'm
already looking forward to the next one from Matthew Stokoe."
Michael Connelly, author of *The Gods of Guilt*

"... heartbreakingly powerful contemporary noir..." "Stokoe stays true to
a bleak vision of the world as he enmeshes his characters in the kinds of
tragic setups reminiscent of a Thomas Hardy novel."
Publishers Weekly (starred review)

"The tension builds unbearably in this magnificent 'Sierras Noir' novel. Stokoe writes damaged people worthy of James M. Cain and Jim Thompson. His star-crossed lovers and broken families will steal your heart, even as Stokoe drives the knife home."
Denise Hamilton, author of the Eve Diamond Series

"This book has everything a good crime novel should: a suspenseful story with violence at its core, characters driven by lust, love and guilt, propelled with prose that's poetic and profound."
Carole E. Barrowman, Milwaukee Wisconsin Journal Sentinel

Cows

"If you enjoy the sensation of your jaw dropping to the floor in a combination of stupefaction, hilarity, and shock, *Cows* is your book. Matthew Stokoe has written a novel like no other I've ever read – appalling, funny, and possessed of a sense of outré violence that makes Joris-Karl Huysmans read like Louisa May Alcott."
Scott Phillips, author of *The Ice Harvest*

"… takes what the Marquis de Sade did and pushes it down the road a little farther. Stokoe is an able craftsman, which makes the content all the more horrifying as he blasts through boundaries and finds increasingly twisted ways of making readers squirm."
Publishers Weekly

"The word is out that *Cows* is every bit as dark and deranged as Iain Banks' classic *The Wasp Factory*. It's not: it's even more so. Possibly the most visceral novel ever written."
Kerrang!

HIGH LIFE

MATTHEW STOKOE

For Richard. Let this be your howl at the world.

CHAPTER 1

A hot rain blew in from the sea. It hit Ocean Avenue in sticky washes of reflected neon that took the colored light from the hotels and stores and ran it into the gutters with the trash. In Palisades Park a fat tramp stood staring down at something by his feet. The way he held his head made him look like a hanged man. He swayed slightly and I imagined a rope stretching from his neck to the sky. I pulled over, wondering if he'd found what I was looking for.

It was hard to see clearly, the sodium spill from the streetlights didn't make it very far across the corridor of parkland and the outline of the tramp's bulk was broken by the drifting shadows of hibiscus bushes. I squinted, wiped rain from my eyes and saw him stamp his foot. A shower of golden drops erupted from the ground. I relaxed – the moron was standing in a puddle, making his reflection explode.

Each time the surface settled he did it again, like he didn't want to see what was there. Maybe it was some symbolic destruction of self. Maybe he thought it looked pretty. To me it was just sad. Not because his behavior was particularly aberrant, but because it was too easy to picture myself taking that final small step out of the mainstream and into a world where puddles held secrets that could make you stand still in the rain.

I looked beyond the tramp, deeper into darkness, and saw bodies. But they were all alive, or what passed for alive on this nighttime strip of California. They lay under the shelter of trees or beneath benches, wrapped in cardboard and plastic sheeting, searching for a blank hour of rest. The longer I looked,

1

the more of them I saw – patches of shadow dissolving into cursing human forms that fought their own bones in an effort to find some impossible position of ease. Occasionally a cigarette glowed orange against the glass of a wine bottle.

These homeless people, these drunkards and junkies, these fucked-out hookers and runaway teenagers, these ex-cons and cons-in-waiting – all of them patinated with the violence of their despair – lived out entire lives on this dog-shitted margin of grass. Lived and drank and fixed and fucked here, and wondered what they might have been if things had been different.

Yeah, fuck.

A small, final step.

It doesn't take much.

I pulled away from the curb, slow-wheeling south. Wipers on interval, curtains of rain sucking up sound. The car felt safe, a padded steel cage insulating me against the city.

On my right, thirty feet below the edge of the park, Santa Monica pier stuck into the ocean like a thorn. Its burger stands were closed and the carousel was dead, but lights still burnt along its length, throwing an unpleasant nimbus of useless wattage into the wet night air.

No sign of her.

I U-turned and cut right into Santa Monica Boulevard. Stupid to expect she'd be down here on a night like this anyway.

It was late enough for the traffic to be light, sometime around three a.m. I smoked and drove one-handed through the long spaces between drifting red taillights. On either side of me buildings advertised themselves – pie houses, motels, office blocks, low-level thirties deco to millennium mirror glass. Packed close at the beach, they relaxed and stretched out somewhere past Lincoln, losing height as real estate prices fell.

Santa Monica. SaMo. User-friendly L.A. Shining malls, chichi cafes, Third Street Promenade with its ivy dinosaurs and high concept restaurants. All of it a plan for the way everyone with money wanted everywhere to be.

My eyes burned. Last night had been the same – trawling the streets, totally fucked but unable to sleep, cursing Karen and cursing myself and cursing our whole fucking life together. She'd disappeared plenty of times before, but I had a feeling about this one.

Eight days and counting. I didn't know what it meant.

But I had a feeling....

Santa Monica blurred into West L.A. – no markers, no separate identity. Too late for the Drag, business there was so desperately urgent it burnt itself out around two a.m. But there was a chance she'd try for a drunk outside one of the clubs on the Strip.

Hollywood here I come.

The dash lights glowed comfortable and orange. I wanted to believe what they said, that everything was running smooth and correct. I wanted to, but I didn't. She'd been gone too long.

I concentrated on driving and tried not to think.

The rain stopped.

Century City looked as sterile at night as it did by day – office towers and a mall and nothing human. Twenty stories up, behind the spotless glass, massive amounts of money brooded, waiting for the employees of Warner Bros. and Fox and Sony to pick up where they left off the day before and continue channeling it into footage of other people's lives. This was where the dreams of the planet's population were given life, not in the screenwriter's mind, not in the studios of Burbank or the Amblin offices over in Universal City Plaza, but in the machinery that made the green-light money available.

Dreams. The Dream Factory. Most people thought its product was a form of entertainment, maybe a pointer to fashion or lifestyle. Most people went home from the movies and said, "Wow, that was great. Man, that guy is so cool, that chick is so sexy, that house was so big, did you see that fucking car? But, shit, it's only a film...that ain't life."

But I knew better. I knew that it was, and that films were windows into reality, not distortions of it – views of the only worthwhile way to live. Everything else was a river of shit.

Movie stars gazed down from their billboards, ten times as big as anyone else, ten times as real – the only people who counted for anything. If there was a God, these were the children he loved the most.

3

I crossed into Beverly Hills. The streets were wide and quiet and lacquered with the rain's aftermath. Tall palms doubled themselves in wet reflections along the perfect edges of perfect roads, and in the gardens of flatland mansions soft lighting turned foliage gentle and friendly. No shit here, these people lived in a film.

A stretch greased past on the inside, long and polished, one of its black-glass windows down. Inside, a flawless dark-haired man spoke on a mobile, two implant-blondes pressed close. Billboard people – the colors of their clothes and bodies more intense than mine, their forms more sharply delineated in the golden cabin light. Unlike the white-trash-slope-nigger-spic masses that made up the greater part of L.A. they meant something to people other than themselves.

Money is part of the architecture of the city and mostly you learn to co-exist, blinkered in self-defense to the reality of its beauty. But there are times when it won't be ignored, when it rears up and pushes itself forward and makes damn sure you haven't forgotten that it's all still there – a passport, a reward, a validation that some people, certain people, can just reach out and pick up.

And as I watched the limo, as I watched its taillights slide deep into the night ahead, full of mystery and purpose, all I wanted in the world was to be inside it with those people, gliding to whatever marble-lined, sea-front palace they were headed for. To be their equal, to own a similar or greater amount of possessions.

To live life as it should be lived.

But I was a thousand light-years away.

So....

Cut north on Fairfax, right at Sunset, and head on into the Strip.

They say it was better in the seventies, but I was five years old and somewhere else.

Flashy fronting, famous names in light bulbs – The Roxy, The Viper Room, Whiskey a Go Go. A place where Johnny Depp and Dan Aykroyd and plenty of others made a hobby of playing host to a tight community of friends. A place for River Phoenix to die and for plaid-jacketed, out-of-state conventioneers to get ripped and score some pussy. Karen had milked it for plenty in her time. Whoring in front of tourist attractions worked – the punters had money to spend and an excuse for being away from home.

Outside entrances to clubs, dissolute knots of temporary Californians tried to argue their way past doormen for a last drink, or stood around thinking of home and waiting for cabs. The earlier rain had killed whatever action there might have been at the ass end of this midweek night and the street was pretty much deserted. If sex was selling at all, it was doing agency business – phone calls and taxi rides to hotel rooms and private houses.

I carried on, took Fairfax north and the most famous street in the world east – Hollywood Boulevard.

When the stars were still black-and-white it must have been clean and relaxed and bursting with its own desirability. Coleman and Flynn and Crawford and all the others had made America a hit with the world, and the crowds clamoring outside the Chinese Theater to see them participated in this success by proxy. Back then, the country was a place where anything that wasn't American wasn't good enough, and where individual achievement reflected on the entire population.

Pre-dawn in the last quarter of the nineties, the boulevard was a flashing, anxiety-ridden nightmare. The restaurants that once captured the nation's imagination as backdrops for celebrity trysts had long ago made way for T-shirt stores and sunglasses emporiums. The hand prints had spit in them and the brass stars were spotted with gum. And if success was ever rash enough to take a trip down from the hills, the industry made sure it was too well armored to ever share itself around.

But it was still Hollywood Boulevard. Still the draw card, the iceberg tip of the Californian legend that shone out to small towns across the world, ruining whatever complacency they had won from the past with the notion that there was, without doubt, somewhere more exciting to live.

Sometimes Karen came here to score or to hang out. Or to look for rich out-of-towners to sugar-daddify for a couple of days. But it was too late and too dangerous now. I should have started searching hours ago, but the ocean had kept me – I'd had a feeling she'd turn up in one of the picnic huts on Venice Beach, spliffing and drinking with whoever she could find to keep her company. Now I felt stupid for wasting my time.

The Drag wasn't far from the boulevard, I could have checked it on the off chance, but I'd had enough. Karen would have to haul her ass home from wherever it was herself.

The drive back to Santa Monica was blank. My eyes felt charred and the cigarettes had eaten into my throat. I bought a cold coke from a machine outside a motel and chugged it till my eyes watered. Coke and damp night air, and the slowed pulse of the city around me. For that moment, for that snap-shot, micron-thin slice of time, I was free of the past, free even of the present – just the sweet caustic singe in my mouth and the loose quietness of being up and alone when most other people were asleep.

Five minutes later, back on the road, the sugar and caffeine kicked in and perked me up a little. But there was nothing to look at, so I ran Calvin Klein perfume commercials in my head.

Around Franklin I started taking notice of things again. Santa Monica Boulevard was clear down its last long sweep to the ocean and I was glad not to have the hassle of dealing with other drivers.

My back ached, I pressed it into the seat. The upholstery felt good against my shoulders. The wheel felt good in my hands. Honda Prelude, five years old, low mileage, not a scratch. Not a Porsche, but I wasn't complaining. I was lucky to have a car at all.

A month back, after my uninsured Ford had been stolen, my only chance of getting back into the personal transport loop had been the bus, double shifts, and the hope I'd get enough cash together before the hours or some crazy on the back seat killed me. Karen could have kicked in, but I didn't ask her. By then we were way past the stage where she contributed to community property – everything she got hooking went on drugs and partying. Besides, a car didn't mean much to her, she didn't have a license.

Turned out, though, I'd written her off too soon. Turned out she felt the need to indulge in a single, inexplicable, act of generosity.

Ocean Avenue, an hour before dawn. Inland, a runtish light was starting to seep into the sky, outlining a few of the clouds that had brought last night's rain. Too late for sleep now. I figured, check the park again and maybe the beach below it, then back to Venice for a shower and something chemical before go-time at Donut Haven.

But it didn't work out like that.

As I was passing the camera obscura I heard a siren. A couple of seconds later a paramedic vehicle pumped by on the inside in a sudden compression of light and sound. It hung level for a few yards then cut into my lane and pulled ahead.

There was no reason for this ambulance to mean anything more to me than the hundreds of others I'd seen since I arrived in the city, but after it gained a quarter-mile and I saw where it was headed, I had a bad feeling I wasn't going to be able to dismiss it as part of someone else's horror.

Activity on the edge of the park, about opposite where San Vicente cuts off inland. A couple of police cars were already there, turning the street into a movie set with their roof lights. Dark shapes of people moved around, silhouetted against the blue and red glare. The foliage back from the street rippled under the sweeping colors like there was a high wind blowing through it.

The paramedics slowed, curved across the oncoming lanes, parked next to the cops and added their lights to the rest.

I had an urge to turn around, to head home and escape knowing what it was that had brought this group of emergency vehicles together on a parkland bluff at the western edge of a country of 300 million people. But I didn't. I had to know if they'd found what I'd been looking for all night.

I left the Prelude a little way north of the commotion and walked back.

This was the shitty end of the park, where the tramps came to dump and screw – a ravined and collapsing patch of dirt without sidewalk that sloped toward the cliffs in a shallow network of gullies and depressions. There weren't many trees, but low bushes grew densely over much of the area, nourished by scraps of junk food and the droppings of withered bowels.

A small crowd of early-morning joggers and rejects from the park had gathered along the roadside and were craning their necks, trying to see into a gully that ran from the edge of the road, back into the park about five feet below ground level. They weren't having much luck. The police had the scene locked down. They'd run a horseshoe of yellow tape around the gully and strung sheets of blue plastic between a couple of bushes to block the view from the street. Going for a side angle further up or down Ocean Avenue wasn't much use either. The depth of the gully and the bushes that grew along both sides of it made viewing pleasure an impossibility.

Flashlight beams flitted about behind the plastic sheeting, throwing the shadows of cops against it – hunched shoulders, hands rising and falling with cigarettes. Whatever had dragged them here at this hour was probably lying at their feet and, as the paramedics were sitting on the step at the back of their van drinking coffee from a flask, it was probably also dead.

I stood for a while with the other people, listening to conversations, hoping for information. Nobody knew what had happened, but they all knew what that yellow tape meant. And they knew if they waited long enough something would come out in a bag. But that was no good to me. I wouldn't be able to see the face.

The alternative was simple enough. The cops had a couple of men making sure no one got too inquisitive, but they were only guarding the street edge of the scene. So.... A quick walk twenty yards south, cut into the brush and circle back deep enough into the park to hit the gully somewhere on the other side of the plastic sheeting. It took a while because I had to crawl in a lot of places to keep my head below shrub level, and because I had to concentrate on avoiding turds. But I made it eventually, right up to the tape, the last ten yards on my belly. I got a good view through a gap between two bushes.

The gully had been reinforced with concrete to make a trough for a storm drain outlet. A shallow stream of water spilled from the mouth of a large pipe and made rills around the shoes of four cops who were standing in a group telling jokes. All of them were in uniform and didn't seem too bothered about the thing on the ground. I figured they were killing time until the detectives showed.

The thing on the ground....

It was much worse than I'd expected.

I lay there and watched the water wash against it for a while, then I inched back the way I'd come.

Away from where my dead wife lay.

Back on the street. The leaves in the park went copper-red as the sun rose, and the sky started moving through a spectrum of pastels toward its daily trademark blue. The policemen were still telling jokes and their laughter carried well on the warming air. It came in snorts, like animals grunting.

I drove to Venice as the world woke up.

The picture in my head was pornographic in detail.

Chapter 2

Speedway runs parallel to Ocean Front Walk, one block back. The beachfront buildings are several stories high and the only time you can see the ocean is when you pass a cross street. Further back, the houses and apartment blocks are funkily shabby and sun-bleached and dusted with salt. It isn't a ghetto, but you don't see too many photo shoots from *Architectural Digest* setting up.

Venice has a reputation for being wacky and fun and full of counter-culture freaks. But like Sunset Strip and Hollywood Boulevard a lot of this is just PR to drag the tourists in. What Venice really is, is a lot of different places. Bohemia for artists, rich pickings for the renovation-mad people they used to call yuppies, a place of sandy roots for the old folks who've been there forever, a carefully dressed-down place to have a pad if you're on the way to celebrity. And it's cool to watch the women rollerblading on the weekends.

For me, when I moved there, it had had the scent of possibility, of potential. The colors – the blue ocean, the white walls and red roof tiles – the soft air, the unexpected lushness of the vegetation, all that space on your doorstep stretching out across the water to China, had all been ingredients I'd mixed into a metaphor for my future. Optimism, bright light, movement, success.

I'd lived there two years and all of it had been unhappy.

I parked the car between two garbage dumpsters and just sat – windows tight, engine off. I felt zoned, separated from all human babble and activity. A riot could have broken out around me and I wouldn't have seen it. The only thing I was looking at right then was what had been in the park.

I'd recognized Karen instantly, though of course she'd been very much changed.

Faceup, laid out as heavy and awkward as all the corpses on TV. I'd always imagined a real dead body would impact on the senses more violently than the slumped and spattered actors in cop shows. But Karen had seemed robbed of color, even of some amount of substance, compared to those nightly small-screen copyings.

She was naked, too, sports fans. Legs spread, one arm crossing her chest below her breasts, the other flung straight out to the side. Her eyes were closed, but her belly was open – sliced from sternum, through navel, to a couple of inches above her pubic bone, then T'ed there with a horizontal stroke to make flaps of her abdominal wall. It looked like the left flap had had a piece cut out of it.

I stayed in the car a long time trying to work out how I felt. In the end I gave up, my ambivalence was insurmountable. Instead, I thought about how easy it must have been to dump her – just pull up, open the door and give her a shove. She'd disappear from view immediately. And how she must have looked as she fell, her legs falling loosely apart.

After that, I figured I should hold a picture of her face in my mind – it seemed to be what people on TV did when they'd just lost someone. But the only picture that came to me was of water running between her legs, out over the wet concrete of the drain.

The apartment was the apartment. As it always was. Second floor in a poorly stuccoed fifties block. One room with a bed and a couch, kitchen and bathroom off it.

The place smelled stale. I could have opened a window for air, but that would have meant letting the world in, and this was one Venice morning when I needed to shut it down.

I fired up the VCR and ran last night's edition of *28 FPS*, a weekly late-night movie-gossip show, pumped out by a small cable station. The presenter was a punky blond chick called Lorn. She didn't care much about the actual movies people made, but she went all out for the people themselves – the actors, directors, producers, anyone rich and connected in the industry.

Relationships, money, houses, cars, practices and preferences, addictions and detoxifications – she was jacked on all of it. I never missed a show.

Robert Downey Jr. was having hassles over drugs and guns and Don Johnson had broken his ankle. On a lighter note, Ray Liotta and Michele Grace were engaged, Mickey Rourke and Carré Otis had been spotted looking totally cool in New York and Goldie Hawn was in London for the premiere of *The First Wives Club*. At Heathrow Airport she wore a cute black see-through number that gave a fetching glimpse of her nipples. Back in L.A. at House of Blues, Noah Wyle and Anthony Edwards were hanging out at some MTV gig. Anna Nicole Smith was writing the story of her life and George Clooney had gotten pissed off over intrusive TV journalism.

The tape finished. I wanted to run another one, but I couldn't concentrate – thoughts were starting to break through.

My wife of a year was dead and I hadn't told the police she was mine. Anyone else would have burst through that tape shouting incoherently about wife and relationship and OH MY GOD....

But not me.

And it wasn't like I could brush it off with the knowledge that they would be coming around to the apartment anyhow. Because they wouldn't.

She hadn't used her married name since the novelty of it wore off a few weeks after the ceremony, and she'd never converted any of her ID to my name or address. And getting a make on her from someone around where she was found was unlikely, no one knew her in Santa Monica – she hung out almost exclusively in West L.A. and Hollywood. Even if they did find someone who recognized her, the chance of me being located was still almost zero. We lived separate lives, she never brought her friends back to the apartment. As far as the world at large was concerned, there was very little connection between us. And anyhow, what was one more dead whore to Los Angeles?

We met in a bar. I'd been in L.A. about a year and I wasn't making much of a success of it. Beyond evening courses in telehosting, held in small private sound stages whose only business was evening courses, I hadn't integrated. I knew how to hold my head so shadows didn't form in my eye sockets, I could read an autocue and I could keep a smile in place. I could project that flawless, unflagging vitality so important to holding an audience. But plugging myself into the city just wasn't happening and my contact with the general population didn't rise much above sitting on a stool in a bar with a beer in front me.

I'd come west shackled with the usual dream of making a lot of money fast then spending the rest of my life in the sun enjoying it. But it hadn't happened. In the absence of being mythically rags-to-riches discovered by some part of the media industry, an unskilled thirty-year-old tends to be channeled toward the dish washing end of things. And I didn't get discovered.

So I got a job at Donut Haven. It meant I could survive. But even by the time I met Karen, after I'd been a doughboy for almost a year, I didn't have a pot to piss in. My only financial achievement was that I'd stayed out of East L.A.

She'd been working, that night. I'd never been with a hooker, but I said yeah when she stumbled against me and slurred that I could do her if I had the cash. Why not? After a certain point, city depression makes almost any offer of physical contact attractive. We went to my place and when it was over she stayed the night. She didn't have a place of her own.

Karen was a short skinny blonde who lived on the streets, a twenty-two-year-old with a collection of borderline addictions. When she didn't have a trick she slept in all-night theaters or under a bench in the park. She smelt so bad that first time I had to make her take a shower. It was pretty obvious she was on a downhill run.

I needed company. And Karen needed a place to put the brakes on and get herself together if she was going to see her next birthday. I guess I just saw my chance and took it. But then, so did she. I paid her a few more times, then asked her to move in. She didn't hesitate.

The first month and a half was great. She stopped hooking, we went places, I started living interactively. L.A. became a place I could call home, instead of a wasteland of envy. Karen scaled down her drug use and regained her health. Each of us got plenty out of the other, a situation we fooled ourselves into calling love. And, to put a tightener on it, one deluded weekend we got married. Something Karen looked embarrassed about the next day and would only rarely admit had happened.

She made a mission of avoiding her present, but her past was even more thoroughly sealed. The only thing of any personal weight I learned about her in our year together was that her father had been a cop and that she'd run away from home when she was fifteen and never gone back.

Maybe it was something in this shitty past, some need for attention, that made her start hooking again. More likely it was just that I was not a rich enough vein of disposable income.

It was a bad time, it was the beginning of the end, it happened early in our marriage and it didn't stop. If she'd been all one thing, if she'd been slutishly callous in her pursuit of her preferred lifestyle, maybe I could have called an end to it and walked. But along with all the absences and the fucking of other men, she still talked about love, still said she wanted to stay with me.

Most of me knew she just wanted to have her cake and eat it – screw for her money, get stoned, hang out, and at the end of it all come home to some sucker who'd provide a domestic recharge situation. But there was another part of me that so desperately wanted the whole couple thing that I couldn't rid myself of the idea everything would come right in the end.

It wasn't easy, though, this attempt to hang on. The first few times she came home from a gig it was all I could do not to hit her. I'd wait up, stupidly hoping she'd fall into my arms and tell me how glad she was to be back. But what usually happened was she'd walk straight to the shower and wash. So I'd follow her in and watch her undress, see the dried come on her belly like shiny, flaking scars and think I was going to puke.

Eventually, though, I got numbed to it. I grew an insect shell over my boiling sadness and I stopped waiting up. It wasn't that the pain was any less real, it was just that I didn't have the energy to keep confronting it so actively. For a while I conned myself into thinking I could separate things, that I could section off the Karen who went out and sucked cock from the part-time wife who still declared an interest in me.

But that state of self-induced stupidity didn't last. It might have been possible to maintain, perhaps, if things had stayed low-level, but she increased the pressure – escalating her whoring from the odd daytime stint to regular week nights, then on to sleepovers and more. She mentioned a doctor, a policeman....

Toward the end she was disappearing for a week or two at a time without warning. And I, of course, was self-destructing with a rage that had gone beyond jealousy into the realm of hate and self-loathing. Through it all she kept telling me she hadn't stopped caring, that she owed her life to me for pulling her out of the gutter. But by then I was too far gone to believe it.

When she went missing eight days ago, I'd had a feeling something more than the usual call-out might be involved, something a lot more illegal and a lot more dangerous. But I didn't call the police. I went searching for her eventually, but that was out of guilt, not love.

Now I'd found her and death, that ultimate clarifier, hadn't done a thing to change the way I felt. Her corpse could have been made of rubber for all the emotion it evoked in me.

And it was this unveiling of the crushing pointlessness of our time together that had stopped me from announcing our connection to the police. I just didn't care enough anymore to put up with the hassle it would bring.

Eight days ago.

She'd come home late-night after a two-week absence and she didn't look good. Her skin had gone beyond its usual gothic paleness to pallor, she'd lost weight and her hair was dull. Nevertheless there was a jagged energy about her, like she was a kid at a party about to give the best present, but to someone she didn't really like. And basically that's what she did, took me outside and gave me a present – the Prelude.

I knew by the look on her face she wanted me to be pleased and, shit, I wasn't going to kick about being given a car, but the gift confused me. I said all the right things, though, the things she obviously wanted to hear, and we took it for a spin to Santa Monica. All the way, I couldn't stop trying to figure out what particular variation of sexual commerce had been necessary to get that kind of money together in two weeks.

Back in the apartment she sprawled on the couch, legs apart, leather mini riding up. I started to ask questions, but she drew me down. I wanted to pull back and hassle her, or at least grasp after dignity by firing off something like, "I wouldn't defile my cock in your semen-soaked guts." But I hadn't had sex for two weeks and the feel and the smell of her was too much. I kissed her breasts through the cotton of her singlet and slid my hand between her legs. She used to moan when I did this, but now she was quiet, waiting for something. So what? I carried on, pulled her briefs off, pushed up her skirt and rammed myself into her. I tried to ignore how distant she felt, after all I wasn't expecting a valid emotional exchange. I just wanted to unload. Dealing with the emptiness that would come later was something I was used to.

But then I reached up under her skirt to get a better grip and the palm of my hand brushed against something that shouldn't have been there. A swollen ridge, spiky along the top. It stopped me dead. I jerked out and had a look. Karen watched me closely.

"What happened?"

"It's where cars come from."

A twelve inch horizontal scar curving from the left of her belly to her back, between hip and ribs, puckered and purple and still cinched with half-embedded loops of shiny black surgical thread. It made me think of *The Fly*, the remake with Jeff Goldblum, where some kind of obscene bristle things start growing out of his back.

But this wasn't a film, it wasn't even happening in Beverly Hills. This disfigurement had none of those ameliorations. It was stark and brutal and she'd wanted me to see it.

"What do you mean?"

"I sold my kidney."

"Huh?"

"I sold one of my kidneys. Don't look at me like that, they do it all the time in India."

"I don't understand. How can you sell a kidney?"

"You've got two of them."

"I mean, who buys them?"

"A doctor."

"*The* doctor?"

"Yeah, the doctor."

The latest client getting the sleepover treatment. Someone she'd been seeing more and more of over the last few months.

"You sold your kidney to a trick? This is like, some kind of extreme
BDSM thing, right?"

"I knew you'd be a prick about it."

"Well, Jesus, don't you have any self-respect?"

"Shut the fuck up, okay? It's my body, my kidney. Like it's my pussy. For
thirty grand I wasn't going to say no."

That froze me and for a moment I couldn't think of anything to say.
On one hand, selling an organ was a bizarre thing to do, but on the other it
wasn't. Not in L.A. Not for someone like Karen. Thirty thousand dollars is,
after all, a lot of money.

"What did he want it for? What do you do with a kidney?"

"I don't know, give it to a hospital. Who cares? You want a blast?"

As she reached into the pocket of her jacket I noticed she was wearing a
gold bracelet I hadn't seen before. It had a lot of filigree engraving on it and
looked antique.

"My, that's pretty."

"A get-well from the doc."

"Very nice."

She sighed tiredly. "Do you want a hit or not?"

Karen didn't own the usual glass tube with kitchen scourer stuffed down
the middle. Too easy to start carrying around and, like ID, too much of a
giveaway if she got busted hooking. Instead she made her own pipe.

Foil stretched and held with a rubber band across a glass of water three-
quarters full, a small oval of needle perforations on one side of the circle, a
half-inch slit on the other. Pile up cigarette ash and a piece of crack. Then
burn that sexy little volcano with a disposable lighter and suck pure white
smoke straight into your head.

When she couldn't hold anymore she handed it over. I fresh-ashed and
reloaded. Cool smoke going in, dead mouth, lungs stretched to burst, let a
little out and suck in even more. Dab the coal out with a pearl of spit. And
hold, and hold....

And then breathe out, nice and slow. Curl up, close eyes. Nothing exists. Only you, floating in some totally painless void. Better than smack, better than love. An adorable distant nausea. Given the choice, you'd choose this over any sensation in the world.

Ten minutes max, that's all you get before you hit earth and find nothing changed. Guts knotted, jaws clenching, anxiety riding in steel-shod. Not the best condition to be in to deal with tales of kidney excision.

We didn't talk anymore right away, we knew we were too fritzed to do it safely. So we bounced around the room instead. Stand, sit, stand again. TV on and off. Booze from the fridge. Meaningless surface babble.

Then an explosion of sex, a few minutes escape from cocaine revenge. Bent over the table, stabbing it in from behind, both of us grunting like animals. The faint shitty smell of her ass on the air. When we'd finished we weren't any closer than we'd ever been.

She lay on the bed, naked from the waist down, and there was something about her unconcerned positioning that right then, to me, was a fresh and unbearable reiteration of just how little I meant to her. She seemed to be screaming that she didn't care anymore how I saw her, that maintaining some measure of grace in my presence was no longer worth the effort it took.

Jitters of anger were already running up my arms as I started to speak, but I got a whole lot angrier thirty seconds later.

"That car's the first thing you've given me."

"I know."

"Making up for lost time?"

She rolled off the bed and pulled on her briefs.

"It's a thank-you, Jack. And a goodbye. I'm leaving."

"What?"

"We're quits. I've got some money now, I can move on. Living like this isn't good for either of us."

"I don't believe this."

"I like hanging out, getting stoned. I like fucking for money. It's real. You live in this bullshit movie-star fantasy world. We don't connect."

Around me the world seemed to slip sideways and all the things in the room looked suddenly flat and sharply defined, like high-resolution photos of themselves that were too intensely concentrated to recognize. I stood in a synaptic freeze and catalogued my idiocy.

I'd dragged her back from the edge of narcotic self-destruction, I'd given her a place to live, I'd fed her and clothed her. And all through her whoring, the year of lying awake nights imagining those endless insertions, I'd hung in there, figuring that someday it had to end and that when it did I'd come out of it safely locked into a partner for the rest of my life.

Maybe it was because she was leaving just when she'd gotten some money, maybe it was the coke in my system. I don't know. Maybe it was just the fear of being abandoned. Whatever, when I routed back into the flow I kind of lost control and hit her.

She shrieked at me and I shrieked back, we grabbed each other and lurched around the room, and out of anger and desperation I hit her some more. It wasn't a pleasant scene, in fact it was very, very bad, and it ended with her running out of the apartment, bleeding from the mouth. I didn't try to stop her.

"You can keep the fucking car."

It was the last thing she said.

I stood in the middle of the suddenly silent room, under an unshaded bulb that was too bright. Night air came in through the open door and something by my feet moved in the breeze. I picked it up – a crumpled piece of paper that had my name on it – the pink slip for the car. It made me feel pretty bad.

Chapter 3

I checked the clock. Already too late for work. Tough. I wasn't going, I had an excuse – a death in the family.

A death. Her death.

How far did she make it? How much time passed between our fight and the carving of her belly? Maybe she got it straight away, hacked up just half an hour after she stormed out into the night. But the body in the park hadn't looked eight days old.

If she'd been killed sometime last night and the police did find me, things could get difficult – I had no way to prove where I'd been after I left work.

My pill supply was in the icebox – a biscuit jar full of blister packs and brown plastic vials Karen had accepted as payment a month or two back for taking a shit in front of a room full of doctors up from San Diego on a stag night. They were all downers of one kind or another and they were all past their use-by date. But they still worked just fine. I swallowed 20mg of Valium and thought about phoning Donut Haven. Explaining why I wasn't there seemed like such a hassle, though – better to sit with a beer in front of morning TV and wait for the benzodiazepine haze to wrap me up. Then just drift....

Scenes in the park. Scenes of her leaving the apartment. A question of consequences, of meaning, of how I felt. Would she have ended up dead if I hadn't exploded? I guess I had to assume some responsibility – but I was only a link in the chain. I forced her out of the apartment and sometime later she died. But I forced her out because of the things she'd done, and she, in her turn, had done those things in response to a lifetime of earlier events, back down the line to childhood. In the grand scheme of things, I don't suppose either of us was entirely at fault. But we both played parts and each part carried its measure of guilt.

And beyond this vaguely apportioned blame, the issue of grief. Slumped on a couch in a furnished room while the day stoked its furnaces outside and bustling, self-improving Californians carelessly let snatches of their conversation and laughter float up to me, I can't say grief was paramount in my emotions. There was shock at violent death, of course, and there was my own fear of being alone and adrift in the city again. But a devastating sense of loss? No.

There was relief, though. It sounds foul to say, but it was there – an obscene voice of truth shouting that the unmanning was over, that the nights spent waiting for the sound of her feet on the steps outside the apartment were finally at an end. The hideous compromise I'd had to make to hang on to a soulless and incomplete replica of a relationship was finished. There was certainly an element of relief.

But as much as I wanted to bathe in this traitorously comforting emotion, Karen's last gesture made it impossible to avoid an artesian seepage of self-reproach. If she had been all bad, it would have been easier. But putting the car in my name raised doubts about the completeness of her cold-heartedness and, by extension, any justification I might unearth for my violence.

I tried to force something more definable out of myself, a few tears or a sob. The best I could manage was an anemic self-pity just before the pills kicked in and made manufacturing emotion redundant.

Next morning I woke in a post-Valium languor and found that I was changed. I'd had to hit the pill jar a second time around ten p.m., but that had seen me through. One whole day gone AWOL, twenty-four hours that had been unable to find purchase upon me. Time during which my head had finally let go of those ideas that had been steadily bleeding themselves dry through all my time in Los Angeles – the notion of what ought to be done, what ought to be felt.

I hadn't pulled the blinds and the sun lay across the room like a brand. Cali sunshine – envy of the world, a go-get-em flux of ocean, brand-new cars, money, and a channeled energy generated by millions of western seaboarders who were so damn sure they were going to make it. I felt like rolling around in it like a dog, trying to rub it into my coat so I smelled the same way.

I lit a cigarette and went to the fridge. Out back, across the street, a girl was sitting on a balcony. I was naked and she could see me through the kitchen window, but I didn't care. I looked at her sitting there in her high-cut swimsuit and sunglasses. She had arms and legs and a face, and her pussy was probably getting a little sticky in the heat. But trying to invest that collection with anything approaching personality or significance seemed like the biggest waste of time. After a moment it became impossible to distinguish her from the bricks and the peeling iron railing that surrounded her.

I went back to bed with a couple of beers. Outside, people would be blading along the edge of the beach, sitting in open cafes drinking juice and fresh coffee, sunning up and hanging out. Fuck 'em. This morning, California and all its manic enthusiasms could slide into the ocean for all I cared.

At one time I'd bought full-scale into that same sunny optimism. I'd figured as long as you got a job, worked hard at it and didn't cross the police, you had a chance at some sort of a life. A chance at a decent relationship, a house in a nice place, a car, the occasional holiday.... Not a big life, perhaps, nothing of movie-star incandescence, but one that at least offered a measure of protection against the world's cold winds – an entry-level prize for playing inside the rules.

But that was gone forever now. Last night, while my drugged blood went endlessly round and round, the last reactionary part of me had finally accepted a truth that had been screaming itself hoarse all my adult life: that chances didn't exist, that they'd all been used up by people who made it into movies or onto TV.

I fired up the VCR and loaded one of my perfume commercial tapes. Ads for high quality cosmetics are some of the best pointers to a proper life. The people in them are perfect – you can tell just by looking at them. Their bodies are desirable, they wear the most expensive clothes, and they don't even think about money. They live in a world where problems are dealt with by other people, where it is impossible to doubt yourself, and where no one can see you without loving you and wanting to be like you.

The Obsession series was very good, but my favorite on this tape was a Sun and Moon and Stars clip with Daryl Hannah – dreamy soft focus, floating through the universe, free of worry about anything that might happen back in the world. You couldn't beat it, a Hollywood star playing what she really was – a goddess.

I didn't get out of bed all day. I wanted to sleep some more, but I'd already had too much, so I read the gossips and watched the episode of 28 FPS again. Lorn looked good in a white tennis skirt and a sleeveless top that showed glimpses of the sides of her breasts. Once when she was bending over I thought I saw one of her nipples. I couldn't stop thinking about it.

About ten that night Rex came around. He was zipped on coke and all finger-snapping, joint-popping energy. He was wearing a long, lightweight cashmere coat over a casual silk-blend suit and he smelled like an expensive clothes store. The feel of the fabric when he hugged me was comforting and clean.

Rex made his money fucking. Blond hair, white teeth, slim and sexy. At first glance a boy with everything Californian. But his skin was pale and the blue eyes didn't really do that "have a nice day" thing. When you paid attention, when you didn't just skim the surface, it wasn't hard to believe the history of suicide attempts he liked to trot out whenever he got the chance.

Karen had brought him home one night after they'd connected in a shared role on a porn flick. It was just work to them and they were never going to be friends, but he and I had hit it off well enough to generate one of those satellite relationships that exist only within certain parameters – always at my apartment, always when Karen wasn't there. We didn't go out together, didn't buddy up for a ball game or sink brews on a standing Friday night bar date, but it was still friendship of a sort.

He threw himself down on the couch.

"Whew, man, I'm flying. Called in today, you weren't there. Wanted some donut action. Needed that sugar. Well, didn't need it, I guess, but I wanted it, man. I wanted it."

Rex took a breath and ran his hand over his face. I dug some pills out of my pocket. Rex shook his head.

"What happened with work? It's not like you."

I swallowed a Valium and told him Karen was dead, that she was found in the park murdered.

He was glitteringly aghast, his mouth open and his white teeth shining. He shifted quickly to where I was sitting on the bed and put his arm around me. He held me close and I was tempted to interpret it as genuine commiseration. In a way it was. I'm sure he felt sadness at what he perceived to be my loss – sadness for me, sadness that someone he knew was dead. But at the same time I couldn't rid myself of the suspicion that what he was really plugged into was a resonance between the loss he imagined me to feel and his own black void of unhappiness.

"Wow, man.... I don't know what to say. I mean, Jesus...."

"It's not like it wasn't going to happen someday."

"Sure, sure. But it brings it home, dude, it brings it home."

"Mortality?"

"How everything fucks up. How *we* fuck up everything."

He was silent for a moment, then: "What happened? I mean, can you talk about it? Is it too soon?"

"You know how we were. I can't tell you I'm dying inside."

"But it's something to assimilate. It's something to come to terms with."

At this point I was pretty certain I was right, that Rex was all set to use this situation as a windfall opportunity. He was after a little transposition. He wanted to project his own pain onto the backdrop of Karen's death and watch it play. But that wasn't going to work for me. Too complicated. He was going to expect me to be intensely genuine and introspective, and I wasn't going to be able to explain to him how the death of someone could feel so...peripheral.

"You know, maybe it *is* too soon."

"Oh.... Okay. Sure."

He looked robbed and for a moment I could see into him, see the horrible twisting beast he had to struggle with each day, and absurdly I felt guilty about not giving him what he wanted.

"They found her in the park a couple of days ago. Before it happened she sold her kidney. Maybe that had something to do with it."

"Sold her kidney? Like....*sold her kidney?*"

Rex couldn't help a quick snort of laughter.

"Now that's what I call hooking."

He caught himself, was immediately concerned and shocked again.

"Sorry, man, too much blow. God, that's terrible. But I can dig it. Sometimes you feel so disgusting you want to have part of yourself cut out. I mean, you know what I'm talking about, right?"

"She just wanted the money."

"Nah. It might not have been conscious, but she was making a statement. She was saying how ruined she was, paying for being bad."

This looked like a long road to travel and I started to feel a little less guilty. I got up and took a few steps around the room so I didn't have to answer.

"Still, she's got to be better off now, huh?"

"Oh, please...."

"Come on, you think this is all there is?"

"Pretty much."

"You don't think there's some kind of...continuation?"

"If you get on TV."

"Hey, it's your night, but...."

He looked down and busied himself with a vial of coke. We charged up and I talked a little faster.

"I mean it. Only half a dozen people remember my father, right? It's like he never existed. But someone like Dean Martin, say, is still here. It doesn't matter if he's dead, he's still in his records and his movies. That's life after death. That's as close as you get."

"I wonder if Jerry sees it that way."

"Of course he does. Same thing's going to happen to him."

Rex nodded like he was taking this in, but I knew he thought it was a pile of shit. After a moment he cleared his throat and stood up.

"Got a gig, dude. You want another hit?"

I felt a quick fizz of affection for him because I knew he wanted to argue with me but was holding back, despite the coke.

Another snort and he split to service the wife of a director who was shooting nights over at Warner Bros. We hugged at the door. I heard his Porsche start down on the street and the breathy clatter of its engine turned the salty night air hollow.

The sound died quickly as he turned a corner somewhere out in the city, and with it went the illusion of his company. He'd been there in my apartment and he'd heard about Karen, but it hadn't gone very deep. Where were the questions about my long night being grilled down at headquarters, about the arrangements I'd made for her funeral, about all the other things that also hadn't happened?

The truth was, I guessed, that his capacity for caring had already been pretty much exhausted by the demands of his own depression.

Later, I walked around to an all-night Korean store for beer and food. On Main the restaurants glowed with indirect lighting – smooth interiors full of happy people spending money, drinking good wine, making plans for the future. Parked cars down both sides of the street looked shiny, looked like they belonged in three-car garages surrounded by exotically stocked gardens. It all made me feel outnumbered and vulnerable.

Back in bed. I stared at the ceiling for a while then dialed a twenty-four-hour shoot location service – recorded info on where in Los Angeles current productions would be filming over the next week. The trades reported an exodus of film-making from the Hollywood teat, out to places like Seattle and Canada, even to Fox Australia. But it was still easy to find several shoots a week within driving distance. A lot of these were TV cop/action series, or straight-to-video dross filmed out in the Valley – but the big budgeters were there too, trying to find a new angle on the landmarks of the city.

And that was why I phoned. Not because I had any interest in the mechanics of putting a movie together, but because I found it comforting that Willis and Travolta still occasionally walked the same unremarkable streets as me. Late at night, with enough pills, booze and self-delusion I could turn this into a point of connection between us.

I fell asleep with the phone against my ear, listening to its endless reassurances.

CHAPTER 4

Next morning I was slumped on the toilet feeling rough, working my way through a shit, when the door of the bathroom banged open and I met Ryan for the first time. He stood for a moment staring at me, like some kind of spree killer deciding whether or not to pull the trigger, then he flipped open his cop ID.

"Wipe your ass."

It looked like I'd underestimated the investigative ability of the city of Los Angeles. I used a few sheets of paper, but I felt pretty exposed and didn't really do much of a job. When I started to pull my pants up he stopped me.

"That last wad was still dirty. You don't want an itchy crack. Give it a decent scrub."

Right then I knew I had much more of a problem than just being found by the police. I'd drawn a member of the force who got off on what happened in toilets. I checked him out while I was making sure I was properly clean. He looked like a plump Bela Lugosi – pale skin, black suit, soft body, dark receding hair slicked straight back. I put him at an unhealthy fifty.

"That looks a lot better. You know, it's a good thing you're not doing the whole 'What's this about, officer?' business. I'd be insulted. What do you call your dick? Average? Or a bit under?"

After that we went downstairs to a gray Plymouth and drove up to Santa Monica.

Weekend traffic made the boulevard busy. Sunlight bounced off wind-shields and fenders, hurting my eyes, making me wish for somewhere dark and silent to strain last night's booze and pill sludge from my system. The air stank and it was too hot.

I stayed quiet most of the way. If the police had found some sort of link between me and Karen I figured there wasn't anything I could say that wouldn't hurt me. I certainly couldn't tell them I'd already seen her dead. That would have looked somewhat odd. By the time we hit Palisades Park, though, I was so tense I couldn't help myself blurting:

"Is this about Karen? My wife? I mean, she's been gone like two weeks now. Did something happen to her?"

Ryan turned his head and smiled at me.

"That's good, Jackie. I like that."

The morgue was on Euclid – a street that, unlike its parallel brothers, had a name rather than a number because it fell thirteenth off Wilshire Boulevard. Squat and gray it crouched between a dress wholesaler and an auto parts complex, like an animal hunched over food. On the grass verge out front, a bunch of kids were doing something unpleasant to a dog.

Ryan didn't use the main entrance; instead he took me around the side of the building and down a concrete ramp to where the ambulances dropped their cargo. Into the basement.

The place where they kept the bodies looked like a public toilet, all white tiles and hard strip lighting. Rows of square, stainless-steel panels with handles like old-fashioned refrigerators ran three-high down opposing walls. It was cold and unwelcoming, but I guess the meat on the shelves didn't care.

The room was empty, Ryan whistled for the help. I closed my eyes and listened to fluid move in pipes that crisscrossed the ceiling. Poison being sucked out of dead people behind the panels, leaving them clean and de-stressed at last? There were other sounds too – the ticking of whatever gigantic refrigeration system stopped things going off down there, air blowing through a vent, a game-show-tuned TV blatting away through an open doorway at the end of the room.

A fat Japanese guy carrying a clipboard and a can of Diet Pepsi ambled out to meet us looking back over his shoulder like he was missing a Mars landing. He wore glasses and his grubby white lab coat had a piece of dried noodle stuck to it. His black hair was plastered back in a Jack Lord style with something that made it shine.

"BMW three series and a round trip to Florida for a family of four. Some people have all the luck. Never me. How you doing, Ryan?" He flicked a look at me. "This business today?"

Ryan's voice was hard, like he was steeling himself for something.

"The girl they found in the park. Wednesday."

The Japanese face softened up and went sickly genuine. He made a small, nod-of-the-head kind of bow to me.

"Oh, so sorry. You here to identify? Nobody figured, so she already autopsied."

"Jackie's a tough guy, he can take it. Bring her out."

We all walked to a wall and the Japanese guy jerked a handle, swung open one of the steel panels and rolled out a long drawer. TV hadn't got it quite right. I'd been expecting the buffer of a white sheet, maybe just a peek at her face. What I got was a naked, uncovered Karen lying on something that looked like a thin air mattress with the edges turned up – to stop any collected body fluids leaking into the drawer.

I glanced across at Ryan. His face had lost what little color it had and his breathing was strained.

Karen looked different than she had in the park. She looked worse. Like I thought I'd seen, part of her left side had been removed – a curving strip a few inches wide that ran from the cut on the front of her belly to halfway around her back. The doctors had extended the main wound on her belly up into her chest to perform the postmortem. They'd also cut away the back of her head. I could tell because it lay too deep in the rubber of the mattress. As a result, the skin on her face was loose and her features were blurred.

She wasn't beautiful anymore, but it was her all right. The anchor points of the matrix were still there – the short blond hair, the pale anti-Californian skin, the pierced nipples and navel. Only now they looked like they'd been stuck on a side of beef, some sort of bizarre decoration that had lost its significance.

I wondered, as Ryan and I stepped closer to the drawer, if proximity would release the emotions that had seemed so completely cauterized that night in the park. After all, a year together should have left me with at least some memories worth cherishing. But looking at that life-size monster doll, all the times we'd spent together, all the fucking and the fighting, felt like a movie about someone else.

She'd been cleaned with something antiseptic and the hospital stink masked whatever personal odor there might have been. I longed for a living smell, some olfactory mnemonic of close times – stale shit, dried piss, sweat, anything. The musk of her cunt would have been best. But it was all gone.

I pressed a fingertip into the side of her breast. When I took it away the flesh was slow returning to shape. Ryan was staring at me. I didn't know why he was acting so jitzed, but when our eyes locked I knew I was in deep shit. Because his had tears in them.

The orderly shifted his bulk from one foot to the other, picking up on the tension.

"She a pretty girl, this one. Must have looked very nice before this."

Ryan snapped out of the look of death he was giving me, dragged himself back to realtime, and scanned the body.

"Yeah, she was pretty all right."

When he started running his fingers gently over her pussy I thought the orderly would step in, or at least shout some kind of outrage, but it didn't seem to faze him in the slightest. Ryan carried on for a while, looking sadly at her face all the time. The orderly just watched. And I stood there and felt vaguely jealous.

Ryan took his hand away.

"You're quiet, Jackie. I brought Kleenex, you know."

"What happened to her?"

"Word at the station is someone cut out everything she had inside."

The Japanese guy flipped through some papers on his clipboard and started reading.

"Twenty-three centimeter vertical incision of a surgical nature. Intersecting lateral incision above the mons of eighteen centimeters. Excision of left abdominal wall between hip and lower ribs. Area of skin approximately eight centimeters square missing from the right shoulder blade. No other cuts or abrasions. All internal organs, except heart and lungs, removed."

"Sounds thorough, wouldn't you say, Jackie? Let's take a look."

Ryan nodded and the orderly wedged his things between Karen's legs and peeled open the part of her wound that hung together above the hole in her side. The edges of the cuts were smooth and in cross section they carried the same striations of white fat and red muscle as meat in a butcher's shop.

"See?"

He looked at me like I might not understand.

"See? Empty."

It was true. Below the last rib there was very little left – no blue-gray pulp of intestines, no sticky lumps of offal, not even a pool of collected glit. Under the hard lights a butterfly of pelvic bone shone whitely beneath a thin layer of tissue. There was no blood, everything was clean.

Gutted like a fish and hosed out.

Ryan shouldered the orderly out of the way, took hold of one of her arms and pulled it across her body until she lifted enough for me to see her shoulder blade. It looked like someone had used a cheese-slice on her. A rough patch of skin was missing, right where her tattoo had been.

The Japanese guy looked back toward the room where his TV waited.

"Listen, guys. I got things to do. You wanna see anyone else?"

Ryan shook his head.

"Okay. Shut her up when you go. Make sure the handle clicks, or could get smelly."

He touched hands with Ryan and took his drink and clipboard out of the room, back to the TV noise. I heard him flipping channels, then things stabilized on Pamela Anderson's voice. His Pepsi can had left a blotch of moisture on one of Karen's thighs.

I knew it was cinematically mandated that I show some sort of grief, so I hung my head and tried to look like I was struggling manfully with my emotions. Until Ryan told me not to bother and we left.

Out in the car we sat in silence while Ryan wheezed and sweated and eventually put a pill under his tongue. It worked so fast it must have been nitro. When he had himself fixed he slid his arm around my shoulders and squeezed the side of my neck.

"What was today's lesson? C'mon, I know you were paying attention. No? It was about me telling you something."

"Obviously that you found Karen and she's dead."

"Oh, I didn't need to tell you the dead part. You already knew."

I tried to protest, but he cut me off.

"The way I feel right now it'd be safer not to shit me. Today's lesson was about me telling you that I know."

"Know what?"

Ryan took a breath, held it in, then let it out like he didn't want it to get away from him.

"With me, Jackie, trying to see how far you can push things isn't something you want to do."

He took his arm away and put the key in the ignition. I was sitting next to a frightening man and I was starting to get frightened.

He dropped me at the corner of Santa Monica and Lincoln. We hadn't spoken during the drive, but as I was getting out of the car he stopped me.

"Jackie, the part of her shoulder that was fucked up, did she have a mark there? Something distinctive that might have been cut away for a reason?"

It was a simple question. The answer was yes, that was where she'd had an Egyptian scarab inked into her skin. But I wasn't going to tell Ryan that. He was too fucking odd. The pussy-stroking scene wasn't any kind of forensic procedure I'd ever heard about.

"Not that I can think of."

"Sure about that, now?"

"I think I'd know."

"Yeah, Jackie, you'd know."

He pulled away from the curb and left me standing there feeling like I should have said something different.

I walked downhill to look at the sea. There were white-caps out beyond the breakers and the water looked uneasy. Even so, it seemed to me that underneath those waves the world would be a whole lot more peaceful than here on dry land. I spent a long time staring at them, then I took a cab back to Venice.

The phone was ringing when I got in – Donut Haven wanting to know when I'd be back at work, sympathetically informing me that if it was any later than tomorrow I'd be fired. I broke the connection without answering. I wasn't going back, ever. The rent was paid till the end of the month, and the month after that was a problem I'd worry about later.

I ran a tape I'd rented on the way back – Jennifer Jason Leigh in *Rush*. I felt like watching cops get fucked up.

Chapter 5

Days passed. I'm not sure how many, they were all pretty much the same. Beer, junk food, pills. Sprawled on the bed, shades down but the windows open for air. I sweated and didn't wash. I wanted to be dirty. I wanted to be caked in filth.

In the kitchenette things rotted.

Crushed cigarette packs and empty beer cans made walking around the place hazardous. But that was okay because I didn't do it much. The bathroom thing was a drag, so mostly I leaned over the edge of the bed and pissed in a bottle. Once I took a shit in a plastic bag.

The TV ran eighteen hours a day, from the moment I could coordinate sufficiently to thumb the button in the morning, until the daily buildup of tranq and booze reached a level that interfered with vision.

A couple of times, when it was dark and quiet, I went outside to check the car. Once, I got in and drank a beer and listened to the radio.

I guess fugueing out this way was a reaction to something. Maybe a shrink could tell you. I put it down to my newly hatched rejection of the mainstream. And to something else a lot simpler to understand – fear. Fear that Karen's death might bleed forward in time and fuck me up.

I was already the object of Ryan's attention. I had no idea where the whacko play at the morgue was going to lead, but even a best-case scenario was something I could do without. And I kept thinking about Karen's tattoo. It hadn't meant anything to me when she'd had it done. She'd come home with it one day a few months back, I'd had a look, made the usual comments, and that was that. She told me she'd had it done with a friend. What did I care? It was just another bit of body decoration.

So it would have been easy enough to tell Ryan what had been on the missing square of skin. It would have been, so to speak, no skin off my nose. Just like I could have told him she'd recently had her kidney removed.

But I hadn't. And despite my gnawing three a.m. fears, I wasn't going to. I was out of that world now. Out of the world where sniveling Joe Citizen did his best to be a good boy.

Plus, same as already knowing she was dead, letting on about the kidney now would only make me look more suspicious.

A market on Lincoln, evening coming down. I was out of the apartment for the first time in four days and I had no feeling about it. The paranoia I'd experienced on Main the night I stocked up at the Korean store had been replaced by a numbed insularity. I moved, but I didn't feel the air against my skin. I heard the sounds of traffic and people, but they were filtered through some muting device that rendered them meaningless. The colors and angles and planes of the surrounding buildings were indecipherable.

None of this bothered me. I wanted booze and food, I wasn't thinking about much else.

Until a wino hassled me for change as I approached the sliding doors. He was one of a group of four, all of them crusted like forgotten, turn-of-the-century statues in that brown semi-gloss accretion cities use to camouflage the homeless. Their clothes – all of them wore too many for the summer heat – had the slickness of oilskin, their hair looked like something dredged from the bottom of a river and smeared into place with a trowel. They stank of shit, garbage and genital cheese.

The guy in my face was about fifty and pretty close to the edge; sores around his mouth, the shakes, liquid eyes, that blank expression beggars get after years of having to ask other people for money. It looked like he needed a drink pretty badly. It looked like the hope of getting one was the only thing holding him together.

I pushed past him into the cool interior. Produce section. I felt a stab of guilt as I moved past the fresh, crisp, tastefully arranged bins. Every famous person on the planet ate a super diet of carefully balanced fruit and vegetables, unrefined carbohydrate and hormone-free protein. It was important. It meant you stayed looking better than everyone else. And my telehosting course had stressed the impact of good skin tone and clear eyes on the projection of personality. But I just couldn't do it.

I went to the chiller cabinet that lined the rear wall and leaned against it, face on glass, exchanging heat. Packaged meat, low-cholesterol dips, zero-cholesterol cakes, naturally extracted juices.... Most of the food had product photos on the front and I got hung up for a while picturing the homes they must have been taken in. Soft lighting, tasteful decoration, high-income furnishings. Successful homes where life was fulfilled and comfortable. I quit when the security guys started to hover.

Inside this hangar-sized supermarket the feeling of detachment that swaddled me increased. The overweight women, the tired men, the whining kids – all the fucking, guzzling, calibrations of moderate income humanity – trundling their carts up one aisle and down another, seemed so pointless and disgusting it frightened me to consider I was part of the same race. They were fairground constructions, papier-mâché models drawn in shopping circuits by a network of hidden cogs and chains. Things to be shot at or knocked over with baseballs.

I hit the snack and convenience food sections heavily, then moved on to liquor. Bud was reduced so I took a couple of six-packs. On my way to the checkouts I had to pass the spirits. Brandy, gin, vodka, all the rest. On an impulse I added a half gallon of generic whiskey to the beer.

The girl at the checkout swiped my Visa and we had a few seconds' wait for authorization. Time to worry about credit balances and to wonder what her cunt looked like, and if sitting on it all day crusted up her briefs. I was putting my stuff into paper sacks when she handed my card back. She smiled. I smiled too.

"Spare change, buddy?"

Same wino as before, the fuckwit didn't realize he'd already asked me ten minutes ago.

"Spare change, buddy?"

Muddy voice. All clogged mucus and collapsed nasal passages.

"Buddy? Buddy? Just something so's I can get something to eat."

I looked past him, at his three derelict companions slumped against a wall twenty feet away. They were watching expectantly, gearing up to grab a share. I spoke quietly so they wouldn't hear.

"You don't want anything to eat. But I bet you could use a drink."

"Well, to tell you the truth...."

"Sure. It's a hard life."

"Damn hard. Takes it out of a man just sucking in your next breath. I don't suppose you got a bottle in one of them sacks, do ya?"

He couldn't take his eyes off the bags in my arms. When he spoke it was to them. His lips were cracked and he licked them constantly.

"A fine young man like you, mister, sure to be taking maybe a bottle of wine home for dinner. A fine, civilized young man like yourself."

"Are they your friends, over there?"

"Yes, sir. We been watching out for each other a few months now. Lots of others come and go, but we stuck together."

"Ah.... See, I'm thinking there won't really be enough to go around. What do you want? A few mouthfuls for everyone, or something more sensible?"

The wino flicked a quick look over his shoulder and licked his lips some more.

"Well, mister, I sure wouldn't want to do nothing that weren't sensible. What exactly is it you got in there?"

"I think we want somewhere more secluded."

"Can I take a peek first, mister? Just to kinda fortify myself."

I let him see the whiskey.

"Holy Jesus Christ! Come on, there's a place around back."

He took off at a trot, coat flapping, skinny arms jerking crazily. It looked like the sockets of his hips were filled with broken glass. He made about twenty feet, then stopped when he realized I wasn't beside him and waved frantically for me to catch up.

The market kept its garbage hoppers in a three-sided brick pen. The walls were about six feet high and, crouching at the back, we were pretty much shielded from view. Cars in the parking lot were visible through the open end but the sky was getting bruised around the edges by then and I figured the evening shadows would hide us well enough. Besides, I wasn't going to do anything that bad.

When I pulled the whiskey out of the paper sack the wino almost lost control. He grabbed for the jug, but I held it out of reach.

"You a hard drinking man?"

"Mister, I'm the hard-drinkinest man you ever met. How much of that hooch you figure you want to take home?"

"Have a taste."

"Sweet Jesus."

I kept hold of the jug but let him pull it to his mouth and take a small swallow. Then I took it away.

"Oh, Jesus, mister, don't do that to an old man. You know what they say, a taste is worse than none at all."

His laugh was so laden with need I felt like squirming.

"Maybe I should get your friends. It doesn't seem fair to leave them out."

"You don't want to do that. No sir, not if you want to keep any for yourself. They'll drink it dry. I seen them fuckers do it before. Just you and me's best. Believe me."

His eyes flicked back and forth between my face and the jug. He was dribbling and it looked like he was on track for some kind of wino anxiety attack.

"Want some more?"

"Fuckin' A – I mean, damn straight I'd like some more. You can spare it, can't you, mister? For this old bastard?"

"Two conditions."

"Whatever you want. I'm happy to oblige."

"You get five minutes with the bottle. Five minutes only."

"Ok. Sure, sure."

"And you stop drinking longer than twenty seconds, I take it away and give it to your friends."

"All right, mister, whatever you say. Let me at it. Let me at it!"

I gave him the jug. He held it with both hands, tipped his head back and started to gulp. He got about a quarter pint inside him before he stopped to take a breath.

"Whoa, buddy, that's the right stuff. That hits the spot for sure."

His eyes were watering a little, but he seemed okay. The only immediate change was he looked a bit healthier.

"Ten seconds."

"Just getting my wind."

"Fifteen seconds."

He stuck it in his face again. His swallows were a little slower this time, but he was still going for it.

"Fucking Jesus, I ain't been let loose on this much hooch for a long time. I gotta take my coat off. Won't be more'n a few seconds."

"Take your coat off."

He was sweating. When his coat came clear, the stink of his body filled the space around us. Mostly piss, but a lot of other rotted-down stuff as well.

"Better start again."

"A few more seconds."

I reached for the jug.

"Okay! Jesus Christ, what's your hurry?"

He clutched the whiskey to his chest like he was holding a baby.

"I said there were conditions. If you don't want any more...."

"Shit, who said anything about that? Just trying to pace myself, is all."

"Give it back."

He jerked the jug to his mouth so fast he cut his lip. Blood ran around the bottle and down one side of his chin in a thin red line. I don't think he noticed. He was trying to use a few brains this time, making his mouth small and taking shallow sips. His thin arms shook with the effort of keeping the jug steady.

When he came up for air he made a sort of hooting noise. I guess it was a laugh.

"Phew, buddy, I think I'm getting the hang of this. Got a smoke?"

"You don't have time."

Under the dirt his face was flushed. He grinned stupidly, shrugged like he had a man's job to finish and raised the whiskey again.

This time some of it went down the wrong way and he spluttered violently, trying to clear his throat. Something ran out of his nose and he stuck his head between his knees and coughed for a while. When he straightened, the skin around his eyes looked swollen and there was a caul of spit across his chin. About a quarter of the jug was gone. He dragged his sleeve across his face and started humming snatches of some tune to himself.

"How much of it are you going to drink?"

"All of it."

"Half a gallon?"

"You just watch me."

And away he went again.

A little while later he started puking. I heard his teeth crunch against glass as his head jerked forward and a fountain of booze sprayed around the neck of the jug. He managed to get it away from his face, but his guts didn't stop heaving. Dark gouts of whiskey and whatever else he'd had in his stomach splatted onto the concrete between his knees and ran into the V of his crotch. The liquid foamed at the edges.

"Bit ambitious, the whole jug."

"This make you feel good, you pitiless prick?"

"Have some more."

"You think I won't?"

Loops of viscous puke hung from his chin, they swayed as his head moved. He looked a lot less healthy now.

"I'm waiting to see."

He tried to keep belligerent eye contact with me as he went back to the booze. But it didn't last. He puked again. Swallowed and puked, swallowed and puked, until the cycle exhausted him and the vomit-slick jug slipped from his hands.

He collapsed sideways and his head made a thunking noise as it hit the concrete. I stood up and watched him convulse, he looked like a dog having a nightmare. Between his retching he cursed me – strange old-man curses from a previous era that made him sound like Elmer Fudd.

The jug of whiskey stood where he'd dropped it, upright, unbroken, almost half empty. When his body would let him, he stared at it as though it were some reliquary for the whole of his life. He tried to reach for it. I thought he was going to make it, but a few inches short the strength left him and he closed his eyes and let his arm fall. Without lifting his head he puked a stream of blood that gathered itself into a chest-sized ink blot and washed against the base of the whiskey bottle.

He wasn't dying – I checked his breathing – but it looked pretty much like he'd fucked an already fucked stomach. I left him with the remains of the booze and headed out into the parking lot. The last sound I heard him make was a prolonged wet fart as his bowels let go.

I had a bit of an erection all the way to the car.

I'd almost gotten the door of the Prelude closed when a plump white hand reached out of the corner of vision and stopped it. Ryan moved into frame, backlit by the mercury wash from the street.

"Jackie-boy. It's that man again! Don't start the car."

He walked around to the passenger side and got in. He settled his bulk comfortably into the seat.

"This is cozy."

"Have you got some news about Karen?"

I tried to sound tiredly grieving and expectant at the same time.

"Interesting thing to do to a tramp."

"Huh?"

"I let you have the dumb act last time, don't push it. I was watching. Been watching a couple of days. You don't get out much."

"He asked for a drink. I gave him one."

"Yeah, I saw."

"He could have stopped."

"But you knew he wouldn't."

I had the interior light on, it made shadows of Ryan's eyes, outlined the pouches of fat beneath them. He looked even more unhealthy than before.

"Aren't you here about Karen?"

"Oh, you want to talk about Karen?"

"Of course. Why wouldn't I?"

"Boy, let me think.... Maybe because you weren't surprised when you saw her at the morgue? Maybe because you had something to do with putting her there?"

"Get real."

"If I got any realer, boy, you'd be face down bleeding through both sides of your head. I know you lied to me.... Didn't she ever tell you about us? Didn't she tell you who I was?"

"What are you talking about?"

"I knew her, you asshole. She was a whore, I used to buy her. I liked her because she went that extra mile, didn't have a problem with those frills most cunts get all precious about. She used to call me Daddy while we were doing it."

"You're old enough."

"Yow, Jackie, bitch-ee! You oughta be more respectful, I must have been a regular source of income for you two."

I wondered if this was all just cop psych to freak me into confessing to something. I'd never heard Karen mention Ryan's name, but that didn't mean anything. She might have hated the police but she'd fuck one of them if there was money in it.

The next thing Ryan said, though, cleared things up considerably.

"You look like a smart guy. Given that seeing her on her hands and knees wasn't an unusual occurrence for me, it shouldn't be too hard to figure that I know what you said about her shoulder was a little inaccurate. One of those Egyptian bugs, if I'm not mistaken."

"Oh, shit, yeah, the scarab! Fuck, I'm sorry, I must have been in shock, or something."

"Ooo, that's upsetting."

"What do you want? I'm sorry. When I saw her body I just froze up."

"Or maybe the tattoo connected to something you didn't want me to know about."

"Like what? Why would I hide anything?"

"Right now I don't know, Jackie. But if I gotta take a guess I'd say because you killed her."

You have to think of the exact right comeback to a statement like that. Surprise? Indignation? Outright denial? Something that will make him stop believing what he so obviously does. I couldn't do it. So I lit a cigarette and stared out the window at the floodlit cars. Through the glass of the market people moved around all purposeful and clean, safe in whatever lives they led. And for one brief moment I was envious of them, of their acceptance of the rules of the world they found themselves in. I'd been like them once, but not anymore, and I'd moved too far away to ever go back. Now I was in some alien place, sitting next to a cop who wanted to fix me for murder.

A woman in shorts that cut into the crack of her ass walked across the parking lot to her car. Ryan watched her like some flabby predator. When she bent over to put her shopping in the trunk he rubbed his balls.

"Look at that. What sort of beard you think she's got? Real hairy, or just one of those wispy things around the outside of her hole? Whaddya say, Jack? You shack up with someone like Karen, I know you gotta like cooze."

"My wife's just been murdered."

Ryan laughed. "You ain't in mourning."

"Maybe it just doesn't show."

"Maybe it's just that old shock thing again, freezing you up. Where were you Monday before last? Evening into night."

The quick change threw me for a second, then the meaning of the words sank in. Monday night. Two days before she was found in the park. Totally cool, I had an alibi.

"That was when she was killed?"

"Answer the fucking question. And you better hope it's checkable."

"I was working. Donut Haven on Wilshire, West Hollywood. Four till midnight. You can check it with the guy who runs the place."

"I will, but I gotta check something with you first."

"What?"

"They found come in her guts."

"She was a hooker, what do you expect?"

"I'm not talking about her pussy. I'm talking about that big hole in her tum-tum. Looks like after she was gutted someone relieved themselves at close range. Know what I'm saying?"

"Me, I suppose?"

"I'm hoping. But I tell you what, Jackie, I'm a guy who tries to see all sides of a problem, you know, consider all possibilities. So I'm gonna give you a chance to settle the spunk aspect."

"Er...how?"

I had a feeling something bad was coming, and it did.

"We got come in her guts. The obvious step, obvious to me anyhow, is get a sample from you."

"Sure, anything to help the investigation. What do I have to do, give some blood?"

"I'm kinda picky about these kinda things. We find spunk, we should match it against spunk. Call me old fashioned."

"You're kidding."

"I'm giving you a chance."

"Jesus, all right.... Where do I go?"

"Shit, Jackie, I don't want to put you to any trouble. You can do it right here."

"Are you serious?"

"It's up to you. Of course if you refuse it's going to be difficult for me not to draw the obvious conclusion."

"You want me to jerk off in the car?"

"Why not?"

"No way. This is too weird...."

"Say, have I shown you my gun?"

Ryan leaned over on one side of his ass and pulled a short revolver out of a belt holster. The metal was dull. It looked well used. He twisted it in the cabin light.

"Thirty-eight. Not as powerful as the Glocks the young guys carry, but it does the job. Know how many people I've killed with it? Enough so I have to use my toes to count.

"That's like a subtle threat, right?"

"When I was fucking her I used to wonder what her old man was like, what I was competing with, so to speak. Turns out he's a worthless fuck who won't even cooperate solving her murder. I got two reasons to shoot you, Jack. First, it would close the case. You tried to escape – you musta been guilty. Second, I'd just like to do it. Now, if I was a guy sitting next to a guy like me, I wouldn't be arguing over a couple of teaspoons of love juice. Get my meaning?"

"Okay, okay.... Will you at least get out while I do it?"

"Can't. Sorry. You might contaminate the sample in some way – cigarette ash, say. And I don't want to have to do this all over again. Here, you can use this."

Ryan took a plastic pharmacy jar from his pocket and handed it to me. It was a safe bet that no cop on a bona fide investigation was going to collect evidence like this, but there wasn't much I could do. His gun was pointing in my direction and I'd already painted myself into a corner by lying about the tattoo. So.... I got my dick out.

The starter bone from the tramp was long gone and getting hard was an impossible task. I rubbed for a while and tried to think of something dirty, but Ryan staring at me made it difficult to concentrate.

"I can't do it with you watching."

"Sure you can, you just need a kick-start."

He took a photo from his inside pocket and held it out. It showed a rear-end view of a naked young woman, face down on a concrete floor, knees drawn up under her chest, arms thrown stiffly out to each side. The angle of the shot made it possible to see the blood that had run out of her mouth and pooled around her head. She had a crowbar sticking out of her ass.

"Gang killing. South Central squadies like to pass these things around. Kinda erotic, huh?"

Despite the sickness of the subject, Ryan was right. The flat, pitiless quality of the lighting, the thick flesh of her cunt, the violated anus – all of it combined to produce something that made my head swim. The horror of it drew me out of the world for a while, blocked out Ryan long enough for me to pump up.

After that it only took a minute to spurt into the jar. There was a lot, and some of it missed and splatted against the dash. The intensity of the orgasm surprised me, but as soon as it was over I felt disgusted. Being watched while you wank is as bad as taking a shit in front of someone.

"That's the spirit, Jackie."

Ryan put his gun away, screwed the top on the jar and held it up to the light.

"Nice and thick. Must have a high sperm count."

"Can I go now?"

"Soon."

"Jesus, what now? A stool sample?"

"Getting smart with me ain't smart, Jackie. Did she know any doctors?"

"Her client list wasn't in my top-ten of great books to read."

"I'm trying pretty hard here, Jackie. Right now it's the only thing pointing away from you."

"How's that."

"You saw the way she was cut. Coulda been someone with surgical experience. A doctor, no?"

There was something so majorly unkosher about Ryan I was reluctant to tell him anything, let alone stuff about illegal kidney operations. But I figured a little info might put me in a better light.

"Maybe she did mention one. Over in Malibu, I think."

"Oh, really? Got a name? An address?"

"No. She didn't talk about him. It was just like comments she made. I don't even know if his place was on the beach or in the hills."

"You get a look at him? He ever come by to pick her up?"

"No."

"Did she keep an address book, any sort of record of the guys she fucked?"

"Not Karen. She wasn't that organized."

"This ain't good. Not for you anyway. Doesn't give me anything to go on. I guess I'll just have to stick with you. Tell me, what was it like being married to a whore?"

"Not good."

"Could be it pushed you a little too far? Maybe she fucked a guy with a big dick one night, came home and told you about it. And 'cause you ain't so long you flipped out with something sharp?"

"I didn't kill her, Ryan."

He smiled for a moment then nodded at the photo of the dead girl.

"A present."

He got out of the car and walked off into a night that wasn't distant or insulated anymore. Everything in it was sharp and immediate and dangerous. The kind of environment that looked like it would suit Ryan just fine.

CHAPTER 6

Daytime, on the bed. I was interfacing, but at one remove, blurred and border-line irritable behind a filter of pills. Lorn on the TV, on a tape. As perfect as the teen sex visions on Nintendo. Talking about things which possessed me. I lay on the bed like one of those slovenly filter-feeding fish, gulping it in too fast to taste, but drawing bedrock nourishment from it all the same.

Then Royston turned up to collect the rent – a little weasel of a guy who owned a couple of properties along the coast and liked to keep a personal handle on things. He had a habit of pushing his head forward and up that made the front of his neck bulge like the underside of a penis. Black-framed Coke-bottle glasses, hair that looked synthetic, a thin white body that seemed to be always coiling and twisting and trying to escape its clothes. He was in his thirties, but it was hard not to think of him as a child – an idiot child, protected from life by his inability to appreciate the hassles the rest of the world suffered.

I found it almost impossible to stay civil around him.

"Hiya, Jack, it's that time of the month again."

He laughed like he'd made a joke, a sort of braying noise.

"Yeah? I haven't started bleeding yet. I must be late."

"Oh, Jack, you're wild. Come on, you know what I mean."

He threw an air punch and made a growling noise like he appreciated me playing along with him.

"This isn't a good time."

"Oh, wow, I can see that. You really should try to keep the place a bit cleaner, you know. Is that chocolate pudding on your chest?"

"Didn't you hear me?"

"Why don't you open the blinds? It's such a lovely day outside. The sun's shining, the birds are singing and God's in his heaven. That's what my mother used to say. The sun's shin—"

I walked out of the room to get a beer from the fridge. I looked at the pill jar and wondered if I could take enough to pass out before Royston managed to bring himself to say the R-word. Unlikely, so I flipped a single DF 118 and went back and fell on the bed. I was wearing stained, stretched-out briefs that let my cock swing around. Royston avoided looking at my crotch.

"You don't look happy, Jack."

"I got a few problems."

"Oh, problems.... Don't we all? But, Jack, you know? Problems are just things to overcome. Even the tough ones go away if you give them enough time. Like, I had some water damage at my other property? And the living room carpet was completely ruined. I could have let it get to me – I mean it was really nice carpet – I could have agonized over it and wondered why something like that had to happen to me. But I chose not to. I made the decision. Instead of letting it achieve major proportions, I acted straight away, went right out and replaced it. End of problem. Say, where's Karen?"

"Dead. Somebody cut her open, pulled out her guts and blew a load into the hole."

For a moment his mouth worked silently, like he had to chew my words out of the air to get past them. Then his voice started again on the end of a shocked, indrawn breath.

"Didn't your mother ever tell you not to say things like that? They might come true."

He was sitting on the couch, he bounced up and down on the cushion.

"The springs are going in this."

"Replace it, then."

"Oh, it's not that bad. I mean it's not out of place."

"What do you mean?"

"Well, you live at a certain level."

"Everyone lives at a certain level."

"You can't expect a brand-new couch."

"I'm not asking you to give it to me. This is a furnished apartment. I pay rent, the furnishings should be at least halfway decent."

"That's what I'm saying. They are decent...for your level. I'm not being shitty, Jack. It's just the way of things. Come on, dude, this isn't important. Let's do a number. I got this South African stuff. Total head. If I'm lying I'm flying."

Royston thought smoking was the height of hipness and was prone to OD-ing on slang when the subject came up. He pulled out a bag of grass and some papers. Sharing a joint had become a habit on rent days. It made him feel better about asking for the money, like we were really friends and the rent was just incidental.

I didn't like grass – too much love and too many flowers in its history. Give me a member of the benzo family any day – something made in a clinic, not a fucking herbal accident. Something with a zero paranoia quotient. But I figured if he was stoned he might be more flexible on the issue of money. Plus I knew the asshole would keep whining until I agreed to get fucked up with him.

"Get on with it, then."

Royston dropped the bag of weed twice in his eagerness to get one rolled.

We smoked and coughed and smoked. He didn't know to take the seeds out, so the joint exploded periodically and showered the carpet with burning ash. Each time it happened he got down on his knees, clucking like a chicken, and rubbed frantically at the singed spot.

By the time the joint was finished we were both pretty much confused. Royston had a couple of hacking fits and kept taking his glasses off to wipe his eyes. I got up and went to the kitchenette for another beer. My face felt like it was sizzling and things darted about at the edge of vision. But they were hard to catch and when I turned head-on they disappeared.

Out the back window the girl I'd seen before was on her balcony again. She wore a few more clothes this time and was bent forward painting her nails. The THC riding my bloodstream made it easy to project all the sadness of the city onto her. With the glory of the setting sun thrown orange against the walls around her, working so hard at something like painting your nails seemed such a desperate thing to do. My thoughts chained out along dope corridors and I was sure if I went over there and put my arm around her she'd break down crying and everything would be all right in her life from then on. I began to feel an overwhelming kinship with her.

Until she looked up, saw me watching her and gave me the finger.

And then I was suddenly tired of it all – of other people, the noise of the outside world, the evening light, fucking Royston and his fucking rent.... What I wanted was to drift, maybe watch some more TV, maybe look at the picture of the dead girl with the crowbar up her ass.

I went back to the lounge with my drink.

"You were a long time, Jack."

"I don't have the rent."

He looked like I'd slapped him, like it was something I just should not have said.

"Oh.... Well, er.... Gee, Jack, that's not something there's much leeway on. You know? I mean it's not that difficult, is it?"

"Karen really is dead."

"Oh, Jack...."

"I mean it. She was killed."

"Oh, boy."

Royston started rubbing his palms backwards and forwards along the tops of his thighs. He looked uncomfortably around the room like he was hoping someone would come in and rescue him.

"That's.... Oh, boy...."

"Yeah, it's pretty bad."

He stood up and scratched his head, other hand on his hip.

"I feel a bit manipulated here, Jack."

"What?"

"Well, first you don't have the rent, then you tell me Karen's dead."

"Well it's true. I don't have the rent and Karen is dead."

"But you're putting them together. There's an implication."

"I was only going to ask if I could make it up next month. You won't lose anything. It's been a difficult time."

"That's not the way things work, Jack. That's not the way of the world. We have a contract, we have to work inside the rules it sets out. What would happen if everybody did this? Chaos. Nobody'd pay rent."

"I don't believe this."

"I don't either, Jack. I'm really disappointed."

"Jesus, Royston. A few weeks. Is it that much to ask?"

"It's the principle. If I can't trust you to pay on time, how can I trust that you really will make it up?"

"I promise, okay? This is the first time in two years for Christsake!"

He shook his head like this went against everything he'd ever held dear.

"I can't give you another month. It's not possible. I'll give you two weeks, and that's a favor, Jack. Okay?" He walked to the door, still shaking his head. "Jeeze, I feel pretty upset."

After he'd gone my rage boiled over. I felt belittled, I felt demeaned. Something as trivial as an extension on the rent.... I walked around and around the room clenching my teeth, but it wouldn't go away. In an effort to calm myself I took out the photo Ryan had given me. I was instantly transfixed. I held it with one hand and jerked off with the other. Standing in the middle of the room. My spunk made a pattering sound when it hit the carpet.

And later I separated myself still further with gossip magazines – a plunge into the pool of a better way of being.

Tom Cruise had booked the honeymoon suite at the Ritz in Paris and filled it with flowers for a second honeymoon with Nicole. While in the City of Love they spent a quarter of a million bucks on new clothes. Rumors flew that Heather Locklear was pregnant, but the star herself was being coy. Farrah Fawcett danced the night away at a Hollywood gay bar, as sexy and athletic as ever. Tim Allen gave his wife a brand new Jag for her birthday and Antonio Banderas and Melanie Griffith spent twenty-five grand on furniture for baby Stella's nursery. Ted Danson and Mary Steenburgen dealt with marital tension arising from working on the same TV show by sleeping in separate rooms on the weekend and not talking to each other on Saturdays.

A few days after Royston's visit I realized I was bored. Booze tasted stale, my body felt soft and the pill fog around my head was starting to bug me. The fugue of the last week and a half had burnt itself out and I was suddenly tired of lying around. Like some cathartic dawn, the desire to be out in the world again threw its light over me. I wanted a more active distraction than just watching TV. I wanted to participate in what I saw on the screen.

I shaved, showered and dressed. Late night. Black sky powdered orange. Outside, taillights would be streaking the roads with journeys far more exciting than those of the day – drug transportation, deals in the back seat, fucks to be tracked down in bars and clubs and nailed on the wet tiles beside pools in the hills, meetings to be kept or deliberately broken, steps to be taken toward success or someone else's destruction. Ah, the L.A. night!

I stood on the steps out front of the apartment and breathed it in. It smelled different. It was a different place to the city I'd known before Karen's death. Without the daily grind of a job, without the headfuck detrition of worrying about accepted patterns of behavior, it had changed from impenetrable monolith to become again a place where anything might happen – a glittering arena of streetlights, headlights, lighted windows and neon.

The Prelude fired up first go – smooth function Nippon tech. I let it idle and thought about Karen.

Dead in a park shortly after an illegal kidney operation. The scar on her belly and all her organs removed. It wasn't hard to come up with a scenario – Karen dumps her kidney, comes home and tells me about it, we fight and she splits, she gets back in touch with the doc, then something goes down and he kills her. Seemed logical to me. The operation and the murder were close in time. The wounds might have been made by a surgeon. And who better to have a motive for such thorough body emptying than someone who wanted to obliterate all traces of an illegal operation?

I had a feeling I'd linked these thoughts for a reason, but right then I wasn't sure what it was. So I rolled the windows down and hit the road and hoped the night air would blow them away.

For a short time I felt free. There was nothing to stop me driving forever if I wanted to – no alarm clock, no donut boss. My actions had so little impact on the world around me I felt outside time. What did it matter when I stopped, where I went, what I did? Without ties to one of the visual media industries I was irrelevant to the city.

North on Lincoln, east on Santa Monica, all the way to Hollywood and the Drag.

Prime time, around twelve. Parallel with Hollywood Boulevard, a few streets south, the Drag was hot. Its littered half mile of fake fronting and excessive wattage crawled with buyers and sellers like a radiant, maggot-riddled carcass. Porn theaters, fast-food joints, a couple of bars, hard-eyed men with rough skin and too many rings on their fingers. And hookers, hookers, hookers.

Cars rolled slowly, close to the curb, viewing the trade. Cunt, pussy, snatch.... Hunted by all the types the city could throw up. College kids crammed six to a car, hanging out the windows, whistling and yelling and banging the door panels with the palms of their hands, bringing with them the only innocence the Drag ever saw, out to get a friend laid, or find someone who'd do a carload cut price. The pros, the regular customers, confident and relaxed, alone or with a buddy, calling the girls by name, cool in their negotiations, explicit in their demands. They were going to get what they paid for, sure as shit.

And the guys who took it a whole lot more seriously. Always alone, windows shut, until the need got bad enough to force that final swoop up to a woman they'd already passed ten times that night. Hot in the car, sweaty, driving with a hardon, risking a job or a wife or the house or the kids, but unable to stop themselves. Sex as a drug, dirty and dangerous and built on fucked up psych foundations – shit hanging over from childhood. Sickos and sneaks, yeah, but they were the real face of Drag consumption. Unlike the kids and the goodtimers whose laughing transactions did not cut beyond the flashy first layer of the whore animal, these desperate men were its bone and muscle. They were the truth of what went on here, the true counterparts of the whores. Pain slotting into pain.

The pimps in their cars. The junkies sitting hunched over untouched black coffees in tired diners whose toilet walls were smeared with carbon from the bottom of spoons and laced with the red feather-trails of flushed syringes. The odd old guys who always hang near pussy or drugs, feeding off a nerved voracity they mistake for excitement and youth. The liquor store owners with their shotguns – pilot fish around the shark – who prayed at the start of each night to just make it through one more alive. The Mexicans who slopped out and swept up in the porn shows and the fuck rooms, smoking roll-ups or small dark cigars in a snatched five minutes on the steps of a side entrance, leaning on their brooms, so tired they might never move again. The cops, few and far between, mirror shades even at night, thick forearms pale from long-term night duty, chewing gum. And cruising like all the rest.

I parked at the western end of the street, in the lot of an abandoned dress factory. Around here the Drag false-started with a handful of fast-food vendors and fuck-mag shops, hauling itself out of a shadowed nothingness of low-rise office blocks and failed businesses like some beast from a swamp – the start of a curve which peaked about a quarter mile east, then tailed off again into other unlit and forsaken nighttime areas of the city. There were fewer people here, the trawling cars cut in from cross-streets further up. It took about five minutes' walking to get to where the action started.

The Drag wasn't new to me. On really bad nights when my imagination ran wild and the hours gorged themselves on my loneliness, I'd sometimes come looking for Karen here, full of doomed persuasions to bring her home. But this was the first time I'd come to willfully immerse myself in its two-way tug of avarice and desire. I wanted reassurance, some sort of affirmation that the city existed as more than a work ethic-ed middle-class construction. And the Drag was the place to get it. The rabid, hungering impulses that shaped people's behavior ran closer to the surface here. They made it a big fuck-you to the mainstream.

The whores stood like bored hitch-hikers at the curb or lounged against the walls of sex shops and nude encounter parlors in clothes designed to attract attention and give quick access. Around them light and sound moved like the weather – sequential waves of glare from bars and theaters, the bellowings of strip-show callers who stood like small tugs in greasy dinner jackets and went on about snatch and ass and complementary drinks. Some of the girls were dogs and some of them were beautiful, they all looked like they'd rather be someplace else.

Sex was graded on the Drag – normal-ish hetero action where all the light was. And then in the small streets that ran away from this light, stuff that was a whole lot heavier – specialist basement theaters that ran BDSM, animal, shit and piss. And lurking in the shadows near these places, people who could make the images real. Further east, the pedestrian traffic all but died out and the Drag foundered in a stretch of vacant lots and occasional bars. But it wasn't dead. The boys kept it alive.

Jeans and T-shirts, the occasional gleam of leather. Most of them young. On corners or against chain-link fences, one knee bent, foot flat against a wall, thumbs in belt loops, fingers straying to brush crotches if a car slowed, purposely stereotypical. Here there were no theaters, no shows, no specialty rubber-goods stores, no pimps, no criers. Just men, smoking and waiting.

I'd never been this far along – it was hardly a place where Karen would have had much success – and it felt weird knowing men in cars might be looking at me and contemplating sex.

About ten yards ahead, a Merc SEC 560 pulled up opposite a guy with a blond crew-cut and slid its window down. I stopped to watch. It seemed things went pretty much the same as with the female whores, only it was quicker and there was less jive. I couldn't hear what they said, but it must have been cool with both of them because the guy in the car opened the door and the crew-cut climbed in. As the Merc pulled away I could see the silhouette of the driver's arm through the rear window, reaching across the seats.

I watched the car disappear wondering what, exactly, they were going to do and how much money was going to change hands. I'd never fucked a man, but I was down to my last twenty, facing possible eviction. And it seemed simple enough. You stood around, the business came to you. And once you got in the car? Mostly sucking and yanking, I guessed – actions with about as much significance as shaking hands. Easy money.

I found myself an empty stretch of wall and leaned against it. I had no real plan, I just wanted to see what would happen. A few of the closest bum-boys looked sideways at me, but it didn't mean much. If looks could kill the whole world would be dead.

Cars rolled by like counters in a game. Guys on either side of me got lucky. I was better looking, but they were younger. I didn't care, the night was warm and it was better out here with the freaks than guzzling beer I couldn't afford in a sweaty apartment.

Nothing happened for a while. And then it did.

"Hey."

A black Lexus had pulled up and a heavy-set guy in his forties was leaning across the passenger seat, pointing his face at me.

"Yeah, you. You want business, or what?"

Now it was happening it didn't seem quite so simple. I thought about walking off, but that would have meant kissing goodbye to the money, and it would have been embarrassing in front of the other guys.

"Come closer for fucksake, I'm not going to shout across the fucking street all fucking night. You don't like money, or what?"

I walked over and bent to window level. He was bigger than me, too big to beat the shit out of if things went wrong. And things could go wrong, I realized suddenly. There might be plenty of things I wouldn't want to do with a guy like this, and saying no when his dick got hard wouldn't cut much ice.

"How much you got?"

"Huh?"

"How big's your fucking dick?"

"About average, I suppose."

"In inches."

"Seven."

He looked a little dubious.

"That ain't so big. But maybe we can still do business. You spunked up already tonight? If I'm paying for it I like a good solid wad. You driving with a full tank, or what?"

I was close enough to smell him and he didn't smell good. In fact he smelled of shit. I was becoming less enthusiastic about the whole thing by the second.

"What do you want to do?"

"Get in the fucking car. You're going to get us busted. How old are you anyway?"

"I want to know before I get in."

"Jesus fucking Christ. I could find someone else."

I just stood there and looked at him and hoped he would. After a moment he shrugged.

"Felching. I pay good money and that's what I want."

I decided right then to walk. Sticking my head between the sweaty, hairy, shit-stinking cheeks of this guy's ass and sucking my come out of him wasn't what I'd planned as my introduction to male prostitution.

He must have read my face.

"What's the matter? You think there's something wrong with that? It's a normal impulse! What the fuck are you out here for anyway? You think it's funny jerking people around?"

He had his head almost out the passenger window. Some of his spit hit my cheek. I backed away and headed up the street, opposite the flow of traffic so he couldn't follow me. I heard his engine roar. He was still yelling as he took off. The bum-boys loved it.

I circled the block, came out back on the Drag a hundred yards further east of where I'd been standing, and found a bar. It didn't feel particularly welcoming, but I was tired of walking and there wasn't anything else close. I bought a drink and took it to a stool near the front window.

I was pissed off about the Lexus episode. If the guy had wanted a simple blow job I'd have been sitting there with extra dollars in my pocket and maybe the start of a new career under my belt. Instead, I was burning up what little money I had left just to have somewhere to rest.

Around the borders of the window neon beer signs ticked on and off. I stared blindly out at the street, drinking my beer, wishing I had enough money to get drunk. Until someone did a double-take outside and tapped on the glass.

Rex.

He came into the bar, Rodeo dressed and looking polished enough to pass for healthy. Same as every time I saw him, I wondered why he wasn't on TV.

"Dude. Maintaining?"

"Sort of."

"Strange place to find you."

"Yeah, well...."

He looked knowing, then leaned over the bar and ordered doubles and chasers for both of us. When he handed mine over he looked concerned.

"Do we talk about Karen?"

"We don't have to avoid it, if that's what you mean."

"Cool. I wasn't sure.... I keep thinking about her."

"Hey, from the start? We both know you weren't superfriends."

"Well, Jeeze, man, I know that. But it doesn't stop you caring."

"I know. I'm just saying."

"That's okay. The proprietary thing's normal early on."

"Proprietary thing?"

"Wanting to own the dead person. Not let anyone else feel she was as important to them as she was to you."

"I don't want to own her. Fuck.... I'm glad she's gone."

"Okay, okay...." He held his hands up, backing off. "Maybe when I said I'd been thinking about her I meant not about her, but about, you know, actually dying. About the reality of it. You know what I see when I think about it? I don't see her. I see the edge of a cliff. You know? A precipice. And it's like there's this huge gravitational pull on me to jump off. I'm trying not to, man. But, I don't know.... Every day's the same. You know what I mean? It's just the same thing every day. Even if something really different happens, even if it's something really good, it's still the same."

"I saw her body. I went to the morgue."

"Fuck that must have been a trip."

"Yeah, she looked pretty bad."

"Wow...."

Rex drank silently for a moment, then:

"You have to talk to the cops or anything like that?"

"I talked to one guy."

"They okay with you? I mean they don't like suspect you, do they?"

"I don't know.... It was so left-field, so unofficial. I mean this guy was fucking weird."

"Maybe it's better that way. Less shit for you to deal with. Wasn't her father one?"

"Fuck, who knows. She said something once, but you know what she was like."

"Well, not really, man. I wasn't like her superfriend, after all."

He smirked and punched me lightly on the arm. And I laughed and felt good that there was someone close enough to me to make that kind of joke. Rex tapped his shot glass on the bar.

"Your round, dude."

"Can't, sorry. I quit work."

"Ah...."

Rex ordered the drinks himself, then turned back looking satisfied.

"Time to fess up, dude. What are you doing down here?"

"Hanging out."

"No one comes here to hang out. I was scoring, but you don't have the money for that. So if I had to take a punt, I'd say you were looking for an alternative source of income."

"I was thinking about it."

"Hah." Rex clapped his hands. "It's about time, I never could understand why you stayed poor so long. You're great looking, you've got a nice body."

"It's taking that final step, I guess."

"What step? It doesn't mean anything, Jack. You don't get struck dead for it. And you might as well be able to buy drugs and nice clothes as not. You're wasting your time on the Drag, though."

"Why?"

"It's a place for junkies and losers. You trick here if you've got nothing else going or you don't know any better. Those guys out there'll be lucky to have five bucks left tomorrow morning. I know, man, it's where I started.

You can survive, but you won't make any real money. Agency work is where the bread is."

Rex looked at me for a moment then swallowed the last of his drink.

"You got a car here, right?"

"Er, yeah."

"Okay. I got a gig off Mulholland. The Porsche is in the shop and I was going to take a cab, but I'm going to do you a favor instead. Come on."

"Where are we going?"

I was a little drunk by this time and things seemed to be accelerating.

"To take some money off someone who can afford to give it to us."

"You want me to fuck someone with you?"

"If you want to get into it, this is your chance. Don't worry, I know these people, they won't mind an extra bod, believe me."

"They?"

"A couple."

"Shit, I don't know...."

"What are you going to do if you don't? Go home broke and have a wank? Come with me and you get to fuck a woman, take drugs and make some money. I'll split it fifty-fifty. Where's the choice? Come on, dude. Time to shit or cut bait."

Put that way it seemed stupid to refuse.

"Got any coke?"

"But of course."

We walked out into the tawdry Drag night.

Chapter 7

West on Hollywood, then north up Laurel Canyon and into the hills. A cool drive through some of the best of L.A.

The road twisted as it climbed. Tight one-lane streets veined off it into gullies or up rises where box-sided sixties and seventies architecture leaned against the slopes on death-wish stilts. Flatland Beverly Hills had more ostentation and the money in Bel Air was older, but you couldn't beat the Hollywood Hills for atmosphere.

From the street the houses didn't give much away. They were built with their backs to the world, screened by eucalyptus and pepper trees. If they showed any windows at all, they were narrow and the light coming through them was gentle and masked. Driving through the area was an exercise in imagination. Whoever they were, whatever they did, it was a sure bet the people here lived lives worth filming, that they had strings of lovers and unlimited earning potential.

The booze from the bar and the night air blowing through the open windows made me feel young. I was alive and excited, it seemed absurd to me now that I had spent the last two weeks lying in bed when I could have been doing something like this – rubbing up against the outsides of perfect lives.

"I'm a little over the limit."

Rex smiled dreamily. "Who cares? I always feel kind of hopeful driving pissed. Increases your chances of winning that lottery."

"You might hit someone who doesn't want to die."

"True, but if you drink enough you don't worry about that."

Rex got his coke out. I closed the windows and he stuck some on the corner of a credit card under my nose. The road was straight for a little way so I held the wheel with my knees and did it. Call me irresponsible.

A few minutes later we hit the Hollywood Bowl overlook and the city lay spread out below us like a carpet of jewels, an infinite sprawl of light that rose gigantically at its center in the towers of downtown. I pulled over. The gates to the overlook were locked but there was space at the side of the road. We got out, hooked our fingers through the mesh of the fence, and gazed.

At any time the city was awesome, but at night, when darkness removed the comparison of the horizon, it became a construct of light that simply overpowered vision – a glittering prize for all the owners of the houses in the hills.

"Incredible."

Rex grunted. "Gives me the creeps. All those people spinning around as fast as they can go. I mean, you figure when you think about yourself there's some importance to being human. But when you see it like this and there's so many people.... We can't all be worth something. We're ants, man."

"Not if you're Bruce or Arnold."

"I reckon it's all hell on earth, no matter who you are."

We did some more blow at the fence then got back in the car.

The house was at the end of a quietly lit lane off the downhill side of Mulholland. It was large and white – replica Spanish surrounded by subtropical foliage. Two wings angled back from a central block, away from the road, like arms open to the city.

We left the car in the drive and headed for a black oak door that had iron studs in the wood.

"Isn't it a bit late?"

"This kind of thing happens when it's late."

"Looks like money."

"They're industry."

"Cool. How do you know them?"

"They ring the agency and order what they want. If they like you, you get to come back. For fucksake don't start asking them what they do. How do you feel?"

"Pretty fast."

"Just go with it. They'll love it that you're new."

The door was opened by a small-boned man of medium height who looked extremely wired. He wore a carefully faded cotton shirt open halfway down his chest, his hair was sandy and thin. I didn't recognize him. If he worked in film it had to be on the other side of the camera. He waved us in and closed the door. He moved in an abrupt, exaggerated fashion, like he found it difficult to control his limbs.

"Well, it's about time. And who's this young man?"

He smiled at me and jerked his hand forward. His grip was way too tight.

"Ron, this is Jack. I had car trouble and he gave me a ride. You get him too, no extra charge."

"Hello, Jack. You look like a healthy fellow. Do you like teaching people how to behave? Of course you do, of course you do. You wouldn't be here otherwise, would you? Yes, I'm sure you know how to treat people who haven't been quite as good as they should have been."

I looked at Rex and saw his left eye twitch.

"You bet."

After that the three of us stood in a brittle silence. Ron shifted from foot to foot, like he'd forgotten what to do next.

Rex cleared his throat. "Er, Ron...."

"Oh, yes. Jesus. God, sorry. Money first, of course. Nothing extra for Jake, you say? I mean Jack. Sorry Jack. Nothing extra?"

"If you feel you'd like to, Ron. It's entirely up to you. Don't feel pressured."

"Well, maybe a little something, then."

Rex took the folded bills Ron held out and slipped them into his pocket without counting them. Everyone acted as though the money didn't matter. I tried to check denominations, but it happened too fast.

"So, let's go through."

At the end of the entrance hall we went left through an arch into a high-ceilinged room that ran clear to the back of the building and ended in a glass wall that showed L.A. floating above a stretch of dark canyon.

Harsh light, white stone walls, varnished blond-wood floor. Very little furniture – a bar in an alcove, a white leather couch against one wall, a low coffee table that held an oversize douche bag, fat with water. The room felt like an art gallery without paintings.

Centered in the barren expanse of floor was something that looked like a customized gynecological examination table – three feet high, four feet long, surrounded by a chrome-steel framework that held a pair of stirrups.

And on the table, a naked woman.

From her body she looked to be mid-thirties, good condition. I couldn't tell from her face because she was wearing a fitted black leather hood. It didn't have any eye-holes, but it had a couple for her nose and a closed zipper over her mouth. Her feet were strapped into the stirrups and pulled so far back her knees almost touched her shoulders. Her anus was plainly visible. Handcuffs locked her arms to another part of the framework behind her head.

Rex took off his jacket and sat on the couch.

"Does she need the same as last time?"

Ron was over at the bar picking up glasses and things.

"I think she deserves it, don't you?"

"I certainly do."

Rex grinned at me while Ron's back was turned.

I stayed standing and looked at the woman on the table until Ron brought the booze over. Under the halogen she didn't look real, it was hard to think of her as human.

The drinks were strong – vodka, lime juice, ice. Rex watched me over his glass to see how I was taking it.

"Do you hear us, my love? They're here, two of them this time. That'll teach you, won't it? We're all looking at you."

Ron's voice rose as he spoke, he had to struggle to keep himself from shouting. He paused for a second to regain control.

"In a little while I'll let them start, but first we're going to have a drink. Don't worry, we won't leave you alone."

The woman's tits lifted rapidly with her breathing.

"Okay, let's get you fellows fired up."

From a drawer in the coffee table he took a bag of insulin syringes, a few vials of sterile water and a couple of gram wraps of coke.

It was hot in the room – Californian nighttime balminess on top of under-floor heating. Outside, deep night silence ate away at our connection with the rest of the world.

Ron watched the woman flinch at the small sounds he made opening the vials. Her tension seemed to please him. When the water was a quarter inch deep in the bottom of a tumbler he opened one of the wraps and dumped it in, stirring with a syringe plunger until it was dissolved. The rubber end squeaked against the glass.

I helped myself to the vodka bottle, chugged a couple of mouthfuls. It burned my throat and made my eyes water, but things were hotting up and I wanted to be loose. Ron handed out the works.

"Don't worry about a filter, this stuff's pharmaceutical. Help yourselves." Then, calling across the room: "These boys are going to be ripped, pussycat. I hope I can control them."

The woman shifted position slightly. The stirrups and the handcuffs clinked.

Ron had to tie off, but Rex and I could find veins by making a fist.

I slid the needle in, a slight sting in the crook of my elbow. Pulled back a little on the plunger to check I was connected – blood expanded in a thick contrail through the clear solution. I looked over at Rex before I let rip. He was waiting for me. We hit simultaneously, Rex giving me a smile like, here we go, dude, hang on.

Bang. Head and chest expanding. A pleasant flash of nausea that fades as soon as it comes. Superman. Clarity and blurred reality at the same time. I wanted to do it. I wanted to fuck the woman right then, before the rush wore off, before my scrubbing organs robbed me of its insulation.

Ron's forehead shone. Eyes on stalks, no irises, bunched muscles at the corner of his jaw. We were all the same.

"Get ready, darling, here they come."

The woman opened and closed her legs as much as the stirrups would allow. Rex nudged me, stood up and stripped. He was half hard already. I dropped my clothes in a pile on the floor. Ron was still sitting and my dick swung in front of his face.

"This first."

He handed Rex the douche bag.

"Clean her out before you start."

All three of us stood around the woman. She knew we were close. Troughs appeared on her thighs and arms as she strained against her bonds and the different muscle groups separated. Ron hadn't taken his clothes off and his hardon stretched the material of his trousers.

Rex was acting like he knew what to do and I wondered how often he'd played this part. Ron's apparent hatred of the woman looked real, but there was something calculated about the scene, something arranged. Fit and fighting, she would have been too much for our host to maneuver into bondage. She must have allowed it to happen.

The booze and the coke were peaking, making things easy for me. Rex, all business now, moved in with the douche bag.

"Hold her open, dude."

Her cunt was wet and my fingers slipped twice before I had her spread. The white plastic nozzle slid between my fingers and into her. Rex squeezed the bag.

She took about half a pint before it started to come out, gushing around the edge of the nozzle and drooling off the table to spatter on the varnished floor with a sound like thick rain.

"That's right, Rex, wash the bitch out. How does it feel to be clean, bitch? She wants to be clean. Don't you my love? You want to be clean?"

The woman made a noise that sounded like yes.

When half the water was gone, Rex did the same thing to her ass. This time the water didn't come out.

Ron had a cigarette going and was smoking like someone unaccustomed to the habit. Short drags with his eyes screwed up. Puff, puff, puff. He handed it to me and nodded at the woman. I looked at Rex.

"Her foot."

"With this?"

"It's what they want."

I hesitated, the cigarette's tip glowed bright red through a gray dust of dead ash. I scanned the room for a sign to tell me whether or not I should go through with it. But nothing hinted one way or the other. And at that moment I was overwhelmed by the pointlessness of trying to choose right over wrong. Why bother? What possible difference could what happened to this woman make to me?

"Do it, dude."

I felt like a puppet, something without choice.

I pressed the cigarette against the tender skin on the arch of her foot. She convulsed, lifting herself into the air, blasting water from her ass in a stuttering, shitty gout that arced several feet beyond the table.

"Yes! Goddamn, she needed that."

Ron hopped from foot to foot and actually clapped his hands. Inside her hood the woman shrieked. Rex raised an eyebrow at me.

"Interesting, huh?"

Ron produced a couple of novelty condoms, one with a head like an elephant, one like a chicken.

"These boys are pumped, pussycat. You're going to get reamed. You want the new one first?"

She moved her head in an awkward nodding motion.

"Yes, I thought so. In you go Jake. Let me help you."

I stood at the end of the table, Ron took hold of my dick and guided it into her. His fingers lingered for the first few strokes.

"That's it, fella. Give it to her. Jam it in as hard as you can. That's the way she likes it. Harder. Burn the shit out of her."

I made it pretty energetic, but it wasn't good enough for Ron. He shouted and waved his arms like he was rooting for a football team until I was slamming it in so hard my thighs made a slapping sound against her ass and the table rocked. At each impact the woman grunted. By the time I'd finished her gash looked raw and slack.

"Feel cleaner, my love? I hope so, because here comes number two."

Same thing, with Ron jigging about and the woman making animal noises, except Rex was in her ass. After a while she started to fart with each of his thrusts.

We broke for booze and another shot of coke, then swapped holes and did it all again.

When we were finished, Rex and I stood like drooping matadors over an exhausted bull. Ron lit another cigarette. He had his dick out and looked slightly ludicrous wanking and jetting smoke at the same time.

"Don't keep me waiting, man."

He held the cigarette out to me. I felt drained and jittery from the coke, stale from the booze. I wanted to be gone. I started to take it but Rex pushed me aside.

"I'll do it, Ron."

"Whatever. Just do it, for Godsake."

Ron stood by the woman's head, up on his toes, putting all of himself behind his dick. Rex blew on the end of the cigarette, then, avoiding my eyes, spread her labia and pushed it against her clit. I heard a small hiss as the coal hit pussy juice.

She pissed herself and jerked around on the table like she'd been electro-cuted. The sounds she made behind her mask were really quite frightening. Ron groaned and spurted white come over the black leather of her face.

Out in the night again.

Rex said, "I'll drive."

"Sure."

I wasn't going to argue. My body ached and my head hummed with post-coke emptiness. I could do without the hassle of driving.

"Got any Valium?"

"Jacket pocket."

Rex pulled out onto Mulholland and headed in the opposite direction to home.

"Wrong way."

"Helps me unwind. Just for a while, okay?"

I tapped out two yellow pills from a brown plastic tube and swallowed them with some of the vodka Ron had let us take when we left. Two didn't seem much, so I did two more. Rex took the same and finished the booze. I chucked the bottle out the window and watched it explode against the side of the road like something heavy thrown into a lake. There was a long hour until dawn and the sky was a sick gray lid. Around us the hillsides were developing like some scene in a retarded Polaroid photo. We drove in silence for a couple of miles, letting the pills take hold.

"What did you think?"

"Was she really into it?"

"Of course. Easy money, huh?"

"Are they all like that?"

"Some are, some are different. You did good."

"What's she look like under the mask?"

"I've never seen her."

"They must have an interesting relationship."

"I guess it's one way to keep a marriage alive."

"Sure, as long as you've got the money to feel safe doing it."

"What safe? They're not killing each other."

"Yeah, but to be okay with it you've got to be able to step outside the usual morality. And that's not something everyone can afford."

"You're saying money buys them out of right and wrong?"

"Out of other people's ideas of it."

"Man, you romanticize it too much. When it comes down to it, they're just people, same as everyone else."

"Bullshit. Can you see some guy, like some sanitation guy or something, coming home and his wife, who's been scrubbing floors all day, letting him tie her up and burn her cunt with a cigarette? Fuck, there'd be all kinds of shit to pay. Police, domestic violence, sexual abuse.... That one act would change everything for them. But rich people aren't affected the same way. They can segment. They can indulge without fucking up the rest of their lives. Tomorrow, Ron and his wife will wake up and she'll be sore as hell, but

I bet they'll be having breakfast in some chichi nook off Melrose as though nothing ever happened."

"Well, I won't be out looking for them. Jesus I'm wrecked."

He U-turned and we tried for home. Pilled out, it didn't matter to either of us that our speed was below twenty-five. Five minutes later Rex nodded off at the wheel and it became obvious we weren't going to make the distance. I elbowed him awake.

"Pull over."

He snapped his head up and did his best to focus. When he spoke his voice sounded like mine – slurred.

"Are you hungry, dude?"

"I can't tell."

"Me either."

"We did too much Valium."

"Nah, not after that coke."

"Let's pull over."

"Yeah."

We drove for another half mile while Rex summoned the motivation to change from a mobile situation to a stationary one. By the time he managed it we were back at the Hollywood Bowl overlook. We parked up close to the fence.

An angled vista of city dawn.

Engine off. Systems shutdown.

"Holy fuck."

"These seats recline."

"Thank God."

The sun was high when I woke and the air in the car was stale. Through the windshield downtown L.A. was a dark ghost behind a curtain of smog.

Rex was gone, but he'd left a business card and some money on the dash. I counted the money – three hundred dollars – and read what he'd written on the card: "Use the number. Getting a lift with tourists." I flipped it over. Black on white, expensive letters. A phone number and the words *Bel Air*

Escorts. The area code wasn't Bel Air, though. I stuck it in my pocket with the money.

The overlook gates were open now. I got out of the car, walked through a group of sleek Japanese in the parking lot and climbed the steps to the top of the sandstone outcrop. Cicadas buzzed in the scrub around me and down in its dirty brown bowl the city hustled ten million people through another day.

Despite the body mileage I'd clocked up last night I felt good. I ran scenes in my head and marveled at them – my cock, the chromium stirrups, my fingers holding the cigarette against her foot. I'd done it, I'd crossed the line between accepted behavior and behavior most of the population would consider a lynching offense, and that morning I felt as real as any of the men in the Escape commercials. It had been dirty and nasty but I wanted more.

I looked over my shoulder to check the car. Another coach-load of tourists was squeezing its way through the gate and I was worried about my paintwork. Reflected sun made bright ovals on the windows and heliographed memories of Karen at me. She would be underground by now, flapping chest and skinny limbs bundled into a county grave that I would never visit.

But she'd bought me a car with money earned by selling her kidney and I couldn't forget her completely. Same as I couldn't forget I'd forced her from the apartment that night – an action which almost certainly had its place in the chain of events that led to her murder.

I realized then why yesterday evening I'd put together what I knew of her death. Karen to live with had been a nightmare, but Karen dead could be used as an escape. Tracking down her killer wasn't something I expected to succeed at, but the simple doing of it, the attempt alone, had the potential to give me again what I'd experienced at Ron's – life outside the mainstream.

If I ever found the person responsible I wouldn't know what to do with them, but that didn't matter. What I wanted from her death was a reason to move in a world where the usual social obediences didn't apply. An excuse to go places, to ask questions, to do something other than lie in bed all day.

And to finance this withdrawal from all things good and clean and American? I had three hundred bucks in my pocket and the number for Bel Air Escorts. Rex had told me I'd be good at it. Man, I'd be a natural.

Down from the lookout. The first cluster of Japanese had been replaced by another. I walked through them, half a foot taller and full of alien thoughts about the pointlessness of community.

Inside the Prelude I felt protected.

The seats were warm, they wrapped around.

CHAPTER 8

A **phone booth** in West L.A. I'd stopped because the confidence I felt at the overlook had become infected with thoughts of Ryan. Maybe it was just chemical residue paranoia, but I couldn't shake the feeling I should tie up the loose ends of my old life before embarking on a journey out of it. By now Ryan would have confirmed my alibi, and that my spunk wasn't the same as the stuff they'd found in Karen. I knew I'd check out okay, but I wanted to hear it from him. I needed to be reassured he wasn't going to be following me any further down the line.

His ID badge had made him part of the Santa Monica Police Department. I dialed info and asked for the Homicide section. And things got immediately weird. He didn't work there. The guy I spoke to said the only Ryan at the station was a member of the Minor Vice team.

"Would they be dealing with that girl who got killed in Palisades Park a couple of weeks ago? The one that was cut open?"

"Not a chance. We catch all the murders. If you got information you better talk to Detective Sullivan, he's the officer in charge of that case. What's your name?"

It seemed so much simpler to hang up rather than answer. So I did. Then I rang the switchboard again and asked for Ryan in Minor Vice. The extension rang for a long time before it was picked up.

"Yeah?"

"Ryan?"

"Not in. Try tomorrow."

"Ryan's like this fat guy with black hair, right? Takes heart pills."

"Yeah, that's him. Who's calling?"

"I've got some info on that case he's working. The murder in Palisades Park."

"Murder?" The man laughed. "You got the wrong guy."

"I'm sure it was Ryan."

"Not unless it happened in a porno store. Try Homicide."

I didn't have to hang up this time, the guy beat me to it.

I stood in the booth for a while trying to decide whether I should be relieved or frightened. I hadn't heard from anyone called Sullivan, and he'd had plenty of time to show up. So I figured the Police Department as a whole didn't have a handle on me. That was cool, but what did it leave? A psycho like Ryan gone rogue, with me as the focus of his obsession? Had I become his independent pet project?

I got back in the car and headed home. I needed a shower and some sleep.

On the ocean side of Lincoln Boulevard that morning Venice had a dusty feel, like a reluctantly reinhabited ghost town. Maybe when I first moved there it held some kind of mystery or romance for me. But that had changed. What had not been gradually eroded during my time with Karen had now, I found, been finished off in the incinerating flash of last night's sex and this morning's epiphany. Now it was hollow and untenanted, a place to pass through, to move away from.

I'd caught a radio rundown of the latest news on the way back from the hills. Mel Gibson was getting twenty-five million for *Ransom*, Macaulay Culkin was hanging out for his eighteenth birthday when he'd get his hands on sixty of the same, and Michael Jackson was estimated to be personally worth two hundred and fifty.

The sums of money jammed my head. When I was younger I used to play the game of deciding what I'd do with ten million dollars, certain that one day I'd have at least that much. I'd plan in infinitesimal detail the exact steps I'd take, the order of my purchases, the choices between the unlimited alternatives so much money would open up. But now, at a failed thirty, those kind of hyper-realistic imaginings brought with them a depression too exhausting to bear. Along with the news about Ryan, the reports of other people's wealth fucked my mood completely.

I took two Seconal and climbed into bed. A shower would have to wait.

CHAPTER 9

It was dark when I woke. I lay for a while watching the colored washes of light that the cars down in the street threw across my ceiling like opening Japanese fans. My head was clear. I ran my hands over my body. It felt ready for action.

Time to motivate.

Shit, shower, teeth, shave. A can of cold Pepsi and two cigarettes in the warm night air by the window, silent TV alight in the corner of the room. People moving outside. I imagined how they felt – suntanned skin smooth and dry after day-long beaching, frictionless under freshly washed denim and soft cotton, happily heading for bars and movies.

I ate some food in front of the open fridge and thought about Brad Pitt and Johnny Depp and Tom Cruise. How much more keenly they must be feeling the same night air that lay against my skin. Their senses would be more finely attuned to it than mine, undulled by the exhaustions that plagued the poor – food, rent, taxes, tires for the car.... And if anything like that did make it into their world, they had maids and personal assistants to deal with it.

I got kind of caught up with those thoughts for a while and it was pretty late by the time I left the apartment and started the game of looking for Karen's killer.

I didn't know any of Karen's friends well enough to have their phone numbers, but from the early days, when she and I were still attempting the charade of a shared existence, I had an idea where I might connect with one or two of them. Karen had been part of a loose-knit group that hung out in the same places, listened to the same music and shared similar interests – drugs, money, leather clothes....

Unless what was hip had changed since we terminated our joint socializing, I figured a tour of certain bars ought to turn up someone who knew her. And if I found someone who knew her, then maybe I'd get a pointer to the kidney man.

The first couple of places didn't work – an espresso bar on Harper Avenue, where I was a little reckless with caffeine, and a live music joint near Paramount where I did what I could to antidote myself with vodka. Third time lucky, though. At a place on Detroit Street, not far from the Drag.

The club didn't make much of a fuss about its entrance, just a door between two businesses, propped open with a chair, giving onto a flight of steps that led below street-level. It wasn't mentioned in the entertainment listings, and it wasn't at the cutting edge of any musical trend, but it had its attractions for a certain kind of person nevertheless. Because, along with an almost nonexistent policy against substance abuse, it had a gimmick that was just so terribly wild, man – it was cool to jerk off there. Or jerk someone else off. Or get jerked off. And you didn't have to hide in a toilet stall either.

At the bottom of the steps I got frisked for weapons, paid the twenty dollar entrance fee and pushed through a set of padded double doors. Simultaneous high-volume sound and low-power lighting – so low, in fact, it took a couple of seconds for my eyes to adjust. The music was pretty much industrial and it created a jagged atmosphere that I figured was designed to get people so tense they had to beat off for relief.

Small and dingy, everything black. The dance floor held about eight and the top of the bar looked like it had been cut from the side of a Russian freighter. The air stank of fish. I bought vodka and watched some girl in latex pump spunk out of a guy into a glass that was already a quarter full. Then I checked out the crowd. It was hard to make out faces, so I concentrated on haircuts. I found two I recognized sitting together in one of the booths that ran down a wall.

Jimmy and Steve were rock star wannabes who'd come over from England a few years back only to find that California already had about a million unemployed musicians of its own. They'd adapted pretty well, though, and moved swiftly on to an area in which they excelled – taking smack. Mid-twenties, leather head to toe, dyed-black hair.

Their faces went blank and guarded through a moment of image search when I walked up. But after I said Karen's name they remembered who I was and let me sit down. The first thing they asked was if I had any gear. It wasn't a particularly safe assumption, but I took it to mean they didn't know about her yet. On the junk front I didn't disappoint them. I'd scored a quarter gram at the beginning of the evening for just such an ice-breaking opportunity. Even in that place, though, cooking up in public would have been a bit much, so we had to duck our heads below the table and snort it through a bill. After that we were friends, mates, buddies – long-time acquaintances chewing the fat about this and that.

Half an hour later, when a chick in the next booth had finished screwing herself with a bottle of Rolling Rock, I started in on the real business of the evening.

"How long since you guys seen Karen, then?"

The smack had taken hold and their responses were pretty relaxed. Steve looked like he'd done a tad too much to continue active communication, but Jimmy was functioning reasonably effectively.

"Dunno. When'd we last see her, Steve?"

Steve managed a shrug. "I dunno. A while."

"Yeah, be a while now. How is she?"

"I haven't seen her for a month."

"A month? You split up or something?"

"Not that I know. I thought she was on a job."

"Long job."

"Yeah, I'm getting worried. You haven't seen her?"

"Nah. Hey, Steve, you know where Karen's at?"

"Huh?"

"Karen. D'you know where she is?"

"Haven't got a clue."

Jimmy lifted his hands and let them fall.

"Sorry, pal."

"She was going on about this plan she had. I don't know if it's got anything to do with anything."

"No offense, man, but she's always fuckin' on about one scam or another. They're bullshit. Never happen."

"This was, like, about kidneys or something."

Jimmy laughed and slapped the table.

"Oh, fuck, not the kidney thing! Man, she was hot for that one. No offense, but she's a mad cunt sometimes."

Jimmy's reaction jerked Steve out of his stupor. He opened his eyes and scratched his forearms.

"I know someone who did it."

"What are you talking about, you dumb cunt? Go back to sleep."

"Nah, you know him too. That geezer who used to score off us. What was his name? The fuckwit with all the earrings."

"Joey."

"Yeah, Joey. That's how he reckoned he got his bar."

"Bullshit."

"He showed me his scar."

"And that makes it gospel."

"I'm only telling you what he said."

"He was shitting ya, for fucksake."

Jimmy shook his head and got up to go watch a circle of guys who were starting to group around a girl.

I asked Steve how much Joey was supposed to have been paid for his kidney. When he said thirty grand it seemed smart to ask for the guy's address as well.

"I don't know where he lives, but his bar's on Pico. It's got all this bullshit Egyptian stuff on the front. Look for a little guy with a goatee. And lotsa earrings."

Chapter 10

Dead beat. Late night back at the apartment. Head still swaddled in smack. The place looked worse than ever, dingy under light from a naked bulb. Even the furniture was unpleasant to look at. One piece in particular, because Ryan was sitting in it. Flabby body sagging into cracks between cushions. Same black suit, a clean white shirt, hair slick and gleaming, flat against his head.

"What the fuck—"

"Hiya, Jackie. Where you been? I was out in the car, but you took so long I thought I'd come in and make myself to home."

"What do you want?"

"Oh, touch base, look the place over.... Where were you?"

"Out."

"Put a bit more effort into it."

"I was with friends."

"So soon after Karen's death? My, my. Got a drink?"

"What?"

"A drink. Liquor, booze, firewater."

"It's like three o'clock."

"So we'll have a three o'clock drink."

Arguing obviously wasn't going to make things any easier, so I got Southern Comfort, ice and glasses from the kitchenette, poured a couple of drinks and sat down on the bed, opposite him.

"Is this going to take long? I'm tired."

Ryan ignored me and scanned the room.

"Not much to show for a life, is it?"

"No, it's not."

"You should have tried harder, Jackie, given her something better. I would have."

He drifted off then for a couple of seconds, like he was remembering something. When he came back he wasn't any better. He knocked back his drink and screwed up his face like it was painful going down.

"I heard they make this stuff from orange peel."

He poured himself another and looked at me speculatively.

"Know what I used to think about when I was fucking her? I used to think what it'd be like having her all the time, like you did."

"It was less fun than you might imagine."

"Yeah, she said your relationship wasn't too hot. But that sort of thing don't mean shit after fifty. You get someone her age who isn't hideous, you're ahead of the game. It makes it like you haven't gotten older. Feels good just walking down the street with something like that, believe me."

"How interesting."

Ryan moved surprisingly quickly for a fat man, lunged forward and dragged me upright. His fingernails scratched my chest. The back of my head hit a wall.

"Don't ever think I don't matter. I spent thirty years shoveling shit in this town and at the end of next year I'll get a pension for it that'll rent a two-room dump and buy a piece of second-rate ass once a month. Facing that, Jackie, I won't take attitude off some waster fuck like you."

If we'd gone at it I would have come out on top, easy. But he was a cop and he had a gun. So I stood there and let him breathe heavily into my face. A few seconds later he went back to the couch and sat down abruptly, rubbing his chest.

"Get me some water."

I brought him a glass. He took a few sips then put a pill under his tongue. His face looked congested.

"Are you okay?"

"Yeah. Pour me a drink."

"You think that's wise?"

"Yeah, it's wise. Pour me a fucking drink."

I splashed out Southern, trying to figure if him dying in the apartment would be a good thing or a bad thing. Ryan held it up to the light.

"I gotta cut back on this shit."

"You get the results from my sample yet?"

"Maybe...."

"Or maybe you never put it in to be checked."

"Really? Now what does that mean?"

"I called your station. You're not on the case. You don't even work Homicide."

"Jackie.... That wasn't very smart. That wasn't very smart at all."

"I didn't say anything to them, but I mean, shit, you work porn or something."

"If you ever do anything like that again, I'll kill you."

"I want to know what the fuck's going on."

Ryan sucked in a breath and held it for a moment. He let it out slowly.

"So you can understand, so you can appreciate the potential for something very bad happening to you, I'll outline the situation. I knew Karen, I already told you. I see some crime-scene photos on a desk and I find out she's dead and that no one can get a handle on who she is. I not only know who she is, but I know plenty about her background. Probably more than you, Jackie.

"I know she's married 'cause she told me, and I know where she lives because I followed her home one time after I fucked her. Call it idle curiosity. I know other things too, but I'm not Homicide, I'm Minor Vice. So I got a choice. Let the murder guys have what I know and hope they don't fuck it up. Or go out on my own and make sure things get done properly."

"But why? So you knew her. Big deal. I don't see the motivation."

"Well that's something you'll have to puzzle over, isn't it? And while you're puzzling, it'd be smart to remember that me not being hooked up with the department on this one don't have too many advantages for you. I don't have to worry about all those pesky regulations and codes of practice, get my meaning?"

"I figured that when you made me wank in the car."

"I needed a sample. Don't worry, it didn't go to waste. I might be operating unofficially, but I got people who owe me favors."

"Then you know it wasn't my spunk in Karen. You check my alibi too?"

"Yeah, I spoke to the guy. You got lucky both times."

"Then why are you still hassling me?"

"'Cause things are never as simple as they seem. Time of death can be thrown off by a lot of things, maybe you kept her in the fridge a few days before you dumped her. And your come? You could have had an accomplice and it was his. Doesn't stop you being involved. You know something, Jackie, and I'm going to keep turning up and turning up till I find out what it is."

"This is insane. I could call your station right now and get you seriously fucked up."

"But you won't. One, you'd have too much explaining to do – like why you didn't report her missing, like why you lied about her tattoo, like why the whole thing seems to mean nothing to you. And two, because I'd kill you. You think things are insane now? Wait till I really get pissed off."

He pushed himself to his feet, but he must have done it too fast because he had to bend at the waist and take a few deep breaths. He straightened after a while and blinked rapidly a couple of times.

"Fuck, I must be getting old. Got any coke?"

"I wouldn't give you the steam off my shit."

He laughed at that, then ran his hands over his hair and pushed his way through the door.

Look out world, asshole re-entering.

I slept and the night rolled over into day like a dog. Another postmeridian awakening – sunshine on empty bottles, tangled clothes. I dozed while the temperature rose.

Sometime around one Royston phoned and whined about his money. I told him I had it and to come around tomorrow morning. He sounded pleased and tried to make out we were buddies again. I hung up on him, then dialed the number of a house clearance company.

Sucking cathode. Lucky people on the screen, going back to their trailers after each take to be pampered, to rally the army of friends and associates necessary for the movie-star night ahead. Or to hold conversations on their phones that would shift large amounts of money and equipment around the world, conversations that would affect the lives of other men.

I burned up an hour with longing. I dreamed I was one of them. But after a while it got too painful.

To distract myself I bagged up Karen's stuff and took it down to the garbage drum at the back of the building. I heaved the bags over the steel side and looked in after them. One of them had split and spilt its contents across a previously dumped family of cats. The animals were rotting and badly torn. I stood there watching maggots crawl over panties, cheap cosmetics, Kotex.... Then I got in the car and caught a movie at a multiplex on Third Street.

The clearance team turned up at the end of the afternoon, some cowboy outfit that didn't ask questions as long as they made a profit. I put the stuff I wanted to keep in the closet and told them to take everything else. They offered me four hundred and seventy-five bucks, not a huge sum for the contents of an apartment, but it didn't seem too bad to me, considering none of the stuff was mine.

I left them to it and killed what was left of the day in a bar on the promenade. Around seven I used the card Rex had left me and made a call.

CHAPTER 11

Bel Air Escorts was a telephone service with the end of the line in a Wilshire district apartment. Nice area – wide road with no loiterers, wide balconies, plenty of glass. Hardly Bel Air, but clean and quiet and anonymous – fine for a business that dealt in take-out sex.

My intercom buzz was answered immediately – they were expecting me. Up fifteen floors in a mirrored elevator that smelt of pine disinfectant. Deep-blue carpeting along the hall. No people, no sound. Faceless and sanitized, like the passageways of a hotel. I pressed a white button next to the door and waited.

A lean, bald guy in leather trousers and a black vest opened up. He had the air of a favored slave, proud and dedicated, but kind of reined in. We walked down a hall of closed doors to a room that had probably been a bedroom but was now an info-teched office. Minimalist decor – gray slate floor, white walls, a big carbon fiber desk across one corner, a spray of black twigs in a smoked-glass vase. The windows were opaque, tinted slightly orange by streetlight from the road below.

There were two people in the room; a sleek Latin guy about forty tapping away on a laptop behind the desk, and a girl with perfect blond hair and an even better body sitting on a black leather couch placed midway between two of the window panels. She wore a tight red lycra mini-dress and held herself with confidence. Thousand bucks a night, for sure.

The Latin closed his screen and slid his eyes over me.

"You know Rex."

He had a rough voice, like his throat had been damaged in some youthful Central American skirmish. And I didn't like his eye contact, either – too direct, too long. No one asked me to sit down, so I stood in front of the desk feeling uncomfortable.

"Er, yeah. Rex said he thought I'd be okay at this kind of work."

"And what kind of work would that be?"

"The kind Rex does."

"Be more precise."

"Well, hustling, I suppose. Going round to people's places for sex."

"Oh, no." The Latin shook his head sadly. "Oh, no. That is not what Rex does at all. Hustling—"

"Rex fucks people for money. He said I should get in touch with you."

"Do not interrupt me. I am making a point. This is an operation with class, there is no room for the hustling mentality. My clients pay a lot of money and they expect something more than ten minutes in the back of a car. I am not in the business of selling what can be found on any street corner."

"Okay."

"Understand also that sex is sometimes only part of what you will be paid for. Some clients wish to be accompanied to dinner or to a party first. You must be discreet and pleasant, even if they are old or unattractive. Can you do this?"

"I can do anything you want."

He nodded to the girl on the couch. She stood up and moved close.

"Good. Indulge me."

"How do you mean?"

"Grace."

The girl took hold of the hem of her dress and peeled it up over her head. She was naked underneath, tanned without break from head to toe, pussy hair shaved into a tight wedge.

"You've taken me a little bit by surprise. I'm, er, not exactly sure—"

"If you can't do it here, how can I trust you to perform in the bedroom of a rich woman whose looks are nowhere near as...perfected as Grace's?"

This wasn't the same as the night with Rex. This was cold and demanding and hadn't had time to grow into shape. And my blood was relatively free of liquor and drugs. The potential for humiliation was high, but I had no choice. I needed money. And more than that, I'd committed, up at the Hollywood Bowl overlook, to a certain kind of life and this was one of the ways it was lived. If I backed away now I'd be forced to reevaluate myself, and I had nowhere left to reevaluate to.

Grace came close, she smelt of something dark and expensive. She smiled a small kind of smile that didn't help much.

When she pulled my jeans down the air in the room felt unpleasantly cool on my balls. I pressed against her, seeking heat. Hard back under my hands, firm ass, breasts against my chest. If I could jerk off in front of Ryan, I had to be able to do this.

I blanked out the Latin and the bald guy and pushed my face into her hair. When I touched her she was wet. She made a small sound of pleasure. It sounded so genuine, so wanting, that the primal fuck-urge overrode my worrying brain and pumped my cock full of blood.

She put a condom on me with her mouth and we fucked standing up, me behind and her bent forward, hands braced against the edge of the Latin's desk. He watched me carefully over her shoulders, but not like it was giving him a kick.

When it was over the bald guy gave us both a small towel. Grace wiped herself, pulled her dress back on and took her place on the couch. She didn't light a cigarette and she didn't fix her make-up. She just sat there, letting her eyes drift around the room.

"How fast do you recover?"

"You want me to do it again?"

The Latin smiled, slightly.

"I have a job for you. Tonight. A nice job. Big house, good money, not too bad looking. Start you off easy."

The clearance guys had done their work well, the apartment was gutted. They'd left the phone and the light bulbs, but that was about all and I had a momentary pang when I realized I'd forgotten to tell them to leave the TV – a friend in the corner would have been nice while I got ready.

The Latin's gig was a deep night number – dick on call to chill some woman when she got home from a premiere or charity function or a Hills party where absolutely everyone was there, darling. Or whatever. That meant I had some hours to kill – time to take a stab at tracking Joey down. I showered and changed, then started on bloodstream preparation.

I still had some of the three hundred I'd earned with Rex, plus the cash from the contents of the apartment, and as it looked like I'd be getting more tonight, I decided to blow a little of it down at the beach front.

I could have had coke, but I went for sulfate instead – bathtub amphetamine. Quarter the price and a lot less fun, but it had its advantages. Half a gram would wire you all night and make you horny as hell. It also gave you a stressed-out edge that communicated itself to people, made it harder for them to be certain of your reactions. Just right to fritz Joey if I found him.

Back at the apartment; a couple of lines, two Southerns and a Bud took me close to the terminal velocity of mood necessary to make it out into the city and do the things I'd set myself to do. A minute of air punching to limber up in case Joey got difficult. Almost there, almost there.... Something missing.... Yes, a cigarette! Stick one in and fire it up. Check eyes in the mirror – yep, pupils at maximum dilation, skin tight, jaws clenching.... Ready to energize.

Into the Prelude. Driving felt like fun, but all the other cars were going so goddamn slow. I tailgated along Lincoln. Everything was crystal, like the air had been sucked out of the spaces between things, like that awful, beautiful clarity you get in pictures taken from the space shuttle.

Litany in my head; take it easy, take it easy, watch that car ahead, that other guy's making a right, tap the brakes, indicate, smooth swoop around, straighten up, take it easy, next guy ahead, pass the sucker, no competition, nothing touches this Jap technology. Switch lanes, switch lanes again, perfect highway positioning. At one with the car – a Zen state inside a machine from a polluted Zen race.

Pico Boulevard, a tertiary road, narrow but pretty straight and not too busy. Fine for dawdling along, looking for a place I'd never been. Four blocks past chunky Santa Monica College, on the corner of Clover Field Boulevard, I found Bar Ramses. Like Jimmy said, bullshit Egyptian – plaster pharaohs on either side of the door, floor to ceiling windows in the shape of ankhs, hieroglyphics over everything.

I parked in the lot out back – not much light, plenty of trash – and did another line. By the time I got out of the car I was grinding my teeth and the booze in the bar had as much pull as the possibility of finding Joey.

Inside. Not what the flashy front suggested, just a neighborhood bar. Booths, wall alcoves, a couple of pool tables in the rear, a scratched-up open space where the clientele danced sometimes, perhaps. A lot of tobacco smoke and very little mineral water.

Scanning didn't do any good, so I chilled at the bar with shots of vodka until I'd had enough contact with the barman to feel comfortable asking after Joey.

It went easier than I'd thought it would – no movie-style shifty eyes or sudden tightening of the mouth, no dive under the counter for a gun. Just: "Joey? Yeah, he's around. Try back there by the pool tables. Middle booth." Bit of a letdown, really. I'd been all set to faze him with something neat about old buddies or wanting to pay back a loan.

Joey was sitting by himself. He had a bottle of beer and a contact mag in front of him. Steve's description was accurate, the edge of his left ear was rimmed with nickel-sized silver hoops and the bottom of his face ended in a triangle of dark hair. He wore a Hawaiian shirt and he was short and scrawny, a lot smaller than me. Things looked good.

He jerked when I sat down opposite him.

"This is private, fuck off."

"Hi, Joey. How ya doin'?" Big smile.

"Do I know you?"

"No, but we're connected."

"I don't know you, but we're connected? The fuck's this, a game show?"

"I want to ask you something."

"I don't do handouts. Fuck off."

"Steve gave me your name."

"Who?"

"English Steve, long black hair. Hangs out with Jimmy."

"Never heard of him."

"I don't want to be indelicate about this, Joey, but you used to buy from him. All I want is some information, it's important to me."

"I could give a fuck."

Being reasonable obviously wasn't going to get me very far. Time to push a little harder and hope my balls held up.

"Could you give a fuck about telling the IRS how you financed this place? Or the police maybe?"

"I could give a fuck about calling some friends over."

Joey jutted his chin at a group of men playing pool.

"Remember the story you told Steve?"

"I told you, I don't know Steve."

"Don't be a prick. I can freeze you with a word."

"Yeah?"

"Kidneys."

Joey stepped his attitude down just a notch.

"What about kidneys?"

"Removal. Selling. Don't act stupid, I haven't done this sort of thing before. I might flip out at any moment and get all amateur and violent. Tell me how to connect and I'll walk out of here. That's the last you'll hear of it."

"I can't tell what I don't know.

Enough was enough. I leaned across the table, took hold of his Hawaiian lapels, and pulled. The material made a nice ripping sound and buttons flew out of the booth. I ran my hand down the skin of his chest, down the left side of his guts, down to the scar that ridged his pasty white skin.

"Hey, fuck off, man!"

He started to push himself upright, ready to make an unwelcome scene. I didn't have much choice, I hit him hard enough to make his mouth bleed.

Hitting someone was new to me, but it meshed perfectly with the way things had been going since Karen's death. I'd seen the situation a million times on TV so I knew it was the right thing to do – I didn't feel bad about it at all. I guess I was growing as a person.

A quick glance at the bar, no one seemed to be paying much attention. But Joey looked like he might be thinking about yelling, so I talked fast.

"This kidney thing connects to a murder, and if I don't get what I want you're going to find yourself involved. I got one super-fuck cop on my ass about it and he'd just love to get a taste of you. You want to lose your liquor license? Man, it'd be gone the day he came to see you. Now sit down and we'll talk about that scar on your belly."

The mention of cops took the wind out of Joey. He wiped blood off his lips and dropped back into his seat.

"I don't know nothing about a murder."

"I asked about kidneys."

"So I sold one of them. Big fucking deal. The bread was too good to pass up."

"More."

"Like what?"

"Like, Joey, where you went to do it, who did it, how I find them. That sort of thing."

"That's going to be difficult."

"You got a phone in here? Maybe we need someone who's better at asking questions."

"Fuck, man, I'm telling you the truth. I don't know any names or places."

"Tell me how it fucking went down, then."

"Jesus, okay...." Joey raised his hands like he was placating an aggressive retard. "Fuck.... A while back I wasn't set up like I am now. You know the Drag?"

"Yeah."

"I used to hustle down there. I ain't proud of it, but I didn't have a place to live, no family to go to, I was hungry most of the time—"

"I don't give a shit if your dog just died. Get on with it."

Joey looked vicious, then made me wait while he took a slug of beer and sloshed it around his mouth.

"One night this black Jaguar pulls up, I think the guy wants to trick and great because he obviously has bread. But it don't turn out like that, the guy says straight off he ain't interested in sex. He works for a rich doctor who gives free healthcare to homeless people and he's out looking for someone to take up the offer."

"What was the offer?"

"Go with the guy back to the doctor's clinic, get a free check-up, some immunization shots, pills if anything's wrong. Plus a bed for the night and two hundred bucks in the morning. I jumped at it. Two hundred was a lot of money to me then. So I get in the car and after we've been going a while he gives me this bag thing to put over my head so I can't see where we're going. If I don't do it the deal's off 'cause the doctor wants to stay anonymous. I figure what the fuck, a guy in a Jag ain't a serial killer, right? Anyhow I do it and nothing happens and we get to where we're going. He don't let me take the bag off till we're inside so I don't know where we are."

"How long did it take to get there?"

"'Bout a half hour."

"What did it look like?"

"Some kind of private place. No windows, not very big, bits of medical stuff all over the place. He locked me in a room and a coupla minutes later this woman comes in, but she's got one of them doctor's masks on, so I don't get a look at her face. She tells me she's the doctor and takes some blood and piss and asks me a load of shit – medical history, do I have any living family, etcetera, etcetera. Then she makes me strip and gives me an examination. I knew right then something weren't straight. The way she handled me – made me bend over, stuck her fingers up my ass, checked out my balls. She was getting off on it, man.

"Anyhow, at the end of it she says I don't need any medication, but would I like a sedative to help me sleep. I say what have you got? She only lays some morphine on me. Can you believe it? Then she says she has to think about the results of my examination and leaves. Back comes the old guy and takes me to another room with a bed in it. Again he locks the door and there's no windows, no way to get out. I figure so what? Just bang the morph, wait till morning and collect my two hundred. If they've got some security hang-up, it ain't my problem.

"Next morning the doctor chick, still with her mask, tells me she's looked at my results and there's a proposition. I can take the two hundred like they promised and get a ride back to town. Or I can donate one of my kidneys and get thirty grand for it. Thirty fucking grand!"

"Donate it to who?"

"Who knows? Some rich bastard who needed one, I guess. She showed me this operating theater they had there and gave me this spiel about how you can live just the same with one as two. Everything was too real to be weird, I mean they had all these machines and everything. So I said yes. It happened the next day and I stayed about two weeks healing up – wasted on morph the whole time. Then they let me go. With thirty grand in cash. And get this, the night before the operation she came into my room and fucked me. Kept her mask on like always, but she had some bod."

"Could you identify her?"

"Not her face, anyhow."

"What did the old guy look like?"

"Tall, thin. About fifty or sixty. Excellent hair, all silver, hadn't lost a strand. If you want to find him, look for that hair."

"You ever see him again?"

"No. I got this place, I don't need to be doing with the Drag anymore. Hear about him, though, sometimes."

"From who?"

"Fuck, just hustlers. A couple come in now and then, they talk, I listen when I can be bothered. I hear mention of a silver-haired guy in a black Jag, gotta be him."

Joey leaned back and drank beer. He'd got his confidence back with the telling of his story.

"You wanna give out with this murder business?"

"No."

"I figured. What about the cop? I don't want him around here fucking up my life."

"So long, Joey."

I headed for the door. He shouted that I was a cocksucker and a few heads turned, but nobody stood up.

I sat in the car and slow-breathed. My hands were shaking but I felt pretty good about the way I'd carried things off. Playing strong-arm wasn't something I was used to and it had been a lot harder than it looked on TV maintaining the necessary aggression.

I thought about doing a line, but I was wired to the gills already. The adrenaline I'd pumped in the bar hadn't combined well with the speed and I felt nerved. In an hour I was supposed to be fucking some woman in Beverly Hills, if I didn't chill a little I'd spurt as soon as I stuck it in her. And if that happened I'd be fucked with the Latin and a potential source of decent bread would vanish into the sunset. My head said I should eat, but my guts weren't into it. I smoked instead and mulled over what I'd learnt.

Karen had sold her kidney. Joey had sold his. To the same buyer? Obviously. Even in L.A. black market organ acquisition couldn't be that widespread. But as far as Karen had let on she'd gone to Malibu for her doctor fuck sessions. Joey hadn't been in his guy's car long enough to make it there from the Drag. A problem? Same people with two operating theaters? Or did they move about as a precaution? Impossible to know. Right now I'd have to go with Joey's info. A silver-haired old guy in a black Jag. Apparently still recruiting members for the kidney club among the trash of the Drag. Only one way to check it – hang out there and hope I got lucky.

Pulling out of the parking lot, on the way to my gig in Beverly Hills, a complication arose. My headlights caught a gray Plymouth across the street. Lights off, engine dead, but there was a dark man-shape behind the wheel. I looked close and saw a silhouette of slicked hair and heavy jowls paying attention to me. Ryan. Had to be.

Rapid ignition. I got mobile and he wanted to follow, but I couldn't have him click to my sex deal – too much to add to his already skewed imaginings.

He was pointed at Pico. He must have followed me and figured I'd go back the way I came. I screamed right instead, figuring I could take Clover Field straight to Santa Monica and lose him on the way, then be free to motor on up to B.H. He dropped seconds hauling a U-turn and I punched the Prelude down a street of bungalows and over the Santa Monica Freeway. I had a two-hundred-yard lead by the time he'd gotten himself straight.

I split right from Clover Field about a minute past the freeway. Twenty-Sixth Street. The lights phased my way as I crossed Olympic – talk about ass. Ryan caught my turn, though, and on the straight the big engine in his Detroit cop car cut into my lead. No siren, no strobe, still out on his own.

Shaking him by Santa Monica wasn't going to happen. I went cold and dry. I was eyes through a windshield, hands on a wheel, feet on pedals. I knew if Ryan caught me his anger at my having dared to run from him would express itself physically. But if I could lose him maybe there was a chance we could both pretend I never knew he was there, that I was just out testing my wheels. Slim, but better than nothing.

Past Colorado Avenue I was into a grid system. Evasive action. I cut from the straight at ninety degrees. I did it again and again. Ryan managed to make it, I could see his predator headlights in my mirror, but he was later each time, each time a little further behind. Until, on the other side of Wilshire, when I made the second of a series of turns, he hadn't made the first. I was out of his eye-line at last, but he could still make a lucky guess, so I dog-legged it all the way over to San Vincente Boulevard. By the time I reached it, things were fine. No more Ryan. Left cursing in residential SaMo, hopefully.

Wind down. Pull over. Deep breaths, fingers through hair. My stomach felt weird. Into a convenient McDonalds, then back to the car with a chocolate shake and a carton of fries. Forcing down a burger was out of the question.

I sat for a while wondering what the fuck to do. Ryan was snowballing into something it would soon be impossible to shrug off. The semen collection in the market parking lot and the hassle in my apartment had been unpleasant and pervy. But actually being jacked enough to trail me across town and sit outside a bar on the off-chance of witnessing something useful raised things to a more worrying level.

And now I'd just outrun him in a car chase.

The only hope I had was to move fast enough to stay ahead of the game. And pray that if the shit ever hit the fan I had the name of Karen's killer to save myself with.

I started up, nauseous from the shake and fizzing with decayed adrenaline. I drove fast, but not fast enough to attract attention. The last thing I wanted was to pick up a cruiser on my way to Beverly Hills and my first solo performance. Especially as Ryan might catch the radio traffic.

The gig went okay. I got to the place half an hour late, but it didn't seem to matter. Big house, rose stucco, thirties style but fake. Set back from one of the streets north-west of Sunset. She let me in herself, it was too late for the servants. Sharp thin face, sharp thin body, she looked like a woman who lived on cigarettes and pills. Dyed brunette, around forty, maybe a minor tuck behind the ears. I wouldn't choose her, but she didn't disgust me either.

A drink downstairs and small talk that seemed difficult for her, then up to the bedroom. Wild. Floor space for a couple of apartments, a sunken bath in a glass-walled conservatory that looked out over a cleverly lit and expensively maintained garden. A ceiling studded with small bulbs that twinkled like stars.

She wasn't interested in pretend love. We stripped off like we were changing in a gym.

She said she wanted me piss in the bath before we got it on, so I stood on one side of it and let rip. She watched me with what I thought was jaded resignation. I figured it was just more Hollywood, that she'd paid for sex so many times it had lost its edge for her.

The bath was stoppered and when I ran dry she climbed in, got on her hands and knees and started splashing it on her face with one hand. She did it like it was something she didn't want to do, like she knew there was going to be less of her left when this was over. I heard her choke back a man's name and I realized then that it wasn't resignation I'd seen in her, but the kind of raw sadness that comes when you can't escape knowing you've lost something you once had and that maybe meant the world to you.

There was a dildo in the soap tray. I worked it into her for a while, until I got a hardon, then I fucked her from behind. It seemed to be what she wanted. Halfway through she started sobbing and I pulled out. But she shouted at me to keep going.

Twenty minutes later she was holding the front door open and handing me cash – the Latin's forty percent would go direct to him via one of her credit cards. Easy money. I guess. But there were still tears on her cheeks.

Chapter 12

Early a.m. Venice looked blurred and dissolute, already a place I'd left. At least Ryan wasn't waiting there for me. No gray Plymouth parked in the shadows, no disinterred Bela lurking in a stairwell across the street. I went up to do my packing.

The apartment was as empty as I'd left it, but the emptiness had taken on a permanence now that a legion of future tenants would not dispel. At least not in the picture of it I'd take with me.

I filled a couple of garbage sacks with my stuff. There wasn't much to take – clothes, bathroom things, my tapes of *28 FPS*, my gossip magazines, the pill jar, the photo of the dead girl – but by the time I finished I was beat. It had been a long day and there was still plenty to do. I sat on the greasy carpet and smoked. When my body started aching too much to hold itself upright I lay down and closed my eyes and tried to ignore the hissing in my head. At 7.50 the Casio on my wrist went off. Royston wasn't due till 8.30, but I wanted to leave plenty of margin.

I took the bags down to the car, then went back up for a last look around. I stood motionless in the room and tried to suck one small pleasurable past experience from its walls. All I got was stagnation and an old, old life turned to dust.

I moved the car a little way down the street, but still in sight of my door, and waited. It didn't take long. He arrived at 8.15, pulled up in a shiny black Cadillac and bounded up the exterior steps like a dog expecting dinner. His glasses caught the light and his mouth made stretched, spastic shapes as he sucked air. I watched him knock on the door. No answer. Obviously. He knocked again, then brought out his copy of the key and disappeared inside.

Thirty seconds later he stepped quickly out and stood at the top of the steps looking wildly around. He didn't know I owned the Prelude and so didn't spot me hunched down in my seat with a magazine covering most of my face. He re-entered the apartment. When he came out again it looked like he was crying. He walked jerkily down the steps like he couldn't see where he was going.

I felt blood in a hot flush crawl up from my groin to somewhere behind my eyes. It felt good, good, good. I wanted to scream at him. I wanted to stand on the roof of my car and beat my chest. But then he'd get my license plate and be able to trace me. So I just pressed my thighs together and started the car moving. Right outta Venice, toward Santa Monica.

Ripping off his furniture had been revenge for his meanness over the rent, and though I knew it was a petty emotion it still felt eminently satisfying. But its real value lay in that it was another defining landmark along the road out of the mainstream, another irreversible step further away from a pattern of living that had become obsolete. The old me would never have done it. Ergo, I was becoming someone new.

I drove with both windows down to feel the air. At Santa Monica I took the ramp to PCH and kept going. I could have stayed on that road clear to San Francisco and beyond. It crossed my mind. Just drive with the car getting emptier and emptier of gas, and with each mile part of me vaporizing and floating away too, until the car finally crunched to a stop on some graveled coastal overlook and I was completely gone.

Blown away by the wind.

If only.

I drove through Malibu and same as always it wasn't there. Low-level house fronts on the ocean side of the highway, the occasional discreet road winding into low hills on the other. You couldn't see the beach, and what you could see of the houses didn't tell you much. But you knew that wealth was close by, it was part of the legend.

Half an hour north I had breakfast in the diner of some shabby beach town. Home fries, eggs, white toast, crisp bacon. I smoked over coffee and watched the sea through the window. Blue with the morning sun. Local surfers already out, sitting straddle-legged on angled boards, waiting for a set. Easy, if you could just get up in the morning, tool down to the beach and hit the waves. Just do that every day and it be enough for you. A blissful ignorance where the horror of not being as good as a movie star didn't exist. Where you didn't know what you were missing, or if you did, you didn't care.

But I could never be like that, I wasn't stupid enough.

I found a place in a thirties wreck on Emmet Terrace – north of Hollywood Boulevard near the wax museum, east of Highland Avenue. The shell was beautiful – a faded sandy deco, ten stories high. Once it must have been a proud landmark, thrusting its chin out, Il Duce style, over the dream capital of the world. A man with a place here in the thirties would have looked out of his window through glass tinted gold with success and satisfaction. He would have stood on the top floor, impeccably tailored, holding a crystal tumbler of fine whiskey, the balmy air about him lightly hazed with Cuban cigar smoke, and felt that there was no better place on earth to be than right there, in Hollywood.

But that was a different world ago, and the shell was the only thing left. The place had been chopped and divided, and divided again. A palace had been turned into a collection of boxes stacked on a rise above a street of cheap glitter.

Still, I wasn't complaining. I was out of Venice and I had a roof over my head in a part of town where sex and drugs ran close to the surface. One room, kitchen and bathroom. Bare wooden floor, a mattress in the corner, a phone, a table, a chair and, thank God, a TV. Sixth floor at the back, up in a cage elevator you had to open yourself. I had a view of houses going ass first into the hills.

It was around midday and I was broke. Rent and security hadn't left me with much more than two days' supply of coffee, cigarettes and beer. I pulled down the blind to shut out the sun and turned the TV on. But there was a rip in the canvas and I had to position the set so the gash of light it let through didn't fall on the screen. I put it next to the mattress, then lay there and ate my heart out at what I saw.

Rene Russo had bought a six million dollar mansion next door to Dean Cain. Sylvester Stallone and Arnold Schwarzenegger were talking about a two-hundred-million-dollar co-project. Tom Cruise was expected to net twenty-six mil for *Jerry Maguire*.

Alcohol and nicotine. Drift off with the TV on, leave it on forever. If I stay in front of it long enough maybe I'll fall in.

The night before caught up with me and I slept.

A girl moaning on the next floor woke me around nine p.m.

I phoned the Latin and gave him my new number. He didn't have anything for me, but said he'd be in touch. I tried Rex for company, but his mobile was off. There was no one else to call.

I turned on a light and killed the TV, sat back on the bed and stared at it. The dead gray screen looked like all the world shut off, like everything everywhere all over the planet had stopped.

Panic. A feeling of being trapped forever in a room, in front of a blank screen, while life rushed riotously past on the other side of the walls. I got a beer out of the fridge in the kitchen.

Time to be doing something, time to get hold of some bucks. It was a shame the Latin hadn't been able to set me up, I would have liked to mark my first night in Hollywood with a gig that involved a woman and a certain amount of luxury. But, truthfully, being forced into street trade was probably closer to what I wanted that night. Furtiveness, squalor, men – so much more of a fuck-you to the mainstream.

So....

Out into the warm night, a few more beers under my belt and a cigarette between my lips. The pink-lit concrete of the parking lot behind my building had a dusty dryness that made it look like it might be comfortable to lie on. Some nights all of L.A. looked like that – airbrushed, pastel-tinted, something you wanted to run your hands over.

Scoot over Hollywood and Sunset, park within striking distance of the Drag. I was kid-perceiving as I wove through the hookers. Colors, smells, sound, the damn light and the air itself crashed against my senses with a keenness unknown since childhood. I watched the punters jumping out of their lives for half an hour, into this trough of flesh. True colors, baby. This is what the world is. What it would be twenty-four hours a day if it hadn't put a collar on itself.

I felt stoned, though I wasn't, and in a stoned kind of mind-babble I told myself that this slice of society had as much validity as any other, that because of its greater honesty maybe it had more.

But I knew I was wrong, only one level of society had any validity at all – the one at the top. I moved away from the flashy concentration of whores and headed into butt-town, my mood getting rapidly more real.

Last time I'd chickened out, but that was a long time ago. That was before Rex and the couple in the hills, before the Latin, before Joey and his man in a black Jag.

It happened like clockwork. A Ford at the sidewalk, I was there as the window went down. Cool, a guy smaller than me, an easy pummel if things took a wrong turn. I got in. He spoke with a whine.

"Do you know a place? I don't like to do it in the car."

"Drive down an alley. Nobody cares around here."

"I don't like to do it in the car. I don't like people watching."

"Nobody's going to watch."

"They will. There'll be ten people around the car jerking off before we're through. I know, it's happened before. I'm not giving a free show. I mean it. Don't you know a place we can go?"

"Yeah, I know a place. Take a left here."

"Oh, thank you. I didn't mean to be difficult, it's just that it has to be how I want it."

We took La Brea up to Sunset and across. Two streets back from Hollywood Boulevard there was a row of old office buildings – low-rise, six or seven stories of heavy, monoxided stone. The one on the end had its ground floor boarded up, but a black iron fire escape jagged up the side to the roof. Karen had brought me here once with a few of her friends – booze and dope around a hidden fire of orange crates – simple pleasures and good clean fun. Yes, siree, out under the stars.

He parked his car carefully, made sure he'd set all the locks and the alarm. On the steps he kept looking behind him, snapping glances into shadows like he expected this to be a set-up with my gang waiting to roll him. Nervous. But I got the feeling the possibility of danger was all part of it for him. What he wanted was something with an edge to it, something stamped as unmistakably bad.

Welcome to the club, dude.

A small hut stood in the middle of the roof, an elevator housing or something. The best place for what we were about to do – shielded from view, a surface to lean against. It cast a shadow that swallowed us.

"Are you sure no one comes up here?"

"It's safe. Don't worry about it."

"Okay." He nodded like he was giving final permission for things to go ahead. "How much?"

What could I say? I should have checked with Rex. Street trade was a different scene to the Latin's call service. A whole different scene. Karen got thirty K for a kidney. How much for the use of my dick and a spoonful of come?

"What do you want to do?"

He looked at me, working up the guts to ask.

"Blow job?"

I shrugged. "It's up to you."

"And you fuck me afterwards."

"Seventy-five."

"Okay."

He dragged his money out and forked it over. I couldn't figure from the sound of his voice whether I'd asked for too much or too little.

Close, against the wall. He wanted to kiss, but I couldn't cotton to that. I pushed his face away and went for his fly. It felt weird touching another man. I thought it would be the same as grabbing myself, but it wasn't. The squishiness you imagine a woman to feel when she holds your balls through your trousers turns out to be much firmer, like a bag of sand. And his dick, when I took it out, was like some machine-produced rubber sausage, not organic or really part of him at all.

I got to my knees. He curled his fingers into my hair and talked to me like a girl. Near the end he started thrusting and his cock hit the back of my throat. I heaved but managed to control it. When he came I spat it out, he didn't seem offended.

On to the main attraction. Did he want to feel loved-up like a woman, or did he want to be punished? Fuck it. Just skin up, stick it in and do it. What did it matter? The money was in my pocket.

We had gel, but even so it took him a couple of minutes to relax enough for me to get inside. I started off holding him above the hips, but later I leaned over him, braced myself stiff-armed against the wall. The brickwork was rough against my hands. He made noises like a dog rooting through garbage.

Behind me, the city stretched away in an enormous shallow dish of neon and gridded sodium light, so large you had to turn your head to scan it. In front of me, if I could have seen through the hut and two streets of other buildings, was Hollywood Boulevard, and beyond that the hills. Wild to think that in the middle of all that, out in the open air, I was boning some guy in the ass for money. For a moment I felt like the hub of a city-wide wheel, the center of it, pumping this faggot in front of me to keep it turning, like an engine. Absurd, of course.

It finished and I guess we were both satisfied. He was quiet while he fastened his pants and I was glad not to have to put up with chatter, not to have to engage any further. I had my own thoughts.

What had it meant to me? Not much. I could already regard it dispassionately. It was only a question of mechanics after all – rub something until you get a reaction. I didn't suddenly find I liked men, but I didn't feel like I'd done something terrible either. It was a kick, a spike of adrenaline. And I'd gotten paid for it. It didn't need to be anything more.

He wouldn't take me back to the Drag. All he wanted was to get gone. Cool by me. I cabbed it back to the Prelude, but I didn't feel like going home right away, so I cruised the streets for a while. The Drag was still happening – plenty of action, plenty of money changing hands. A lot of different cars trawled the sidewalk. But no black Jaguar driven by a silver-haired man.

Eventually I went back to Emmet Terrace and hit the sack. A few hours before dawn I woke up and jerked off over the picture of Crowbar Girl. Then I slept again.

CHAPTER 13

A couple of days later I connected with Rex. Late afternoon. He was in a bar on Melrose, sitting alone at a table by the window, waiting for a gig. His Californian gloss was a little dull and he didn't seem interested in talking. We ordered some food and watched expensive cars move along the street.

"Hard night?"

He looked at me blankly, then grunted.

"Prothiaden."

"Huh?"

"I'm in a trough."

"I thought you were taking Zoloft."

"Doctor wasn't happy with the results."

"Is it working?"

"Too early to say. They're hopeful."

"And you?"

"I gave up hope for Lent."

"You sure they got the dose right?"

"It's all a fucking joke to you, isn't it?"

"Hey, man, I was just—"

"Joking. Yeah. That's what I mean. Shit goes right past you and doesn't stop."

"Hey, I've got problems. I mean, I've got fucking giant problems."

"But nothing gets past the surface."

"Bullshit."

"Jack, your biggest ambition is to be in a gossip magazine."

"So?"

Rex must have realized how he was sounding because he dropped his head and stared at his plate for a moment. When he spoke again I knew he was trying to repair the damage, but it looked like an effort for him.

"Getting much from the service? He said he took you on."

"One a few days ago, another tonight."

"Mmm. Money." Rex nodded, but his gaze was wandering.

"Not enough. I'm doing the Drag as well."

"Don't let him find out."

"Yeah, I figured."

"It's a dumb move."

"So it's dumb, what the fuck? I moved out of Venice."

"About time. That place is a slum."

"Venice is hardly a slum."

"It's shabby."

"I'm in Hollywood now."

"Actual Hollywood?"

"You bet."

Rex screwed up his face. "And that's not like a giant leap into shabby? All those beggars...."

"Well, yeah, I know–"

"It's so depressing."

"Please, I can only stand so much encouragement."

"Encouragement? Sorry, we're all out."

"Okay. Let's move on. I wanted to ask you about the Drag."

"What about it?"

"Well, like, should I know anything about working there?"

Rex snorted. "You mean apart from it being super-dumb? Nup. Can't help you. What you want to know you can only learn by doing. Figuring who the whackos are, who might be dangerous, who wants something you don't want to give. How to get out of situations without getting stomped.... You have to kind of absorb it, and if you're not quick enough you'll get fucked over for sure. The only thing only thing I can tell you is don't carry ID."

"How come?"

"If you get picked up it means more work for the cops. Some nights they can't be bothered and you walk."

His cell rang then – the Latin with his gig. Before he left I gave him my new number and address. He put it in his wallet without looking at it.

Later that night I made three hundred dollars for fucking a woman while her husband and twelve-year-old daughter watched.

In Hollywood the weeks rolled by. Days blurred into each other. I woke late, watched late-night Hollywood news and gossip on a VCR I'd bought, then soaps and movies. I'd go out to eat, spend most of the night on the Drag. I had no plans to do anything with myself, no formula for self-improvement. I saw what I wanted on TV and I knew I couldn't have it. Everything else was futile.

Work from the Latin was sporadic, maybe once every ten days. I was the new boy, the last in line when the gigs came in. On the Drag I got to know a few of the hookers, they spoke to me when I walked by and I drank coffee with them sometimes. The rent boys were colder. They thought my age put the punters off. Toleration was about as far as it went. I didn't give two fucks, I wasn't there to make friends. The only things I was interested in were money and that intensity of feeling I got when I slid into a car with a guy I'd never seen before, when I didn't know what was going to happen next. I knew it would involve sex, but I was never quite sure how things were going to pan out.

My schoolboy fantasy of tracking Karen's killer, a motivation which had ridden alongside the need for cash and kicks in bringing me to the Drag, faded further into the background with each of these passenger-seat escapes from boredom. I kept an eye out for the man in the black Jag, occasionally I asked about him, but I would have been there even if he'd never existed.

Not long into this time, Ryan looped back in, bristling and gnashing his teeth through an angry trajectory from Santa Monica to Hollywood.

Early evening. The Drag hadn't started to swing. The hookers were out, but most of them weren't bothering much. They just stood around and smoked and talked, staking out their piece of sidewalk for later that night.

Out on the street, heading for a burger at a place that had stools bolted to the sidewalk outside a slit in its front. No gig from the Latin, so fagsville looked like the evening's entertainment.

Wrong.

A white hand on my shoulder, long tapered fingers that were pudgy but shouldn't have been, carefully filed nails. It was that man again. The world moved in jump cuts as I turned to face him, kind of a life-before-your-eyes thing.

"Not smart, checking out of Venice like that, Jackie. You think I wouldn't find you?"

I bit down on the impulse to run.

"Gee, was I supposed to call the station first?"

"I'm still pissed about the car chase. Don't make things worse."

"Oh, shit, was that you? I thought it was someone trying to rip me off."

"Don't push it, Jackie. Where are you living?"

"Over on Emmet."

"Gosh, I'd like to check out the fittings."

We sat at the table like cowboys in a poker game. A bottle of Southern Comfort between us, a six pack of Bud, ice in a bowl – the guts of my refrigerator. Ryan had his jacket off, his shirt was wet down the back and under the arms.

He swallowed a shot of Southern, popped one of his nitro pills and opened a beer. He looked set to be around for a while.

"So, Jackie, how's it going?"

"Okay."

"Okay? That's good. How are you paying for this place? I checked with the donut guy, he said you never went back."

"This and that."

Ryan looked like he was trying to kill a smile.

"What are you telling me? You're working the Drag? Shit, I thought you were just hanging out. You get stranger by the minute."

"What strange?"

"Your wife gets dead. A few weeks later you're living in scum city, taking it up the ass to pay bills? What is it, some kinda PTSD thing? You feel so guilty you're trying to be Karen?"

"What do you want, Ryan? You found out where I live. You obviously don't have anything else on the killing or you would have busted me on the street. This chewing the fat thing is bullshit."

"Wow, Jackie, talk about hurt my feelings."

He dug a bottle of Dexedrine out of his pocket and shook a few into the palm of his hand – flat yellow tablets that look like 5mg Valium. Opposite effect, of course.

"Here."

"I want to sleep sometime tonight."

"You can sleep when you're dead." He did two. "Might as well, Jackie. I got something to do tonight and it'd be just dandy if you came along."

"What is it?"

"Don't worry, you'll find it interesting, I guarantee."

"What if I don't want to?"

"Oh, Jackie, don't say that." He shook the pills at me. "Come on, I don't want you going all droopy on me."

I sighed and took three. Ryan wasn't a guy who took no for an answer and the faster whatever he had planned was over, the better I'd like it. I could always dose myself later with any number of downers.

"Thatta boy, Jackie. You and me together, drinking booze, taking pills, kinda pally, don't you think?"

"Whatever you say."

One a.m. Breeze through the windows, warm and dry and powdered with carbon. Both of us liquored and zipped on speed. Ryan drove one-handed. Two types of cars on the streets – heaps driven by the young and the poor, out looking for some kind of kick; expensive coupes and limos carrying rich people looking for the same thing. The expensive cars looked exciting, like you wanted to follow them and see where they ended up, meet the people they were going to meet. The dented, primer-painted sedans just made the road look ugly.

Palm trees everywhere, quintessential against the mauve sky. We headed east, cut the Hollywood Freeway on Santa Monica Boulevard and plunged into zero land. East of the freeway and south of Griffith park L.A. turns into a million square miles of shit. Unless you're a Dodgers fan heading for Chavez Ravine. I'd never liked sport.

Around Silverlake Ryan banged through a maze of side streets until he found some kind of industrial estate – a compound of single-story breeze-block warehouses with corrugated metal roofs, ringed with a wire-mesh fence that was rusted through in places. The estate was unlit and the driveways of cracked concrete that separated the warehouses turned into black tunnels a few yards from the light of the street.

Ryan drove like he knew where he was going, along one edge of the compound to a gate that was pretty much like the rest of the fence. A high-beam flash brought a heavy-looking guy out of the dark, he looked closely at Ryan, grunted unpleasantly and opened the gate.

We rolled quietly through shadow, past oil-stained loading docks and sinister dead-body piles of broken packing crates.

The Plymouth slid into a space beside a row of other cars. Scratches of light cut a closed side door into a building. In we went, Ryan and me, into sudden light and people. Secondhand furniture storage an obvious function – sofas, couches, upholstered armchairs ranked and racked, back to the walls and up to the ceiling. Cheap velvets, fake leather, stained material – used-up things to sit on that other people's asses could no longer afford.

A square space had been cleared in the center of all this, twenty by twenty perhaps. Around it, most of them standing, about fifty men waited for something. Low talk shivered between them. They smoked and drank beer out of cans.

A man watched by another man with a pump shotgun was taking money and checking faces at the door. When he saw Ryan his eyes hardened but he didn't say anything, just nodded and handed over a wad of folded bills he'd had ready in the pocket of his sport coat. Ryan winked at him, slipped the money into his jacket like he'd done this more than once, and led me along a short aisle of sofas to where everyone was gathered.

At one corner of the open space there was a stack of twelve-packs that looked to be complimentary refreshment. Ryan grabbed a couple of cans and handed one to me. It wasn't cold, but at least it was Bud. I chugged it down. The scene around me was combining with the usual Dex anxiety to make me feel somewhat edgy. I couldn't figure the atmosphere. There was a lot of macho ball-swinging going on, but underlying this there was a current of tension that seemed out of place at a gathering of beer-drinking buddies.

A jackhammer lay against a couch. Its black air hose snaked out of sight, and somewhere back in the furniture jungle a compressor thudded.

"What's this? A bare-knuckle fight?"

"Relax, Jackie, all you gotta do is watch."

I looked at the men around me, trying to guess what they were here for. What I saw didn't make me feel much better. Their faces were slabbed and scored by whatever winds blew when pity was relinquished. Frozen mouths and flat eyes that wouldn't change expression whether they watched young children playing or someone in an alley having the shit kicked out of them. Motherfuckers who took pride in being motherfuckers. And keeping an eye on these motherfuckers, no doubt thoughtfully provided by the event's organizers, were a handful of armed men standing around in conspicuous positions.

"I don't like this. I want to go."

"You know what it costs to get into this place? A grand, minimum. I'm doing you a favor, boy, don't turn pussy."

Two minutes later one of the gun guys walked across the square and disappeared into the furniture. Everyone got quiet. Seconds ticked and some of the hard men did little nervous things like running fingers through hair or pulling shirts away from chests.

Then the guy came back, his hand clamped firmly around the wrist of an anxiously giggling girl. She was about twenty-three and she wore a short skirt and a blue Coca-Cola T-shirt. A large bare-chested man whose face was hidden under an executioner's hood followed them.

I figured some sort of spectator sex gig and relaxed.

The guy in the mask was built like a bull, very little definition but plenty of muscle bulk. He stood in the middle of the square like a rock, the girl looked at the floor and swayed from one foot to the other. She was obviously stoned, but not smack – she was too up for that. After the gun guy left the ring, Bullman grunted and the girl got to work – dragged off the track pants he was wearing and sucked his dick until it was hard. Huge, of course, thick as a woman's wrist.

The routine went on from there – fingering, fucking, sucking in a sequence of positions. At the end of it Bullman pulled his pipe out of her and pointed at the floor. I guess it was a signal, but she just looked unhappy and didn't move. Bullman hit her on the side of the head. She started to say something and he hit her again. A few men in the crowd made turned-on noises. The girl whimpered then bent her legs like she was getting ready to sit on a chair. A second or two later, piss drew a yellow line to the floor, spattering off the concrete and wetting her ankles. A dark pool spread beneath her. When she'd finished, she squatted lower and I saw her face turn red until a shiny bone of shit fell heavy and dead into her piss. I could smell it from where I was standing.

"Totally interesting. Can we go now?"

Ryan seemed fixated. He didn't look at me when he spoke.

"She's somebody's daughter, can you believe it?"

"Huh?"

"Just watch the fucking show."

Out on the square they'd handcuffed the girl to a ring-bolt set into the floor. She was on her back with her arms stretched behind her head, yelling stuff about this not being part of the deal. Two men held her legs – one each, straight up and pulled back. Bullman had a can of lighter fluid and a lighter. It wasn't a joke. He went all the way with it, squirted it between her legs and dropped a match. The noises she made didn't sound human. The men around me yelled like they were at a football game. Bullman didn't let it go on too long, though. When all her hair was gone he put the fire out with his foot.

The air in the warehouse was bad – piss, shit, burnt hair, burnt flesh. One of the men holding her legs had a bloody nose from where he'd lost his grip for a second when she started to writhe.

"This is sick."

"That maybe, Jackie, but this kinda thing happens every day in every country on the planet. It can happen to anyone you know. A few wrong turns is all it takes. Think of it as an eye-opener."

I was going to hassle him some more about leaving, but Bullman was lugging the jackhammer across the floor and I had a feeling there wouldn't be much chance of getting out of there for a little while yet.

The girl sobbed and begged, but it didn't make any difference to Bullman. He rested the jackhammer's chisel on the floor by her legs and gave it a short blast. The clatter was deafening, small chunks of concrete leapt into the air and the girl's ass discharged a yellow-brown liquid.

When Bullman released the trigger silence fell heavily. This was what the men had paid for, and they were waiting to collect – mouth-breathing, blink rate way down, a whole separate reality.

The girl babbled, promising everyone anything they wanted, but it wasn't going to help her. Everyone there knew it. And so did she.

Bullman stood with his dick sticking straight out and waited for her to quiet. When she was down to a weak sniffling he hefted the jackhammer, motioned to the two men to pull her legs further apart, and slid it into her.

And pulled the trigger.

The tool tore into her, blood misted about its pistoning steel. Bullman guided it so that the point forced its way through her back – I heard a metallic rasp as it hit concrete. Then he pulled free and sent it in at a different angle, this time it came out the side of her hip. Blood sprayed through the holes, dripped off the barrel of the jackhammer, off Bullman's forearms. The girl puked over her chin and her eyes rolled back.

Bullman went for her mouth next. Teeth snapped as he put it in.

When the roar started again her head came apart.

Rolling west through the sodium wash. Quiet time. A space between the esu-
rience of night and the yawning kick-start of another morning. Few cars, dry
roads. Mild air whispering of optimism and possibility. I'd watched a girl torn
to pieces, but the city hadn't changed. The money-bathed totem remained
intact despite the furniture warehouse.

And how did I feel? Pretty much like the city. Things happened, other
things went on regardless. The girl was dead, but she would have died whether I was there or not. One more pawn out of the game. Shitty for her, but
what real difference did it make to me?

I drove. Ryan sat in the passenger seat drinking heavily from a bottle of
bourbon he'd picked up at a liquor store a few streets from the warehouse. By
the time we turned off the Hollywood Freeway he was pretty far gone.

"So, you like that, Jackie?"

"Why did you take me there?"

"Wanted to show you what happens to people is real. You think it's a joke,
but it's not. It matters.... It matters to someone."

Ryan shook his head slowly and stared at his knees. I had the horrifying
feeling he was close to tears.

"Stupid dumb bitch. Why did she do it?"

"Didn't look like she had much of a choice."

"Just grow up and piss it away... Life ain't perfect, but she didn't have to
do that."

A little while later he slumped forward against his seat belt and muttered
things I couldn't hear. When he started to heave, I swerved to the curb but it
was too late. He vomited into his lap and passed out.

If he'd been lying down maybe I could have dumped the car somewhere
and hoped he'd choke to death on his own puke. But he was upright and
breathing. Sitting like that, there was no way the fucker was going to sign off
and make my life any easier. So I checked him into a motel on the Strip, paid
for it with money out of his wallet, and took a cab back to Emmet Terrace.

Chapter 14

The Latin called midmorning. He had a gay escort job set for that night. Unusual as most of the agency gigs were hetero, but what the fuck? It was money, and if it was coming through the Latin it had to be reasonably high-class. And high-class in L.A. meant movie people – real people.

I went out and rented a tux. From then until show time I sucked up news – taped late-night gossip and midday broadcast info on current productions. Stallone, Schwarzenegger, Douglas, Roberts, Stone, Willis, Moore.... And on down the ranks. Bit players, rising stars, falling stars, flavor of the month, TV and big screen, the grossers, the flops, bankable, sexy, crumbling, fighting.... But all of them in there, in that glass-sided swimming pool that magnified even the least famous of them into objects of envy for the rest of the world. The quality of their movies wasn't important, all that mattered was being on the screen.

I read glossy housewife magazines. I did the quizzes – multiple-choice star facts, current and past film titles made into crosswords, guess the star, which movie? Has Liz Taylor had a hysterectomy? Who's dating who? I knew 'em all – scored one hundred percent while I preempted small-screen airhead reporters who thought they knew it all. I was better than them, I knew more and I looked good. But they were the ones with lives.

I did a little coke and had a shower. Out of it, dried off but still naked, I walked around the apartment. Smooth night air sliding across my skin, colors in the sky outside. A hole in time, one of those pauses where the day stops and you float, free of the usual trivial bullshit. Tick-tock. Potter about, touching walls and chairs, straightening my few possessions. No thought, just movement. Just peace.

I dressed in the rental and did my hair. Most of the time it didn't matter as long as you were clean, but with an escort gig you had to take a little more care. Besides, who knew what could happen mixing with the rich?

That thought, though, made me nervous. I hoovered more lines and followed them with Valium. A fine combination. A pick-me-up and a take-me-down colliding in a supernova of insular confidence. Yum.

The guy blew his horn about ten o'clock and I walked out of my building to taste another world.

Merc 500 SL with the top down. Latest model, of course. Shiny and red and showroom neat. He said his name was Dean. I told him mine. Gym-hours across his chest and shoulders, good skin, good hair. He spent a lot of time on himself and a lot of money on his clothes. But none of it looked like it ran too deep, he'd put everything into front, into his car and the way he came across.

He leaned back and looked at me as I got in.

"Oh, you'll do just fine."

We breezed away from the curb and took boulevards into Beverly Hills. The night looked polished – chrome, taillights, buffed metallic paint jobs, pastel neon. Silhouettes of palms razor-cut into a warm velvet sky.

"I've seen you somewhere, right?"

Dean smiled. He was pleased. He had good teeth.

"Come on, now. I'm paying, you don't have to do that. You don't have to impress."

"Er, yeah.... But I have seen you, haven't I?"

"Not often enough, baby."

I ran my hand along the top of the door. "You're doing okay."

"This old thing? Six weeks' work last fall. Remember Farrah Fawcett?"

"Wow."

"What do you drive?"

"Prelude."

"What's that?"

"Japanese."

"Like a Lexus?"

"Not really. It's a Honda."

"Oh."

"It must be great being an actor."

"It's the best thing in the world. I mean, I haven't totally made it yet, but it's a very nice thing to have people recognize you."

"And the money."

"Money just buys things, Jack. It's only a way of measuring what you've got. It's how your life *is* that's important. Love's important."

"Love?"

"Being loved. That's what we are, all of us in Hollywood working like whores. We're the love generation. Love, love, love. Gotta have it! It's what we feed on."

"I can dig it."

"I imagine you can."

Dean let out a whoop and gunned the car. Reflected light slid like oil across the smooth paintwork of the hood.

"I want you to love me tonight, Jack. Really love me, like I'm everything to you. Every single thing in the universe. Can you do that?"

"I guess. I've done a telehosting course. That's kinda like acting. Isn't it?"

He slapped my thigh gently a couple of times.

"Good for you. Good for you."

We turned into Beverly Drive and started to climb into cooler air and greater wealth.

The higher you go in the hills, the smaller the streets become, like you're moving away from the thudding central core of some beast toward its skin. Artery, vein, capillary, tighter and more twisted. Until you get high enough and super-money takes over from the double-digit millionaires below. The houses move back from the road, too far to see, and the crowding ostentation of the flats is filtered through acres of lawn and woodland and becomes something beyond dreams.

The drugs I'd taken at the apartment seemed suddenly insufficient. I would soon be in a world where everything was better than me – from the people themselves, down to the fittings in their bathrooms.

We turned off the road and drove up a stretch of private asphalt to a set of white iron gates. A man in a three-piece suit nodded pleasantly at us and checked Dean's invite against a list he had on a clipboard. As he did so, he and Dean exchanged brief but pertinent comments on current affairs. Then the suit spoke into a wrist mic and the gates opened.

And we rolled on into paradise.

From the drive the grounds sloped down to the edge of a canyon in a series of terraces. In green open spaces there were two pools, an ornamental garden, an orchard, a set of tennis courts, scattered service buildings and a number of follies – everything glowing soft gold. Overlooking this, a white Spanish mansion, built in a horseshoe, went up three stories in steps, like the land. Flowers had been braided into ironwork balconies and laced around the outside of every window.

The inside of the horseshoe was filled with coral-pink gravel around a fountain of some ethnic ceramic glazed sea-blue. When we got out of the car it was driven away by a guy in crimson livery.

I can't say I'd never seen a place like it before, because they were on TV all the time, often in made-for-TV movies and nearly always in mini-series. But it was wild really being there. Dean and I entered hand in hand.

Space. Endless stone floors. A central reception that rose the full height of the building and held another fountain. Arches in ranks, one after another, off to other parts of the house. The ceilings were vaulted, like some European monastery.

I stopped and looked around, drinking it in while Dean rubbed the back of my neck. I imagined how it would feel if I lived there – in the morning, getting up and strolling through quiet Spanish expanses, warm air and silk against my skin – in the evening, freshly showered, dressing in perfect clothes, smoking a single cigarette on the balcony of my suite, the sound of a beautiful woman swimming in the pool below me rising into the night, mixing with the scent of honeysuckle.

"Things, Jack, only things."

"Yeah, but it must make being loved a lot easier, owning a place like this."

"That's true. Indubitably. How much do you love me, Jack?"

"Lots?"

"No, Jack, properly."

I stepped close to him, put my hands on his waist and kissed him.

"I love you like anything."

"Will you love me forever?"

"Forever and ever."

"You, my handsome stud, are on your way to a bonus."

We followed a wide corridor down one arm of the horseshoe to a series of interconnecting rooms that looked to be party central. A long way ahead of us the end wall was folded back in a concertina of French windows and the house gave out onto a broad spread of sandstone flagging and a pool the size of a battle ship, burning turquoise with underwater lights. Somewhere a quintet played West Coast jazz.

There were a lot of people there, but the place didn't have the usual frenetic party wildness. It didn't seethe. Instead there was a smoothness to the motion in the rooms, people glided from one flesh cluster to another, their limbs lagging and subtly slowed. I thought at first it was an affected grace, some learned mannerism of the upper class. What I realized later was that wealth and success actually gave these people greater control over themselves, it just happened to show in the way they moved.

Waiters were circulating, but there were a couple of bars too. The one we used was made out of white marble. It looked like it had been imported whole from some turn-of-the-century Italian salon. Spring water for Dean, a vodka, Southern Comfort and champagne cocktail for me. In a tumbler. What I really wanted was to find a little seclusion and armor myself with a chunk of the gram I was carrying, but if I couldn't have one drug, I'd have another.

I leaned against the cool stone and scanned the crowd. There were celebrities there, standing in scrums of hangers-on, but a lot of the people I didn't recognize. I figured the bash was mostly a production-side affair – money men, producers, studio people, the lower profile directors and so on.

Even so, I felt like I'd walked into the pages of a particularly glossy magazine and, God, I wanted to belong. I didn't want to be just watching these people, to be on the outside looking at them. I wanted to be them. I wanted their limos and their palaces and their lack of worry about money to be part of me. I wanted to wear clothes that could buy a car, that I could throw away after a season. I wanted to walk into a restaurant and have people know who I was. For a moment the desire for it all possessed me so intensely I thought I was going to faint.

Snap back. Slug my drink. Order another.

"Whose place is it?"

"A guy."

"It's a secret?"

"Do you know much about the movies?"

"I know everything."

"Really?"

"Well, everything about some things."

"You know Peter Laratin?"

"No."

"Big producer, TV movies. Lots of work."

"Oh."

"He needs a gay guy to play a straight guy playing a gay guy. It's a sitcom. He thinks it'll be more realistic."

"So you're working tonight."

"Not me. I'm playing."

"Listen, Dean, I gotta take a piss. I won't be long."

"Back that way, up on the second floor."

I swallowed the rest of my drink and went exploring. Out to the central reception, through discreet clouds of thousand-dollar perfume. Women everywhere, all of them beautiful. I ran fantasy scenes. Would I fuck this one, or that one, or her, or her? Indubitably. If they weren't rich themselves they'd be connected to someone who was. Blondes, brunettes, redheads, all trimmed down and monied up. Any one of them could take my life up a considerable number of notches.

The washroom off the second-floor gallery had urinals, black tiles and tinted mirrors. I did my coke in one of the three stalls and sat there licking my gums, letting it take hold. On the other side of the door men came and went. Their conversation over the splashing of piss was about imported cars, high-yield investments, films and women. They told jokes I didn't understand.

On the way back to work I passed a woman standing at the balustrade of the gallery. She was alone, looking down at the people grouped around the indoor fountain. She turned as I moved by and it was there that it all started. In the *Godfather* they called it the thunderbolt. Tick, tick, tick. A series of freeze-frames, our eyes tracking each other, locking. Connections completing, switches being thrown. It was all the lead-up, all the courting, all the emotional feeling-out we were ever going to need or have.

She had gray eyes and black hair and white skin and she wore a fitted gunmetal two-piece. She was older than me and she wasn't immediately beautiful, but her body was excellent and she was obviously major money. I went down the stairs and she didn't take her eyes off me. I looked over my shoulder and her lips parted, but then someone got in the way and I was out of the foyer.

Back at the bar Dean was talking to a middle-aged bald guy with rimless specs. He was dressed casually in fawn slacks and a soft wool shirt and he was super self-possessed.

"Jack, I'd like you to meet Peter."

"Peter Laratin?"

The man shook my hand and smiled. "The one and only."

"Wow."

Peter moved closer to me.

"We have been talking, Dean and I. Can you guess what about?"

"Er...."

"We've been talking about love. About how much in it you are with him."

I glanced at Dean. He was looking at me lovingly.

"Oh, I love him like anything."

"And he feels the same. Can you tell me what love means to you? How you...view it?"

"Well, I don't know...."

"I'll tell you what it means to me. I see it as a hunger. I see it as a big bloody roast on which to gorge myself. Thing is, you can never get enough, you can never get full. And it lasts such a short time. Especially Chinese love, eh?"

He chuckled at this.

"Chinese love?"

But he wasn't listening. He'd put his hands out, one on my shoulder, one on Dean's, like a favorite uncle.

"You know, Dean, I'd very much like us, all three of us, to talk this over some more. You and Jack are such a rare example, I'm sure I could learn from you."

"Oh, I could talk about Jack for hours."

So we left all the swinging Hollywood hipsters, all the millionaires and movie stars, and walked back in the direction of the toilets I'd been to earlier. From the gallery, on the way, I thought I saw the woman in the gun-metal two-piece again, standing in a corner on the ground floor. But I couldn't be sure it was her.

The room Laratin took us to had no windows. There was a large bed in the center covered with a cream rubber sheet and the walls were hung, floor to ceiling, with black-and-white enlargements of assholes. Not soft-focus Playboy-style rear-end shots, but closeups of pitilessly exposed anuses – hair, abrasions, and all. There was a camera on a tripod in front of the bed.

"Now I do want to talk, Jack, but I wonder if you'd do me a little favor first?"

Laratin was fiddling with the camera and I could hear the high-pitched hiss of the flash charging.

"Just lower your trousers, will you, and bend over, there at the end of the bed? I like to keep a record of all my new friends."

I dropped my pants and braced my hands against my knees.

"No, no, no, that isn't right. It isn't open enough."

I reached behind and pulled the cheeks of my ass apart. I felt a soft puff of air – Laratin had his nose as close as he could get without touching and was inhaling my butt fumes. He straightened when he saw me watching him.

"Used to do it as a child. We called it sniffing bottoms. You had to see who could get closest. I always won. You smell like a stag."

He moved the camera to within two feet and fired the flash a couple of times.

"All done. Buckle up."

Then the three of us sat in smooth leather armchairs and drank brandy and soda.

"It's somewhat unsettling exposing yourself like that, is it not? It feels like an invasion."

"I don't mind, if that's what you want to do."

Dean tapped my ankle with the toe of his shoe and looked disapproving. Laratin made a point of not noticing.

"No, I think you do mind. Anyone would. Something so intimate. Such things are things you save for special people. People you love. For instance, what you do with Dean, and what he does with you – these aren't things you'd share with just anyone, are they?"

"Well, yeah, you have to keep them for the right time and place."

"Exactly."

Dean chimed in: "Sex is an illustration of emotion."

"Well put, Dean. You like someone, you let them have some sort of average sex with you. You love them.... Well, there are any number of ways to differentiate, aren't there? Different grades of love, so to speak. Jack, how do you know when someone loves you?"

"They do things for you."

"Close, but I think we can do better. They abandon themselves to you. That's what loving another person is – the willingness to give them every part of yourself."

"Oh, we do that, don't we, Jack?" Dean raised his eyebrows and I got the idea I was supposed to act suggestive.

"You bet, *every* part."

Laratin made a small sound and pressed his thighs together.

"Sounds interesting, sounds positively delightful."

Dean leaned forward in his chair and seemed suddenly to want to downplay our positively delightful scenes together.

"Of course, Peter, we keep it all pretty tame."

"You haven't plumbed the depths."

"Jack only wants to give so much. He values me to a particular level. I have to be satisfied with that."

It was obvious that some kind of game was being played here, but what it was I couldn't tell. All I knew was that I wished the sex would start so I could get it over with and get out into the party again and get another look at that woman.

"If Dean wants to show you what he does with me, I don't mind."

"Really, Jack? It would be a privilege to watch two lovers. I have a bottle of oil somewhere, I think."

So Dean and I got bare. He covered me with oil from the bottle Laratin produced, lifted me up like a bride and carried me to the rubber-covered bed. We lay together and he slid himself back and forth across me. There was a lot of kissing, which wasn't too bad with him, and a lot of slow stroking. Laratin just sat in his chair and watched. When Dean flipped me over and went down on my ass, Laratin became a little more involved.

"Oh, Dean, he must love you if he lets you do that. Tell him you love him, Jack. Tell him you love him."

I said it. It was just another step along the road that would eventually lead me out of there. It wasn't hard to do.

"But you know, Dean," and now Laratin had the fly of his pants open, "I think that Jack might have found someone he loves more."

Dean lifted his head out of my ass and looked seriously at Laratin.

"I don't think that's possible, Peter."

"Oh, I think it is. You're not going to deny it, are you, Jack?"

I felt pressure on my thigh from Dean's hand, urging me to reply. The evening's play became clear.

"I love Dean, Peter."

"Of course you do. But you love me too. I can see it in your eyes."

"Yes, you're right, I do."

Dean's grip relaxed. Laratin stood up and began taking his clothes off. His body was firm and tanned.

"Come and show me how much."

Dean gave me a prod and I rolled off the bed, knelt in front of Laratin and sucked his cock for a while. He made noises of enjoyment, murmured endearments to me, but he only got half hard. He ran his hands through my hair.

"You see, Dean, he loves me. You're not upset, are you? After all, one person can love two men."

"I'm okay, I guess."

"You're okay? That's good, Dean. That's very good."

He did some more of the head stroking, then pulled his dick out of my mouth.

"But what if he loved me more than you?"

"I think he loves us both the same."

"No, Dean, he doesn't. You've had a bit of oral, I've had a bit of oral. Even Stevens. But I haven't finished. It'll be best if we show him now, Jack. It'll make things easier on him in the long run."

He took a steel speculum and a tube of lubricant out of a drawer beneath the bed.

"All fours, Jack."

I made like a dog. Laratin warmed up the spreader professionally, like a doctor, rolling the business end between his palms.

Then it was lube time.

Then it was time to open the back door.

The speculum felt enormous going in. Laratin started off trying not to hurt, twisting it slowly like a corkscrew. But I hadn't fully mastered the art of anal relaxation and he got impatient. Once the first inch was inside he put his weight behind it and finished the job with a lunge. It hurt so much I shouted.

And it hurt more when he started turning the knob that ratcheted the two halves of the device apart. Feeling air on the inside of my colon for the first time was unusual, but the novelty was overshadowed somewhat by the sensation that my rectum was about to split.

I shouted again and turned my head, about to tell him to take it the fuck easy. But I didn't say anything because, standing with her back against the door, was the dark-haired woman in the gray two-piece. Dean and Laratin knew she was there but were acting like she wasn't. And she was watching us as though we were part of a show she'd just happened to stumble across – distanced and evaluating.

I wanted to stand up and turn it all around somehow, make it plain that this was all just bullshit to me and I was way above it. But Dean was paying, and I needed the money. So I gave up the dopey dream of connecting with her that I'd been keeping warm all night, dropped my head and figured fuck it, bring it on.

"You see, Dean, what he does with you and what he will do for me are really worlds apart."

Laratin jiggled his now flaccid cock between his fingers.

"Admit it, he loves me more than he loves you. And he only just met me."

And at that point he showed Dean just how certain he was of my love by jetting a stream of piss into my stretched-open asshole. It didn't sting, it just felt warm and heavy. Occasionally he played it across my ass cheeks, but most of it went inside. When he was empty and I was full he closed up the speculum and slid it out.

Dean lay on the rubber bed, faceup, pulling at his hardon, blowing kisses at Laratin.

"I love you too, Peter. Watch this."

At Dean's direction I climbed up onto the bed and got into position over him. I glanced toward the door, dreading eye contact but wanting to see how the woman was taking this scene. I felt an unexpectedly strong wash of relief when I found she was no longer there.

Dean blew his wad and I let go with a torrent of Laratin's piss. I heard Dean gurgle as some of it went up his nose.

After that, it was towels all around, back into clothes and another drink.

"I bet you're marveling at my self-control, aren't you, Jack? Wondering how I could restrain myself."

"If you don't need to shoot it's fine by me."

"Oh, but I do. I'm just savoring the anticipation, leaving myself a treat for the end of the night."

"Oh."

"Why don't you go back out there and enjoy yourself for an hour or two? I need to discuss business with Dean here. I've kept him waiting long enough. But remember, Jack, don't get too friendly with my guests. I won't have anyone go slutty on me."

Dean walked me out the door. When Laratin couldn't see us anymore he handed me a wad of money.

"For services rendered."

"I hope you get the part."

"Thanks. He's as mad as a hatter, but what can you do? You will hang around and let him fuck you later, won't you? There's enough there to cover it."

"Sure, man."

"I hope I can trust you. It'll make everything else a complete waste of time if you don't. You understand how important it is to me."

He kissed me on the cheek and turned back to the asshole room.

I didn't feel like doing much of anything. The idea of hanging around till Laratin worked up a head of steam wasn't particularly appealing. I felt sore and tired and I wanted to head home. But I kind of liked Dean and I didn't want to let him down. So I figured I'd find somewhere quiet to do a couple of lines and take a walk around the grounds.

But then a hand slid into mine and she was there, the woman, stepping in front of me, pulling me along a corridor, smiling quickly back at me over her shoulder. We didn't speak, we couldn't, the air around us moved too quickly. Our world, this space where the two of us were, had started to happen outside time, in some other dimension where all that was necessary was the headlong rush into desire.

We moved deeper into the house – indirect lighting, silk on the walls, objets d'art. Designed and decorated to inspire envy. She wore no perfume but the smell of her enfolded me – her hair, her skin, even a faint tang from between her legs. We moved faster, unable to wait another second, until we were almost running – dogs to food, sharks to blood – primal and unthinking.

Into a brightly lit room where a young Mexican maid was working her way through a pile of ironing. She looked up as we entered, but carried on with what she was doing, silenced by the woman's aura of wealth.

In the back of my mind I thought somewhere else might be cooler, but the woman already had her lips on mine and the need to worry about being sensible was fast becoming less than paramount. The maid did her best to ignore us as we struggled at each other, concentrating on a white shirt she had laid out on the board. But when my dick came out of my pants locked solid she yelped and ran from the room.

The woman had her skirt hiked up around her waist, her blouse hung from her shoulders, open, exposing hard white breasts with dark nipples. I lifted her onto a low cupboard that jutted from a wall. She sat with her body bent back, bracing her arms, legs open and drawn up so that her heels hung on the edge.

We fucked hard, like some need in both of us fed off our sex, driving us deeper into each other. It was the first time I'd done it with anything approaching emotional involvement since the early days with Karen.

She whispered obscenities. She jerked and moaned and came. I was set to pump seed as far inside as I could get it, but then hands on my shoulders wrenched me out of her and the outside of her belly got it instead.

Laratin. In a rage. With a couple of hefty guys in waiter's uniforms, both of them jostling to be the one with the best grip on me.

"You fucking swine! You...*fucking swine!* You said you loved me. I trusted you."

I could see a vein swelling on his bald head. Behind him, through the doorway, the Mexican maid peered in then jerked back out of sight. The woman wiped herself down with a tissue and began arranging her clothes. She seemed supremely unconcerned about the intrusion.

"Really, Peter...."

Laratin turned on her. "This is my house! My house! Do you know how upsetting this is for me? Everyone knowing that he doesn't love me?"

"Of course he doesn't love you, you moron. No one does."

Laratin shrieked and covered his ears with his hands.

"That isn't true, that isn't true. You can't say that." Then, to the waiters, "Get him out of here. I won't stand him in the house a second longer."

I managed to get my pants back up as they dragged me out of the room. The woman didn't say anything or try to stop them. The last I saw of her, she was doing up a button on her blouse. Laratin came out into the corridor and stood there watching as I was hustled along it.

"You slut! You slut!"

He was punching the air as the guys bundled me around a corner.

When we got near the party again the waiters gave me the option of continuing to the door without assistance – supervised, of course. As a result the embarrassment factor wasn't too high. I did feel bad, though, when I saw Dean slumped on a couch with his face in his hands.

Outside. I hung around for a while, hoping the woman would show. She didn't. I looked up at the house and around at the grounds, at the slick cars still arriving. A piece of the world behind the TV screen – straight out of a dream. Right in front of me. And I was as far away from it as ever.

I was tired. I went to the fountain and splashed water on my face, leaned there looking for messages in the drifting reflections. Tough luck – messages are for drunks and madmen. I knew it that night driving along Ocean Avenue, when I saw the fat tramp in the rain. Why should anything have changed?

I walked down the drive. The guy at the gates let me out but wouldn't speak to me. I started the long walk down out of the hills to somewhere I could call a cab from.

Chapter 15

Twilight. Rex had an empty hour before a gig. They'd tweaked his medication and he was a little smoother than last time I'd seen him. We went driving in his yellow cabriolet Porsche. On the boulevards neon glowed in rainbows and the billboard stars looked down without caring what they saw, too far removed from the endless street hassle to understand it anyhow.

The sidewalks were full of girls for a guy in a fast car, but if they weren't paying, I wasn't interested. Californian tits and ass in skin-tight clothes – nice to look at, but only one percent of it could get you anywhere.

Rex said, "You fucked it with the Latin."

"I know."

"He doesn't want you to call again."

"Look, I'm sorry if it comes back on you."

"I only introduced you. You want to chuck it away, it's up to you."

"I didn't want to chuck it away, I didn't have any choice."

"No other agency'll touch you."

"There's still the Drag."

"Jesus, I hope she was worth it."

"She was loaded, man. Loaded. You could tell."

"Don't go looking for a ready-made life, dude, they don't exist. Crawling out of the swamp ain't that easy. And you know what? When you think you've finally made it out, you look around and everything's still exactly the same."

We drove a little while longer, then Rex had to split. I got him to drop me at a drugstore on La Brea Avenue. It was a big place with a lot of displays – photo presentations for shampoo and perfume – dream material that was almost better than the movies. The models were always perfect, always happy in beautiful clothes and exotic locations. One look and you knew what type of lives they led – jetset, million-dollar apartment, nightclubbing, kisses on the cheek, mixing with other people just as good, restaurants, first-class, five-star, step out of a shiny car and snap go the cameras to pay for it all, then, wow, oh dizzy me, on it all goes....

Yeah, perfume ads are the best. Smooth dark guys and windblown women, life in places like Malibu and Beverly Hills and Paris and London. Sure, I knew the pictures were staged, but the thing was, the people in them actually lived like that. The ads weren't fake in any way, they were a true representation of what the world was like for the lucky.

Back at Emmet Terrace I phoned into a radio quiz about movie trivia and won it hands down. The prize was a subscription to a magazine. I got my photo out and jerked off over it.

On the Drag again. For money now, pure and simple. I mouthed cock and jammed it into buttholes – fagboy extraordinaire. I fell into a routine – get up late, hang out until I had some dollars, buy food, booze, occasionally some drugs, make it back to the apartment and fry myself with TV. Then get up and do it again. Simple pleasures. But one night there was a variation.

I was a few paces down from a convenience store, waiting for somebody to rent my dick, when a black Jag pulled up to the curb. I'd been daydreaming, so a fucked-up surfer beat me to it. He leaned in at the window and blathered for a while with the silver-haired driver. I moved closer, like I was bored with standing still, and watched the scene go down. A few bucks changed hands, but too few for any kind of genital interaction. It puzzled me until the surfer headed for the store, then I clicked – a bottle for company.

I was beside the surfer at the liquor counter before the door closed on its pneumatic hinge. A few seconds pretending to check out the high-octane booze to make things look good, then in with a bit of sincere hustler-to-hustler chat.

"Say, did I see you with that guy out there? In the black Jag?"

Surfman recognized me as a fellow bum boy, so his reaction wasn't quite as fuck-off as it might have been.

"Yeah, the cunt sprung for some booze."

I waited while he made an intelligent selection – maximum specific gravity per dollar, change straight into his pocket.

"He's an old geezer with silver hair, right? You want to watch yourself, man."

"Huh?"

"Haven't you heard about him? Fuck, they call him the Silver Slicer."

"Whaaat?"

Surfman didn't want to believe this because a guy in a Jag was certain to lay out bread, but hustling is a vulnerable profession and too many boys turn up dead in vacant lots for advice not to be taken seriously.

"No shit, man. I tricked with him once and I was lucky to get out alive. I'm sucking away, right, and the fucker pulls out this razor and slices me across the shoulders. Right through my fucking shirt."

"No shit!"

Surfman's eyes were wide and round and his mouth hung open like something in a cartoon.

"You want to see the scar?" I started pulling my shirt out of my pants. He stopped me quickly.

"No, man, I don't want to see the scar, he might be looking through the window. And he'll know I know."

"And if he knows, you're fucked. You'll have him on your ass every time you look over your shoulder. It'll happen, man, it'll happen. Look at me, he's been trying to finish me off ever since I split with my back hanging open."

"Motherfuck."

"Yeah, it don't make things easy, I can tell you. But, shit, I was lucky, I didn't get the full Slicer treatment."

"The full treatment...."

Surfman was off in his head conjuring possible Slicer death scenarios.

"Yeah, the full fucking treatment. You hear about that kid they found behind a liquor store on De Longpre?"

"What kid?"

"Young Mexican kid, used to work down here."

"Yeah, man, I think I did."

"The Slicer, man. The full fucking treatment. Cut his dick into strips and peeled it back like a banana. Peeled his whole fucking body like a banana."

"Motherfuck. I'm not getting in that car."

"Fuck, man, don't even go out on the street. Just stay where it's good and bright and pray he ain't feeling bold tonight."

"Bold?"

"Came after me in McDonalds one night."

"Holy shit, McDonalds...." Surfman was momentarily lost for words, then: "I'm taking the backdoor, man. You coming?"

"Can't do it. He got his first taste of street blood through me. I feel like I owe you. I'll hang out here and slow him down if he makes a move. You split. Just.... Just have a drink for me if I end up in the papers."

Surfman gripped my forearm and looked hard into my face like this was all real-life *Dirty Dozen*.

"Thanks, man."

Then he was gone, dust at his heels and me the furthest thing from his mind.

Outside and up to the Jag, looking earnest and like I only wanted to help.

"Er, excuse me. You give that blond guy some bread?"

English coachwork and soft brown leather, walnut dash around LCD readouts. The guy sitting in it definitely the man I was after. Sixty, maybe – but looking good for it – light tan, thick silver hair swept back from the forehead, strong face with noble features, pale eyes that looked odd under the streetlight – less responsive than you'd expect. He wore a dark suit, conservatively tailored, and a tie.

He looked up at me, not fazed at all by a new face at his window, even in that part of town.

"I beg your pardon?"

"That surfer guy, just went into the store. You give him some money?"

"He wanted to buy something to drink. I gave him ten dollars, yes."

"I don't want to offend you, but this part of town and all, you were probably expecting to take a ride with him somewhere. Right?"

"I had something I wanted to talk to him about, though perhaps not what you imagine."

"Whatever it was you can't do it now. He split with your bread. There's a back way out of there."

No anger, just a small "Oh".

"Yeah, I've seen him pull it a hundred times."

"You know him well?"

"I couldn't tell you his name, but you hang around here long enough, you see things."

Silverhair clicked on with a smile.

"Do you spend a lot of time on the streets?"

"Man's got to eat."

"Where are you from?"

"Detroit."

"Ah. That is where your family lives?"

"They're all dead."

"And you live by prostitution?"

"That's what happens on this side of the street, man."

"Of course. I ask only to see if I might be in a position to offer you some help."

"Help?"

"I was about to offer it to our thirsty friend before he ran off. I can see you are in a similar situation, so I'll offer it to you. Would you like to get into the car while we talk?"

"Sure, man." I said it like I knew what he really wanted was to score some butt, and opened the door.

"I'd prefer it if you sat in the back."

"Uh, okay."

Silverhair pulled away from the curb, he talked as he drove.

"I work for a doctor whose usual practice caters to the wealthy of our society, but occasionally we like to do a little charity work. To pass on our good fortune, so to speak. To this end I search the streets for suitable candidates. Are you interested?"

"What do I have to do?"

"You don't have to do anything. We offer a free medical checkup, any minor treatment you might require, vitamin shots, a clean bed and two hundred dollars."

"How long do I have to stay?"

"It usually takes the doctor about two days to run tests and administer treatment."

"No sex?"

"Absolutely not. Hard to believe these days, I know, but all we want to do is to help people."

"This, er, medical treatment, I don't have to have it if I don't want to, do I?"

His eyes flashed up in the mirror, reassuring, shocked at the suggestion that anything might be forced on me.

"Of course not. It's there for you only if you choose it."

I took a long breath and wondered what the fuck I was doing.

"Okay. I could use two hundred bucks. Let's go."

We'd been circling aimlessly during our conversation, now he pointed the Jag out of Hollywood and toward the wide quiet of Beverly Hills. Just after we turned off Sunset he twisted sideways in his seat and stuck his hand out like he was offering me something.

"You should look at this before we arrive."

I leaned forward, trying to work out what it was. He seemed to be holding some kind of aerosol, like one of those purse-size cans of deodorant. When I saw where its nozzle was pointed I started to think that maybe having my head so close to it wasn't the best idea. But it was too late by then. A hail of tumbling pin-prick droplets coned out of Silverhair's hand and into my face.

I jerked back. The stuff didn't hurt, but it tasted chemical, and it went to work right away. Seemed like old Joey had left a little piece out of his story back at Bar Ramses – the part where you got drugged on the way to the clinic. I reached for the door handle. Guess what? Central locking. I tugged weakly at it once or twice, but my motor skills were already too corroded. My body relaxed in spite of itself as increasing waves of anesthetic warmth rippled out from my hips and spine into the soft matter of my cells.

In any other situation the experience would have been yummy, but rolling toward a place where people got things cut out of them it was alarming to say the least. I slumped in my seat moron-style and thought about shouting, until I realized I didn't know what shouting meant. Breathing looked to be about the maximum achievable level of function, so I stuck with that and forgot about things like vocalization and limb mobility.

"Do you like it? Most of you seem to, once you stop panicking. In a minute you'll become unconscious. Don't worry, nothing will happen to you. This is just a precaution to safeguard the doctor's anonymity. I repeat, nothing will happen to you. You'll wake up shortly between clean sheets...."

His words didn't reassure me. I stopped listening. And then I passed out.

Zap. Out of no thought into too much. Too much feeling, anyhow. Hard road surface under me, cutting into my cheek and elbows. Clothes damp, muscle-ache from head to toe. And something tugging at my ass, pulling at the material of my jeans.

I opened my eyes. Dawn light on backstreet tarmac. Weeds growing through cracks. Belly-down between trash cans. And that fucking tugging....

I groaned and moved my arms. The tugging stopped and someone behind me said, "He's still alive." And someone else said, "Hurry the fuck up then." Cracked voices – too much street time and Thunderbird. They started on my back pockets again. Material ripped. My head felt foggy and my eyes were gummed, but gut instinct took over and put my body to work.

I rolled onto my back and kicked without aiming. Thin air. Two scuzzy winos in scuzzed-up coats – gabardine once, perhaps, but now just something to soak up piss and sweat.

They backed off a couple of steps and stood with their red faces and calcified eyes looking down at me – not guilty like they'd been caught at something illegal, but wary and waiting for another chance at whatever they thought I had in my pockets.

Crows.

Hyenas.

I felt zoned, like I'd gotten up too early after a night of speed, but the winos were old and physically fucked and it was easy to get hold of them. At first they thought it was going to be the kind of superficial beating tramps get as a matter of course every couple of weeks – bloody nose, black eye, that sort of thing – and they started to curse me. But that stopped pretty quickly.

The first one collapsed after I laid a fist into his Adam's apple, fell to his knees and made choking noises, contorting his mouth to try and get air past the ball of blood and gristle he'd just found in his throat. Number two backed into a wall and took a few in the guts, stupidly doubled up and got a knee in the face which split his nose and bounced the back of his head off the corner of an air-conditioning exhaust vent.

After that I was too tired to carry on. So I walked out of the alley onto a secondary road and went hunting for early-morning coffee. I had things to think about.

I was in Hollywood, within walking distance of Emmet Terrace. A block east of the Chinese Theater I found what I needed, a twenty-four-hour grease joint; vagrants, whores, junkies and fuck-ups – pinned eyes and sucked-white skin – trying to make believe another day wasn't starting.

"I want my burger, and I want it NOW! I said I want it NOW!"

A black guy, totally fritzed and not in a mood to be trifled with, had a problem with the service. He stood at the chest-high counter sweating and rolling his head, running his palms over the hot glass and polished steel.

"I paid for the motherfucker and I want it. Hear what I said? You think it's funny, holding my burger back there? You think that's funny? I can see it, man. That's my burger right there. What did you say? I need a WHAT? WHAT? Yes you did, you ofay motherfuck, you said NIGGERBURGER!"

He started to climb over the counter, but two cops came in just then and maced him and dragged him out to their vehicle. It was quieter after that.

I ordered a pint of coffee and found that the winos hadn't been the first to come across me in the alley. Small change, keys and wallet – gone. Inconvenient, but not major – nothing in the wallet but twenty bucks and the

Latin's business card. I had a spare for the Prelude back at the apartment, and the super would have one for my door.

I paid with a fifty I kept in my sock for just such an L.A. emergency, bummed a cigarette from a couple of hookers, and found a table in a patch of sun by a window. Outside, the cops had the black guy cuffed and in the car and were feeding him pieces of a hamburger through the open rear window.

Alone – sitting, smoking, stirring sugar into my coffee.

What was the story? One minute, night in the back of a Jaguar heading for Kidney City, the next, flat on my face in dawntime Hollywood with vags going through my pockets. I checked my guts. No scar, no cut. Evidently I had been spared the doc's kidney acquisitiveness. But what about the free medical treatment? The free dope and the horny nurse? Had that happened and been wiped with chemicals? Or had things been interrupted for some reason before the knives came out?

Quick date check with the nearest table. Yep, the morning after. I'd been gone, shit, not even six hours. Maybe less, depending on how long I was out in the alley. Fucking bizarre.

I tried to recall an image, a smell, a sound. Anything. But there was only Silverhair's drug spray and a minute of his babble afterwards.... And something which had to be a phantom memory, the imprint of a past dream. I tried to shake it, but it lingered. The sensation of lips...a mouth...sucking...on my.... On my dick? I'd been drugged and dumped in an alley, scavenged by winos, and the thing that haunted me was the impossible memory of a blowjob?

I needed downtime.

But first there was the hassle of tracking down the super to get my key. No sweat. The washrooms would yield something for sure, there were enough drag-ass, end-of-the-nighters around to make it worthwhile for someone. I finished my coffee.

At the sink in the men's room a Chicano chick was washing between her legs – miniskirt hiked past her hips, briefs around her knees, a lather of soap over her bush and the tops of her thighs. Her hand made sucking noises as she moved it backwards and forwards. Oblivious, baby – on some other planet where you could do this kind of thing. She hummed to herself, something that sounded like *Lover Man*. Her eyes were focused way beyond the surface of the mirror.

A guy in chinos and an Australian surf shirt lounged in an open stall and watched her absently. I scored a wrap off him and did it on top of the paper-towel dispenser.

Bang. Out on the street. The coke had been badly cut, but there was enough of something in it to make getting home and getting a key easier than it might otherwise have been. I moved through the smoggy, sunlit morning air like I was jet-propelled. Over pink concrete and dirty brass stars with the names of famous people on them. I thought about how those people must all be waking up in places a lot cleaner than Hollywood Boulevard, about how they probably shuddered when they had to come down here for a premiere or something.

CHAPTER 16

The Latin called. I had the blinds down against the afternoon sun and the light in the room was calm and isolated. The bleep of the phone made me jump, incoming calls were not frequent.

"You have a job."

"Oh, hi."

"Do not mistake this for forgiveness. The only reason I give it to you is that she insisted."

"I understand."

"Clean up whatever pigsty you live in. She will come to you."

"Who?"

"Someone with money, that much is certain. Of which you will get none. Call it an apology for the damage you did my business."

"What does she look like?"

"I could not say – she phoned. I wanted to send her Rex, but she described you and would not be dissuaded."

The afternoon rotted outside. I lay on the bed and remembered how the girl in the warehouse had looked. Not her actual death, but the way her body had lain so still and heavy on the floor after they put the jackhammer away, like something made of rubber.

My gig turned up around nine.

I opened the door and for a second the world seemed to shimmer in a kind of horizontal vertigo. I had trouble understanding what I saw. Then everything synched up again and I let her in. The woman from the party, of course.

She walked to the middle of the room. I'd made an attempt at tidying it, but with her there it looked as attractive as an open wound. She turned slowly, scanning, and the light blouse she was wearing pulled tight against her breasts. There was no disgust on her face at what she saw, not even surprise, just a neutral taking-in of her surroundings.

It was all scripted and cinematically perfect. The way we locked eyes, the warm breeze through the open window, even the way the evening city-light flung itself across the floor to make a languid pen about her feet.

The quilted Chanel bag she was carrying slid from her arm. She shook her hair free of a small gold clip and stepped out of her shoes. The buttons on her blouse didn't snag as they came undone – TV buttons, doing their bit for this TV scene. The blouse was silk, it took forever to drift to the floor.

Three steps and I was against her. She pressed her face to the side of my neck. All my clothes and the rest of hers fell away. I was solid and she was soaking and both of us were in some twilight heaven of the senses where touch and taste and sight and smell were all one super-sense that did not differentiate.

A leg snaked around my thigh. I lifted her onto my cock. We fucked standing up, jerking and balancing and moaning at each other, straining in the warm air. Sweat ran between her tits and over my stomach. Our faces were wet with spit. Her kisses fell in smears from my forehead to my chin.

Later. On the bed, nighttime L.A. scouting the room – sodium light and dry air that felt freshly washed even though it carried, as always, its signature scents: eucalyptus, exhaust, pizza, donuts, coffee and, even this far inland, something that would have been missing without the sea.

Her name was Bella and she was a few years past thirty. Her skin was expensively healthy and her clothes were expensively tailored. But money had been obvious from the start.

And beyond this, I could feel something intangible – her power, a sense of otherness that rose from her like a dark perfume. There, but potently indefinable.

The sheets were wet. We stank of fish. I blew cigarette smoke at the ceiling.

"How did you find me?"

"Your friend gave me the number of your agency."

"My friend?"

"The man you were with."

"He was paying."

"Obviously."

"You must have been impressed."

"I have the luxury of being able to act on my feelings."

"And what are they?"

She didn't answer, just looked around the room, then:

"Are you really this poor?"

"Poorer."

"Why."

"Because I am. What do you mean?"

Bella twisted to arrange her pillow then propped herself against the wall. While her back was toward me I noticed she had a tattoo at the base of her spine. In the dim light it looked similar to the scarab Karen had had on her shoulder blade. She waved at the apartment.

"You're good-looking and smart. You could do better."

"Everyone's good-looking and smart in California. What's that saying about wishes?"

"What do you mean?"

"If wishes were horses...."

"....beggars would ride?"

"Yeah, that's it. You have money. Obviously."

"Yes."

"How?"

"My mother's family, back a few generations. Water and oil. I'm not talking anything like that, though, just something better than you have."

"If wishes were horses, beggars would ride."

"Do you want to stay a hustler?"

"It's a distraction. But after the other night I don't expect I'll be working much."

"Distraction is important to you?"

"Isn't it for everyone? Sometimes, at least?"

"And how far do you go for it. For this distraction?"

There was something about her eyes when she asked this that made me feel a little out of my depth.

"Oh, just the usual perversions."

"I don't think there is anything usual about you at all. You have a small life, but you want a bigger one, I can tell. And it's possible, Jack. It could happen. All it takes is the courage to push yourself further than the rest of the sheep."

Maybe she thought she'd gotten a little too intense because she paused for a second, then went on like it hadn't been important.

"What would you do, if you had your choice of jobs?"

"Something on TV, I guess."

"What, exactly?"

"I'd like to present a show on movie stars, one of those *Hollywood Report* things. I've done a course in telehosting."

"I don't watch a lot of TV myself."

"Too lowbrow for you?"

"Not really, I just find watching other people a somewhat pointless exercise."

She split later that night.

Five minutes after she'd gone, Ryan arrived. Opened the door with his G-man tool kit and walked straight in. He sat on the edge of the table. I didn't bother to get out of bed.

"What the fuck do you want?"

"And we had such fun together last time." Ryan made a sad face.

"I'm not in the mood for another girlie show."

"This is more in the line of business. I've been talking to some of the hookers who worked the same patch as Karen, turns out she was pally with a couple. Wanna take a stab at what they told me? No? Well, it seems she was loaded just before she disappeared. You know what I'm saying? She was in possession of a disproportionately large amount of cash. Didn't say where she got it, but she flashed it around plenty. Don't tell me you don't know anything about it."

"We weren't close at the end. Whatever money she had was her own business."

"Let's talk about that shiny slope-wagon you drive."

"What about it?"

"Jackie...."

Ryan made himself look dangerous and flexed his fingers.

"Okay. All right. The car was a present. She bought it for me."

"Yeah. DMV lists it as being registered in your name only eight days before she was found. You didn't think that might be important? Like it couldn't possibly have something to do with what happened to her?"

"I don't see what buying a car could—"

"I'm talking about the money, fuckhole. Where did she get it?"

"I don't know. The last time I saw her she split because I was hassling her to tell me. We had a fight about it."

Ryan shook his head and moved to sit down next to me on the mattress. I shifted closer to the wall.

"Jackie, seems like every day turns up something else that don't look good for you. You shoulda told me about the money."

He took hold of the sheet and lifted it so he could look at my body. I knocked his hand away. He smirked and stood up.

"Got anything to drink?"

"Jesus, don't you ever buy your own?"

"Not when I got friends like you."

He went into the kitchen and came back with Southern and two glasses, filled both of them and stuck one out at me. I didn't take it at first, but he kept it there until I did.

"I owe you for checking me into that motel."

I didn't say anything, just stared past him out the window at a night that had no depth to it – a black sheet that looked like it was going to hang there forever. He sipped his drink for a while, then cleared his throat delicately.

"I saw a little thing on the Drag the other night. Maybe you can help me with it."

"Oh, yeah?"

"You and someone in a black Jaguar."

"A black Jag? I don't remember...."

"Yeah, you do. You talked for a couple of minutes, then you got in and drove to Beverly Hills. It didn't look like your average faggot pickup."

"You're still following me?"

"I put my heart into my work. Who was it? Where did you go?"

"If you were following you ought to know."

"The Beverly Hills Patrol thought I looked suspicious trailing such a fine car and pulled me over. By the time we straightened things out I'd lost sight of you."

"Jesus, you're so far gone even other cops don't recognize you."

"Careful, Jackie."

"Well, fucksake, you don't think that's ridiculous?"

Ryan shrugged.

"They're a private outfit. Answer the question."

"Shit, it was just some guy who wanted a blowjob. We parked near Sunset, I did it, then he split. That's all."

"Name? Description?"

"I don't spend a lot of time looking at their faces, you know? Why didn't you check his license plate?"

"I did – no trace. Which means the plates were false. Which means I want to know even more."

I shrugged. "What can I say?"

"Okay, try this one. Who was the slit you had in here? Arrived about nine."

"You've been out there that long?"

"Like I said, I put my heart into it."

"She could have been visiting anyone in the building."

"But she wasn't. Too much money to hang around a place like this, something odd about it. And if it's odd and in this building, my money says it's you."

"I do some work for an agency. They sent her over. I don't know anything about her."

"Looked like a good fuck."

"She was."

"Which way did you give it to her?"

"Fucksake."

"Come on, Jackie. From behind, like a couple of dogs? Woof, woof, woof. Well? Don't tell me you just got on top."

I didn't answer him, so he carried on. Of course.

"How about when she sucked you off? Did she swallow, or did she make you squirt it over her tits? I like it when they let it dribble down their chin."

"You're getting boring, Ryan."

"Really? Well, let's see if I can make myself a little more interesting. I bet I know more about her than you do."

"Sure."

"Like her name, where she lives. You see what she was driving? Beemer, eight-series. I ran the plates through DMV. She's a Malibu baby, prime sector address. Would you like that info, Jackie? Huh?"

"What for? It was work."

I would have liked her address, for sure, but I was fucked if I was going to ask Fatso for anything.

"How about I get her number and you call her up and ask her back for a freebie and I set it up so we can video it?"

"Fuck off."

"That bitch looks like she could lay out plenty."

I put my head back against the wall and closed my eyes. I heard Ryan pour himself another drink. I wished I was someone famous enough to have lawyers and bodyguards to make him go away.

Eventually he said, "Maybe you're right. A scam like that takes a bit of planning."

I kept my eyes closed and didn't respond. After a while he left.

Chapter 17

Rex was up, way up. A brittle high-powered energy that kept him shifting in the seat of the Porsche like his legs wanted to run off by themselves. Dusk. Chasing the yellow burn of the headlights through poorly lit residential streets near the ass-end of Burbank. We had the top off and the stereo cranked up. The air blew in across us like a high-speed dream. All the ingredients for a scene from a teen movie – high school buddies tearing it up after the prom. But there was none of that wild innocence in either of us. I was living in a twilight world. And Rex was roller-coasting between the poles of a deepening emotional imbalance.

We were out for smack. Or rather, Rex was. I was along for the ride and maybe a taste. Outside the car rows of clapboard houses slipped by, neat and well-kept, but you knew every waking hour lived in them was sucked dry by the battle to make ends meet. Front gardens with small dusty lawns and the odd desiccated gum tree, waist-high chain link fences, small cars parked on short concrete driveways, kids here and there, booted out of the house so Dad or Mom could get an hour's peace before the terror of dinnertime.

Rex drove fast, slinging the car around corners, not because we were racing to make a connection, but because there was no other way he could off-load the anxiety that rode him.

"This guy better be in, man, he better be in. I feel like I'm going to come apart."

"I've got downers at my place."

"Not anesthetic enough."

"The Prothiaden didn't work out?"

"It works, man, it works. Why the fuck you think I'm like this? Spins your fucking head around. Up. Down. I can't tell anymore."

"Stop taking it."

"Doesn't make any difference. This does, though."

He stuck his arm out so the sleeve of his shirt pulled back. He had a number of small bruises on the inside of his forearm. Nothing you could call tracks, but I was surprised they were there at all.

"You want to get sharper needles."

"Yeah, man, that's what I want. Sharper needles, bigger bags of smack, something that'll suck my brain out, wash it clean and stick it back. I want a million things, man, a million things and just one. I just want it to stop."

I'd like to think I would have said something sensitive at this point. But I didn't get the chance. Rex had just rocketed around another corner into a street that was mostly empty lots and looked deserted. He was working the stick and doing some mad thing with his head, shaking it like he had a maggot trying to eat from one ear to the other, when a boy about nine years old ran into the street chasing a ball. If Rex had been driving normally he might have had a chance at stopping. As it was, he didn't have time to hit the brakes until after the impact.

The boy came up over the hood, hit the windscreen, and flew. I had an absurd shot of him through the open roof, cartwheeling against the dark sky, head down, blond hair in a fan around his face. Then the brakes took hold, no screech, they were ABS, and Rex slewed the car to the curb. For a moment he sat there gripping the wheel, eyes screwed shut, as though he thought that with enough effort he could close down his senses. Then we were out, running back along the road to the body.

The boy, incredibly, lay straight out, faceup, legs together. The only thing that made it look like he hadn't just laid down for a nap was the way his left arm was twisted sharply behind his back.

But he was dead, there was no question.

A lot of things went through my head. I felt bad that a young life had been snuffed out, I tried to figure possible legal penalties, I wondered how his parents were going to react, if they'd start screaming when they found him. But thrown across all of this was the overwhelming relief that I had not been the one driving.

I looked at Rex. And I felt bad for him. He was gray and all the blood or life or whatever seemed to have withdrawn itself from him. He stood there, head bent, looking down at the boy, arms forgotten at his sides, sucked empty by the world. I thought he might vomit and howl, but he just stood. And then he sighed and his breath caught like he was going to cry. But he didn't. Instead, he turned and walked back to the car and we drove away.

No one came out onto the street. No one had seen us. And somehow both of us knew that nothing would come of this. That we'd skate. Rex didn't drive fast, didn't drive like we had to get away, and we rolled out of the neighborhood, not to accusing shrieks and wails of grief, but to the sound of his German engine and the rustle of wind in dry gum leaves.

We didn't speak, and we didn't turn around and go home. We went on to the connection.

Chapter 18

started the day puking. Rex and I had stayed up half the night shooting smack. When the drugs took hold he'd opened up about the accident. He said he was never going to recover from it. I tried to offer some sort of comfort, but what can you do? It was his bag of misery and he was the only one who could carry it. The amount of difference you can make to another human being in a situation like that is really pretty limited. After a while I'd passed out. He'd left sometime after that. And now I'd woken up with a dope hangover that had turned every cell in my body against itself.

I crawled across the floorboards to the bathroom and heaved into the toilet until all I had left was black bile that stuck to the side of the bowl. It was midday before I could get off my knees. I found a blister of DF 118s and managed to get a handful down. It took a long time for the painkillers to kick in. I spent it waiting next to the toilet. A couple of hours later I woke up with tile impressions across my cheek and shoulder and although it didn't really feel like it, there must have been some improvement because I was able to lurch to the kitchen and make coffee.

I was standing with a cup of it by an open window, breathing slowly and fighting my stomach, when Bella phoned. She wanted me to meet her that night for a media bash downtown and she wanted me to wear a suit. The good news was that she was going to messenger over the necessary bucks. The bad news was that I would have to brave the outside world almost immediately to go get it.

Rodeo Drive. I took a cab. I could have gone somewhere cheaper, but Bella had sent a lot of money and it seemed stupid not to use as much of it as I could. I carried a plastic shopping bag with me for emergencies.

I'd never bought a suit before, but Versace was mentioned in all the mags, so I found the place and went inside. Lots of empty floor space, most of it marble, a few pieces of arty furniture and a collection of very beautiful assistants. Straight, I'd never have had the guts to go in there. As it was, the horror of my hangover and the pills I'd taken insulated me from the worst of my inferiority.

A redheaded girl in leather pants that separated her labia picked out several sets of clothes for me to try on and escorted me to a changing room the same size as my apartment. Every time I glanced at her I caught these looks like she was trying really hard to be as nice to me as she would to anyone who didn't look as though they'd just eaten a plate of dog shit. It was an effort for her but I appreciated it. It was way better than outright disdain.

She told me to call her if I needed anything and closed the door. I didn't need her and I didn't want her. I wanted to curl up into a ball in the corner and never go outside again. I was sweating and all the moving around had made my head start to pound. I made the mistake of bending down to untie my shoes. My stomach roared. The good thing was that I hadn't let go of my trusty plastic bag and was able to catch the jet of steaming gut-acid before it spoiled the floor. The bad thing was that the redhead came in while I still had my face in the bag. She backed out without saying anything, and I didn't see her again until I settled the bill.

I chose a dark, three-button silk number. It fitted pretty well, but the trousers were a little long. One of the assistants offered to have them taken up if I'd wait twenty minutes – an absurd suggestion. So I took the suit as it was, laid down most of Bella's money and split to the street and the cab I'd kept waiting.

I had the dry heaves most of the way through Beverly Hills and I knew I wasn't going to make it through the coming evening without some sort of chemical prop. I had the driver detour through the side streets around the

Drag. When he figured out what I was doing he started to get shitty, but I told him I'd give him a cut of the deal and he got flexible quickly enough.

Eight-thirty saw me downtown, standing out front of the Bradbury Building. The area is a dump at the best of times, but after-hours, when the drones have gone home, it turns into a creepy wasteland best avoided if you aren't carrying a gun. I was safe enough, though. They'd rigged up an entrance awning with a lot of bright lights, and there were enough uniformed guys running to park cars and manning the door to scare away the human shit that would ordinarily have been heaped on the sidewalk.

I felt better than I had earlier that day, the puking had stopped and the pain in my head had fallen to a low-level throb. But between all the DFs I'd dropped and the coke I'd snorted while dressing for this third connection with Bella, I was pretty spaced. I hadn't realized there would be valet parking, so I'd come by cab rather than risk leaving the Prelude on the street, and now I had nowhere to wait until she showed with the invites. I stood and watched the cars arrive.

Black limos, white limos, a few two-door exotics. The people getting out of them glowed with wealth. The women wore pearls and diamonds around their throats, their bodies were toned and supple, they moved with an erect grace, aware of their own importance. The men strode with these women on their arms like sated beasts of prey, sleek with the knowledge that they could have anything in the world they desired. They were a tailored and massaged and personally-trained golden race who had reduced amounts of money that would make an ordinary man choke to nothing more than points in a game they played among themselves.

An auto horn blipped discreetly. I turned to see Bella climbing from a stretch, a chauffeur holding the door for her. She was wearing a short dark skirt and as she scissored her legs out onto the sidewalk I caught a flash of white briefs fringed with black hair.

"Hello, Jack. I've missed you."

She kissed me. I felt the heat of her breasts through my suit coat.

The Bradbury building is one of the most beautiful in L.A. Five stories high, it was built a hundred and fifty years ago out of some kind of brown stone and it looks pretty much Art Nouveau. Inside, things are laid out around a central atrium that rises clear to the top of the building. At each level there is an exposed walkway with doors leading to the offices of lawyers and accountants and literary agents. Dark wood, wrought iron and a set of cage elevators you can watch going up and down. Ridley Scott shot the end sequence of *Blade Runner* there.

Tonight the offices were closed, but the ground floor and the first two walkways were open and decorated in an *Alice in Wonderland* theme. Polystyrene grandfather clocks had been wedged into odd corners, a four-foot automated caterpillar puffed smoke from a water pipe on top of a mushroom, bottles labeled "Drink Me" were scattered around on small tables. Behind the buffet, the catering staff were dressed in character. I thought it looked cool, but Bella didn't seem impressed.

"Do you drink? I don't. Get one if you like, this isn't a sit-down thing."

I scored a couple of vodkas from a waiter dressed like a fat English schoolboy, tipped them into one glass and followed Bella up some stairs to the second of the walkways. Up that high, we were almost alone.

"We don't mingle?"

"With those people?"

On the ground floor men and women chatted in groups, helped themselves to food, drank drinks, laughed and had a good time.

"They look okay to me. What's it for?"

"Profile raising for a cable station. Don't you think they look like pigs at a trough?"

"You really think they're that bad?"

"You don't know them. With all their money not one of them has the courage to look at themselves. They take cocaine, perhaps have sex with more than one person, and they think they know what it is to test the limits of their morality."

We looked down on the people for a while, then Bella asked me if I wanted another drink. I wasn't too bothered about more alcohol, the vodka had burned my stomach and I didn't want to start puking again, but I said yes because it meant we'd be back in the action.

We made the ground floor and headed for the bar. I ordered Coke.

"If you don't like these people, why did we come?"

"For you. Do you know what these people do? The ones that do anything?"

"I recognize a couple of actors."

"Mostly management and major stockholders. You said you wanted to present a movie show, I thought it might be useful for you to have some contact with the people involved."

"Jesus, I was only dreaming."

"How difficult can it be, talking to a camera?"

Bella scanned.

"You see that girl there? In the white skirt? They found her in a pie store. Now she does what you want to do."

The girl Bella pointed out was Lorn from *28 FPS*. White mini, white crop top, punky hair. In the flesh she still looked good, but real life removed some of the definition from her features. Where Bella had a sharp dark radiance, Lorn's attractiveness veered more toward the kind of Californian tomboyishness Heather Locklear had in *Dynasty*, before she bitched up for *Melrose*.

"I watch her all the time! Do you know her?"

"Vaguely. I have money in the channel."

Bella looked at her watch.

"It's getting late. There's someone we need to talk to."

"It's only ten o'clock."

"I have to get back to Malibu."

"Not Beverly Hills?"

"The only people who live in Beverly Hills are those who can't afford to leave and those who don't have the taste to know any better."

Bella beckoned to a thickset man with curly gray hair who was talking to what looked like a group of subordinates. He immediately slapped a few upper arms, worked his way out of the huddle and came over to us.

"Bella, this is a surprise."

He had a fleshy voice that made me think of cigars. He didn't do the usual cheek-kissing thing.

"Hello, Howard."

"What do you think of the decoration? We went all out."

"I couldn't imagine anything less original. How's the channel?"

"Going from strength to strength, baby. Increasing audience-share weekly."

"Good. Howard, this is Jack. He's interested in working on a movie-news show."

Howard shook my hand and glanced at the cuffs of my trousers.

"Good to meet ya, Jack. It's a hard racket to crack. Lot of young people want in on it. Had any experience?"

"Well I've done a tele—"

Bella cut in and nodded across the room toward Lorn.

"That girl does one, doesn't she?"

"Sure. *28 FPS*. Great ratings, lot of interest. We might syndicate next year."

"She's attractive, but do you really think she's right for it? She doesn't look particularly...cerebral."

"This is TV, who wants cerebral? She's young, she's got great tits, she can talk. It's enough already."

"I wonder what she really brings to the table, though."

"Hey, indulge me." And here Howard winked at me. "I've been doing this all my life. I think I can pick people. Gorgeous, lovely people like you provide the bankroll, for which I'm eternally grateful. But running the channel, well, that's what I know best. That's, what do you call it? My forte."

Bella went on as if she hadn't heard him.

"It's my feeling, Howard, that she would benefit from a little assistance. Perhaps a partner on the show."

"You mean Jack here?"

"You should consider it."

"Bella, darling, the girl's doing fine as she is. If it ain't broke, don't fix it. You know what I'm saying?"

"Letting you know my thoughts, Howard. I hope you'll take them on board."

A reasonable tone, but the threat was there. I could see its impact in the tightening of his smile and it made me wonder exactly how rich Bella was that she could use such thinly disguised blackmail against someone who obviously played a large part in channel control.

"Bella, your thoughts are pearls to me. Give me some time with them, I'll bounce them around. We'll talk again soon, baby, huh? Real soon."

And with that he was off, weaving his way through groups of people, escaping.

"Wow. I don't think he liked that. Who was he?"

"Howard Welks, top man at the channel. I have to leave. Walk me to the car, will you?"

"We're not leaving together?"

"I'm sorry, Jack. Not tonight, my father's at home."

"Family visit?"

"Some nights he spends at the house, some at his apartment downtown. Tonight he's at the house."

"And you can't bring anyone home? We could go to my place."

"No, Jack."

At the entrance to the building Bella took a slim mobile from her handbag and told the limo to come around. My disappointment must have shown because she kissed me and squeezed my arm.

"Are you terribly upset?"

"Well, I just thought...."

The limo arrived, the driver stood patiently holding the door open. Bella glanced at the interior, then at me.

"Sit with me for a few minutes."

We climbed in and the car moved out onto the road. Bella told the chauffeur to drive down the street a little way and park, then she slid up the partition. The cabin light threw gold across tan leather and the black glass windows held infinite concertina reflections of ourselves.

Bella took her jacket and skirt off. The seat made a soft crunching noise as she lay back and pulled off her briefs. She ran her hands over the insides of her thighs.

"Watch."

She started slowly, drawing her fingers through her labia, making lazy circles. My dick was painful against my trousers and I undid my fly and took it out. Bella's hand moved faster between her legs. After a while she arched her back and slid a finger into her ass. She moaned and shuddered. Her hand went lazy again, over her belly and breasts. The muscles in her legs relaxed, she sat up and kissed me.

"Maybe I should turn you out now?"

"You're kidding."

She laughed and put her head in my lap. And it was weird. Every woman does it a different way and a lover's blowjob is as distinctive as her voice or the smell of her hair. Bella hadn't gone down on me before in either of our two previous connections, but somehow the movement and the feel of her mouth were familiar to me. It was a dim recognition, one I couldn't link right then to any particular time or place, but it was there nevertheless. A sort of sexual déjà vu.

While her back was bent, I saw again the scarab inked at the base of her spine. Afterwards, when we were finished - as she was reapplying her lipstick and I was tucking my shirt in - I mentioned it.

"I like your tattoo."

"Oh, that.... I had it done with a friend, one of those silly, spur of the moment things. I really do have to go now."

I stood on the sidewalk. As she pulled away, Bella wound down her window and called to me.

"What do you think about love, Jack? Do you think it can happen this quickly?"

Then she was just a pair of taillights getting smaller on a wide city road. I watched them fade, until a gray sedan pulled into her lane and blocked my view.

Emmet Terrace. Home. A room hissing with late-night isolation. I watched gossip TV until the examination of better lives than mine got too much for me and I had to kill the screen. Darkness swallowed the room, followed a minute later, as my eyes adjusted, by the orange glow that seeped through the fabric of the blind. It caught the edges of things, made ochre cross-hatchings of pieces of furniture and the corners of walls. I drifted, exhausted. Thoughts chased themselves through my head.

Bella's blowjob.... Bella's blowjob.... Why was it familiar? As I slipped into semi-consciousness the feel of my cock in her mouth haunted me. I floated with the sensation, trying to focus on it, trying to find some explanation. But I couldn't stop other images creeping in – a car door shutting, flashes of Hollywood through a window, a head of silver hair, gravel against my cheek.... When two tramps made an appearance I came awake with a start. Bella's blowjob matched the inexplicable memory of oral sex I'd woken with in the alley after my abortive attempt to locate Doctor Kidney!

Bizarre to say the least. So bizarre, in fact, it made a couple of other things seem odd. Her tattoo, for instance. Of course, tattooists work from patterns and in the city there might be hundreds of people sporting the same design. But it was strange that both my wife and the first non-trade fuck I'd had after her death should wear identical marks. Then there was the fact that she'd visited my apartment so soon after I'd been drugged and dumped in the alley....

I caught myself. A day spent hungover was obviously taking its toll. I was allowing coincidence to become paranoia.

To channel my thoughts in a different direction, I pictured how she'd looked fingering herself in the back of the limo. But that dredged up a wave of despondency. Maybe it was irrational, but I'd expected to be taken back to her house after the Bradbury thing.

It didn't take too many synaptic firings to realize that if I was ever going to get anything beyond money for a suit, I needed to strengthen my connection with her. That meant I'd have to push myself into her world, instead of letting her just dip into mine.

I woke thinking about Daryl Hannah, about how her mornings must be. How she'd lie on a king-size bed in a pure white room the size of a tennis court with sunlight cutting swathes across the carpet. And just a short distance beyond the floor-to-ceiling windows, a matter of yards perhaps, the sea would roll under blue sky and fat white clouds. The maid would come in with a light breakfast of coffee and croissants and the aroma of the freshly roasted beans and the delicate pastry would mix with the clean salt air and just that, just those three simple smells and the ocean breeze against your skin would remind you that you were a god.

I got out of bed, drank a can of Pepsi, and found Ryan's number in a dirty pair of jeans that lay with all my other clothes in a pile on the floor. I hesitated. It wasn't an easy thing to do, making deliberate contact with Mr. Frightening. But I wanted my mornings to be like Daryl Hannah's and there was no other way to get Bella's address.

I arranged a meet for that afternoon. I didn't say what I wanted. Ryan sounded smug on the phone, thinking, no doubt, I was ready to spill some Karen-related info.

At night, darkness and neon dazzle threw a deceitful caul over the Drag, hiding the patina of blood, semen and shit that layered the sidewalks and the buildings and glued the whole place together. Daytime, though, it was a wound laid bare. Drifts of trash sloped against walls like dunes on a beach. Pools of drying vomit mixed their stink with the acrid burn of piss that drift-ed from every ground-level recess and alley entrance. What little glamour the place managed to disguise itself with during prime-time was mercilessly stripped away the instant the sun rose.

The whores were thinner on the ground when it was light, but they were still there – the more determined or the more desperate – hanging out for the midday trade of office drones who preferred a fast fuck in a closet-sized cubicle to eating salad in the company lunch room.

I had souvlaki and coffee at a counter and watched them parade listlessly along the street, wondering what type I'd need to hook Ryan. A simple fuck wouldn't cut it. He'd get freebies for the asking – flash the badge and any girl would spread herself open to avoid the hassle of a trip to the station and a night's loss of earnings. No, to get Bella's address out of a guy who watched girls do it with jackhammers I'd need something more toxic.

In the months I'd been hanging out there I'd gotten to know things about a few of the girls – maybe you chat with them over a drink while they're between tricks, maybe you overhear gossip, some info you pick up just by watching what goes down on the street. It isn't anything self-improving but it helps pass a slow night.

And that was how I'd heard about Rosie. She was a brunette in her forties who worked more for pleasure than for business – she got off having guys shit in her mouth. Rumor was she had a husband and a couple of kids somewhere, but she spent so much time on the Drag, day and night, I didn't think it was true.

I found her in her usual spot, standing in the doorway of an abandoned corsetry store in a cross-street twenty yards back from the Drag, as though her non-economic motivation segregated her from the rest of the whores. She wore a black latex mini dress and her body looked soft and a little overweight. I'd pawned the suit Bella had paid for, and with the rest of my money I had about three hundred bucks. It was going to take most of it to get her to trek over to Santa Monica with me, but that was the way it had to be.

Her mouth had some sort of nervous tic that made her lips pull back from her teeth when she spoke.

"So who's the john?"

"A guy."

"Yeah, but he does what?"

"Does it matter? I'm paying."

She shrugged. "I'll do it whatever, but lifestyle can make a difference. A man who spends all day sitting on his behind eating refined foods, chances are his output will be less than spectacular. Believe me, I've learned the importance of fiber. Donuts for breakfast, burrito for lunch, fried chicken for dinner, you're going to get a six inch turd if you're lucky. Skinny, too. Someone eats muesli and exercises, well, that's a different story."

"Don't worry, this guy's full of shit."

"That's a joke, right?"

We purred down Santa Monica Boulevard in the Prelude.

Ryan had parked out front of the Senior Citizens Center and was sitting on a bench under a palm. There wasn't a homeless person within thirty yards. I guess one of them must have fucked with him and got burned. I left Rosie in the car and went and sat next to him.

"Jackie, how nice to see you. Tell me about the limo outside the Bradbury Building."

"The Bradbury Building?"

"From where I was it looked like the same bim you had over at your place."

I remembered the gray sedan that had blocked my view after Bella pulled away.

"I'll trade you the limo story for an address."

"Jackie, I don't know if our relationship has reached the trading stage. What address?"

"The woman at my place, the woman at the Bradbury Building. She forgot to pay me."

Ryan laughed.

"I saw she left you on the sidewalk. What happened? Couldn't perform?"

"The address? You got it through DMV, remember?"

"Oh, I got it through more than that. Give with the story first."

I didn't want to give him anything without a guaranteed return, but Ryan had the upper hand and there wasn't much else I could do.

"She called me up and invited me to a party."

"Sounds like she's getting serious."

"She needed an escort, that's all."

"What about those fifteen minutes in the back of the limo?"

"You were counting?"

"I was imagining pictures."

"Jesus...."

"For her address I want details. Tell it like one of those phone-sex things."

"You know what I was doing, you know I didn't go home with her. That's enough. See that woman in my car? She's paid for, and she isn't your usual hooker."

"I can see that. How *old* is she?"

"She comes when you shit in her mouth."

Ryan took a heart pill out of his pocket.

"You're quick, Jackie, but then I never figured you for dumb. Where are we supposed to do it?"

"I'll spring for a room."

Ryan stood up abruptly and started for his car.

"Let's go. Don't bother getting her out, just follow me. You know the Starway on Wilshire?"

"Give me Bella's address and take her with you. I'll give you the money for the room."

"Oh, no, Jackie, you have to come too."

The Starway Motel was a dump that stood across from a shoe retailer on the eastern border of Santa Monica. It was the kind of place where ten-year-old Trans Ams and Camaros pulled up late at night then disappeared before dawn without the owners ever being seen. The rooms invited invasion – the windows didn't shut properly, the doors didn't latch. Inside, the carpet was greasy and the sheets were stained. But it was cheap, and if the other guests weren't actively trying to rip you off they pretty much minded their own business.

Rosie took an eight-foot square of plastic sheeting from her bag and spread it out in the middle of the room. I climbed onto the bed and sat with my back in a corner. I was pissed off. I wanted Bella's address safe in my hand. I wanted to be out, heading toward it. Instead I was stuck here, hanging on Ryan's string, not knowing if he intended to make good on his promise or not.

"This'll be an experience for both of us, Jackie." Ryan glanced across at Rosie and shook his head. "Jesus.... What happens to some people?"

"You're the one who's going to give it to her."

"It's an opportunity. Who wouldn't?"

"Pretty much everyone."

He sat on the edge of the bed and took off his shoes. He had small feet. He laughed.

"You wouldn't take it if it was offered?"

"Doesn't do it for me."

"Probably ain't extreme enough."

"Yeah, right."

Ryan was down to his shorts. He picked up his jacket, took an envelope from it and spun it into my lap.

"Brought you another present."

I looked inside: several glossies.

"Take 'em out, have fun. I won't think any the less of you."

I dropped the envelope on the bed. Ryan made a disappointed face. Over on the floor a naked Rosie was flat on her back, legs spread, talking to herself. The plastic crinkled beneath her. Ryan winked at me, stripped off his shorts, and moved toward her.

"Time to get to work."

From behind he looked like some huge slug heading for food. He didn't have a waist, the fat on his guts filled up what hollows there should have been, and the cheeks of his ass were so full his crack was just a tight vertical line running between his legs to the small of his back.

He stood in front of Rosie for a while and stuck his toe into her cunt. She ground herself against it. Then he got down on hands and knees and crawled up her until his hardon was in her mouth. He pushed it in as far as he could. She took it until she was about to heave, then told him to turn around. The cheeks of his ass stayed together even in this position and she had to use her hands to pull them apart. She pressed her nose in and took a deep sniff. Her tits rose and her eyelids fluttered like she was getting a rush.

Ryan shifted position so that he was squatting over her. Rosie's bent legs trembled. Ryan looked like a small Sumo wrestler, hunkered down over her head, arms braced against his knees. His dick looked ugly and dark against the white skin of his belly. Rosie pressed her mouth home. I watched the sides of her mouth roll as she worked her tongue, but it went on too long to hold my attention so I gave in and took the photos out of the envelope and looked through them.

Five shots of two bodies, different angles. A guy on his back, a woman slumped on top, his bone curving into her. Both of them locked together in rigor. Some hotel room, cheap prints on the walls, pieces of plaster missing. Their heads were covered with plastic convenience-store bags, cinched tight with silver duct tape at the neck. I could see the logo for a liquor company on the one the woman was wearing.

Wild. Real dead people having sex. An image so shocking that for a moment I couldn't make sense of the pictures, couldn't arrange the collection of limbs and asses into two joined people. When I did I got hard, so I put them away for later.

Rosie was murmuring up at Ryan.

"Are you ready? Squeeze it out of that big ass of yours. Come on…come on…."

Ryan concentrated. There was a moment of complete stillness while his face turned red and Rosie lay motionless with her mouth open. Then he grunted and a flood of liquid shit covered her face in a lumpy brown sheet.

She coughed and swallowed and coughed again, blowing shit out of her nose, wiping it from her eyes. Her tongue circled her mouth once, trying to lick more of the stuff in, then she twisted her head away and puked.

Ryan dressed. I opened a window and sat counting the minutes until I could get away. The smell in the room was appalling. Rosie was in the bathroom and the shower was running. I thought I could hear her shouting at herself.

Ryan tightened his tie. "Fucking nitro, haven't had a solid shit for five years. You think Miss Vernier is into this kind of thing?"

"Who?"

"Your piece with the limo."

Ryan took out a small notebook, tore off a page and handed it to me.

"The address DMV gave me, same as where the limo went."

"You followed her home?"

"I'm interested in the company you keep. Dress smart when you go see her, she's big money."

Ryan and I left Rosie in the bathroom and headed back out into the world. Late afternoon, the sky was clear and there was a nice breeze coming up from the ocean. Traffic was starting to pick up along the boulevard.

"You want to grab a coffee, Jack?"

"No."

Ryan smirked. "She forgot to pay you, huh?"

"That's what I said."

"Sure."

"Maybe I just like her."

Ryan laughed.

"Don't get those photos too sticky."

Then he got in his car and drove away.

Chapter 19

O n the flats of Beverly Hills they go out of their way to flaunt their wealth. In Malibu they do their best to hide it. Up in the hills, anyway, where the really big money settles itself. More space, better views, enforceable seclusion. The roads are narrow and winding and they don't have sidewalks. The only things that show people live there at all are the occasional driveways disappearing between screens of vegetation.

Access to the address Ryan had given me was blocked by a pair of black iron gates ten feet high, set into a solid stone wall. Through them I could see redwoods and pines and a lot of other European-looking trees. I parked on a grass verge and thought. How to explain knowing her address? I couldn't tell her I got it from a cop. So I generated some bullshit about knowing a guy in the DMV – which was kind of related to the truth – and when I had it straight in my head I got out of the car and pressed the intercom by the gate.

No one answered, but there must have been a camera somewhere because after a while the gates swung open. I drove through them and along an avenue of trees that opened out, about a quarter of a mile later, into an area of gently rising wild grass surrounded by woodland. I'd expected something more formal, more landscaped and designed, but it looked like Bella's ideas on gardening were strictly low-maintenance.

The house, at the top of the rise, was large, but not obscene. Old stone, slate roof, leaded windows – more New England than Malibu. I rang the house bell and looked back the way I'd come. I could see a slice of ocean above the trees.

Bella answered the door herself and she didn't seem pissed off to see me – the opposite, in fact. I got ready with my story, but I didn't need it.

"I thought that must have been you last night. The driver noticed your headlights."

For a moment I was thrown. Then it clicked, she'd mistaken Ryan's tail for me.

"I don't like sleeping by myself."

She reached out and ran her fingers through my hair.

"Come inside."

The interior of the house wasn't anywhere near as gothic as the outside. Instead of antiques and shadows, the decor was contemporary and there was a feeling of light and space that could only have come from an extensive re-modeling of the original layout.

Bella led me up a flight of stairs and along a corridor to a suite of rooms – bedroom, bathroom, dressing room and another room with the door closed. The windows of the bedroom were on a corner of the building. On one side they overlooked a large rectangular pool, on the other, an area of grass and forest.

"Nice house."

"I like the seclusion. One of the advantages of wealth is the distance it can buy you from other people."

"One among many."

She undid my fly. I came out hard in her hand and we fucked a solid hour.

Afterwards, while she took a shower, I wandered through the suite. The style of the rooms was deco minimalist – smooth unornamented surfaces, furniture with clean lines, nothing unnecessary. In a wardrobe that formed one wall of her dressing room I found her clothes. They hung with department-store precision – a lot of short-skirted suits, dark colors, no patterns, cut from the best fabrics in the world. On the rack they looked almost conservative, but I knew how Bella's body transformed them. The recessed dressing table in the opposite wall was bare of cosmetics or jewelry except for a platinum compact and an eye pencil.

I ran my hands over things, over polished hardwood and flawless joinery, over materials and furnishings the rest of the planet could never dream of owning. I breathed in the smell of money.

The closed door off the bedroom opened onto a small room without windows that held video equipment – a couple of semi-professional cameras on tripods, a two-tape VHS editing desk, three monitors in a row above it.

I was looking at the controls of the editing machine when Bella walked up behind me and touched my shoulder.

"Do you know anything about them? Or are you only interested in the end product? What you see on the screen?"

She was wrapped in a towel and there was still moisture in the hollow of her neck.

"I'm interested in the life around it."

"I spoke to Welks this morning. You should call him, he's warming to the idea of another presenter."

"You pressured him."

"I'm a stockholder, I'm entitled to make suggestions. Did you enjoy mixing with those pigs last night? Is that really the life you want?"

"It'd be better than the one I've got now."

She kissed me and smiled, and it was a smile that unnerved me. Not passion or compassion or pity or love...but satisfaction.

"Go and clean up, Jack, we're having dinner soon. There's someone I think you'll find it interesting to meet."

The dining room was on the ground floor. Bella held my arm as we went down the stairs. I expected to hear the bustle of cooks and maids, but the house was quiet.

"Are you good at surprises?"

"Sure."

"I hope so."

She pushed a door open and we walked into some sort of pre-dining area, a room with couches and a bar – a place for cocktails. A man stood at a window, looking out at the grounds. His back was toward us but he turned as we entered. And in that two-second movement I understood what Bella had meant about surprises.

"Jack, I'd like you to meet my father, Powell Vernier."

There was laughter in her voice, like she was enjoying a joke. But it was lost on me. I was too busy trying to deal with the implications of what I was seeing. The man in front of me had silver hair. He'd picked me up in a Jaguar on the Drag, and later he'd dumped me in an alley. And his presence here moved the thoughts I'd had the night before, about Bella's blow job and tattoo, from bleary late-night brainshit to something with a much more definite connection to reality.

Powell ignored me and looked hard at Bella.

"Is this wise?"

"Whether it is or not, he's here."

"You invited him?"

"Shall we go through?"

Powell snorted and turned away from her abruptly. He stalked through a pair of open sliding doors that connected with the dining room proper. Bella and I followed.

The table was laid with crystal and silver, pale roses were arranged in the center. On a counter under a row of windows, covered metal dishes rested on warming plates. I thought someone might appear to serve us, but Bella and Powell moved to the food and helped themselves. Bella caught my look.

"I don't like other people in the house."

"I didn't say anything."

"We have cleaners and a cook, even a chauffeur. But none of them live on the property. And when they are here I don't allow them to show themselves."

We ate in silence. Bella shot glances at me like she was waiting for something to happen. Powell pretended I wasn't in the room. I just sat there and wondered what the fuck was going on.

After a while Bella stopped eating and said, almost laughing, "Aren't you going to say anything?"

"About what?"

"About Powell."

"Well, I wasn't sure...."

"If I was part of it? I am. What do you think of our...social conscience?"

"I don't have much to go on, do I?"

"I'm sorry about the spray but it's a necessary security measure. Gratitude can turn to greed so easily. And we didn't treat you because it wouldn't have been ethical working on someone I was interested in. Besides, you aren't homeless."

"You're a doctor?"

"I am. But Powell has more experience."

"Why didn't you just let me wake up and send me home?"

"I wasn't sure I knew you well enough. I didn't know how you'd react."

Powell looked up from his plate.

"Do you know him well enough now?"

He'd cut his food into small pieces, but he hadn't eaten more than a couple of mouthfuls. I checked his eyes and realized why they'd seemed so unresponsive when I saw him on the Drag – they were pinned. The guy was smacked. Bella ignored him.

"We're somewhat jealous of our privacy."

"Leaving me in an alley was the only alternative?"

"An alley?"

"I woke up with a couple of tramps trying to take my pants off."

Powell chuckled softly. Bella turned on him.

"I told you to be careful with him."

"What would you have done?"

"I certainly wouldn't have left him in an alley." Then, to me, "Whereabouts?"

"Hollywood."

"Hollywood! For Christ's sake, Powell, what were you thinking?"

"I was thinking of our security."

"Are you sure?"

"Meaning?"

There was a calculated blandness to Powell's expression that made me feel I'd missed something. Bella changed the subject.

"Would you call us philanthropic, Jack?"

"You really do this free healthcare thing?"

"Of course. It isn't anything particularly exhaustive – a checkup, some medication, some money – but I think it makes a difference."

"I thought you didn't like people."

Powell made a short barking noise which I guessed was laughter. Bella looked viciously at him.

"Certain people. The people we help have so little impact on the world it isn't worth judging them."

"As you see, my daughter is completely selfless."

Bella gave him a false smile.

"But you give so much to the project yourself, Father, don't you do it out of a sense of selflessness too?"

"You know why I do it."

"Yes, I do." The bitterness in Bella's voice was unmistakable. She caught herself and looked apologetically at me.

"You'll have to excuse us, we've been working very hard."

Later. Upstairs in her bed. She fucked madly, clawing at my skin, sweating into my eyes. It felt like something was trying to fight its way out of her body and fuse with my heart.

In the dark, afterwards, I smoked and watched the moonlight play against her legs.

"Why did Powell act like a messenger boy when he picked me up? He didn't say anything about being a doctor."

"He thinks it separates him from what we do. A precaution in case anyone recognizes him."

"He doesn't like me."

"He hates you. He's hated every lover I've ever had."

"Have there been many?"

"Would it worry you?"

"I'm just wondering how long I'll last."

"You'll last as long as you want."

"It's my choice?"

"Everything is your choice. It's the same for all of us. Self-determination – it's what makes us human."

"If you've got enough money."

"If you've got the strength to decide what you really want and then to act on that desire and make it a reality."

"Sounds simple."

"Only the weak allow themselves to be thwarted, Jack."

"What did you mean outside the Bradbury building, when you asked me about love?"

"I was asking you to make a choice."

"About us?"

"About what you want for yourself. I can offer you *everything*. But there are things about me you might find unusual."

"Such as?"

"Oh, one step at a time, I think."

Bella smiled and swung her legs out of the bed.

"I have to confess something, Jack. I've been less than frank with you."

"What about?"

I held my breath, wondering if she was going to make some kidney revelation.

"How I found you after the party in Bel Air."

"You spoke to my trick."

"I don't think he was in a mood to do you any favors."

"Yeah. How, then?"

"When Powell picked you up you had a card in your wallet – your escort service."

"Oh."

"Do you remember anything from that night?"

"Between getting sprayed and waking up? No."

"Nothing?"

"Well...."

"Come with me."

In the video suite she pressed part of the wall, it slid back to reveal a shelf of video cassettes. She took one, slotted it into the editing machine and fired it up. I saw myself unconscious on a gurney. Clinical surroundings – green walls, green surgical fabric. My pants were around my knees and Bella had my dick in her mouth.

She killed the tape.

"The drug we use allows certain physical responses. That's one of them."

"I thought it was a dream."

"Does it bother you?"

"Why would it?"

"Taking advantage of an unconscious person might be considered an abuse of power."

"But only the weak allow themselves to be thwarted, right?"

She laughed.

"It wasn't an opportunity I could pass up."

She led me back into the bedroom and began picking up her clothes.

"What are you doing?"

"I have work to take care of."

"What work? It's almost twelve."

"Some results I need to check before tomorrow. I'll be gone a few hours, don't wait up."

She showered quickly and left the suite.

It wasn't what I'd expected on my first night in her house, but then she hadn't known I was coming. I lit another cigarette and lay in the dark thinking.

Both Bella and Powell were involved in the homeless medical care thing. Neither of them had said anything about kidneys, but if the operations were for real it seemed a fair guess that they would both be involved in those too.

A doctor who took out kidneys and who was also one of the clients Karen spent extended time with....

Joey had said he'd been examined by a woman, but after the anesthetic came down he wouldn't have known who did the actual cutting – Powell's messenger-boy act would have fooled him the same as it did me. So who had Karen been fucking? Powell? Certainly his age and general creepiness wouldn't have stopped her if there was money to be had. But then I couldn't rule out Bella either – she didn't strike me as a woman who placed limits on her sexual menu.

What clinched it for me was the tattoo. Karen's had first appeared when she came home from some stay-over fuck job. Bella said she'd had hers done with a friend. Identical designs. It had to be more than coincidence. And you don't go out with someone and get the exact same picture unless you have a pretty strong attachment to them.

If that made Bella the sex partner, did it also mean she was involved in the killing? Lovers waste each other all the time, but I couldn't see what reason Bella would have for murdering Karen. She'd already taken her kidney, after all. And even if Karen came back and started hassling her about the operation, maybe trying to blackmail extra cash, one glance was all it would have taken to know there was no way she'd make good on any threat of going to the police – she just wasn't that kind of person. Still, there could be a whole load of shit I didn't know anything about.

In the absence of knowing any of that shit, however, two things made Powell a better bet as killer. He was male and, for some reason, he hated Bella's lovers. Which meant the semen they found in Karen's guts could have been his, and that maybe he had a motive for the killing.

Of course it could have been a double act – daddy and daughter cooperating in an operation that went a bit too far – but from the vibe between them it didn't seem likely. There was too much antagonism there, too much vicious jousting to figure cooperation was a word they used very often.

I ran my head in circles for an hour trying to figure it out, but I didn't have enough info to feel conclusive about anything. All I got was a panic attack over the thought that, if Bella did turn out to be the killer, things might go terribly wrong before I had a chance to benefit from my association with her.

Chapter 20

Morning light woke me. The windows were open and let in a breeze that carried a taste of the sea. Bella stood next to the bed, she was fully dressed and looked too fresh to have spent all night working.

"I was hoping you'd wake before I left."

"Where are you going?"

"I own a clinic in Brentwood."

"The place Powell took me?"

"No. This one is more orthodox."

"You work full-time?"

"Just the odd day here and there. It keeps me current."

"Even though you don't have to?"

"It has its compensations." Bella smiled suggestively. "Will you stay here until I get back?"

"Sure. Can I use the pool?"

"Of course. And call Welks."

She handed me a business card.

"What time did you come to bed?"

"Late."

An hour or so later I dragged my ass out of bed, had a shower and wondered through the ground floor until I found a room with open French doors and a table laid with breakfast. Cereal, fruit, pastries and coffee for one. The trappings of wealth around me made me feel a little slovenly at being the last to rise.

I ate the pastries and drank the coffee, smoked a couple of cigarettes. There was no TV in the room and after a while I got bored, so I took the French doors and went out to look at the grounds. I was at one side of the house and the garden there was just fifty yards of deep grass bordered by woodland. Thick ferns grew at the edge of the trees. I kicked my way into them, wondering if Arnold Schwarzenegger's estate was anything like this. I'd seen Leibovitz's photos of him on a white horse and had always figured his home life must be set against some transplanted Bavarian forest.

The sun had burnt the dew off the tops of the ferns, but underneath they were shaded and my shoes came away wet as I shuffled through them. It was a childish thing to do, like running through autumn leaves, but who was there to see me? I hadn't seen one servant yet, and Powell was probably occupied mixing up his morning shot. Besides, I liked the sound it made.

And then my right foot got stuck in a dead dog.

I dragged it out onto an open patch of lawn and twisted my shoe clear of the soggy mess of flesh and bone that had been its ribcage. Once, when I was a kid, I found the carcass of a drowned dog floating in a creek. Someone had got to it before me and jammed a piece of wood up its ass and the skin there was torn and had fluttered in the current like tissue paper. It had given me a hardon because I knew whoever had done it must have been turned on too. But this dog looked different. It looked like it had died in pain. The skin of its muzzle was desiccated and drawn back and its eyes had been eaten out. It must have been in the undergrowth some time.

The animal corpse worried me. There were feral dogs in the hills all around L.A. and one of them could easily have picked this place as a jump-off spot for doggie heaven. But I didn't think that was the case here. This dog was a domestic animal and it hadn't chosen anything. Someone had cut it open from groin to chest and pulled its guts out into the air.

I kicked it back into the brush and walked around to the back of the house. Powell was on the far side of the pool, dressed in a dark, conservatively cut suit, staring at some clouds moving across the sky. I called out good morning, but he didn't respond, just fish-eyed me for a few seconds then turned his head back to the sky. I couldn't be bothered with that kind of shit so early in the morning so I sat in a chair near one of the pillars that ringed the pool, pointed myself toward the sun and closed my eyes.

A couple of minutes later a shadow fell across me. Powell, of course, standing there like he was contemplating sticking something sharp into me.

"Come with me, I want to show you something."

In some room on the ground floor, sitting on opposite sides of a low table, a photo album between us, closed.

Powell touched the book like it was a treasure he took pride in owning. He had long slim fingers.

"You expect your relationship with Bella to last?"

"Why shouldn't it?"

"Look at these."

He opened the album and turned pages, holding them so I could see. The pictures were all of Bella. They started off with a run of mid-teen shots. She wore tight jeans and bathing suits. They weren't the type of photos you'd expect a father to take of his daughter. Some things were too obvious – young labia separated by a crotch seam, bending rear shots, a hint of pubic hair around a bikini, nipples visible through a thin T-shirt. But Bella seemed natural enough, as though she was unaware of the focus of the camera.

In the next set she was a few years older, naked and posed – a series of glamour mag copyings in which she either flaunted her body with full-frontal pride, or looked bored.

"I took them all myself. Look further."

He pushed the book across the table to me and I flipped pages into porn territory – legs spread, ass exposed, fingers and other objects inside. From her early twenties to the present. And in all of them Bella looked like she was brandishing a weapon, controlling whatever dynamic existed between her and Powell when the camera came out.

Powell took the book back and closed it.

"Do they shock you?"

"Nothing there I haven't already seen."

His jaw muscles tightened.

"But you find it strange, do you not, that I should take such pictures?"

"I wouldn't call it normal."

"Bella was a willing participant in all but the earliest of them. This estate, my friend, is not the place to look for normality. It is a world within a world, a private universe, and in it we have lived lives outside the rules that govern yours. If you think Bella is just another woman to bed, someone who behaves in an essentially similar manner to the trash you are used to, then you are very much mistaken."

"You're trying to frighten me, right?"

"It will be interesting to see how long you maintain that bravado." Powell stood. "I am going to the city. Shall I leave the photographs with you?"

I looked up at him, at the poisoned hardness of his junked eyes, and I knew Bella had been right when she said he hated me.

After he'd gone I got Howard Welks' card out and found a phone. But I hesitated – the thought of calling the boss of a TV station for a job made me nervous. I punched Rex's number instead.

"Guess where I'm calling from."

"Who's this?"

"Jack."

"Oh."

Rex sounded like there was nothing left inside him. He also sounded more than a little stoned.

"I'm in Malibu, man. At that woman's house. Jesus, you should see the place."

"What woman?"

"The one I got dumped out of the agency for. I tracked her down."

"Jack, is this, like, a joke?"

"A joke? Shit no, it's real. What do you mean?"

"You don't think it's kind of inappropriate, considering the situation."

"Fuck, man, it was an accident. It wasn't your fault."

"I still killed him."

"Yeah, I know. And no one's saying it wasn't an awful thing to have happened. To you and to him."

"But I bet you don't think about it much."

"What do you want me to say for Christsake? I'm not going to make it the central fact of my life."

"Well it's the central fucking fact of mine."

"Maybe you should talk about it with your doctor. You know, get some counseling."

"That won't bring him back to fucking life, will it?"

"What are you going to do, then? I mean, it sounds like you need to do something, man."

"You know what I'm going to do? I'm going to have another hit, then I'm going to take a page out of your book, Jack. I'm just going to pretend it never fucking happened. How's that?"

He broke the connection before I could think of a comeback.

The next phone call I made went a little better.

Howard Welks was in a meeting, but he'd left word with his secretary and she routed the call through to some guy called Larry Burns who turned out to be head of production. Burns wasn't overjoyed about having to make space for a new presenter, particularly one with zero experience, and he worked hard at finding a reason to kill things before they got started. But I'd been following the lives of the stars too long to fuck up on any of his questions and in the end he told me to come in the next day for a dry run in front of the camera.

When I put the phone down my hand was shaking. Two months ago I'd been struggling to make ends meet serving donuts to truck drivers and factory workers. Now I had a chance at what everyone in L.A. wanted – visual exposure. A chance to become someone other people wanted to be.

I knew it had nothing to do with me. If I made it onto TV it would be due to Bella's financial power and nothing else. But what did I care? As long as I got a fast car, a place in the Hollywood Hills and my picture on the pages of magazines, nothing else mattered. Even so, the thought of walking into a studio full of technicians and cameramen made me feel distinctly edgy.

But then, that's what drugs are for.

I swam nude in the pool, then lay with my back against one of the columns and caught some sun. The clouds Powell had been staring at earlier had disappeared and the sky was the kind of blue Californian license plates used to be. Above the trees the slash of visible ocean glittered distantly.

Later I got dressed and went around the front of the house to the Prelude. The photos Ryan had given me were still in the glove compartment. I took them upstairs to Bella's suite and sat on the bed and looked at them – plastic bag lovers, dead rubber bodies joined by a dick. After a while I went into the bathroom and had a wank over the sink.

I spent the rest of the day in front of a TV smoking and catching up on current affairs.

After surviving surgery to remove a brain tumor, Elizabeth Taylor was now facing diabetes. Leonardo DiCaprio had been snapped eating organic popcorn during breaks from work on *Titanic* and, on the set of *Michael*, Nicolas Cage helped with a birthday surprise for John Travolta. Later John dropped four-point-seven big ones on a mansion and twenty-five K on a party where he got down with Tom Hanks, Sean Penn, Sharon Stone, Priscilla Presley and Dustin Hoffman.

Bella came home around five. We fucked and had dinner and sat out by the pool.

"Powell and I had a chat this morning after you'd gone."

"That must have been edifying."

"He showed me some photos."

Bella sighed. "His private collection I suppose."

"I imagine."

"What did you think?"

"Sexy."

"You know why he showed them to you, don't you?"

"I guess he thought it'd put me off."

"He's a consummate bastard."

"You mind that I've seen them?"

"I mind the way they were shown to you."

In the twilight the water in the pool looked beautiful.

"Feel like a swim?"

Bella shook her head and held her hand out to me.

"Come on. This can't happen again."

Up in the video room we sat on black leather chairs. Bella selected a tape from the hidden cupboard and fizzed a monitor into life. A succession of clips, all of them looking like they'd been shot in the house. Bella and Powell fucking, a variety of positions, most of them extreme. Nothing tender – not rape, but definitely not love – more like combat.

"What do you think?"

"He's got a big dick."

"Jesus, Jack, these are now. It's still happening. I wasn't working last night, I was fucking him."

"Oh...."

"I've been doing it since I was sixteen."

"He forced you?"

Bella's smile made me feel naive.

"He didn't have to. My mother was killed in a car accident when I was fifteen. Powell was driving. He was drugged, as usual, and he ran into the side of a truck – he might as well have murdered her. The opportunity for revenge was too good to pass up."

"I don't understand."

"I'd let him do it, then deny him for weeks, sometimes months. It drove him out of his mind. He was powerless against me. He couldn't even coerce me financially because my mother had been the one with money and she'd left most of it to me. On top of that, it was a thrill."

"It turned you on?"

"Not the way you mean. But testing how far I can go has always excited me."

"What about now? It can't still be a thrill."

"Manipulating another person is addictive."

"But it's been going on what, fifteen years?"

"On and off. But you're right, control for control's sake is ultimately pointless."

"Then why?"

The tape had been silently humping away through all of this. Bella killed it, took it out of the machine and put it back in the cupboard. When she sat down again she looked pensive.

"This conversation is happening sooner than I'd planned. Please promise me you won't let it change things between us."

"How bad can it be?"

"Not bad, just...unusual. You might see me in a different light."

"I doubt it."

Bella read my face, evidently found what she wanted, and went on in a rush.

"I opened the Brentwood clinic shortly after I qualified. At first it was just somewhere to pass time. But it didn't stay that way. I became fascinated by what I could do to the patients. Given the right type of person and the right lies, they'd agree to anything. It began with examinations – unnecessary rectal probes, vaginal swabs, colonoscopies.... But, eventually, nothing is ever enough and I moved on to minor surgical procedures, small operations I had no medical reason to perform. Or qualification – I'm not a surgeon."

"How did you know how to do them, then?"

"At that level it's only really a question of mechanics. Once you know the layout of the body and the basic procedures it isn't too hard. And I enjoyed the challenge of working things out."

"And it was sexual for you?"

"Of course. Sex is just one body doing something to another. Most people limit themselves to what they believe is normal. I have a broader definition of the word, that's all."

"Was Powell involved in the clinic?"

"No. Our medical partnership came later, when I realized I was risking exposure. A clinic is never free of scrutiny from one board or another and it was only a matter of time before someone made a complaint. If I was going to continue to indulge myself I had to move out of the public arena."

"That's what the homeless thing is about? A safe way for you to get off?"

"I do also provide a valuable service."

"But essentially...."

"Essentially, yes, it's for my own pleasure."

"What does 'minor surgical procedures' cover?"

"Vasectomies, mole removal, an appendix occasionally. Often I don't go beyond the examination stage. But for all of it I need to maintain my influence over Powell. I need the technical assistance he can give – he *is* a surgeon – and I need him to find the patients."

"So you're going to keep having sex with him?"

"For the time being. But nothing lasts forever. You can handle it, can't you, Jack?"

She said this as though she was already sure of it.

"I can handle pretty much anything."

"Thank you. You should come and watch me with a patient one night, you'd enjoy it. We have a one-way mirror set up. They do the most absurd things for money. Sometimes I think the essence of human nature is venality."

"Whose idea was it to tape the sessions with Daddy?"

"Mine, of course. But he sneaks in here and takes a copy of everything I have. He's duplicated my entire collection. I suppose it gives him back some sense of ownership."

CHAPTER 21

I drove the 850ci. Bella sat in the passenger seat wearing a short iridescent spandex dress she'd picked up at some late-opening store at the Wilshire end of Third Street Promenade. It wasn't particularly slutty, but at least it cost less than five hundred bucks. She wanted to get into a group sex thing and we were out trawling for a victim.

It was too early for the Drag to yield much – only about eight p.m. – so we parked and hit a triple-X store on the outskirts. Inside – a few guys checking cassette covers with tunnel-vision intensity, avoiding any sort of contact with each other. Bella stood next to one of them – skinny, mid-forties, eyes tight in his head, the need for a fuck like a smell around him. She reached down a tape and lingered over the come shot on the cover. The guy noticed her and I guess he thought it was pretty weird, a woman in that sort of place. When she touched his elbow he almost ran for the door. But Bella smiled and talked fast and nodded at me. He didn't need much persuading.

The three of us took a cab to some shitty motel on the Strip. His name was Rudy and he whined about how his wife hadn't let him fuck her since a year ago when they had a kid. He was a weak, greasy man who looked like he ought to be wearing a raincoat. We got a ground-floor room at the rear of the block. I pulled the curtains but they didn't fit too well and I was worried about the parking lot being right outside. No one else gave a shit, though, so I figured the best thing to do was get on with it – get Bella satisfied as fast as possible then get back to Malibu.

We left the lights on and stripped down. The guy had a hardon before he got his pants off. He lay where Bella told him to, on his back on the bed, dick sticking up dark and painful. Bella said she needed a piss first and went into the bathroom, but she didn't close the door completely and through the crack I saw her loading a syringe from a clear glass vial with blue writing on it. She hid it in a towel which she dropped on the floor beside the bed just before she climbed on top of Rudy and stuck his dick in.

When Bella was set I got behind her, greased up and worked my way into her ass. Over her shoulder I could see Rudy's face moving through expressions of rapture – this kind of scene must have fritzed his head every night as he jerked off in front of the mirror. I could feel his cock moving on the other side of her colon wall.

Bella ground away for a while, dangling her tits in his face, then lay right down on top of him like she wanted to snuggle her face into the hollow of his shoulder. But I saw her hand reach for the syringe, and while the poor bastard had his eyes closed she stuck it into a vein in his neck.

Rudy yelped, but that's all he had time for. The drug wasn't tardy. His eyes rolled back and his face seized. Best of all, as far as Bella was concerned, he went into a rapid series of thrusting convulsions. I was a little freaked and my dick started to shrink, so I pretended I'd finished and pulled out. I watched Bella shake her head and yell as he pistoned away, the sound of his hips against her like a fist hitting flesh. She came with a scream and swung herself off him. As his dick slid free it started to spurt, I couldn't believe the amount he got rid of.

His jerking got slower but more pronounced, muscles locking harder each time, taking longer to relax for the next spasm. Until his body froze into a curve, supported only by his shoulders and the heels of his feet. He looked as though he'd been electrocuted. His dick was still hard and there were sheets of come over his belly and the tops of his thighs. Bella was absently wiping herself with the towel.

"I think he's stopped breathing."

She cursed lightly, like this was a minor inconvenience, and pushed down on his stomach to straighten him out. She put her mouth on his and gave him a couple of blasts. The sound of air going into his chest was hollow and sad.

"Here, you do this, he needs cardiac massage. Five breaths then let me pump. Don't worry, he'll be all right."

I did what she said and it felt like I was blowing into the hold of a ship, something I could never fill up if I stayed crouched over him forever. We took turns doing our thing. I was getting worried the guy would die, but Bella didn't seem fazed in the slightest. Her movements were sure and professional, and after a minute Rudy started to splutter and breathe, even though he was still unconscious. As soon as this happened Bella turned away from him and began dressing like he wasn't in the room.

I dragged my clothes on in about five seconds flat and stood waiting by the door. Bella took her own sweet time.

"Relax. He'll be out for two hours at least. I hope you feel proud of yourself. You helped save his life."

"Let's just get out of here."

"Is anything wrong?"

"It wasn't really what I was expecting."

"He'll be all right. The drug's only dangerous with heart conditions."

"How do you know he doesn't have one?"

"He's breathing. Come on, we'll get a cab on the next block."

We left Rudy where he was. His hardon had gone and he looked kind of pathetic, but at least he was alive. Out on the street, we flagged a cab and got in. When it started to roll I asked to be dropped in Hollywood. Bella looked upset and told the driver to pull over. We got out and talked in whispers on the sidewalk.

"What's the matter, Jack?"

"We almost killed that guy."

"No we didn't."

"What do you mean, we didn't?"

"He was healthy enough, there was very little chance he'd sustain any permanent damage."

"It didn't look that way to me. I thought he was going to snap in half."

"Aren't you going to come home with me?"

"I need some downtime. I mean, Jesus.... Besides, I have to test for Channel 52 tomorrow. Burbank's closer from my place."

"You spoke to Welks? That's great. You should have told me."

"I was going to wait and see how it went first."

"Come back to Malibu, you can take the limo tomorrow."

"Not tonight."

"I'm sorry, Jack. I thought it would excite you."

I was tempted to give in, but I had to think of the future. A little bit of playing hard to get could go a long way. At least that's how it went on TV. Plus I knew I'd need pills to make it through the test, and Malibu wasn't the place for a poor boy to score.

"Will you come to the house tomorrow? After you've finished?"

"Sure."

"How are you going to get to the studio? You don't have your car."

"Cab, I suppose."

"Take mine. This too."

She handed me the keys to the 850ci and a wad of hundreds.

We kissed and she got back in the cab and drove away. I stood looking after her, wondering if I'd done the right thing. It was a fine line to tread.

I took a cab back to the Drag and picked up the Beemer. Alone behind the wheel, smelling the leather, feeling the incredible grip the car had on the road, I knew I wasn't going to let anything on earth fuck up my chance at Bella.

Ryan chopped lines out, straight onto the Formica of the table in the kitchen.

He'd rolled up while I was parking in the lot out back of my building and told me he felt good enough to party. So now we were bent over, hoovering caine through a couple of Bella's hundred-dollar bills. When he finished, Ryan didn't bother to give his back. I didn't say anything, I was too busy worrying about exactly where in the course of the evening he'd latched onto me.

"I'm curious about those wheels downstairs, Jackie. In fact tonight I'm curious about a lot of things."

"You know whose they are."

"I know who owns them. What I don't know is how come you've got them."

"We were out. I wanted to come back here, she didn't. Just worked out more convenient this way."

"You two must be getting close. You have a good time tonight?"

"It was okay."

"A woman like that, it's gotta be more than okay. What did you do?"

"This and that."

"Same old same old, huh?"

"Yeah."

"It's an uphill fucking struggle with you, boy, isn't it?"

"What do you mean?"

"You ain't the only one with a new toy."

Out in the main room Ryan picked up a bag he'd left by the door and took out a snappy new video camera, the small tourist kind you could hold with one hand.

"Like it? Took it off a hooker who had this idea she was going to try out the personalized end of the porno market. Thought it might come in handy for what we talked about last time."

"Which was?"

"Your high-ass Malibu bim. Don't tell me you forgot."

"We didn't talk about anything."

"Yeah we did – the blackmail thing."

"You talked about it, not me. I don't want any part of it."

"Well, now, after tonight you don't have a choice. You took a couple of big steps backward in that motel room."

I wanted to say something smart and relaxed, but I suddenly felt too nauseous to open my mouth.

"Let me illustrate."

Ryan fucked about with a couple of leads and the TV then used the camera to drive the mini-cassette. On the screen a cross of peeling paint blurred out of existence as focus went beyond a window frame and through a gap between badly patterned curtains. A cheap motel room – three people on a bed. Me, Bella and Rudy.

"Fuck."

"Fuck is right, Jackie."

"Listen, I didn't know she was—"

"Let's just watch it. Excellent picture quality, wouldn't you say? Amazing what these Japs can do."

He killed the tape after Bella finished dressing.

"That's one good fucking body. Shame I couldn't get more of your cock going into her, but I was kinda limited for angles."

"I didn't know anything about that injection. All she said was she wanted to get it both ways. I almost shit when I saw what she was doing. If I'd known—"

"Slow down, Jackie. This doesn't have to be a problem for you. It can go two ways. First I could add it to the wino thing and all your other bullshit and let it find its way into Karen's file back at homicide. Or—"

"What are you talking about? I didn't do anything."

"But you were there and you didn't try to stop her."

"But we brought him round. If we wanted to hurt him, why would we do that?"

"Yeah, she was cool there. That guy dropping out didn't faze her a bit. She got paramedic training or something?"

I thought for a second about telling him Bella was a doctor – like there was no way she was going to let somebody die and the guy was never in any danger – but with the surgical slant on Karen's killing I figured it would do more harm than good.

"How would I know?"

"What about the shit she hit him with? What was that?"

"Look, Ryan, I don't know anything about her. She's just someone I fuck, okay?"

"I'm glad you feel that way, Jackie, 'cause it brings me to the second option you got."

He stopped to cut out more lines on top of the TV. When he'd done his share he started pacing the room. I could see his jaws clenching under the soft fat of his cheeks. He looked wired enough to start shadow-boxing.

"Yeah, your second option would be a much smarter choice. Ready? We show the tape to Miss fucking Vernier herself. Whaddya think?"

He stopped in front of me with an expression on his face like he really expected me to agree with him.

"Whaddya say, Jackie? That bitch would lay out big bucks to squash something like this."

"You've got the tape, you don't need my permission."

"But I want you involved. It'd buy a lot of goodwill – something you need right now. Plus I'll give you a cut.

"Fuck, no one got hurt, no one got ripped off. Can't you just leave it?"

"Jackie, I'm gonna get something out of this one way or the other. Me? I'd rather have the money but...."

"What do you need me for?"

"To explain things, to smooth the way. You tell her you saw the tape and a genuine threat exists. Then, when we meet, we don't have to fuck about so much."

"You want to meet her?"

"I ain't about to let you do the negotiating. Come on, it'll be fun, something we can share. Like we shared Karen."

"We didn't share Karen."

"Our cocks were going the same place. I'm giving you a chance, Jackie, you oughta take it. All you gotta do is set up a meeting."

He moved behind me and started rubbing my neck.

"Yes or no? Some money from a cunt who can easily afford it, or a shitload of hassle vis-à-vis the murder of your wife."

"I don't know when I'm seeing her again. It might take a few days."

"Hey, do I not look like a laid-back dude? I can wait a couple of days."

Chapter 22

Channel 52 had space on the Warner Bros. lot in Burbank – production offices and a couple of small studios that churned out low-budget programs off-beat enough for the under-twenty-fives, but still far enough infield to mutate into middle-America living room pap if the station ever clawed its way beyond the fringe.

I found Larry Burns' office on the second floor of a prefab building that looked like it was designed to be loaded onto the back of a truck – exterior stairs and walkways, air conditioner vents like ugly afterthoughts under windows blank with wooden Venetian blinds. I had to wait half an hour before the fucker came out to see me.

Larry looked like a guy who lived on his dick. He wore lightweight cotton slacks and I could see it hanging down the inside of his left pants leg. It was big, no doubt about it, but it didn't make up for the mess that was the rest of him. He was pear-shaped and soft and he had dandruff on his shoulders. He had some kind of blackhead problem happening with his nose and he'd broken so many capillaries trying to pick them out that the center of his face looked like a permanent boil. It was upsetting to find someone like him in California. In the film industry.

When he finally showed he didn't say anything, just jerked his head at me and strode outside. I followed him through narrow streets between hangar-shaped soundstages and workshops to a permanent set they used for one of their sitcoms – kind of a cutaway house with no roof or outside walls. Right now it was deserted except for the living room section where three guys and a camera waited at the edge of a pool of bright light. The floor was littered with cables and old bits of silver duct tape.

The guys with the camera introduced themselves as director, cameraman and sound recordist. They pretty much ignored Burns, but they were cool enough toward me. I had to stand out in the light, behind a mark someone had taped on the floor and speak to camera. Under the lens there was an Autocue which the director operated. I guess for a test with a good possibility of bombing they weren't prepared to shell out for extra staff.

The director told me to relax and pretend the camera was a person. But I knew better than that from my telehosting course. I knew to pretend that the camera was a window into the universal living room. That way you kept your appeal broad and didn't become inappropriately intimate.

I felt okay. I knew I could do it. I knew that I *had* to do it. On screen, the projection of confidence is your greatest asset. And I was projecting as hard as I could. Plus the cocktail of pills I'd taken that morning to kill my nerves was kicking in just fine.

Ten seconds in, I realized the Autocue script was one of Lorn's from last week's *28 FPS* show – an investigation into the different types of sanitary napkins used by various female stars. A joke on me by Burns, I suppose, but I remembered quite a bit of it and got it off smoother than I would have cold. After that they repositioned the camera and had me do it again.

Burns sat back in the shadows watching me on a monitor. When it was over he barked at the director to send him a cassette, then powered back out into the sunshine like he had things a whole lot more important than me to deal with. When he noticed I was following him he slowed fractionally.

"I'm not totally unhappy. We'll discuss and let you know. Parking lot's along there, then right."

He didn't say goodbye, didn't wait for me to, either. I watched him take a sharp corner and head for his building. Then I got lost accidentally on purpose and spent an hour or so wandering around, breathing the fresh-cut timber smell of newly constructed sets. Trying to suck in and keep forever the history that was there, the presence of generations of people whose whole worlds had spun within the safely insulated Hollywood perimeter. Who thought anywhere else was just someplace you wouldn't want to be.

On one of the prop streets they were shooting a storefront scene. A guy had to walk out the door, say his line to a waiting bimbo, then freeze looking off into the distance. I watched them go through it a half-dozen times, it got tedious, but the actor fascinated me. His clothes didn't crease, his hair stayed in place, he didn't sweat. The sun that burnt the rest of the crew didn't reach him.

I looked carefully at his face at the end of each take and I knew he wasn't there. He was already in his limo heading into the hills, coke in his nose and a seventeen-year-old on his cock.

And all he had to do was walk through doors in a minor TV movie. I didn't even know his name.

Later, a couple of security guys escorted me off the lot in a golf cart.

I spent the next few weeks out at Malibu. Apart from the obvious advantages, it put distance between me and Ryan. I knew he'd be itchy for the blackmail meeting with Bella and the longer I could avoid telling him I hadn't done anything about setting it up, the longer I'd avoid a beating. He was a pit-bull motherfucker, but I didn't think he'd front up at the house so early in the game.

Bella made it her mission to show me how pleasant money could be and the time passed in a glutted wonderland of consumption. We hit Rodeo for a wardrobe – hip suits with trousers that fit properly, a collection of casual wear the magazines were showing at the time, absurdly priced denim, leather that felt like it was still alive, shoes, shirts, underwear.... A lifetime of clothes that would all be replaced next season.

She wanted me to have a watch, so I chose one made out of platinum. She wanted me to have a new car, so we put the latest Mustang on order – a convertible. Not the most practical choice for L.A., but at her level of wealth practicalities weren't something you had to spend a lot of time worrying about.

With a new sled coming my way I could have sold the Prelude, but I didn't. Karen had given up part of herself to buy it, and for me it was too much of a marker to let go of – a possession that drew the line between the end of one life and the start of another. I put it in an auto storage place near UCLA instead.

Mornings, Bella and I spent in a fug of come and glit, sliding over each other on silk sheets. She told me she loved me. I said it right back and I think she believed me. She was beautiful, but the only thing I loved about her was the potential she had to make my life better. The emotional connection just wasn't there.

Maybe we came from worlds that were too different, maybe the feeling she gave off of being above any of the usual moral concerns was just too intense. Who knows? How can you figure why you love someone or why you don't? And what does it matter anyhow if you can fake it well enough to fool them?

Powell was at the house most nights. Bella had told me he usually spent most of his time at his apartment downtown, so it seemed like an obvious attempt to make his presence felt. It worked pretty well. Having Bella climb out of bed so he could stick his faded old bone into her really pissed me off. It was a constant reiteration of how limited my influence over her really was.

Still, sucking up the good life kept me pacified. In fact, receiving expensive goods and services occupied me so fully that for a while I even managed to sidestep the issue of a possible connection between one or both of this Malibu duo and Karen's murder.

But then Powell had two dogs delivered to the house. Black Labradors. I don't know where he kept them, I didn't see them around the grounds, but two days later I found one of them in the ferns at the edge of the woodland. It had been killed and gutted, same as the one I'd stepped in on my first day at the house.

Larry Burns called Bella on her cell while we were having lunch at a place on Beverly Drive. He didn't ask to speak to me, but she passed on the news, glowing with excitement.

"You're second presenter on *28 FPS*. How does it feel?"

"Fantastic!"

And it did. That one phone call changed the world for me. It lifted me out of obscurity and put my feet on the first rung of the ladder that led to a meaningful life. Anyone in L.A. would have killed for the opportunity, and

I'd got it after a single twenty-minute screen test. It felt slightly surreal. I'd been broke and without a future, now I was sitting in an expensive restaurant, wearing a suit that cost more than four months' rent on my apartment, contemplating the fact that very soon I would cease to be a nonentity.

"One thing, though, Jack, you mustn't mention my part in getting you the job to anyone. Nepotism isn't good for morale."

"Yeah, sure. How much are they paying?"

"I'm taking care of your salary – a compromise for your lack of experience. What do you think? Ten thousand a month? You'll need somewhere to live as well."

"You want me to move out?"

"No, but I want you to have an alternative for when it's necessary. Television is a gregarious environment and you may have to entertain – you couldn't do that at Malibu. It will also take some of the strain off Powell if you're away from the house occasionally."

This conversation resulted shortly afterwards in the acquisition of a three-bedroom house with pool in Laurel Canyon.

All I had to worry about now was Ryan fucking everything up with his pissant blackmail scheme.

At Bella's. I answered the phone. She was doing a half-day at her clinic in Brentwood and Powell, mercifully, was at his apartment watching incest vids or shooting smack or whatever else he did with himself. Someone for me. Not Bella with pornographic endearments to see me through until she got home but, strangely, Rex. Strange because I hadn't given him the number.

"Hey, dude."

His voice was bad – dragging and nasal. Smacked, of course, but worse than that, robbed of even the slightest trace of hope or energy. With the upturn in my situation I could afford to let it make me feel sad.

"How did you get this number?"

"Didn't you give it to me? I don't know...."

He was majorly doped. Words tailing off into whispers. I expected him to fall asleep on the phone.

"You don't sound too good."

"I'm fine. What do you mean?"

"Drugged."

"Oh, yeah, a bit."

"Where are you?"

"At home.... Can you come around? That's why I'm calling, to see if you can come around."

"What's wrong?"

"Nothing. But can you bring some money?"

Rex rented a small run-down house on one of the single-lane streets that wound into the hills out of West Hollywood. The Mustang had been delivered that day, so trucking over there wasn't much of a chore. He took a while answering my knock and when he did it wasn't a pretty thing to see. His face matched the sound of his voice on the phone. Pasty skin, pinned eyes, picked-out zits. He was shirtless and his jeans looked crusty. I'd parked the Mustang out front and he spent some time focusing on it.

"Yours?"

"Not bad, huh?"

"From the woman?"

"Beats sucking dicks."

Rex grunted and turned away. I followed him down a hall that was basically untouched, into a living room that was basically an oasis of shit. Carpet littered with pieces of clothing, dead matches and empty Coke cans. One of the cushions on the couch burnt and the foam inside melted. Bloody syringe sprays on the wall closest to the still-good part of the couch, glasses half full of water on a coffee table, used works, singed spoons, pieces of cotton wool, a small patch of puke under an Ansel Adams photo that had been half ripped off the wall. The room was dark and hot. It felt like somewhere an animal would go to die.

"Did you bring some money?"

"Yeah."

I handed over five hundred dollars.

"Bit of a change, you being broke."

"I'm sorry it's such a hassle."

"I didn't say it was a hassle. I'm just surprised."

Rex counted the money and stuffed it into his pocket.

"They repossessed the Porsche."

Something on the deck out back of the living room creaked. I couldn't see what it was because the curtains were drawn across the sliding glass doors.

"You look like shit."

"That's funny because I don't feel like anything at all."

"You've got to do something, man. Cut down on the gear."

"Nup. I don't have to do anything. I don't have to think about where I'm going, I don't have to self-improve, I don't have to put anything away for a rainy day. They say life's all about the way you look at it. But if you stop looking, it stops being there."

Rex turned away. He picked up one of the syringes from the table and started drawing small quantities of blood from a vein in his arm, squirting it out against a wall. It upset me that someone who such a short time ago was helping me make money, who was the closest thing I had to a friend, could become so distant, so unreachable. But as far as he'd moved from the Rex I used to know, I knew I'd moved further. Into my own new world. Into a place that was so different I could not honestly say I had anything more to give him than money.

"I have to go."

"So soon?"

"Where did you get my number, Rex?"

"The guy on the deck gave it to me. He said I should call."

"What guy?"

"He asked me about Karen, but he's here to see you."

Ryan. It had to happen sooner or later. I started to leave the room, but the sound of the deck door sliding open stopped me. Ryan stuck his head through the curtains and grinned.

"Jackie, how good of you to come. Let's have a little chat out here in the sun, shall we, old man?"

I went out onto the deck, Ryan closed the door behind me.

"I expected to hear from you before now, Jackie-boy. But better late than never. You do have something to tell me, don't you?"

"Not exactly."

"Oh dear, I hope this isn't going to get nasty. What did she say to our little proposal?"

"Your proposal."

"I'm not Mister Lenient today."

"It's not the right time to hassle her about it. It could spoil things for me."

"Whoops, wrong thing to say."

He hit me in the face, a straight hard punch to the mouth. In the freeze-frame seconds it took me to fall to the floor the only thing I thought about was how a split lip might fuck my upcoming TV appearances. I made a lot of noise impacting on the wooden planking. Rex must have heard it inside, but he didn't come out to investigate, or to save me. And free of such bothersome interruptions, Ryan proceeded to kick the shit out of my ribs with his dainty little feet. It hurt a lot. I curled up and closed my eyes and waited for it to stop. It took a while.

"You'll have to excuse me, Jackie, my temper isn't the best today."

He moved away from me, breathing heavily, and coughed something into a handkerchief. I got up and leaned against the railing. The house was built out over a small canyon, one of those things on stilts that cling to the hills, counting the minutes until the big one hits. Below me there was a lot of foliage made soft by the late-afternoon sun. It seemed an oddly pretty place to take a beating.

"Do you see how important this is now? She's only someone you're fucking."

"She's more than that."

"Oh, Jackie, I'm all aquiver."

"If you wait a couple of months I'll be able to pay you something myself."

"But not as much as she could. No deal. Have we communicated?"

I ran through the possible progression of events – I tell Bella Ryan's got a tape of us doing our thing in the motel room with Rudy, she starts wondering how come he just happened to be there at the right time, realizes I'm carrying some extra baggage, gets nervous that a cop has gotten so close to whatever illegal medical activities she's engaged in, and figures it's time to end a beautiful friendship. Adios life at Malibu – the car, the money and, worst of all, the chance at TV entry.

But what was the alternative? From the look of Ryan, something life-threatening.

I nodded painfully. My mouth was already beginning to swell.

"That's my boy. Let's sit awhile with your friend, I need to unwind."

"How did you connect us?"

"Once you shacked up with your cunt I knew you wouldn't be in any hurry to get in touch, so I pulled the phone records on your Hollywood place. There were only two addresses to trace – here, and some fuck-service in the Wilshire district. Soon as I saw Rexy I got a feeling this was the one to go with."

Back in the lounge Rex was sitting on the good part of the couch. His eyes were closed, but he was awake and as we came in he dragged them open and looked at my mouth.

"Sounded noisy."

"But you didn't feel like checking."

"Thought I was dreaming."

We sat in the chairs that went with the couch. All I could think of was getting into my car and heading home, but Ryan, pumped from his recent violence, wanted diversion.

"How about some gear, Rexy old boy?"

"Haven't got any clean works."

"Foil will do. I'm sure you've got some of that. Go find it."

Rex took a long time getting to his feet, then disappeared to some other part of the house. I heard things crashing around – pans, plates, glasses.

Ryan stretched in his chair and scanned the room.

"Looks like your friend's got a problem or two."

Rex came back with a crumpled square of tin foil and Ryan and I chased brown smack. No rush, just a low-burn stone that doesn't really punch home until you stand up or try to remember something. Mostly a waste of an expensive drug, but Ryan probably drew the line at syringes. I wouldn't have bothered with it at all except my mouth was hurting and I felt a little humiliated by my beating.

"This is fun, us guys together. Could do with some pussy, though. Whaddya say? Three on one. A hole for everyone."

Neither Rex nor I made any response.

"Did some checking on your bim, Jackie. Strange coincidence. You know she's a doctor? Got a clinic in Brentwood."

"Of course I know."

"Interesting, huh? Karen was cut up by someone with medical knowledge – you're going out with a doctor. A doctor who likes injecting people in motel rooms."

"That doesn't make her a killer."

"It doesn't make her not a killer, either. She tell you about Daddy?"

"He's a doctor too."

"Not quite, fuckhole. I did some checking. He used to be a surgeon, but he fucked up."

"Oh yeah?"

"She didn't tell you, did she? Shit, Jackie, it don't sound like you rate too high."

He giggled and shook his head.

"Seems, a long time back, he developed a habit of visiting the restricted medicines cabinet between operations. He got caught. The hospital didn't press criminal charges but the AMA disbarred him, or whatever they do to doctors, and he couldn't work anymore. What he does now I don't know, but it ain't doctoring."

Ryan rubbed his balls and nodded at Rex.

"Been buddies long?"

"A while."

"You came running plenty fast when he called."

"So what?"

"Just wondering how close you really are."

"Jesus Christ...."

"Hey, Rex, you like men or women?"

Rex had been nodding again, but mention of his name jerked his head up. "I'm ambivalent."

"Ooo, sounds promising. You feeling sexy, Rexy?"

"If you feel like paying."

"You call that enthusiasm?"

"I call it business."

"How about a free introductory offer?"

"Get fucked."

Ryan took out his gun and waved it loosely around.

"You could always go to work on this."

Rex sighed, pushed himself off the couch and dropped to his knees between Ryan's legs. When he started unzipping I got up to leave.

"Sit down, Jackie. You ought to know by now I like to share these special moments with you."

Ryan's dick came out of his pants soft, like a large white slug, and Rex had to suck it for five minutes before it got hard. Ryan tilted his head so he could watch it going in. He started to sweat.

"Hey, Jackie, get me one of my pills. In my pocket."

"Get it yourself."

"Jackie...."

There was a dangerous edge to his voice. I got up and felt through his pockets until I found the pill bottle. When I held one out to him he wouldn't take it.

"You do it."

The sight of his open mouth, tongue sticking out all wet and red, was more disgusting than his hardon. I dropped the pill in and moved quickly back to my chair.

Sex on smack is a drawn-out affair and Ryan didn't seem to be making much of an effort to hurry it along. Rex sucked until his spit ran down the side of Ryan's cock.

"Okay, Rexy, time to change ends."

They moved into the middle of the floor. Rex stripped down and got on all fours. Ryan heaved into position behind him.

"Whoa, looks a bit dry to me. Come over and spit on his ass, Jackie."

"What?"

"You're on that tape as well as your girlfriend. Don't piss me off."

I stood over Rex's ass, getting ready to dribble a gob down, hoping it would find its mark. But that wasn't good enough for Ryan.

"Get close. How many times do you want to have to do it?"

I leaned down until I could smell asshole funk and let fly with a mouthful.

"Oh, no, no, no. Not that thin white shit. We need something better than that, don't we, Rexy? Get some green back-of-the-throat stuff. I'm talking high-viscosity, boy. Go on, lay it right there, right on the old bull's-eye."

I hawked and snorted a wad together, then pumped it out. It hit pretty much dead center.

"That's the ticket."

Ryan smeared it around with the end of his dick, then pushed himself inside.

They fucked for a long time. Ryan dripped. Rex looked like he was dozing. I counted syringes until I realized Ryan was talking to me again.

"—round here and get in his mouth."

"Huh?"

"Both of us together. Come on. You in his head, me in his ass. It'll be like we're fucking each other."

Ryan's gun was on the cushion of the couch. He reached out and cocked it, kept his hand on it, looking at me.

This kind of scene was nothing new to Rex. He'd sucked a million cocks. But I wasn't a trick. We knew each other, we'd been friends. The act would carry a shitload of weight and I didn't want to be part of it. But it was clear Ryan was going to make it an issue if I refused. So I cursed, got up and put my dick in Rex's mouth.

I was beyond boredom, beyond protest. Smacked and drained by the whole scene. Rex was so stoned he didn't even open his eyes when he felt the end of my dick against his lips. He just opened up and started to rock his head. Ryan watched me with a half-smile – my face, the motion of my hips. We synchronized – him holding onto ass flesh, me to shoulders, both of us jamming into Rex so that I imagined he must be compressing somewhere in the middle.

We finished and pulled out. Rex climbed onto the couch and started cooking up a shot like nobody was there, like nothing had happened. His depression seemed to have rendered him completely neutral, a being at the whim of any force that chose to move him.

When Ryan and I left he glanced at me like he was going to say something, but halfway into it he ran out of steam and couldn't carry through.

Out on the street I dawdled, hoping Ryan would fuck off and not notice the Mustang, but that was pretty much impossible considering where I'd parked it. He ran his fingers over the glossy paintwork.

"A little love gift? You know, Jackie, I've got a good feeling about what we're getting into. If this is what she drops to say thank you for a fuck, the cash she'll lay out for our tape could be considerable. Don't make me come looking for you."

Chapter 23

Bella was swimming naked when I got back to Malibu. I sat in a chair at the edge of the pool and waited for her to notice my swollen lip.

"Jack, what happened? Have you been mugged?"

Her body came out of the water shining and white. She stood in front of me, dark hair plastered to her shoulders, water running between her breasts, from the matted peak between her legs.

"Are you all right? Let me see."

She bent down to do the professional doctor thing, but I stopped her.

"We have to talk about something. It isn't good."

Bella frowned, then pulled a chair around and sat facing me. She didn't bother with a towel.

"There's a video of what we did to that guy in the motel."

"No there isn't."

"There is. I've seen it. You aren't the only one with a camera."

For a fraction of a second Bella's face betrayed panic, but she killed the reaction before it had time to take hold. I could see her locking herself together against it, containing it in favor of a more productive alternative.

"Tell me about it."

"A guy was hanging around outside. He saw the three of us go into one room and figured it was going to be a sex thing. He found a gap in the curtains and now he's got a tape to sell."

"Who is he?"

"I don't know. Some guy who gets off peeping into bedrooms. He said his name was Ryan."

"He wants money?"

"What else?"

Bella ran the problem for a while, then something occurred to her.

"How did he contact you?"

"He phoned while you were at Brentwood. He wanted me to meet him at some motel. That's where I've been."

"How did he get the number?"

"I don't know. Maybe he followed us back and got it from the address."

"It's unlisted."

"Well, however he did, he got it. And he's got a tape and it's us on it, the whole injection bit, everything."

"Does he know I'm a doctor?"

"He didn't mention it."

Bella did some more thinking, then pushed the wet hair back from her face.

"I want to meet him."

It surprised me she was so eager, but it saved me the hassle of persuading her to agree to it.

"That's what he wants. Are you going to pay him?"

"At the moment it would seem to be the easiest thing to do."

"But what if he comes back for more?"

"I have a lot of money. And if it gets beyond a joke we'll find another way of handling it."

Two days later Ryan met Bella and me in my new house on Willow Glen in Laurel Canyon. I hadn't had time to furnish it yet and the place was empty except for a TV and VCR that Bella had had delivered.

When I'd made the arrangements with Ryan the day before I'd asked him not to blow the Peeping Tom story I'd given Bella. He hadn't made any promises but I couldn't see what he'd get out of telling her about our previous connection. He might even figure having a man on the inside would be beneficial to possible future transactions. But that didn't stop me shitting myself that he'd do it simply out of spite and I'd had to watch TV almost constantly after speaking to him to keep my anxiety in check.

The walls of the lounge were white and the floor was bare polished wood. Bella and Ryan stood close to each other in front of the TV, watching the tape. I walked around the room, looking out of windows, listening hard for anything either of them might say.

Bella didn't seem angry or disgusted by Ryan, in fact it looked like she was too entranced with the image of her own double-penetration to bother defining an attitude toward him. When the show was over she stared at static, absently touching herself under her skirt. Ryan glanced over at me wide-eyed, then spoke to her.

"The sex doesn't mean much, but that injection.... Was he dead there for a minute?"

"You don't need to emphasize anything. I'm aware of what it shows. How much do you want?"

"Fifty thousand."

"That sounds possible. I have something I'd like you to watch first, though."

Bella smiled at him, her eyes had the heavy dark look they got when she wanted to be fucked. Whether it was real or faked I couldn't tell. She took a cassette out of her bag and had him load it. I didn't have any idea what she was doing.

The tape ran. I recognized the sitting room in Bella's suite at Malibu. She was on her back, legs spread to camera, fucking herself with a vibrator. Ten seconds in, I realized the action had been paced for maximum cinematic effect, her movements were too extravagant for a simple wank. I wondered if Ryan noticed, but he was so locked into the scene he probably didn't care one way or the other. Bella leaned against him, whispering into his ear, stroking the front of his pants. Mister Frightening, the man who watched women get jackhammered, seemed robbed of self-will by her voice and the pressure of her hand.

I heard his fly open, saw one of his legs tremble. I moved further around the room so I could watch. His cock looked thick in her hand. The skin under its head bunched and stretched as she stroked. She timed it to the video and he spurted across the floor as she came, or fake came, on screen. She flicked her fingers and wiped her hand with a tissue while Ryan stuffed his cock back inside his trousers.

"That supposed to make me drop my price?"

"Not at all. I just thought that where a sum like fifty thousand dollars is concerned, we should connect on a personal level.

"Right...." Ryan sounded a trifle uncertain, like he had no idea what the wank had been about. "How do you want to do it?"

"Jack will call you to make the arrangements."

"You don't get the tape till then."

"It hardly matters. You can't exactly give me the negative, can you? It's time for you to go, Jack and I are expecting some furniture."

"Will you come along with the money?"

"Perhaps."

We watched Ryan's gray Plymouth pull out of the drive. Halfway down the hill it passed two large delivery trucks coming the other way – possessions for my new life.

We detoured for dinner on the way back to Malibu, down to the shitty end of Melrose and a Mexican joint with good food and a lot of photos of famous diners on the walls. A little down-market for Bella, but I wanted a burrito and the dimness of the place made me feel less exposed to the uncertainties her interaction with Ryan had raised.

"What were you whispering to him?"

"Nothing important."

"But what?"

"I was just describing how the vibrator felt."

"Do I ask why?"

"Same as I told him, I wanted to create a link other than the money. It may be for nothing, but if he becomes a problem it could give us an edge."

I drank a bunch of margaritas in celebration of the fact that Ryan hadn't yet fucked up my progress toward the high life. Bella had to drive us home in the 850ci.

Next morning Larry Burns' secretary phoned and told me to turn up at the Warner Bros. lot by midday to start work.

CHAPTER 24

Makeup was in a block-mounted trailer outside a sound stage. The seats weren't padded and I couldn't smoke, but it felt great to have skinny girls fussing over me, to be the center of attention in a town where the ability to attract attention is the single most important attribute a human being can possess. They cut my hair, angling it in above the ears because it looked better on TV that way, and put a load of stuff on my face. The director came in for a thirty-second hello and a script girl gave me a couple of pages to get familiar with.

While I was reading them, a messenger arrived with a card from Howard Welks welcoming me on board. It came attached to a brown plastic tube of 10mg Valium. I wasn't sure if it was a hint that I wouldn't be able to hack it, or whether it was just a cool present at a time when doctors were getting reluctant to prescribe downers. Whatever, I was reasonably coked and adding a little benzo to my bloodstream didn't seem like a bad idea.

I looked good in the mirror. They'd given me drops to clear my eyes and mousse to thicken my hair. Foundation and powder made my skin look smooth. For no reason at all I felt like jerking off over Ryan's photos.

Inside the subdivided sound stage the assistant director had me run through a series of link shots. He told me it was all I was going to do for a while until I got easy in front of the camera. I didn't care. If it went on too long I'd get Bella to call Welks.

A moron could have done the work. All I had to do was stand in front of a blue screen and read a couple of lines at a time off the Autocue, the same stuff I'd already half memorized in makeup earlier. There were a lot of people in the studio, but the cocaine and the radiance of the set lights insulated me from them, formed a dazzling cocoon that sealed away my self-consciousness and prevented it sabotaging this, my first step toward celebrity. I was on. I was up. I threw out vitality with halogen intensity. Shit, anyone can make an effort if it means getting on TV.

I finished everything they needed me for around three. The director had a break then, too, and took me to a bar off the lot. His name was James and he said he loved what I did, but it was pretty obvious he was drinking with me to see how much I knew about film. I couldn't match him on who directed what, or when a particular process became available to the industry. But I beat him hands down on who was fucking who and how much they paid for their houses.

After a while he left to get back to the studio – Lorn was coming in to do some cutaways. I stayed to get another Southern and one of the makeup girls came in with a friend. We drank together, then I let her suck me off in the toilets. Not because I was attracted to her, or even because I felt like having sex, but just because it was one of the things you could get if you were on TV and it seemed stupid to turn it down.

Outside. Afterwards. The air was heavy and the hills around Burbank were hazed. All the dead people up on the slopes of Forest Lawn made me think of Karen. I had ten grand a month and a place in the hills now. It would have been enough to have kept her with me, to have made her whoring un-necessary. Money solves all problems. It makes people love you. It makes them stay with you when they would otherwise leave. With ten K a month I could have given Karen a life so good it would simply have cost her too much to leave me.

The adrenaline from my first day shooting started to turn bad, mixing with the burnt-out coke, Valium and booze, making me feel stale and vulner-able. I wanted things to be simple, to have Bella and what she could do for me without the danger of Ryan and Powell and blackmail and murder.

I went back to the parking lot at Warner Bros. and sat in the Mustang watching the traffic pass outside the gates, wishing I could be free of the past, but keep the present.

Bella called me on my mobile as I was about to start the car. We chatted about the day's taping, then she told me Powell had located a candidate for their healthcare scheme and that I shouldn't bother coming to Malibu that night as she wouldn't be home. I didn't care. I was too tired to make the slog out to the house anyhow – all I really wanted right then was to shut myself away and go to sleep.

The house on Willow Glen was open-plan with a lot of glass. I'd chosen it because of the amount of air and light that went with the rooms. Everything in it was new. I'd left the walls bare – no pictures, no ornaments – but I'd picked the furniture and the technology carefully, they were all the decoration I needed.

Early evening. I drank a bottle of Gatorade and went to sleep on top of a Japanese quilt that cost two thousand dollars. I didn't wake until the phone rang around eleven.

I couldn't assimilate at first. I knew the voice, but the fact that it was calling me caused momentary brainlock. Powell. Sounding as smug as he had when he asked if I wanted to see his photos of Bella. He told me to meet him in front of the Beverly Hills Civic Center in half an hour. He hung up before I could ask questions.

I showered, dressed, put the top up on the Mustang and powered down Laurel Canyon through the still-warm night. Sunset to La Cienega, La Cienega to Santa Monica Boulevard where the streetlights ran in soft orange disks over the polished hood of my car and the wind of my passage drew cigarette smoke through my open window, out into the city.

I was ten minutes late. I wanted to pretend I didn't give a shit, that whatever he wanted to see me about couldn't possibly be worse than the tape of him with his dick inside Bella. But this time of night, with Bella apparently out of the loop, I couldn't shake the feeling that I might be heading for info relating to Karen's death.

I pulled up beside his Jag and he ran the window down. Dead eyes turned on me like something out of *The Terminator*. His smile looked cut into his face. He said to follow him. Then he ran the window back up again.

I tailed him through the flats and on up into the hills. At the edge of Beverly Hills we took San Ysidro Drive along Peavine Canyon for about three miles to a narrow track called Apricot Lane.

Apricot Lane was marked as a private road but it didn't have a gate. It cut right off San Ysidro and a couple of hundred yards later cut right again. I noticed one or two houses, but they were set way back off the road and almost hidden by shrubbery. Powell drove past them to the end of the lane and a large squat building that hadn't been built to be looked at. Vines had been planted to break the monotony of its slabbed sand-colored walls, but they couldn't disguise the fact that the place was essentially a bunker. The few windows I could see were barred and a tall fence of steel rails ran around the perimeter of the property.

We drove immediately into a four-car garage. The door rolled down behind us automatically and I knew right away no one lived in the house. There was none of the crap that usually accumulates in garages; no tools, no beach equipment, no boxes of junk. The only other thing there besides Powell's Jaguar and my Mustang, was Bella's 850ci.

Instead of a door leading into the ground floor of the house there was a concrete ramp that sloped to the basement. Powell led me down it, told me not to make any noise and unlocked a steel-plated door. We went through it, into something that resembled a micro-hospital – green walls, vinyl floors, overhead strip lighting. Powell locked the door behind us, held a finger to his lips and motioned me to follow him along a corridor. We passed a couple of what appeared to be examination rooms with reinforced doors and security locks, then a set of double swing-doors that gave onto some sort of pre-op area.

Through the small windows in these doors I caught a glimpse of something that looked like a covered body on a trolley. A little further along the corridor there was an ordinary wooden door, unlocked. Powell killed the ceiling lights and eased it open. A small room, space for two people to stand, a window like cop show interrogation rooms. He put his lips to my ear and whispered:

"The glass is one-way. Do not make a sound or she will know you are here. Do not leave this room. I will come for you after we finish. Watch your lover carefully."

He left and I looked through the glass. On the other side a hard white light fell on a small operating theater. It looked like a scaled-down version of something out of *ER* – a lot of stainless steel, a lot of equipment that flashed lights and fed into monitors, trolleys that held rows of shiny instruments on squares of green material and a big light cluster on a movable arm. There was no one in the room right then, but ten minutes later Powell and Bella, wearing caps, gowns and masks, wheeled an unconscious naked man through a pair of connecting doors and positioned him under the lights. He lay on his side and had a drip in his arm. The space between his ribs and hip bone had been coated with yellow-brown antiseptic dye.

Powell sat at the man's head, put a gas feed over his face and started turning knobs on a trio of cylinders while Bella hooked the guy up to a couple of machines. They talked to each other as they worked, but with their masks and the glass between us I couldn't make out what they said.

When she was ready, Bella nodded at Powell, picked up a scalpel and started cutting. I couldn't see too well because her back was toward me, but it looked like she made a long horizontal incision under the ribs. Her concentration was intense, she moved quickly and economically, discarding one instrument after another, plucking fresh ones from the trolley at her side. I saw smears of blood on her rubber gloves.

The precision of the process fascinated me, but for some reason I couldn't rid myself of the feeling that operational efficiency wasn't the only thing happening in that room. The way Bella held herself, the way she pressed her pelvis against the side of the gurney, the grace of her hands and arms...all of it suggested a sensuality that was out of place amongst the hardware of surgery.

It went on a long time and I got tired of standing still. I had to shift position occasionally to stop my legs aching and once, when I did this, I bumped the glass of the window. In the operating room Bella froze and flicked a hard look at Powell, but he was busy concentrating on the anesthetic. After a couple of seconds she relaxed and continued what she was doing.

Sometime later the operation hit its peak. Bella reached inside the man, made a few final strokes with her scalpel and appeared to cut something free of whatever held it in place. Then, using both hands, she lifted a curved thing about five inches long out into the air.

A kidney.

Big surprise.

Deposits of hard yellow fat clung about the base of a severed stem which protruded from the middle of the inside curve and had obviously been the thing's main connection to the body. Thin blood dripped from strands of tissue that wrapped the smooth organ like a ripped caul. It was a lot pinker and softer than the ones you see at the meat counter, maybe because it was so fresh.

Bella put it in a plastic container, clipped a transparent lid over it and handed it to Powell. He looked uncertain for a moment and said something to her. Bella shook her head, turned back to her patient and started putting in some internal stitches. Powell spoke to her again but she didn't answer, and after a moment's hesitation he carried the kidney across the room and put it in a fridge.

I stayed a little longer, but it was obvious they were on the home stretch and I couldn't see the point of standing around just to watch the mop-up – I'd been in the room close to two hours already. As I eased open the door Bella was sewing up the guy's stomach.

I couldn't get back out into the garage because the steel door needed a key to be unlocked even from the inside, so I decided to go exploring. At the far end of the corridor a flight of steps led up to the ground floor of the house. There was another steel door at the top, but this one was unlocked. I wandered through the rooms on the other side of it.

A lounge and two of the bedrooms were furnished – carpets, drapes, soft chairs, all the comforts of home – a facade of normality in which to recover from those tiring kidney excisions. Everywhere else was bare and looked permanently uninhabited. The cupboards in the kitchen held cans and packets but nothing fresh. I locked myself in a bathroom and lit a cigarette.

So, now I knew for certain that Bella took kidneys out of people. And it was plain that, out of the two of them, it was she, not Powell, who was the driving force behind the operations.

She'd told me the free medical care thing was her idea, and as a result
I'd taken her involvement in the kidney removals pretty much for granted.
But I'd been hoping she played only a minor role in this darker side of their
philanthropy – as an assistant to Powell, say. Or, even better, as an unwilling
participant in the old man's obsession.

Now I knew differently. And it worried me. Karen's death was connected
to the sale of her kidney, I was sure of it, and, without anything to say otherwise, it didn't seem absurd to suppose that whoever played the dominant
role in the operations might well have played a similar role in her murder. A
logical train of thought, but not one I wanted to pursue. Not while Bella's
freedom meant I appeared on TV.

I concentrated instead on wondering what Powell had been so eager to
reveal to me. It couldn't be just that Bella was performing an illegal operation.
After all, his role as procurer and anesthetist made him as guilty as her in that
respect. Maybe he thought seeing her open someone up would turn me off
her. But she was, after all, a doctor, even if she wasn't a surgeon, and wasn't
that what doctors did?

The only thing I could think was that something else was supposed to
happen in the operating room but didn't because, after I'd knocked the glass,
she'd known she was being watched. But what the fuck could she have been
planning to do?

I went back out into the lounge to wait for them, I couldn't see any reason
why Bella shouldn't know I was there. Half an hour later they came up the
stairs. Bella didn't seem surprised to see me.

"Powell brought you?"

Before I could answer, the man himself cut in.

"It was time he knew."

Bella rounded on him.

"How dare you make that decision?"

"Shouldn't one's lover know everything about one?"

Bella smiled mockingly.

"You think if he does, it will end the relationship?"

"I think he should be given the information necessary to make an in-
formed choice."

"You are so transparent it's absurd."

"Nevertheless, I know the whole of you. And there is nothing I could learn that would turn me against you. It may not be so with him."

"Whether it is, or is not, is no concern of yours. Remember that or you might find your bed suddenly empty."

"There are only two kinds of days for me. Those when you allow me to be with you, and those when you do not. Without you there is nothing more I can lose. So you should remember that if my bed is empty, your operating table will be in a similar state. Or do you think he will search the sewers for you as I do?"

For a moment Bella looked at him like she couldn't think of an answer, then she turned abruptly and walked to the head of the stairs. She paused at the doorway.

"He'll be conscious soon. Check the pain relief. Come on, Jack."

She disappeared down the stairs. As I started to follow, Powell caught my arm and hissed in my ear.

"What you saw was nothing, she knew you were there. You are a child playing with a very dangerous toy. Be careful it does not turn on you."

"Get fucked."

I shook him off and went to join Bella. We kissed in the garage, but we didn't talk until we'd driven our cars back to Malibu and gotten naked in the pool.

Bella swam a few yards breaststroke. The sky was black, dawn still two or three hours away, but the pool lights made it easy to see between her legs. She flipped onto her back and floated, the hair on her cunt rose above the surface of the water. I moved close and she wrapped herself around me. Her breasts slid against my chest.

"What did you think?"

"It can't be legal."

"It isn't. But everyone benefits from it. What I told you about the treatment I give the homeless wasn't the whole of the truth. I buy their kidneys from them. It's completely voluntary. Powell finds someone on the street and if I think they can stand the operation I make them an offer. It's their choice. Losing a kidney won't really affect their quality of life and the amount of money I give them is more than they are ever likely to see at one time. Most of them won't reach forty anyway, so they don't have much to lose. You'd be surprised how many of them say yes."

"What do you do with the kidneys?"

"Waiting lists for transplants can run into years."

"You sell them to people?"

"Of course not. I donate them to various public hospitals. Anonymously."

My cock was hard, Bella started rubbing it under the water.

"You don't strike me as the Robin Hood type."

"But look what I'm doing for you."

She said it nicely enough, but the message was clear – don't get difficult with someone who's putting you on TV.

I didn't say anything else.

Bella moved her hand faster. I closed my eyes and saw the girl with the crowbar up her ass, the bag-head couple fucking each other. I tried to imagine what it would be like to lie against those bodies, to feel that quiet flesh against mine. I spurted. My come made white streamers in the clear pool water.

I woke in the half-light of a false dawn. Bella was asleep on her stomach, sheets kicked off the bed, the split between the cheeks of her ass filled with shadow. Outside an animal screamed – not a far off coyote howl somewhere back in the hills, not a natural woodland waking call. The sound I heard was close by and full of pain.

I got out of bed and went to the window. Bella didn't wake. Stars and a paling sky. The grass that surrounded the house was gray with a light that sucked the life out of things, left them two dimensional and unpleasant.

Outside, where anyone at the window would see him, a naked man crouched over something that kicked. He was working on its belly, pulling out steaming handfuls of guts, throwing them on the grass around him. Powell. And the second of the two dogs I had seen delivered.

When the animal was empty he lifted it above his head and held it so the flaps of its stomach gaped toward my window. I knew the darkness in the room would hide me but I couldn't stop myself jerking backward, out of his line of sight.

Even after I climbed back into bed the image stayed with me – the ruined dog, Powell's white body smeared in places with dark blood, his flaccid cock swinging.

Bella and I ate breakfast together by the pool. The air was silken. I blew cigarette smoke into it. The sunlight made patterns on the surface of the water.

Sometime before we finished, Powell came out of the house and told Bella he wouldn't be staying at Malibu any longer. He looked more smacked than usual and had scratches on his hands and face. It sounded like he wanted some reaction from her, like maybe he wanted her to ask him why. But she hardly raised her head from the newspaper she was reading and it occurred to me that last night had been the first time she hadn't left me to join him in his bed.

I hadn't told her what I'd seen from the window.

After he'd gone, we walked in the grounds, holding hands. I steered her to the patch of grass below her bedroom. The blood looked like thick oil and the scattered mounds of dog offal were covered with flies. The carcass itself had disappeared.

Bella groaned in a kind of resigned way. She didn't seem surprised or appalled. I prodded something that looked like a length of intestine with the toe of my shoe.

"I saw him do this last night."

"He feels threatened. He's frightened you'll take me away from him."

"That's a pretty violent reaction."

"It's only a dog."

"It makes me wonder what he's capable of."

"What do you mean?"

"One day dogs might not be enough."

Bella looked at the mess on the ground.

"There is an element of ferocity to it, isn't there?"

She turned away and walked back to the house. I stayed outside, wading through the edge of the forest until I found the body of the dog. Slit from balls to ribs. I looked, but it was hard to tell whether there was semen inside it or not.

Same type of wound, though. Same disembowelment. Surgical skill. Tailor-made evidence to tie Powell to Karen's murder. And the motive? If Karen and Bella had been lovers and he'd known – and living at Malibu, even part-time, it would have been impossible for him not to – it was simple enough. Sexual jealousy.

The day seemed suddenly glorious. The hacked-open dog at my feet out-weighed Bella's leading role in the operating room ten to one. It tipped the scales so far away from her they'd never come back. Even if she'd been aware of the murder, it had to have been Powell who actually committed it, the wounds were just too similar.

Added to the spunk in Karen's guts it meant I could go on sucking up Bella's money and influence without fear of it one day being stolen away from me by some judicial inconvenience. It also meant I'd have something to unseat Ryan with if he got bored after he'd finalized his blackmail scam and decided to start riding the frame-Jack-for-murder trail again.

Bella sat in a gray deco chair in the drawing room of her suite, staring out of the window. She seemed a little distracted and jerked when I came in.

I said, "It's time I called Ryan. What do you want me to tell him?"

"Tell him to meet me tomorrow. The same motel will do."

"I can't make tomorrow, I'm taping."

"I'll go by myself."

"Are you sure? He looked pretty weird."

"You're not jealous, are you?"

"After Powell and that guy in the motel?"

"Good. You have no reason to be. I'll give him the money and hopefully we won't hear from him again."

"Unlikely."

"Yes. But money is a powerful thing. With enough of it you can make anything happen, one way or another. Let me play you something."

In the video suite Bella fired up the machine and loaded a tape.

"These are some of my donors. Everything I'm doing to them is medically unnecessary. They must suspect it, but they talk themselves into letting it happen because they want the money."

She ran the tape. A series of zero-income types, men and women, in one of the examination rooms at Apricot Lane. Bella in surgical gown and mask, hair pulled tightly back. The donors naked. From the way they behaved I assumed the camera was hidden.

A man undergoing a rectal examination, Bella's fingers in rubber gloves slick with lubricant. The same man crouched over a pan on the floor producing a stool sample. A young woman with track marks on the insides of her thighs, Bella administering a douche. A girl on her hands and knees, gritting her teeth while Bella took vaginal swabs with long-handled Q-tips.

"You have to admit there is something intensely erotic about this level of invasion."

I was going to make some noise of agreement, but the action on the tape jump-cut to another scene and I couldn't stop myself tensing up. Bella was no longer gowned and masked, but naked, stretched full-length over another naked woman, head to toe on the examination bench. They were going down on each other and the woman's face was hidden between Bella's legs, but when she lifted her head to work her tongue in deeper I saw her shoulder blade. And the tattoo of a scarab on it.

"What's the matter?"

"Nothing."

"You recognized her.

"No. It's just...different. Was she a donor?"

"She became a donor, yes."

On screen, Bella's hips jerked, then grooved slowly, relaxing. After a while she climbed off and the woman on the bench turned her head toward the camera and smiled – Karen. Bella froze the picture.

"She was my lover."

"What happened to her?"

"What do you mean? If you know her, Jack, I'd like you to tell me."

"I only meant why did the relationship end?"

"Do you know her or not?"

Bella was too hot for the question for me to avoid some sort of answer.

"She looks like a girl who works the Drag. Maybe I saw her down there once or twice, that's all. What's the problem?"

"We had a rather intense relationship. I'm still a little sensitive about her."

"Why did it end?"

"I don't know. One day she just stopped coming around. I never saw her again."

"Didn't you try to get in touch with her?"

"She never told me anything about herself. I didn't know her last name or where she lived, so there wasn't much I could do."

Bella rewound the tape and started it again. She sat on my lap, facing the screen, and put my cock inside her. She moved hard against me and when Karen's face smiled at the camera she came.

Later I phoned Ryan. The Starway Motel was cool with him. When he heard I wouldn't be there it was even cooler.

CHAPTER 25

Bella left the house late morning the next day, first for the bank, then for the connection with Ryan. Powell hadn't come back to Malibu during the night so I guessed he was still sulking in his apartment downtown.

My call for *28 FPS* wasn't until twelve. I used my time alone to do a couple of things.

I took Bella's donor tape from the concealed cupboard in the video suite, cued it to the segment with Karen and copied it onto a blank cassette. It took me about twenty minutes – ten minutes to figure out how to route the signal from one video deck to the other, and another ten for the copying because I couldn't find the high-speed dubbing function. I shat myself the entire time, listening for cars in the drive, footsteps in the house.

There were other tapes in the cupboard, two I'd already seen – Bella and Powell fucking, me unconscious having my dick sucked – and three I hadn't. I spent another jumpy half hour fast-forwarding through them – a solo sex exhibition by Bella, another collection of losers undergoing sexually toned medical examinations, edited highlights from various fuck sessions that Bella and I had taped since I'd been out at Malibu. Nothing that linked to Karen. I rewound and put everything back the way it had been.

I had two reasons for wanting my own copy of Bella and Karen yumming each other. First, the tape proved they'd been lovers, or at least that they'd had some kind of sexual connection. Added to the snippet Bella had let drop about Powell sneaking copies of every tape she had, it backed up my jealousy-as-motive theory about him being the killer. If he had a copy in his possession it would show he'd been aware of their relationship, and if he'd been aware of their relationship he may just have done something about it.

My other reason was a little less Bella-friendly – insurance against her ever changing her mind about how nice it was having me around. If she did have some knowledge of the murder, her rolling around naked with the victim wouldn't be a scene she'd want left anonymously on a police station doorstep.

I put the cassette in the trunk of the Mustang and headed down to PCH. It was a hot day and I felt excited. Lorn and I were going to be working together for the first time – a duet interview with some chick who was going stellar in the porn industry. Not a name recognizable to anyone outside certain video circles, but someone who could provide enough titillation to interest the *28 FPS* target audience.

It was an easy way to start me off – Lorn there to hold my hand, no big name to get pissed off if I blew my lines and forced too many retakes. I told myself to be cool. I'd been watching Lorn on TV and drooling over her for the last twelve months and I didn't want her to think I was a dick.

The girl called herself Mistral. I don't think she knew what it meant, just saw it somewhere and liked the sound of it. It hardly mattered. When you function primarily as a collection of orifices, nobody gives a shit how smart you are – especially if you're a platinum blonde with implants.

She lived in a narrow house that went toward the beach in a slope – one of those places where they're all built so close together along the highway you can't see the ocean. Not a big house, no grounds or garden to speak of, but it was Malibu, and that kind of area code is important on the way up.

There were a couple of vans parked outside when I got there. I did makeup in one of them then wandered into the house. The crew was setting up out on the deck. Mistral was in the lounge, smoking a long thin cigarette and chatting to Lorn and James, the director I'd worked with on my first day taping.

We intro-ed. James told me to relax, that he'd guide me through the whole thing. Lorn said she thought she'd seen me someplace before and gave me a question sheet with J marked next to about every third question.

"They're yours. She knows what we're going to ask—"

Mistral blasted smoke through her nostrils and broke in.

"Yeah, I don't wanna answer no questions that aren't on that sheet there. My agent said I wouldn't have to."

She had a high whining voice that sounded like it came out of a bad part of the east coast. She was close to the top when it came to humping on screen, but it was a cinch she wasn't going to cross over making a noise like that.

Lorn patted her knee.

"It'll be just how you want, honey. Don't you worry."

Lorn looked good, like she always did. Black leggings, Reeboks, a tie-dyed vest that was tight around her tits and showed off her shoulders.

"You wanna see some of my stuff before we start? I got a tape right here."

James left to make some calls, but Lorn and I had nothing to do until shoot time. Mistral was already thumbing the remote.

"This here's me and Paco Rondello. Boy, when he comes in your mouth it's like having a meal. See how my hips are moving there? That's something I do, kinda adds sensuality to it, dontcha think? Oh, and now this, this is one of my favorite takes, 'cause it's so artistic. When I was starting off I wouldn't do an anal sandwich, no way, but after a while I loosened up and thought what the hell? So it's two at once, big deal. To get to the top you have to develop a few specialities.

"Mind you, I ain't into none of that shitting or puking nonsense. Nah, it's gotta be tasteful or I walk right outta there. See, where I am now I can dictate my terms. Hey, did you go to Charlie Sheen's party?"

Lorn nodded distractedly, the stuff on the video seemed to bore her. After a while she stood up and jerked her head at me. We went outside and walked down some sun-bleached wooden steps to the edge of the beach. The sun on the water made a hot path to the horizon that hurt to look at. There were a few rich people swimming and some more lying on the sand under umbrellas. They looked relaxed and healthy, satisfied with themselves, like this time lazing had been well earned.

I wondered how the tramps and the other fuck-ups in Santa Monica felt today. It seemed a long time ago that they'd been a reality I was sliding toward. I had a sudden urge to drive down the coast and look at them, to use them as a gauge for how far I'd come.

"Nice spot."

Lorn was doing calf stretches on the bottom step. She snorted.

"You've got to be kidding. This end of the beach is for wannabes. Where do you live?"

"I've got a place on Willow Glen."

"The Hills?"

"Laurel Canyon."

"Got a pool?"

"Doesn't everyone?"

"Did you think her pussy looked slack in the closeups?"

"Er—"

"I'd have it fixed if it was mine."

"I heard you used to work in a pie shop."

"Really? Where did you hear that?"

"Around."

"Well, I haven't heard anything about you. How'd you get on the show? It's not like we needed anyone else."

"Good honest hard work."

"Like?"

"You know, this and that."

"You know how I got here? Merit. I worked my ass off in local radio for six months. People who get TV handed to them because Daddy knows the producer piss me off."

"Hey, same here."

She looked at me like she couldn't figure out whether I was joking or not, then she did a couple more stretches and sat down on a step.

"How long have you been on the coast?"

"A couple of years."

"Let me give you a tip, new boy. Don't ask people about their past, it doesn't mean anything here. What you're doing right now is the only thing that counts."

"Sure. I didn't mean anything by the pie shop."

"Yeah, right."

"Do you think we're going to get along?"

"I don't know. Do you?"

"Why not? We're both shallow enough."

"Are you trying to be funny?"

"Do you want to run me through what I'm going to be doing?"

"Just wait till your questions come up then ask them. Don't worry about the camera, it won't be on you. We'll do reaction shots after. Jesus, I hate doing these no-name bimbos. They can't introduce you to anyone and they never have any decent coke. You better go back up, James'll want to prep you."

Out on the deck the camera guys had erected a canopy thing made of gauze to soften the sunlight. I sat under it on a short calico couch facing Mistral and felt Arabian. Lorn was next to me. I could smell the perfume of the styling product in her hair.

It went well enough. Lorn asked questions, I asked questions. Mistral talked about the way her childhood had forced her into pornography but how she was glad now because it had a valid place in our society today, about the money she made, what her artistic goals were.... At one point she wanted close-ups of the implant scars under her tits. They let her have them. Why not? It made good TV.

I blew a couple of my lines and we had to retake. Nobody seemed to care, and when Lorn did it once herself I realized working in front of the camera required even less talent than I'd thought.

When there wasn't anything more to be milked from Mistral, they shot Lorn and me asking our questions and reacting to supposed answers. Lorn had about four stock facial reactions. She ran through them for me, one after the other. Mistral, who was standing out of shot on the other side of the deck, saw her and came across to show us her four stock orgasm expressions.

Then she went inside and I heard snatches of her voice as she explained to one of the crew that she always used a silicone gel so her cunt looked wet even if she wasn't feeling in the mood. Which, of course, was most of the time because she was a professional and being sexually aroused wouldn't give her the distance she needed to be truly creative.

The crew packed away their gear. James gave me the thumbs-up and climbed into his Porsche. Lorn hung around the cars clustered out front of the house, looking superfluous now that the shoot was over. She watched traffic swish by on the hot afternoon asphalt as though it was a reminder that between the highs of shooting, parties, premieres and talking to the stars, the underlying foundation of life was a gray rolling mundanity, the meaning of which she was unable to access. She came over to me, wanting to fill this downtime.

"Are you going to Sub tonight?"

"No invite."

"You can come with me if you want. You should anyhow, it'll be a good opportunity to hustle interviews."

"Okay."

"I'm empty for the rest of the day. We can get something to eat first."

"Sorry, I'll have to meet you there. I've got stuff to do."

Lorn didn't look disappointed so much as anxious that she might not have anything to occupy herself with until evening. It wasn't a move I wanted to make. Despite our fencing on the steps, I was as attracted to her in the flesh as I had been to her on the screen, and I didn't want to get off on the wrong foot.

But what could I do? I had to get over to Rex's and stash the tape. I couldn't risk leaving it in the car or at Willow Glen or any other place Bella might stumble across it. And on top of that, for the last few days I'd been feeling that I needed to see him, needed to talk through my last visit.

Lorn and I arranged our meet. I started up my car and drove away. She went back to watching the traffic.

Rex didn't answer his door when I knocked, but it wasn't locked so I pushed in and went down the hall to the lounge. He was slumped on the couch, it didn't look like he'd moved since last time I was there. The room stank of unwashed body. There was more dried blood on the walls and he'd added empty cream pudding pots to the litter of cola cans on the floor. The blinds were drawn and the curtains across the sliding doors at the back of the room were still closed. Dim light came in around their edges, more of it came from the TV.

Rex looked at me blankly, like you'd look at another person in a bus station. He waited for me to speak first.

"Hi, dude."

"Hey."

"This place is...not much better."

"I've achieved stasis. Negative buoyancy. I'm floating under the surface."

"It doesn't smell good."

"Jack, it doesn't matter. It's my world. I'm acclimatized. Nothing is any better or any worse than anything else. The only thing you can say about anything is that it goes on. And it goes on until it stops and then it's finished."

"Rex, you need to see someone. You need to stop taking so much smack."

"Nah, you're wrong. I need to take a whole lot more."

"Look in the mirror, man. It's not doing you any good."

"Oh, but it does. It stops me loving so much."

"Loving what?"

"Everything. I know you hate a lot of things. You hate being poor, you hate not being famous, you hated Karen, you hate most people you pass on the street. But I was never like that. I realized it when I hit that kid. I kind of dug everything, good or bad. I didn't have to judge it like you. Things, people, they were just there. And if I wanted I could take the good from them. And if I didn't I could just pass by.

"But you know what, man? Not everyone's like that. And loving a world that doesn't love you back the same way, that is so fucking conditional all the time.... That gets tiring, man. You can only do it for so long."

"But you were earning good money. And no one's ever going to bust you for that boy. I mean, can't you just think yourself out of this? You could clean up."

"Don't be an idiot. There's nothing to go back to."

"Are you angry about the other day?"

"Like I said, nothing's any better or any worse than anything else. But, yeah, it was kind of a shitty thing to happen. Where is your friend anyway? Shame he's not here, we could do it all over again."

"Jesus, Rex...."

"No, man, I mean it. I like being degraded further than I can manage myself. It's an added bonus to a dull afternoon."

"Why did you set me up?"

"You're pissed off with *me*?"

"You could have warned me."

"He had a fucking gun. What did you want me to do, die for you?"

"You could have dropped a hint."

Rex started laughing when I said this. It started out sarcastic but it ended up sounding sad. He shook his head slowly, then took a wrap out of his pocket and tapped some smack into a spoon. We were in the same room, but he was a million miles away. At that moment I knew I could spend the rest of my life trying to reconnect and I'd never do it. The guy was gone.

"Rex, I need you to hold onto something for me. I can't risk Ryan tossing my place and finding it. Can you do that for me?"

"I could be persuaded."

"You want money?"

"Like I told you, man, we don't take love here no more."

"No problem. Do you want to know what it is?"

"Just give me the money and leave it."

"I'm sorry about what happened with that kid. And with Ryan. But it wasn't my fault, you know?"

"Who said it was?"

"You're acting like it."

Rex shrugged and started cooking up. I dropped the tape and all the cash I had on me next to him on the couch.

"It's important that it stays safe, Rex."

He was too busy with his lighter and spoon to answer.

"Rex?"

"I said I'd look after it. Now can you please fuck off?"

Back in Laurel Canyon, Willow Glen looked good. It looked like the home of a star on the rise, maybe someone who'd just moved from a video soap to their first feature role as support. An optimistic place full of light and excitement and youth.

I had a shower and a Coke then sat up close to the TV and watched a tape of an old Escape perfume commercial, the one with a couple dreamtiming on a boat and a small jetty. Drifting images of happiness and ease. I wanted to be the guy with his thick dark hair and his confidence and his solid unthreatened existence. I wanted to be the girl with her unassailable beauty, her excitement and laughter, that flash of white bikini between her legs.

I had the ad back to back for half an hour. Ten minutes into it I got up and stuck my photos around the edge of the screen. It made an interesting juxtaposition. Dead bodies and a perfect way to live. I jerked off and spurted over everything.

Bella called while the tape was still playing. I watched my come drip on the floor while we spoke. She told me she loved me. She told me the payoff to Ryan went fine. She told me he was coming out to Malibu the next day with a present for us both.

When I put down the phone I felt cold. The present was another tape, apparently, not of us, but of some other people doing wrong. Bella said it was the best thing that could happen because it would give us something incriminating to use against him. I knew that he wasn't that stupid and that he'd have his own dangerous reasons for this continued contact with her. Same as I knew Bella had begun to play a game of her own with him.

I walked around the house for a while. Then I lit a cigarette, turned on the pool lights and went outside to look at the patterns on the surface of the water. A breeze made the fronds of the palms in the garden rustle.

Chapter 26

The toilets at Sub were unisex stalls – black laminate walls with swirls of glitter embedded in them. Lorn and I shared one and did a reasonable amount of the coke I'd brought with me – I'd cut it with a little white smack, but I didn't think she needed to know that. Then we kissed and I fingered her, but it didn't mean anything and we went out into the main bar area, got drinks and hung out.

Lorn knew a lot of the people there and after half a vodka and lime she wandered off to mix with the famous. It was a big place – bars, dance floor, a raised dining layout – and pretty soon I lost sight of her.

I stayed where I was and watched another race at play. They glowed, they possessed a vitality the rest of the world was denied. Their eyes shone, their hair was good, they moved easily in perfectly fitting clothes. And when they talked it wasn't about the weather or how the car needed fixing, but about things that were monumental – six weeks shooting in the Andes, a crowd shot that involved two thousand extras, the manipulation of astronomical amounts of money – lives lived every minute of every day at high speed.

Sub was better than the reception at the Bradbury building, better than being on the Warner Bros. lot. This was where people who had their faces on billboards came to be with others like themselves.

I didn't see Lorn again that night and I didn't make an effort to meet anyone. It was enough just to be there, to feel their otherness around me. I left quite early, afraid too much exposure might overwhelm me.

One last drink at the bar. The barman looked at me for a moment then asked, hadn't he seen me on *28 FPS*? His question almost short-circuited my head, and as I left through the metal-flake entrance hall, pretty well ripped on booze and blow, past the crowd that had gathered to celebrity spot in the warm night air, my blood fizzed with the knowledge that I had taken the first steps toward belonging.

The morning, though, was different. I woke feeling uneasy and hungover. The euphoria that had wrapped me at the club was gone. Instead, my guts were knotted with a gnawing anxiety at the prospect of Ryan's Malibu visit.

I hauled myself out of bed and fell into the pool. I floated facedown. But it wasn't enough to blot him out, so I blew air and sank to the bottom. And lay like a corpse, looking up through ten feet of water at a warped and distant sun. I wanted to stay down there, insulated from all the dangers of the planet, the whole fucking hassle of living – but after a while water pressure and lack of air made me feel nauseous so I got out.

On the ground floor at Malibu.

"I know a guy in the security business. He passes things on from time to time."

We were sitting in front of a TV – me, Ryan and Bella. Outside it had started to rain. People on the slopes were probably freaking at the unseasonable wetness and worrying about mud slides, but in that room the rain just drew things closer about us – the heavy stone walls, the furnishings.... Bella's protective isolation.

Ryan's latest cassette was in the machine and ready to run. He held the remote and talked to Bella like I wasn't there. It was obvious he was fixating, that he thought he had a chance with her. I'd watched him take things in when he'd turned up half an hour earlier – the house, her BMW, the pool, the acreage of the grounds. His eyes had catalogued possessions, and the desire I saw exploding in him confirmed my fear that allowing him up to Malibu wasn't the smartest move Bella could have made. But then, she didn't know him as well as I did.

"When I saw that stunt with the guy in the motel I knew you'd be into what I've got here."

He looked at me and kept his face straight.

"What was your name again?"

"Jack."

"Jackie, yeah, that's right. Well, this is a few steps further down the road so to speak, but I have a feeling you're a man who appreciates extremes. And I expect that goes double for Beauty here."

He smirked at Bella and started the tape.

"This came out of a security camera. The girl's some Hispanic who cleaned the joint after hours."

On screen two men in ski masks walked into view carrying shotguns and shoulder satchels. They looked tense, wired for signs of danger. Glass-fronted display cases bordered the space around them, evidently the showroom of a small jewelry store. From our point of view, looking down from a corner of the ceiling, it was possible to see the lower corner of a door open. The feet of a woman walking backwards came through it. She was dragging a vacuum. One of the men lunged half out of shot and wrestled a pretty Mexican girl into view. She looked about twenty and had great hair that shone even on videotape.

They hit her a few times and pointed their guns at her. She had blood on her mouth and the crotch of her jeans went dark as she pissed herself. One of them used duct tape to gag her and bind her hands behind her back, the other one pushed up her T-shirt and rubbed her tits, then hit her so hard on the side of her head that her legs buckled and she slid to the floor. She just sat there looking vacant, like her brain was off somewhere else, desperately rerouting in an effort to restore function.

The men started on the business of the day, and Ryan fast-forwarded through five minutes of display-case smashing and jewelry theft.

"All this is just straight robbery bullshit, but things start to happen just about...here."

The figures on the screen stumbled back to normal speed. Their bags were full and the showroom was trashed, bits of glass and wood everywhere. The girl had curled up on the floor, trying to be invisible. But she couldn't quite manage it, and as the men started to head out of shot one of them paused and said something to the other. The second man checked his watch then dropped his bag and together they began stripping her.

The girl tried to struggle but after a few kicks in the stomach she stopped and they draped her facedown over the remains of a display case. Both men got their cocks out and the taller of the two started giving it to her from behind. The other guy stood in front of her face masturbating and rubbing the end of his hardon across her eyes and over the tape that covered her mouth. He had a hunting knife in his free hand.

The men moved faster. The guy in the saddle fucked so hard the display case rocked, and the one with the knife looked like he was trying to rip his dick off. A few seconds later he spurted over the girl's face, did up his pants and stood with his knife under her chin, looking at his buddy like he was waiting for a sign.

It came soon enough, a rapid nodding of the head, and probably a lot of shouting too, but there was no sound on the tape so I couldn't hear it. The guy with the knife cut the girl's throat. Blood came out of her neck in a wave and made a wide path across the floor. She shuddered violently like she was having a fit, dragging her tits across the broken bits of glass that still stuck from the sides of the display case. The guy fucking her slammed in a few final times then threw his head back. From what I could see through the hole in his mask it looked like he was howling.

After the men left, the girl's body flopped about weakly once or twice, like a fish dying.

"Ever seen anything like that before, Jackie?"

Ryan knew I had. He knew I'd stood with him and watched a girl get taken apart with a jackhammer.

"How about you, Beauty?"

"Of course not."

"But you like it, don't you?"

"Too primitive No distance, no control."

"Jackie?"

I didn't answer. Ryan chuckled.

Bella got up and killed the TV. Ryan tracked her, his eyes pushing into the creases of her body.

"Maybe it was too much for you, Beauty. Maybe injecting people is okay, but killing them crosses the line."

Bella stood in front of him, all of her body behind her cunt, like she had a hardon.

"You'd be surprised at the lines I've crossed."

Then she lifted her skirt and let him go down on her. Later, after she'd faked an orgasm, she had the limo brought around and we went over to some vegetarian place in Rustic Canyon for food. The restaurant had only recently opened and the air stank of money.

It was too early for the dinner crowd, but there were still plenty of sleek-looking industry types in professionally selected clothes and five-figure watches winding up working lunches. They used a lot of hand movement when they talked. Cell phones went off every thirty seconds.

Ryan took it all in with the same hungry look he'd had on his face when he walked into Bella's house. Watching him sitting there, talking to her like a normal human being, was unsettling. I knew that he was simply not going to let things go at fifty grand now.

An expensive restaurant, the house at Malibu, sex with Bella – these were all tastes of a world that would possess him as much as it did me. I couldn't understand Bella. She was too smart to misread him, to pigeonhole him as some petty criminal of limited threat, but that's what she appeared to be doing.

I ordered grilled fish. It was the closest thing they had to meat.

Me and Ryan, alone in the men's room. Our dicks out at a glass urinal that had fish swimming behind it. Mr. Frightening and me. I was glad that my clothes were so much better than his. I looked like I belonged, Ryan looked like he got lost on his way to a beer joint. It gave me an illusion of security.

But it didn't last.

"I'm getting closer, Jackie."

"To what?"

"Hand job first, then today. Next step's gotta be some deep mattress action, whaddya say?"

"Don't hold your breath."

"Oh, Jackie, don't tell me you're upset. I thought it'd turn you on. I don't see how I could have been so wrong."

"Fuck off."

Ryan looked hard at me. "I like it up here with the money. It'd be smart for you to make things easy for me. I can send you straight back to selling your ass any time I want."

I zipped up. Ryan kept talking.

"You and me are partners, don't forget it. You think I'm going to stand around with nothing, while you suck up everything she puts in front of you? I'm entitled, boy. I spent my life cleaning up other people's shit and I'm fucked if I'm going to miss out on this."

He stepped away from the urinal, fists clenched, dick still hanging out of his pants. His breathing was ragged and he was sweating. I knew whatever Bella gave me, whatever life she made possible for me, was never going to be safe as long as he was around.

"Take a pill and put your dick away."

"I got a lever on her, Jackie, and I'm gonna use it till it's all used up. You can come along for the ride, or you can go back to the gutter. It's up to you."

"You're underestimating her if you think she's going to keep paying out for that tape."

"See, now that's the kind of approach that's gonna keep us tight, you giving me useful advice. I like that about you, Jackie – you learn fast. But don't you worry, that tape was only a foot in the door. Shit doesn't happen in isolation. All I gotta do is look around a little more and something else'll turn up, you can bet on it."

He put his hands on my shoulders and shook me. I thought maybe he was going to kiss me, but then a guy came in and Ryan just zipped up and walked out. I stood in front of the mirror for a little while, looking at the lines on my face, listening to the sound of piss going down the drain.

CHAPTER 27

For *28 FPS* I did more segment intros in front of the blue screen and spent a day hanging around out front of Chateau Marmont trying to get footage of Johnny Depp and Kate Moss. All I wanted were a couple of kissy shots as they climbed into a car or something, perhaps a quick question about marriage plans. I didn't get anything. I'd been tipped they'd be there, but by the end of the day and no show it was obvious I'd been bullshitted.

Still, I got to do the promo for next week's show. James shot it with me talking to camera in front of a wall covered with gang graffiti a couple of streets south of the Marmont. He said it'd help hook a particular demographic.

Lorn was out of town in Palm Springs trying for nude footage of movie stars taking mud baths. When she'd told me she was going I'd had a sudden image of her naked, black mud sliding between her thighs. The more time I spent with her the more I wanted to fuck her. She was good-looking and she was on TV. Plus, getting cozy with her might make it easier to con a few extra minutes from her share of *28 FPS* screen time. As a permanent replacement for Bella, though, she didn't cut it. Not enough money and not enough power.

I hung out at Malibu, swam in the pool, made pornographic home videos with Bella and learnt how to edit them on the machinery in her suite. Between taping my segments for *28 FPS* and her occasional visits to the clinic in Brentwood, we did restaurants and shopped. I hardly thought about my photos of dead people.

It could have been a good time. It could have been real good. Except that it wasn't. Ryan shit right in the middle of it and turned it all septic. It wasn't another demand for Rudy money that brought him back into our world, though. It was something much worse. Even Bella seemed a little fazed.

She arrived at her clinic one afternoon to find that a guy who could only have been Ryan had been there earlier that day asking questions. He'd had a photo with him and he'd wanted to know if the staff had ever seen the blonde in the picture. And if Bella was qualified to perform surgery.

"They said he told them he was a policeman. Do you think that could be true?"

Bella stood side-on to a window that overlooked the grounds and the early evening light made a silhouette of her profile.

"Making a little extra on the side? It wouldn't surprise me. But what does it matter if he is? There's nothing wrong with you knowing Karen, is there?"

"Of course not, but I'm in a vulnerable position, my work with the homeless might be misinterpreted."

"Did something happen with her that would involve the police?"

"What do you mean?" Bella's tone was sharp and for a moment her eyes narrowed.

"Nothing. I'm just wondering how he connected the two of you."

"I don't know. And I don't know what reason he has to ask about her. She left after her operation and I never saw her again. Is that clear enough?"

"I was only asking.... What about the other thing? Why would he want to know about your qualifications?"

Bella moved away from the window and sat down.

"I can only think he knows something about my operations. The question is whether this is going to evolve into another blackmail demand, or whether, if he is a policeman, it's part of a genuine investigation."

"It'll be him on his own."

"You seem very certain."

"I don't think you realize the effect you have on him. He wants you, I can see it in his face. He wants to fuck you and he wants your money. You were mad to bring sex into it."

"If he's acting alone it's the best thing I could have done."

"Jesus Christ—"

Bella cut me off impatiently. "You say he wants to get his hooks into me. Well, all right, let him think that's what he's doing. I may not know everything about him, but I know what kind of man he is, and sex with me will make him a slave. Given time, whatever he thinks he has on me will be useless to him, because he won't have the will to use it."

PCH at sixty miles an hour. Top down, wind in my hair, sun scattered across the ocean in drifts of golden petals. Fine fabric, perfectly cut, against my skin, the crystal of my watch catching the light, turning to a disc of mirror that somehow took all my Californian dreams from the air about me and held them there on my wrist so I could see them. The money in my English calf-skin wallet, the spending potential behind my credit cards – a financial virility translating into feelings of physical well-being as I headed north for no other reason than to delight in these things.

That morning it felt necessary, like it might be the last chance I'd get to indulge myself before the shit came down, the last chance to be willfully blind for a few hours.

A fast car along the edge of the ocean. If I'd had a blonde beside me I could have been in a movie. I wished I had a camera set up on the hood. That way I'd be able to watch myself and see if I matched my possessions.

It was an important thing to know. I had a small amount of recognition and a reasonable level of disposable income, but *28 FPS* ran too late at night and in too limited an area to attract an audience large enough to generate fame on a *Friends* or *Melrose Place* level.

As a result, I hadn't yet reached a point where I could define myself by other people's perceptions of me. Next to Bruce Willis or Brad Pitt I was nothing. Even guys like Judd Nelson were a million miles ahead of me, safe with their lives already hacked into the fabric of Hollywood; their fans, their agents, the waiters and producers who told them endlessly that they were better than anyone else in the world.

I started to toy with the idea of stopping somewhere to get a Handycam to balance on the dash, but then a gray Plymouth closed in behind me and flashed its lights and I forgot all about recording myself.

No point trying to run, he could find me any time he wanted. I drove for another half mile just to piss him off, then pulled into an overlook that had been built on a short spur of cliff about fifty feet above the sea. I got out, stood against the guardrail, and waited for what was coming with an unlit cigarette in my mouth.

Ryan heaved himself out of his car like a fat woman, twisting sideways first to swing his feet out. I didn't bother trying to read his expression, whatever it was it wouldn't mean anything good.

"Oh, I love the sea, don't you?"

He leaned on his elbows next to me and gazed off across the ocean. His stomach hung under him like a sack of grain.

"Bet you been thinking about me, haven't you?"

"Yeah, right."

"Look, don't get all embarrassed or anything, but I set you up a little treat down at the morgue."

"What do you mean?"

"I mean the real thing. Cold and laid out. Those photos have to be getting a little worn out by now."

I didn't say anything. I couldn't. The thought of getting close to a dead body changed the whole world around me. It dragged me out of the sunshine dream I'd wrapped myself in on the highway, back to a dark place of murder and desires I didn't understand. Ryan put on a cheesy grin.

"Yeah, I thought it was the least I could do considering you got such shitty friends."

"Huh?"

"Old Rexy."

My guts went cold. I lit my cigarette.

"You know what's coming, don't you, Jackie boy?"

"You want another payment for the motel thing."

Ryan snorted. "I guess you had to try. No, this ain't about that poor bastard. Don't you know you can't trust a junkie?"

"Get on with it."

"You're not enjoying this? Gee, I am. Okay…. Rex had my number. A couple of days ago he used it. He had something to sell, and after I saw what it was I was happy to buy. I bet you could take a real good guess what we're talking about here."

I didn't answer.

"No? A tape of our two favorite girlfriends pleasuring each other. Only about ten minutes long but, boy, does it sizzle. Don't bother looking vacant, Rex told me where he got it. You know what it means, don't you?"

"So they knew each other, big deal. Karen was a whore and Bella likes sex. It's not impossible they met."

"But you and I know it ain't as simple as that. That tape proves a sexual connection between a murder victim and a woman whose behavior is suspect to say the least. A connection you didn't want me to know about. Why was that, Jackie?"

"Just because Bella was fucking her doesn't mean she killed her."

"Surgical type wounds, professional evisceration, a sexual link. It isn't what I'd call tenuous. And then there's you — another connection between them. You know, Jackie, you oughta be more helpful. It don't take much of a leap to put you and this doctor cunt together in a plan. Maybe that's why you didn't let on about the tape."

"The first time I met Bella was when some faggot trick took me to a party in Bel Air. Two months after Karen was killed. And the reason I didn't tell you about the tape was because I knew you'd jump to some bullshit like this."

"You say she didn't do it?"

"Of course she didn't. She was in love with Karen."

Ryan looked measuringly at me. "I know about the operations."

"Operations?"

"Don't act dumb, I wouldn't want to get pissed off on such a nice day. When I saw the tape I thought it might be worthwhile checking out your movements after Karen died a little more thoroughly. Remember that bar on Pico, the Egyptian place? The night you thought it'd be so much fun to try and lose me? I went back there and spoke to a guy called Joey. Man, you think you know L.A."

Ryan laughed and shook his head.

"So, we got this Joey in a secret clinic somewhere selling off one of his kidneys. It's a bummer the doctor was antsy about being identified and wore a mask and a gown all the time or we could be a whole lot more certain about things. But we got a couple of pointers. On account of him having sex with her, Joey was pretty sure it was a woman. Ain't that a kick? Just like Bella. Plus, those gowns do up down the back and Joey couldn't be completely sure, because there wasn't much of a gap, but he thought maybe she had a tattoo there, something all black."

"Bullshit. You're making it up."

"Now why would you say that, Jackie?"

"He didn't know anything about a tattoo."

"Just 'cause he didn't tell you, don't mean he didn't know. You gotta learn to be more forceful, boy. Of course I can understand you getting upset because, correct me if I'm wrong, didn't I catch a flash of something on Bella's back when you and her fucked that poor cunt in the motel room? What was that, exactly?"

"You got me."

"You telling me you've been fucking her all this time and you haven't seen anything? No ink? Really? I'm going to find out sooner or later, Jackie. You might as well spare yourself some grief."

"Okay, she's got a tattoo, so what?"

"That's better. I didn't get much of a look, describe it for me."

"I don't know, some kind of beetle or something."

"Wouldn't be an Egyptian kind of beetle, would it? Like Karen had?"

Ryan started to laugh, deep belly chuckles like he was immensely pleased with himself. It took him a while to quiet down.

"Okay, Jackie, here's how it looks to me. You tell me that, first off, Karen went away for a coupla weeks – long enough to have her kidney cut out, I'd say. Then she turns up flashing way more cash than she could have got hooking. Shit, she even bought you a car. Add that little scene with her and Bella on the tape and the picture draws itself. Bella's a doctor, she's fucking Karen. Karen wants some extra cash. Bella knows a way.... How am I doing?"

"You're fucking mad."

"You better hope I'm not, 'cause the stuff Joey told me that you asked him is the only indication I got that maybe you weren't involved in the murder. See, those kinda questions, one way to figure it is you were out looking for the killer. Now, are you going to level with me about Beauty, or not?"

"All right, all right.... Karen did sell her kidney, it's true. When she came back to my place she'd already had it done – that's what we argued about the last time I saw her. And Bella did the operation, yes. But that doesn't mean she killed her."

"That's better."

"It doesn't mean she killed her, Ryan."

"Could point to it, though. Karen's sexing up to Bella and Bella with all that money – maybe after you and her had your tiff she went back to the honey pot once too often. Shit, when it came to money she wasn't what you'd call shy. Could be she decided her kidney was worth more than she got. Maybe Bella didn't see it that way and did something about it."

"She's trying to help people. She pays for the kidneys herself and donates them to welfare hospitals. Is that the sort of person who kills someone?"

"Whatever she's into it ain't helping people. I checked her out, Jackie. She ain't a surgeon. She's a doctor, yeah, but that's all. She's got no more right to do those kind of operations than you or me. What does that say to you?"

"That she's really clever?"

"She's a fucking psycho. She enjoys cutting people open. Could easily be she just went a teensy bit too far one day."

"Couldn't happen. She doesn't do the operations by herself. Her father helps her, and he *is* a surgeon."

"*Was* a surgeon. And that doesn't mean anything, anyhow. Karen wasn't killed during an operation. You said she'd already had her kidney out last time you saw her alive."

"What about the spunk? Bit difficult for Bella to come up with that."

"The come don't necessarily mean anything. Could be someone wanked into the body after it was dumped. Could be a million explanations. By itself it don't rule her out."

"But it could mean someone else was involved."

"I just bet you got a suggestion."

"Her father."

"I don't like that suggestion."

"What do you mean, you don't like it? The guy's a junkie."

"It's been fifty years since you could hang a murder rap on someone just because they like to unwind with something stronger than booze. Don't get simple on me, Jackie."

"He's got a major sex thing going on with Bella. I'm telling you, he could easily have killed Karen in a fit of jealousy over it. He cuts open dogs when he gets pissed off. I've seen him do it, exactly the same as Karen was."

"I got Bella doing the operation illegally – which, by the way I wasn't sure of until you told me, 'cause Joey never actually saw who did the cutting. I got similar tattoos and I got a tape of them having some girlie fun. I got nothing between Karen and this guy Powell except what you say. And forgive me, Jackie, but you got what we call in the business a vested interest."

"But if he's involved in the kidney thing too, it could just as easily be him."

"It wasn't him in that motel room stopping some guy's heart."

Ryan shoved himself away from the rail and headed for his car.

"Come on, I want to give you this present. Things have been working out pretty good since you and me hooked up. I want to show my appreciation."

I didn't move right away. I watched some gulls circling over a patch of water and thought about Lorn. All I wanted at that moment was to be with her in a big bed, in a room filled with sun, the world shut outside and the smooth whispering of our skins against each other drowning out the shit Ryan kept forcing me to listen to.

But I also knew I couldn't turn down what he was offering.

Euclid Street. Memories of Karen on a slab. It seemed like a long time ago, but then a lot of things had happened.

The sun was low in the sky as we arrived and the haggard palms made long diagonal shadows across the concrete of the road. We went in the same way as before, down the side ramp. The front office was shut anyhow. Ryan was acting like a guy playing Santa Claus.

The body room hadn't changed – same fluoro light, same coolant hissing in the same pipes, same TV babble from the attendant's room. A place out of time, a place where the temperature and the cool motionless air never changed, no matter how many days went by outside.

Ryan whistled and the Japanese guy shambled out to meet us. He looked pleased to see Ryan.

"You got her ready? My friend here's kinda anxious to start."

"Sure. She all ready out back. One sweet honey. Say twenny-five, look real nice. Big tits, but she got a lot of hair on her pussy. I have to shave her first, but you western guys maybe different. Anyhow, still plenty fresh. Rigor all gone. Mouth nice and clean so you can kiss her too if you want."

Ryan handed over a thick fold of cash, the Japanese guy gave him a key and went back to his TV, unwrapping a candy bar.

"Outside again, Jackie, too much traffic in here. They start coming in from rush hour soon."

He led me out of the body room and around the back of the building to a square concrete block that looked like it had been tacked onto the main building as an afterthought.

"This is where they used to keep the blacks in the old days. The only time it's used now is when Kung Fu needs a few bucks. Praise the Lord for more liberal times, eh?"

He used the key on a recessed steel door that was rusting at the corners and pushed his way inside. The place was windowless and the lights were already on. Not fluoros, but a line of clear low-watt bulbs that hung from the ceiling on dusty flex and threw an ochre pall down the center of the room.

One wall had the same fridge doors as the main building, but there were a lot less of them. The other three walls were marked with trails of powdered plaster that spilled from blisters in the peeling green paint. There was a pile of junk in one corner – old paint cans, a tarpaulin, a few pieces of what was probably refrigerator machinery. It looked like they used the place to store shit they couldn't be bothered to throw away. Today, though, it was going to serve a different purpose. Ryan locked the door behind us.

On a gurney something lay heavy and still and covered with a sheet.

"She's all yours, Jackie. Whaddya think?"

He pulled the material away with a flourish, like a stage magician. Big tits and a lot of cunt hair. I couldn't argue, she was good looking all right, even dead. Along with Karen and the jackhammer girl, this was the third corpse I'd seen. Maybe it was the increasing familiarity, maybe it was because of the photos Ryan had given me, but the sight of her didn't make me feel like puking or any of the other things you see on TV. Instead, it was like when I'd watched Ryan stroking Karen's pussy – I wanted to touch her, to see what her flesh felt like, to run my hands over her belly and the tops of her thighs. I knew she'd be smoother than any other woman I'd ever been with. My cock felt like it was carved from stone.

"Look at that fucking beard. Let's see what's in the middle of it."

Ryan pulled the woman's legs apart. One of them swung off the edge of the gurney and made tight rubbery arcs in the air for a while. The motion made her pelvis grind.

"Whoa, look at that. She wants it, Jackie. The bitch is dead and she still wants fucking."

In the center of the dense black hair I could see a pale tear-drop of meat, about the color of skin on a side of beef. I wondered if she'd be slick inside. A smell came off her, but it wasn't fish. It was more like the fragrance cheap soap leaves behind.

Ryan used his thumbs to pull her open, she looked dry. I spat on my middle finger and pushed it into her. She was tight, but what struck me more was the cold, synthetic feel of her, like she was some injection-molded dummy that had never been alive.

"I bought her just for you, Jackie."

"You expect me to fuck her?"

"It's what you want. Might even do her myself after you've loosened her up."

I pulled my finger out of her. Before I could wipe it, Ryan grabbed my hand and stuck it under my nose.

"Smell that? Know what it is? That's the smell of what's inside you, Jackie. All the stuff you want to do but don't. Not because you think it's bad or wrong or evil, but because you think you might get caught."

"You don't know what's inside me."

"Oh, you're wrong there. I spent too many years looking at people. I've seen the things they want and there's nothing that sets you apart from them. Everyone's the same, only difference is some are less frightened of getting caught than others. I know you want to do it so stop shitting around. Your pants look like they're gonna rip."

Ryan was right. I wanted to fuck the woman. I wanted to be on top of that body, pumping away. And I was going to do it. Right then there was nothing that could have stopped me. Maybe Ryan had set it up to seed another blackmail scam, maybe someone was getting ready to kick in the door and bust me – I didn't care. In that dingy light my desire to make real what I'd seen in Ryan's photos was overwhelming.

I moved up to her head and looked at her face – white like the rest of her. Her eyebrows and lashes stood out so starkly they could have been painted on. Her eyes were closed, her mouth was slightly open and I could see the glint of teeth. I kissed her. Her lips gave against mine, but they didn't spring back, they stayed wherever I pushed them.

I forced her mouth open with my tongue and searched for hers, but it had fallen down the back of her throat and I couldn't reach it. Her teeth were sharp and hard, like small rocks or pieces of bone. I knocked them with my own and her head felt dull, as though all the spaces in it had been filled with cement.

I took my face away and held her breasts, they moved sluggishly under my hands, cold bags of flesh. It was weird knowing I could squeeze them as hard as I wanted and no one would complain – she wouldn't shout, and Ryan certainly wouldn't move to stop me. But I didn't do it, I couldn't spare the time, I had to get inside her.

The gurney was too narrow and too high to be any good as a bed so Ryan and I lifted her down. We got the tarp off the junk pile and spread it out first, though, to stop the dust and bits of grit that covered the floor sticking to her back. When we had her ready I took off all my clothes – I wanted maximum contact. Ryan ran his hand over my ass then sat on the gurney and took a nitro pill.

I got on her. She felt solid and round, like something I'd fall off if I wasn't careful. My weight on her chest made her sigh, a hollow gust of air that smelt like garbage. Her cunt had stuck together again when we moved her and I had to cover my dick with spit before I could get the first couple of inches in. After that it wasn't too difficult, except that her pelvis was at the wrong angle and I had to put my arms under her knees and pull them up to her chest.

The impact of my body made her head loll in quarter circles, back and forth with each stroke. With her mouth open it almost looked like she was enjoying herself, but the only sound she made was an occasional gurgle, like she had something trapped deep in her throat.

I held onto her as tight as I could and concentrated on sensation, on the feel of her cold thighs against the sides of my chest, her belly and breasts under me, the stale hairspray smell of her hair, the taste of her neck, slightly soapy where it met her shoulders, my dick enclosed in dead tissue. I wanted to drive myself into her and never forget what I found there.

Some time in, Ryan got down off the gurney and started wanking himself over her face. He came pretty quickly and I had a closeup of his semen disappearing down her throat. When it was my turn, I must have gotten a little too energetic and disturbed something inside her because foamy white liquid started boiling over her chin while I was spurting. I thought maybe she was going to cough herself alive like a drowned person, but it was just some gassy reaction to the shaking I'd given her and after it was over she was just as dead as before.

I put my clothes back on and stood looking down at her, not really knowing what to do next.

"She liked that, Jackie. Look at her, she's smiling. Fucking slut. You take her legs."

We heaved her back onto the gurney and Ryan wheeled it over to a large white sink at the far end of the room. A length of hose was connected to the cold-water tap. He uncoiled it and handed it to me. I didn't have a clue what he was doing and by this time I didn't care, I was feeling a little spaced by the whole episode.

"I've had enough, Ryan."

"We gotta wash her out first. Stick that end in her cunt."

He turned the tap on then came around and took over from me, jetted water into her until it started coming out again in fast swirls that spilled off the gurney and onto the floor. It reminded me of the first time I'd gigged with Rex up in the hills – the masked woman strapped into a harness, blasting douche water out of her ass.

Ryan pulled the hose out and turned it off.

"Okay, get on the gurney and lift her up."

"Huh?"

"Lift her so she's standing up. We gotta get the rest of the water out of her."

"Fucksake. Let's just go."

"It's part of the deal."

"Christ...."

Doing what he wanted looked like the fastest way out of there so I climbed up and got my hands under her arms. As I lifted, Ryan yanked her legs sideways off the gurney. I almost dropped her and he had to step in and put his arms around her waist. Her legs splayed on the wet floor, but we managed to get her pretty much vertical and water ran out of her gash. Ryan held her open with his fingers so it could happen faster.

"Look, Jackie, she's doing wee wees."

When she was empty Ryan turned the tap back on and hosed out her face. It sounded like she was gargling as her throat filled up. We bent her over the gurney to drain her, only there was some kind of blockage and Ryan had to sit on her back to force the liquid out. Bits of food came with it.

CHAPTER 28

Ryan and I split outside the morgue. The episode with the corpse had left me relaxed and kind of floaty and I didn't want to head back to Malibu straight away. I thought about paying Rex a visit and confronting him about the tape, but there wasn't much point. It wouldn't erase what Ryan had already seen. So I drove down to the ocean instead and parked on Ocean Avenue, near where Karen had been found.

The sun was touching the horizon, bleeding orange light across the water, turning the palms into black cutouts that would have looked good in tourist photos. The place hadn't changed, the tramps were still lurching alcoholically from one pointless activity to another, the cardboard shelters still cowered against bushes in the quieter areas.

I phoned Bella to tell her I was heading back and to give her some bullshit about why I'd been gone so long. She was home from her Brentwood clinic, but just about to leave again – Powell had a donor lined up. She didn't have time to speak and told me she'd see me tomorrow. We blew kisses and hung up.

I sat in the Mustang and thought things over. I'd hoped Bella had suspended contact with Powell after he'd taken me to watch the kidney operation, but it seemed now that wasn't the case. Obviously the lure of a donor was strong enough for her to forgive him, at least temporarily. But why should that be? Providing one more kidney for the less fortunate of Los Angeles couldn't be reason enough to set aside the anger I'd seen displayed at Apricot Lane. I was missing something. And with Ryan trying to tie her into Karen's murder, that wasn't a good thing. Knowing in advance what he might possibly uncover was the only way I'd have a chance to protect her.

I was starting to feel drained from fucking the dead girl. I wanted to go home to Willow Glen and sleep. Instead, I pointed the Mustang up Wilshire, scored half a gram in West L.A. and sat in a Taco Bell there for a while killing time and pumping up my blood sugar with cola. When I figured Bella had had long enough to make it to Apricot Lane, I headed there myself. On the way I tuned into a radio show that was running through the various pairings around town.

Kate Moss and Johnny Depp had been seen on Hollywood Boulevard looking happy and relaxed. Lisa Rinna wanted her long-time fiancé to marry her or walk. Brad Pitt and Gwyneth Paltrow were still beautifully blonde together and almost certainly to wed. Cindy Crawford and her barman boyfriend had just bought a house. Sylvester Stallone and Jennifer Flavin, Arnold and Maria, Pamela and Tommy.... On and on, beautiful people doing beautiful things with each other. It depressed me that I wasn't one of them. Even though I was clocking up screen time on *28 FPS*, I had a long way to go before anyone would be interested in who I was seeing.

I parked on San Ysidro so Bella and Powell wouldn't hear my engine, put the top up and did some coke. Then I got a tire iron out of the trunk and walked carefully along Apricot Lane. This far up the canyon they didn't have street lights and I was glad of the darkness. Down at the dead-end I climbed the fence and managed to work the garage door up high enough to roll under. Inside – the black Jag and Bella's 850ci.

The steel door to the basement was a bitch to open, especially because I had to worry about noise, but I got it done eventually and made it into the corridor on the other side. It wasn't hard to remember where the observation booth was – it was the only door that didn't have a lock. I turned out the corridor lights and stepped quietly into the small space.

Same bright light through the one-way glass. A body on the table, skinny, male and white. Powell sat at one end, behind the head, doing his anesthetic thing. And Bella worked away in the middle.

This time, though, things had a different feel. Bella moved as swiftly and as carefully as before, but as the operation progressed the sensuality I'd seen hinted at during my first visit to the clinic grew into something more overt. Her hips ground against the edge of the operating table as she cut into the body, forcing her cunt hard against the chrome steel framework, and even though it was difficult to tell because of her gown, I was pretty sure she was pressing her thighs together most of the time. Once or twice she threw her head back and I thought I heard her moan.

Powell looked like he was wanking. I couldn't see properly because of the angle of the table, but when he wasn't involved with his gas cylinders his hand dropped between his legs. Unlike Bella, though, it wasn't the open abdomen of the donor that interested him – his masturbation was fueled by his daughter's own excitement.

An hour later Bella lifted a kidney out into the world. She let it lie for a while on the man's chest while she did something inside his guts, then she picked it up and rubbed off the shreds of membrane that clung to it. I waited for her to put it in a container and store it in the fridge like before. But that wasn't exactly what happened.

She stepped away from the table, pulled her mask down and examined the organ closely, not like she was looking for anything in particular, but like she wanted to absorb as much of it as she could through her eyes. The surface of it shone under the lights and I could see a delicate network of dark blood vessels embedded in the pale tissue. It moved in her hand like a small slippery sack, something that might fly from her grasp if she squeezed it too hard.

She hiked up her gown and turned to rest her ass against the edge of the operating table, she was naked underneath and her cunt hair looked like coal against the halogen burn-out of her skin. For a minute she played lazily with the kidney, running it over herself in slow strokes – across her belly, up the insides of her thighs, leaving a trail of rosy smears. Then she got serious, reached between her legs, held the lips of her cunt apart and began rubbing herself with it. Her knees trembled and I heard clearly a sound in her throat.

Powell had rolled his stool out from the end of the table so he could see better and was pounding away at his long white cock. But the scene in the operating room wasn't a shared experience. Bella was occupied only with herself, with the sight and feel of the pink organ sliding between her labia and over her clitoris. As she pressed harder, red juice ran between her knuckles and dripped from her wrist.

After a while she started to shudder too much to stay standing. She lay down on the floor with her knees hard up against her chest. I could see straight into her cunt. The blood and the small rolls of tissue that were beginning to break off the kidney made it look like a wound. Her moans became continuous and her hand started to blur.

At the end of it all she shrieked and jammed the thing inside herself. Powell lurched upright and spurted across the floor, then collapsed back onto his stool and sat looking at her as though he wanted to get up and hold her, but knew she would not allow it. Bella lay where she was, breathing deeply with her eyes closed, stroking the outside of her pussy and the short curve of kidney that protruded from it.

Nothing happened for maybe thirty seconds, then Powell checked a couple of gauges and said something. Bella stirred, looked around like she wasn't sure where she was, then pushed herself to her feet and stood braced against the edge of the table, head drooping over the donor's open abdomen. The kidney fell out of her and landed heavily on the floor. She stared at it until Powell spoke again, then shook herself, put on a fresh pair of gloves and started stitching up the man on the table.

I got out of the observation room, out of the clinic, and walked back to the Mustang. I didn't notice what the night was like around me, I was too busy assimilating.

The story Bella had spun me about helping the homeless with medical care, and low-income people on kidney waiting lists, hadn't really been so bad as far as murder linkage was concerned, even if the operations were illegal. But now it was obvious I'd been bullshitted. Cutting 'donors' open to use their kidneys to wank with kind of punctured the philanthropic cover story she'd used to sucker my acceptance of her extracurricular medical activities – the organs would hardly be much use to anyone after being stuffed up her cunt.

Add the fact that she wasn't qualified to perform that kind of surgery and you had a level of suspicion that was up there with Powell's doggie antics. Not such a great development when Mister Frightening was doing all he could to upscale his Malibu contact.

I didn't feel like hanging around Willow Glen or Malibu by myself, so I figured I'd make the trip to Rex's that I'd put off before. My anger toward him over giving the tape to Ryan had burnt itself out, but I still felt a little face-to-face was called for. I turned the key and L.A. went by outside my car windows – lush trees under a night sky that glowed with reflected light, as though the molecules of air over the city had absorbed so much of its scrabbling desire they phosphoresced with it now of their own accord.

Rex answered his door out of it. As soon as I saw his pinned eyes and his drooping face I knew I shouldn't have bothered. I couldn't say anything that would make him my friend again, or that would persuade him to reduce his drug use and save himself from what he obviously intended to be a terminal degeneration.

I wanted to make him feel bad for hurting me with the video tape, but there was no way the notion of remorse was going to penetrate the cloud of smack and disaffection that wrapped his head. Still, I was there, it would have been a wasted journey if I didn't at least try.

He gave me a dead look for a couple of seconds at the door then went into the lounge and sprawled on what was left of the sofa.

"Go ahead, get your whining over with."

"You don't think I'm entitled?"

"You should have paid me more."

"Giving Ryan that tape could have fucked everything for me."

"I didn't give it to him, I sold it."

"Yeah, I figured, but why?"

"I needed money."

"Did you watch it first?"

"No."

"Why didn't you call me? I would have paid you. Jesus, man, we were friends."

"Because I can't stand the way you look at me. You think I'm fucking up, but I'm not. What I'm doing is the only sane response to life in this city. You're so fixated with your TV bullshit you're incapable of seeing it."

We stared at each other for a few seconds but I knew he wasn't seeing me.

"I ought to kick the shit out of you."

"I wouldn't feel it. But if you want something else to make you feel important you could leave some money on your way out. I'd feel what that'd buy."

I stood there for a while trying to decide on a course of action. In the end I gave up, there was no way to get satisfaction. In that kind of situation words and violence are equally ineffective.

Before I left I tossed a wad of bank notes into his lap. I don't know why. Maybe I did it just because I could. Maybe I thought it would shame him. I don't know.

Chapter 29

Malibu. I hadn't slept and the room with the French windows alongside the pool stank of cigarette smoke and strong coffee gone cold. Outside, though, the sky was a crisp blue – one of the first cool days on the slopes above the sea – and everything looked fresh. I'd called in sick on a shoot to be there. Lorn could handle it alone, but it wouldn't do me much good with the channel – a measure, I suppose, of how urgent I thought it was that I talk to Bella about sex with kidneys and Ryan's latest discovery.

She came home midmorning. If she was surprised to find me sitting there, covered with ash, watching TV on a set I'd dragged in from somewhere else in the house, she didn't show it. In fact it looked like she expected to find me there. She settled next to me on the couch, thigh to thigh, perfect white legs stretching long out of a short black skirt.

"You were there last night. You saw what I did."

"Sorry about the door."

"Why didn't you wait for me? You must have had questions you wanted to ask."

"I didn't want to do it with Powell around. Where is he?"

"Keeping an eye on the recovery. Finding a donor last night was an attempt to reestablish himself with me. Don't worry, it won't work."

"Your story about giving kidneys to hospitals was a lie."

"Are you terribly shocked?"

"I'm wondering what else you do that you haven't told me about."

"What do you mean?" Bella looked shocked. "I'm not a monster. What you saw last night is everything."

"You told me you weren't qualified as a surgeon."

"Powell is a good teacher, when he's forced to be. No one is in any danger. But you want to know why I do it."

"It would help."

"I like it. I like doing it. When I take a kidney out of someone I change them forever. Physiologically it's far more profound than rape. And it takes a monumental effort of will – to go against the law, to go against everything we're taught about not hurting people. It's a test. It's a test of skill. It's a test of courage. It's like I take a torch and shine it into the darkest part of my soul. Everyone has secret thoughts, thoughts of murder and torture, but they won't admit to them. Or, if they do, they pretend they're a momentary aberration, something separate from the person they consider themselves to be. But we are the sum of our thoughts, Jack, whether we admit to them or not, and the most potent of those thoughts are the ones we prefer to keep hidden. I've found a safe way to access them, that's all."

"It all sounds so reasonable."

"You're not convinced?"

"What I saw was too primal."

"All right. What I said was true, but if you want it in different terms, I do it because I can't fucking live without it. Some people like pissing and whipping and bondage and animals. I like cutting kidneys out and masturbating with them. It gets me off. It's the only thing that does what it does to me. Is that a better explanation?"

"Ryan knows about the operations."

Bella had been steaming along with her little speech, but that slowed her down a tad. She looked ill. Her mouth worked silently.

"Not what you actually do with the kidneys, but the whole donor thing. He pulled me over while I was out yesterday."

When Bella spoke her voice sounded thin.

"How could he possibly know anything about them?"

"He found a guy you operated on, a bar owner or something. Maybe he identified you. It wouldn't be hard for Ryan to get a picture of you somewhere."

"I never uncover my face in front of the donors."

"You did with that girl Karen. If she's still around somewhere he might have got it out of her. She saw your face, she knows where you live. Do you think she might have talked?"

I watched Bella closely as I said this, but her reaction was only what would have been natural if she thought Karen was alive.

"No. If she's spent all her money she might try to get more by selling the information. But she'd sell it to me, she knows I'd give her whatever she wanted."

"At least it figures why he was at your clinic showing pictures. They must have been of her."

"But how would he even know about her?"

She put her face in her hands and was silent a while. Then she lifted her head and looked intently at me. Her eyes glittered with buried excitement.

"Why did he tell you? About the operations. Why would he let you know he'd found out? He must know you'd tell me."

"Of course."

"He's thinking of blackmail again. That's all it is. Thank, God."

"That makes you happy?"

"When the alternative is going to jail, yes."

"It won't be fifty thousand this time."

"The more he asks for, the deeper the hole he'll be digging himself. But I don't understand how he found out about the operations in the first place."

Bella put her head back against the cushions of the couch and stared at the ceiling. I lit another cigarette and wondered how long it would be until she caught me out.

A day later, Lorn and I finished a piece on a penis-implant clinic and the more high profile of its clients. I'd been rocking up in the breaks between taping and was pretty fritzed, I needed to make it to a bar and booze off the edges until I could find something more effective. Lorn told me to forget it, that she had Librium at her place – an apartment in a court off Melrose.

Vodka and pills, one way to kill the end of an afternoon. Another is by fucking, which we did for the first time in her bathroom after I walked in while she was finishing up a piss. After that we did it in her bed. The walls were a collage of magazine cut-outs, lacquered so close together there was no space between them – every Hollywood star under thirty-five. It looked like the inside of my head.

It goes without saying that screwing the anchorwoman of a show in which I participated purely as a result of Bella's influence was a potentially dangerous thing to do, stupid even. What can I say? It was a hot day, I was out of it, I'd wanted to fuck her since I met her.

We'd grown closer working together, Lorn and I, after all we had a lot in common – we'd both lucked into the media and found it the only world whose reality was worth having. And while our humping that day might have been largely due to boredom and blood chemistry augmentation, there was something within each of us that recognized a key part of the other.

Chapter 30

Bella had fish with herbs and a selection of undercooked vegetables, I had steak and a bottle of wine – all of it prepared by invisible hands and waiting for us when we came down from upstairs. Candles burnt in the lingering twilight. Our table stood on the flagging between her house and the pool. The white columns around the water were lit and the scene made me think of a European set for a Jackie Collins miniseries. Rome or Monte Carlo, maybe. We crooned endearments to each other.

Until Ryan waddled around a corner, dragged up a chair and helped himself to a drink.

"Don't look so surprised, Beauty. You must have known I'd be paying you another visit. Got anything else? I don't like wine."

"You shouldn't be drinking."

"It's nice you're concerned, but save the doctor shit for the suckers who don't mind losing a kidney."

"Jack told me you had the strangest notion."

"Notion nothing. You're performing illegal operations. There's no two ways about it."

"You have another video tape?"

"I got a witness."

Bella laughed.

"Maybe he can't pick your face, but that don't make what he saw any less useable. Leastwise for me. How does an Egyptian beetle sound? Right in the small of your beautiful back?"

"It sounds like something anyone with the price of a tattoo might have."

"I don't want to flatter you unduly, but not a lot of people have a body like yours. I guess my witness would recognize it if we stripped you down in front of him. The way he tells it he got a pretty good look. And then there's the guy who picked him up. Distinctive silver hair, easy to ID. I checked some old newspaper photos back when your father had that accident with your mom. He was gray even then. Plus he wasn't wearing a mask when he talked my friend into selling his kidney. You got a black Jag registered in your name?"

"No."

"How about Dad?"

"No."

"Yeah, I already checked. But I bet if I went looking it wouldn't be too hard to find. Might even be in the garage here."

"Have a look."

"I don't need to, do I? You already know I got enough. So, here's the plan...."

It wasn't what either of us was expecting. It wasn't just money. It was way worse than that. On top of a million bucks, he wanted to come and live at Malibu. He wanted to share our lives.

"Not forever, of course. A coupla months, say. Shit, the place is big enough, it's not like we'd be in each other's pockets. Don't you think it'd be fun? We could all go out places together. Whaddya say?"

"Why on earth would you want to do that?" Bella's voice was cold.

"Well, see, when you give me that million I can't exactly go out and start blowing it can I? Not a fifty-year-old cop. People would talk. But with you I can walk into any place and all they'll think is I got lucky with my cock."

"You don't need to live here for that."

"But it'd be so much nicer. See what I want is the same thing I figure old Jackie here wants – *Lifestyles of the Rich and Famous*. You know? Restaurants, premieres, charity parties like Steven Spielberg goes to. Those kinda things, you need connections. And I know you got connections, Beauty."

Bella didn't have much choice, she knew he had enough to fuck her up. So she said yes – yes to the million, yes to him living at Malibu. And she didn't say no when he put his hand between her legs and started stroking her thigh.

Later, Ryan split for home saying he'd pick up some things and move in tomorrow. I walked down to the gate with him. He'd had to haul his fat ass over it to get in without us knowing. His car was parked on the road.

"What are you doing, Ryan?"

"Gee, Jackie, I thought I explained. Beauty looked like she got it."

"You know what I mean."

"You can figure the money, but not the moving in."

"Unless it's just to piss me off."

"You know what a hidden agenda is? Like the politicians have? That's what I got."

"Meaning?"

"Meaning I ain't forgotten Karen. That bitch up there is hiding something and the closer I am to her, the easier it's going to be to find out what it is."

"Isn't that shooting yourself in the foot? Look what she's giving you."

"I liked Karen."

"I could tell Bella what you're up to."

"And I could tell her about you. I bet she don't know you two were married. I bet you ain't even told her you knew each other."

"Of course I haven't."

"So if I tell her different she won't like you so much, maybe. Don't be dumb, Jackie. There's no point in fucking each other up before we have to. You want something out of her? I don't have a problem with that. As long as you don't get in my way."

Ryan winked and got into his car. Before he pulled away he wound down the window like he'd just remembered something.

"I checked what you said about the kidneys, that she gives them to welfare hospitals? Don't happen. There ain't that many on this side of L.A. and none of them ever received anonymously donated organs. I hope you're playing straight with me, Jackie-boy."

Chapter 31

So a pretty bizarre time started. Bella put Ryan in a suite on the other side of the house, gave him a suitcase full of money and a set of keys. During the day things ran on the same as they always had – Bella hit her Brentwood clinic a couple of afternoons a week and I backed up Lorn on reports for *28 FPS* and did a few solo slots. Ryan got on with whatever pig business he had happening at the time. But downtime, that's when the new situation really showed itself.

Bella's preference was to stay home most nights, but Ryan was hot to get a taste of society. So every evening those first few weeks the three of us were out dining and turning up at glitzoid parties from the Malibu beachfront to the Hollywood hills. I didn't mind the socializing, it was all more California to me, but the way he jammed himself next to Bella was a major pisser.

I didn't spend much time at Willow Glen around then. I didn't feel comfortable with the idea of Ryan and Bella alone together, consequently I had to suffer the greater part of his onslaught.

The time after our outings was generally the sickest – him, Bella and me in a knot on the floor, or bed, or by the pool, or wherever else the connection occurred, grunting away at each other in a kind of incestuous frenzy. Bella had let him fuck her as soon as he moved in and Ryan had never looked back. He sweated and popped nitro and rolled around in an ecstasy of dreams come true. And didn't notice that Bella lay underneath him completely self-contained, unaffected by his penetrations, even by his presence in the house, it seemed.

Sometimes I'd leave them to it, rock up some coke in the microwave and smoke it out in the garden. Other times I'd sit and watch them writhe. Ryan got a lot out of the sex – a beautiful woman with an incredible amount of money, she was as much a badge to him as she was to me.

"Aren't we two lucky guys?"

We were alone drinking coffee by the pool. Bella was out and Powell still hadn't shown his face at Malibu since the first kidney operation. Ryan wore a white toweling robe and sat close to me. I could see fine black hairs against the pallid skin of his calves.

"Whaddya say, Jackie, are we sitting pretty, or what?"

"She isn't stupid, she'll figure out why you're here."

"If she's guilty she's gotta know already. But what's she gonna do? Call the police? Take my money back? Don't worry, Jackie. Her running scared will only be good for us."

"For you. It won't do me a shit of good."

Regular sex must have softened him because he smiled then like he really didn't want me to feel so bad.

"Look, I gotta admit I'm getting kinda fond of Beauty. I'm not going to do anything unnecessary."

"Fond? You're blackmailing her, for fucksake."

"Things don't always finish the way they start. I think she's into me too."

"Oh, Jesus...."

"Hey, you don't fuck the way she does without feeling something."

"I guess you're not after her for Karen anymore, then."

"I said I wouldn't do anything unnecessary, but if she's the one, then she's the one. But I been thinking about what you said about her father. It'd be a nice solution – Bella skates, you're happy, I'm happy, justice gets done, the money keeps coming.... Persuade me."

So, off we went, Ryan still in his robe, tramping through the undergrowth at the edge of the grounds. Until we found the carcass of a dog. By then it was just a collection of eaten-out bones wrapped in skin.

"I found another one the first time I came here."

Ryan squatted and poked it with a stick.

"Sorry, Jackie, this don't tell me much. It's too far gone. Impossible to determine the exact nature of the wounds. You say they were the same as Karen's, but then you would."

"Doesn't it tell you something about him? Bella said he does it when he gets jealous."

"We must be pissing him off plenty then."

"Are you listening to me? A guy who does this because his daughter's fucking someone obviously has a major problem. Don't you think it's conceivable it could have something to do with what happened to Karen?"

"It's a dog, Jackie, not a person. And we got nothing to say he knew anything about Karen at all. I'm not saying he didn't, but we got no proof."

"Fucksake! They do the operations together, he would have to have known about her."

"But only as someone selling her kidney. And Joey's living proof that being a donor don't have to mean you wind up dead. Beyond what you say, there's nothing that gives him knowledge of any affair between them. So we got no jealousy motive."

"Bella's into videoing stuff, right? You got that tape of her and Karen."

"So?"

"So she told me Powell sneaks copies of all her tapes. If he has a copy of the one you've got, it'd mean he knew about the affair."

"It still wouldn't prove he killed her."

"But it'd point in that direction."

"Maybe."

Powell's suite at the house was paneled in wood. It had olive carpets and brass fittings like a gentleman's club. Ryan went through it without making any attempt to hide his tracks. What we wanted, though, wasn't hard to find.

In plain sight in the bedroom, a wall-mounted rack held an exact duplication of Bella's video collection. Ryan worked his way through them. He saw me unconscious getting my dick sucked, he saw me performing actively in a more recent tape. He went slowly through the donor tape, trying to recognize faces of unsolved homicides as Bella performed her examinations.

"I gotta say, Jackie, this ain't helping Bella any. She's getting off on it. That plus the kidneys just disappearing doesn't inspire confidence."

I took the remote off him and fast-forwarded to the section with Bella and Karen.

"There. You can't say he didn't know about an affair between them now."

"Depends if he got it before or after the murder. If it was after it don't mean shit."

"I don't fucking believe this!"

"Hey, Jackie, I'm trying, but I gotta consider all angles, especially in a situation where a man's liberty is at stake."

I handed Ryan the last tape on the rack. I knew what it would be and I didn't know whether he'd read it as for or against Bella. But there wasn't much I could do to stop him watching it.

Bella and Powell fucking, a selection of their sessions together.

"Oh, Jackie, what have we got here?"

"Daddy's favorite pastime."

"Look at the old bastard go."

"He's obsessed with her."

"With a body like hers, who wouldn't be? If you've been saving this to ace me with, I'm surprised at you. You should know me better than to think a little incest would shock me into jumping on him."

"You're doing this to fuck me up, aren't you? You don't want it to be Powell. Because if it isn't him, then it has to be Bella. And if it's Bella and you take her down I lose everything. What does it take to satisfy you? You want to destroy me? Why? You must know by now I didn't have anything to do with Karen's death."

Ryan killed the tape and turned to look at me. For the first time since I'd known him he looked sincere. More than that, in fact, he looked conflicted.

"Jackie, it hasn't got anything to do with you. I'm being straight. You think I want it to be Bella? Shit, no. I like living here, and you know I like fucking her. Add to that she's a goldmine I haven't even scraped the surface of yet, and I'd be insane to fuck her up for no reason. But I gotta have someone for Karen and I gotta feel confident it's the right person.

"Sure, there's shit about Powell that looks plenty suspect, but without something to tie him directly to Karen it's just dead dogs and nudie pix. With Bella we got a definite connection and we got stuff that's just too weird to ignore. I don't know what the story is with the kidney thing yet, but those examinations make it look like some kinda sex trip for her. And if that's what happens when she's checking them out, what the fuck happens when she's cutting? You said Powell's involved too, but it ain't him sticking his fingers into those people on the tape. And it wasn't him in that motel room. Shit, that was almost a murder right there."

"She didn't kill Karen."

"I hope you're right, I really do, but unless you can find me something more than Fido out there, you better start looking for another source of income because the one you got ain't gonna last."

I went back to Willow Glen later that day. Alone, I looked at my pictures and remembered the feel of the dead woman in the morgue. I wished I could have taken a photo of her to help me. Better, I wished I had a video of us doing it that I could splice into a Calvin Klein commercial. The dead and the living together – hard to think of either of them as important if their images aren't recorded and available for viewing. I spurted then took some pills and fell asleep thinking about Lorn. We shared an obsession with a better way of life. In Los Angeles that was probably as good as love.

Chapter 32

Life goes on. Short of suicide there isn't much you can do about stopping it. Knowing Ryan was watching and waiting and counting the minutes until he could take Bella out of the game kept me in a state of permanent anxiety. But not everything that happened around then was bad.

On *28 FPS* my share of screen time took a small hike as market research indicated acceptance of my face and personality by the target audience. The mid-twenties son of a snack food magnate caught one of my slots and suggested me to his father. As a result I got ten grand for a couple of rushed fifteen-second commercials that screened on the cheaper local stations – the first money I'd earned in a visual medium without someone else's help. The ads were good for exposure, but I worried about being trivialized.

Meanwhile, Ryan and Bella played their respective games. He for Karen's revenge and a lifestyle he never expected he'd have, she for God knows what reason. They fucked, they talked and, despite his mission to destroy her, I could see his infatuation grow. But she sat a long way back behind her eyes when she was with him, calculating things I couldn't fathom.

I carried my photos with me now most places I went. Wanking over them gave me a kind of relief from worrying about the end of money and TV-time that Ryan's plotting against Bella seemed destined to bring about. But the relief was only temporary and as time passed my anxiety built to a point where I knew I had to either act or perish.

I formed a plan that required a confession to Bella and the sacrifice of another human being. Neither were things I would have involved myself in voluntarily, but I no longer had the freedom to choose. The taste I'd had of the high life made it impossible for me to give up the chance at becoming someone special without a fight.

Out in the workplace, Ryan was busy closing cases in preparation for a move to retirement. Some nights he worked late. On one of them I took advantage of his absence.

A small, exclusive restaurant by the sea, a table by the window, just Bella and me in the early twilight. There were reasons for doing it like this. Her breeding would prevent a screaming match in public, Lorn and I had interviewed Laura Leighton there about her days as a waitress and I figured the manager might recognize me and dish out a little preferential treatment. And if everything did have to end, I wanted this memory of California to take with me – an expensive place, beautiful people, soft light, gentle music from the trio in the corner, a view of the ocean, my reflection in the glass, beautifully dressed.

I was clear-headed. No pills or powder, just a Wallbanger – vodka, orange juice, Galliano – a taste that made me think of summer nights for some reason. The cuff of my shirt looked crisp as I raised the glass to my lips, my nails were manicured. Bella glittered. Men at other tables glanced at her. She smiled at me.

"This is nice, darling. But I sense something."

"Do I look that nervous?"

"You're not going to ask me to marry you, are you?"

She laughed in a way that made me think the subject might be open to discussion if I wanted to pursue it. But small talk was only going to make things worse, so I jumped straight in.

"You're in danger. Ryan thinks you killed someone and he's trying to frame you for it."

She gave me a blank look for a couple of seconds, then a puzzled smile like I was joking.

"I'm not sure I heard you properly."

"Karen. The girl in your video. She was killed about four months ago. They found her in a park in Santa Monica and Ryan thinks it was you."

She knew I was serious now. She pressed her lips hard together. She didn't start crying, but most of the blood left her face.

"That can't be right. How can you be certain it was the same girl? I don't understand."

"It's very hard for me to tell you this...."

I took a swallow of my drink, it didn't taste like summer anymore. It didn't taste like anything.

"There are things about the way she was killed that Ryan thinks point to you."

"I asked you how you know it was the same girl."

Her voice was cold and there was an anger in her eyes that wasn't going to let me skate.

"Jesus Christ, Bella, I'm sorry.... I used to go out with her."

She froze.

"You mean you had an affair with her? You were lovers?"

"It didn't last long. It finished months before she was found. But she'd used my address once when she got busted for hooking and they traced me through it. They suspected me for a while."

"They meaning Ryan, I assume. He really is a policeman, then?"

"Yes."

"Why didn't you tell me when you saw her on the tape?"

"I thought you'd think it was all too much of a coincidence. You know, me and her being together, then her being your lover and dying, then me turning up.... I thought you might think there was something planned about it, and I didn't want to risk losing you. Then, when I realized you thought she was still alive, it just seemed easier to forget the whole thing and keep my mouth shut. Until Ryan turned up, of course."

"I thought the episode at the motel was a little too pat."

"Yeah, he's been keeping tabs on me since the murder. I should have told you when he started the blackmail thing, I know, but I never thought it'd go this far. I had no idea he'd try to connect you to the murder."

"So you lied to me."

"There was no way I could explain Ryan without telling you about Karen. Christ, Bella, I didn't want any of this to happen, it all just kind of snowballed around me. I wanted it to stop, but it kept getting worse and worse and there was nothing I could do about it. If I could change things I would, but I can't."

Bella studied me. I must have laid it on thick enough because after a few seconds she reached across the table and put her hand on mine.

"But what made him think I had anything to do with killing her? Is it because you and I are together?"

"It's more than that. He knows you took her kidney out, so he's got the two of you linked in something illegal. On top of that, her body was cut open and eviscerated. Professionally, like a surgeon would do it. He figures she came to you and sold her kidney, then sometime later you killed her."

"He's insane. I removed her kidney, but she left in perfect health. I didn't see her again. Are you sure you're telling me everything?"

"What do you mean?"

"He knows about my operations and he knows you had a relationship with Karen, but how could he possibly know she was one of my donors?"

"After she died he checked around and found out that before it happened she'd been boasting about making all this money from selling her kidney. He checked further and found his "witness", and that led to your tattoo. And, unfortunately, Ryan was apparently a client of Karen's, so he knew she had the same design. That's all it took for him to figure you two had history."

Bella looked genuinely shaken. She ran her hands along the edge of the table, smoothing the tablecloth over and over. Then, as though suddenly drained of energy, she dropped them into her lap.

"What am I going to do? I didn't kill her, but I won't survive an investigation. The operations alone would ruin me. Will he take more money?"

"He'll take it, but it won't fix things. Karen's death is personal to him for some reason and he won't let it go. But if you listen to me and try not to freak at what I say, I think there's a way out."

"A way to make him see it wasn't me?"

"Not exactly. Jesus, I don't know what you're going to say to this.... I swear I wouldn't suggest it if I could think of anything else at all."

"Go on."

I took a deep breath.

"I've been looking at things and thinking about things and it seems to me there could actually be a connection between the kidney operations and Karen's murder. Not you, like Ryan thinks, but Powell."

"You think Powell killed Karen?"

"If you were having an affair with her, he had to know about it, right?"

"Of course."

"Okay, and I know from experience how much he hates you to be with anyone else. Isn't it possible your affair pushed him over the edge? That he got so twisted about it, the only thing he could do was kill her?"

Bella was straight in her chair and her eyes were narrow. I took it as a good sign.

"He's obsessed with you, and more than that he used to be a surgeon, easily capable of inflicting Karen's wounds. I think he killed her in a jealous fit, then removed her insides to hide the fact she'd recently had her kidney removed. For Christsake, he cuts up dogs exactly the same way."

I stopped and drank some of my drink. It tasted better.

"What do you think?"

Bella spoke slowly.

"It's possible.... That bastard.... All this time I thought she'd left me."

She drifted for a while. The waiter brought me another drink and took away our untouched food. Then Bella snapped back.

"Your solution is to give Powell to Ryan."

"If he killed her, he deserves to pay for it. Assuming you're willing to take that step."

"Have you talked to Ryan about it?"

"I told him about the dogs and the jealousy. He knows Powell's background – the drugs, his medical training."

"Was he receptive?"

"He didn't think it was enough."

"I'd hardly call it a solution, then."

"It will be if we can find some proof. Shit, you've seen the way Ryan looks at you. Sweet-talk him. He says he wants to take you down, but I think secretly what he really wants is to find a way around it. Explain about Karen, who she was, what she meant to you. Lay it on about Powell's jealousy. It won't take much. Meanwhile, I'll try and find a tie between Powell and Karen, there has to be something. All we need is one piece of evidence."

"I hope you're right, Jack. If you're not, both of us could lose everything."

Chapter 33

On the strength of my TV exposure over the last few months I got an agent. They had offices high up in Century City, nice and flashy and reassuringly successful – you could see the Fox studios from them. I didn't tell Bella anything about it. With the unstable state of things at Malibu it seemed smart to lay the foundations for an alternative future. Also, after the earlier increase, my share of air time on *28 FPS* had hit a plateau.

The channel only allowed Bella so much for her money and from the planner on the wall of the production office it was plain I'd reached that limit already. A few more people recognized me on the street, but I didn't think many of them wanted to be me yet. I hadn't had the steamroller exposure necessary to become part of their desires.

So, fronting for a major product – something expensive and fashionable – looked like the best remedy. You didn't have to put in the legwork you would for a part in a movie and you didn't have to establish the kind of marketable personality the TV shows demanded. All that had to happen was some casting guy liked your face and away you went. Not as heavy-duty as movies or a show, but a real quick way of getting seen. And with Bella balancing on a knife edge, speed seemed most definitely to be of the essence.

Right at that moment, though, the agent didn't have anything for me and I had to content myself with whatever slots I was tossed on *28 FPS* and the occasional photo that appeared when the gossips had a slack week and had to cull visuals from the minor league. And even then I was usually riding Lorn's coattails, accompanying her to some function and standing too close to crop out when the bulbs went off.

The fuck we'd had at her place had repeated itself several times during the intervening weeks. Our connections occurred in those hidden times when the two of us being alone together wouldn't raise eyebrows – in our trailer while everyone else was setting up outside, on the back seat of a limo when we splashed out and hired one to attend some career-furthering do.

I would have liked to have done it more often but the fear of Bella finding out put a serious dent in my motivation. And besides, opportunities for sex were becoming limited because I couldn't stop myself scurrying back to Malibu immediately after each taping session like some hack reporter waiting for a disaster story to break.

Even when we did manage a bit of action, it wasn't what you'd call emotionally satisfying. I thought of my humping at those times as an act of evacuation, as though I'd stored up poison from the anxiety pervading Malibu and the only way to get rid of it was to empty it into Lorn.

I don't know if she noticed, maybe she thought it was just the way I fucked. When we'd finish she'd stare out the window with a look on her face that made me think what she saw out there and the fucking we'd just completed bored her equally. At these times it wasn't hard to imagine some essential part of her was missing.

Nevertheless, one day while we were waiting to interview Willem Dafoe as part of a piece on Hollywood guys with good hair, she asked me if she could crash the night at my place. We'd never gone further with each other's life histories than that first conversation on the steps of the porn star's house and she didn't know anything about Bella or the role she'd played in getting me the *28 FPS* gig. Explaining it all and outlining how dangerous it would be to allow her so close to home right then would have taken more energy than I was prepared to expend. So I refused and made up some bullshit about being a very private person. She listened to me with less attention than she'd give a weather report.

The pool at Malibu had a spa built into one end. Bella, Ryan and I sat in the bubbling water one afternoon, naked and wearing sunglasses. Ryan and I poured drinks from a bottle of Southern. I tried a cigarette, but the water kept splashing up and getting it wet.

Bella sat opposite Ryan with her legs apart, he had the start of a hardon.

"Jack tells me you suspect me of murder."

Ryan wasn't fazed. We hadn't spoken about it, but he must have known I'd tell her. The fat on his chest jiggled in the swirling water. I wanted to leave it all up to Bella, but I had to cover my ass, I couldn't have him blowing the lies I'd told her. I talked fast.

"She didn't do it, I thought she should know. I told her about the short affair I had with the girl. I told her how you used to suspect me."

"Oh, yeah, that short affair you had...."

He hid his smirk behind his glass. I leaned back and rested my head on the tiles. Blue sky, the occasional cloud, inland the tiny black speck of a hawk circling. I closed my eyes and wished I was a thousand miles away. Bella took over again.

"I didn't have anything to do with her death, Ryan. In fact I didn't know she'd been killed until Jack told me."

"It's a nice afternoon. The water feels good, nice company, good booze – if you want to tell me something, I couldn't think of a better time to do it."

"What do you want to know?"

"How did you meet?"

"Not in the usual way. I mean it wasn't because she wanted to sell her kidney, she didn't know anything about that. She was a prostitute. I picked her up on Santa Monica Boulevard one night. We had sex. I was attracted to her and I asked to see her again. Over time we developed a relationship. We fell in love."

"Musta had some pretty hot nights."

I heard Bella sigh with annoyance and I opened my eyes. She was sitting higher in the water and her breasts showed above it.

"She visited regularly, she'd stay for several days at a time. She said lived with some awful man in Venice but I never found out where, she wouldn't talk about herself. I think coming here was an escape for her."

"She said he was awful, huh?"

I avoided the glance Ryan threw at me.

"That was the impression I got."

"Go on."

"She wasn't high-class. She worked the streets, she had a drug problem – but perhaps I'm telling you something you already know."

"I could listen to you forever."

"She always needed money. I gave her some, but it never made any difference, she always needed more the next time I saw her. One day she told me she had to buy a car. I suggested she sell her kidney."

"Why didn't you just give it to her? You got enough."

"I was afraid if I gave her that much she'd either overdose or end up getting killed for it. I thought if she had to go through an operation and give up a kidney she might value the money enough to be more careful."

"Gee, it's nice how you rich people look after us poor folks."

"I cared about her. I didn't want to see her ruin herself."

"I'm touched. Go on with the kidneys."

"She jumped at the chance. I paid her well. Thirty thousand dollars."

"And?"

"And nothing. After the operation she stayed here for two weeks, then she said she had to visit home. I didn't want to let her go, but she promised she'd come back. There was nothing I could do to make her stay. I never saw her again."

"Didn't she have stitches or something? Wouldn't they need to be removed?"

"They dissolve by themselves. She should have been monitored, of course, but...."

"And you didn't see her again? Not even once?"

"No. I remember the day she went. She'd hocked all her jewelry sometime before – for drugs, I suppose – and I gave her an antique gold bracelet. She liked it very much. Do you remember if she was wearing it when she was found?"

"What I remember is the hole where her guts should have been."

"I only took a kidney."

"Then who took the rest?"

"My father."

"Now there's a surprise. Jackie's been trying to sell me the same deal. Where is this Powell guy, anyhow? He's got rooms here, but he's never around."

"He's unhappy about my relationship with Jack. He has an apartment downtown."

"You mean he doesn't drop around for the odd fuck when I'm not here?"

Bella looked sharply at me, but Ryan carried on before I had to say anything.

"Jackie showed me your video collection. Don't blame him, though, he thought it'd help you."

"Then you'll understand why Powell might have an objection to me taking a lover. You know about his mutilation of dogs, you know he used to be a surgeon. Can't you make the connection? My relationship with Karen was significant. Doesn't it seem plausible to you that a man who has an erotic fixation with me might snap and commit murder to remove someone he saw as a rival?"

"Yeah, but it could just as easily have been you had a lover's spat with Karen and butchered her yourself. I'm not saying it was one way or the other, but if you want me to believe it was your father, you're going to have to show me more than your spread pussy. Speaking of which, you got any more videos of Karen getting all sexy?"

"You've seen everything in my video suite?"

"Everything in that cute hidden cupboard."

"That's all I have. Karen felt uncomfortable being filmed. The only segment I ever took of her is the one you've already seen."

After that nobody said anything for a while, the water bubbled and Ryan and I had another drink. Then Bella spoke again.

"I have a question for you, Ryan."

"You only gotta ask."

"Why did you never mention you knew Jack?"

A question like that could only mean she wasn't entirely certain I'd been telling her the truth about my connection with Ryan, maybe even about my connection with Karen. And asking it in front of me meant she wanted me to know it. Ryan stayed silent for a while like he was considering his answer, doing it to make me sweat, no doubt.

"We're dealing with a murder. To anyone who knew anything about it, Jackie plus me equals Karen. It would have been stupid to give that away so early in the game."

Bella didn't look convinced. She kissed me on the cheek, got out of the spa and walked nude into the house.

"Saved your butt there, Jackie, boy."

We stayed in the water while the afternoon decayed. There wasn't much else to do, so I drank enough Southern Comfort to get moderately sloshed.

That night, for the first time, Ryan got to sleep with Bella. Not just a fuck, but the whole eight hours, dusk to dawn, lover style. I looked in on them once, but the sight of that fat animal nuzzling into her armpit like a gigantic baby was just too obscene. I took some pills and passed out in another room.

Ryan slept late next morning so Bella and I got to have breakfast alone together. She was waspish and impatient.

"He doesn't seem particularly interested in Powell."

"Is that why you let him sleep with you?"

"It was a logical step."

"Really?"

"I don't want to go to jail. And you don't want to lose your TV time. We've got to take care of this thing, Jack. You've got to see the big picture."

"Okay, okay."

"He needs something concrete to persuade him."

"Like what? We've been through Powell's rooms."

"Here."

Bella handed me a key ring. There were three keys on it.

"Building, elevator, apartment door. Powell phoned earlier – he's found another donor. We'll be operating this evening, his apartment downtown will be empty. Take Ryan and search it."

Around midday Ryan surfaced in fine spirits, in fact he was almost bouncing. I figured he was so unused to love that the pseudo emotion Bella had dished out through the night must have made him think someone cared about him. He wanted to go shopping and he wanted me for company.

Only it wasn't your usual department store shopping. It took a couple of hours trekking from showroom to showroom, but at the end of it Ryan was the owner of a late model, slightly used convertible Bentley turbo coupe. I didn't see what he paid for it, but it must have been a reasonable chunk of the million he got from Bella. It made me wonder how soon he'd be asking for another installment.

We went cruising and the car turned heads. It felt good to know people were thinking I was someone important.

A little after three we parked outside a high school on Fairfax Avenue. The sidewalk was busy with kids heading home. Ryan was in predator mode.

"Always wanted to do this, how about you? Sure you have. What guy hasn't, huh? What we gotta look for is two together so they feel safe. Slutty types, you know? The class bikes. Nothing over fifteen, though."

Kids were checking the car. Young males whistled, the older ones wanted to trash it. Two girls passed by wearing tight T-shirts and lycra shorts. They looked like maybe they'd just got out of gym class. Both of them were smoking and wearing makeup. Best friends for sure, the kind that shared adventures. Definitely not virgins.

They saw the car, our clothes, our wrist watches, and there was a subtle change in attitude, in the way they held themselves, the way their walk became exaggerated and their tits stuck out. Ryan slipped into drive and kept pace with them.

"You girls wanna lift?"

They giggled and kept walking.

"No, come on, I'm serious. Look at the car. You think we're maniacs or something?"

Ryan was half leaning across me, speaking in a light friendly voice I'd never heard before. The girls whispered to each other and stopped. Ryan nudged me.

"We just come in from outta town. We got plenty of money. Wouldn't mind spending some of it on a couple of girls as good looking as you two. You know how to have a good time?"

"How much money?"

"Hey, whatever it takes."

They whispered together. Getting into a car with a couple of men wasn't a problem, it just had to be priced right.

"Five hundred," one of them said, like maybe she was asking for too much.

"Each? Sure. But what do we get for that?"

"Anything you want, but we gotta be home by six."

Into a motel on the edge of Hollywood where no one gave a shit about questions of age difference. Coke, booze – the chicks got wild and naked. Their bodies were smooth and slim, the hair on their cunts was silky. Ryan was right, every guy wants to.

We fucked one each. Mine had long blond hair and a few zits on her chin. She looked good, though. She looked like she spent a lot of time at the beach. I couldn't believe how firm her body felt.

Later, out in the world again, Ryan said, "Jesus, I feel loose."

The girls were in a cab somewhere, counting their money, and we were in Ryan's obscene car gliding downtown to Powell's apartment.

"Don't you worry about doing stuff like that? I mean they were pretty young."

"Shit, Jackie, you oughta spend more time in the real world. Another birthday or two, they'll be standing on street corners. Ungrateful fucks."

"What?"

"Forget it."

I glanced at Ryan. He had a bitter look on his face that didn't make sense after the fun we'd just had back at the motel. He stayed silent a while, concentrating on driving. Left out of Fairfax, then Wilshire all the way. Somewhere around La Fayette Park he took a heart pill and started speaking again.

"Kids think they know everything. They see how they think something should be, and they never forgive you if you can't make it that way for them. No point trying to explain life ain't simple like it is on TV, they won't listen. Those two cunts are probably the happiest they've ever been right now – a grand between them and laughing about how pathetic we are. But give them a few years and a social worker, they'll be moaning how being whores is all Daddy's fault, like they woulda been nurses or something if he'd loved them better."

"What's this, your PhD in Child Psychology coming out?"

"I had a kid once."

"Bullshit."

He stared through the windshield at the evening traffic, but he wasn't seeing it.

"Whatever you say, Jackie."

Only someone as rabid as Ryan would drive a convertible downtown after dark. Even so, he parked in the basement rather than on the street. I'd handed over the keys Bella had given me and he used one of them on the elevator. We stood in the middle of it and watched the numbers change.

"Beauty seems gung-ho for this idea of Powell being the killer."

"What do you expect, that she should take the fall herself?"

"Not if she didn't do it. But there's usually a bit of reluctance between family members."

"If they like each other in the first place. They don't. He's hung up on her pussy, and she hates his guts. It's not what you'd call a happy-family scenario. Plus she blames him for her mother's death."

"There better be more to this than payback for Mommy getting scrunched."

The apartment was empty and quiet, its décor an exact copy of Powell's suite at Malibu. I followed Ryan around while he tossed the place, praying for a miracle. It came in two doses.

In the drawer of a writing cabinet we found a Polaroid – a dog cut open, a dick dropping semen into the bleeding split, held by a hand that looked old enough to be Powell's.

"See? Exactly how it happened with Karen. She was cut open and someone—"

"I don't need it explained, Jackie."

Ryan looked at the pic for a moment then held it out to me.

"You like this kinda thing. You want it? No?"

He smirked and put it in his pocket.

A room with a big-screen TV gave us the clincher. A selection of videos – a duplicate collection of the ones we'd already seen in Powell's Malibu suite and Bella's video room. Plus one more. A tape that was new to both of us. It showed Karen nude on her side, a back view, one leg pulled up, ramming a dildo in and out.

In front of her on the wall there was a mirror that reflected occasional glimpses of the front of her body as her movements rolled her in and out of its range. The angle of the shot was tight, but there was enough wood paneling and olive carpet around her to make the location of the scene unmistakably the apartment in which we now stood.

The plastic cock looked slippery and her hand moved fast. Sometimes the crack of her ass pulled open. It was obvious she was into what she was doing. It was also obvious from the glances she threw over her shoulder that she was performing for someone.

I found myself incapable of reacting sexually to this scene of my dead wife masturbating. Karen had changed from something human to a counter in a game, a piece of a puzzle, the solving of which would determine my future. Her image on the screen held about as much interest as a documentary on animals in Africa. Until something on her wrist shifted and caught the light. I almost yelped.

"She's wearing a bracelet."

"So?"

"It's the same one she had last time I saw her. It has to be the one Bella told us about."

"The goodbye present."

"Bella said she gave it to her when she left Malibu, the last time they were together. That means this video was shot after the operation."

"Maybe she wanted to give Beauty something to remember her by."

"But that's it! Bella doesn't have a copy of this tape, if she did we would have found it with the others."

"Who says?"

"You saw the stuff she had – me fucking her, Powell fucking her, even her goddamn donors fucking her. If she was going to hide anything, she would have hidden all of that as well. She was in love with Karen. This would be top of her playlist, for fucksake."

"So after she got her kidney cut out, Karen just dropped around to give the old guy a thrill?"

"She would have spread her legs as soon as he opened his wallet. You know she would. Maybe it wasn't the first time, maybe they had history. It doesn't matter. What matters is that this tape shows there was some connection between her and Powell *after* the operation."

"It ain't conclusive."

"Look at the way she's fucking herself. She's got to be pretty well recovered, and that doesn't leave a whole lot of time between when this was shot and when she was killed. I think she had the operation, got well enough to leave Malibu and come back to see me – we had an argument and sometime later, whether she had anything going with him before or not, she connected with Powell. After that, there's two ways it could have gone. Either she tried to put the bite on him or, what I think's more likely, he figured that as long as she was on the scene his access to Bella was going to be threatened – she was always going to be taking his daughter away from him. Either way, his solution was to kill her."

"If Powell shot this tape, why is there no camera here?"

"Jesus fuck, Ryan, it could be in his car, it could be somewhere at Malibu, he could have thrown it away. Does it matter? You said before, if there was something to connect Powell with Karen then it's possible he could have killed her. What do you call this? It's a fucking connection, for Christsake."

"Calm down, Jackie."

Ryan rewound the tape and played it again. He watched it silently and I held my breath.

"Something about this bugs me."

"What?"

"I don't know, but something feels wrong."

He rewound and played it a couple more times, searching the screen for whatever it was he thought he ought to see.

"Can you imagine how grateful she's going to be, Ryan, if you make all this murder hassle go away?"

"You'd love it to be him, wouldn't you?"

"And you wouldn't?"

Ryan stared at the TV for a little while longer then killed the set.

"Okay, we'll see what the old fuck's got to say for himself."

"You agree it could be him, then?"

"The only way we're gonna know is if we DNA him against the spunk in Karen."

Back at Malibu I split from Ryan. He was waiting like an expectant schoolboy for Bella to come home so he could get a bit of action in, but I knew with a donor she wouldn't be back for ages. I fired up the Mustang and headed for Lorn's place.

I felt good on the drive over. The tape we'd found at Powell's was better than anything I could have hoped for. It was going to make all my problems go away. Ryan would have his killer and wouldn't be able to lay the murder on me or Bella anymore. And with Powell out of the picture, I'd be free to mine his daughter for all she was worth. The only remaining hassle, of course, would be Ryan's presence at Malibu. But, same as I knew Powell's spunk would match what they found in Karen, I had a feeling that problem would resolve itself too.

Lorn was in the lounge watching tapes of herself when I got there. She was a little distant at first, still low-level pissed at me for telling her she couldn't sleep over at Willow Glen. But after a while I managed to smooth the evening out. We talked about work and movie stars then fucked on the floor. Later we watched *Pumping Iron* and lost ourselves in a firestorm of envy at Schwarzenegger's rise.

CHAPTER 34

It was a nasty scene, four of us in a room full of books and leather furniture out at Malibu – me, Ryan, Bella and Powell. Three ganging up on one. I hadn't bothered with this room before, there was no TV and the books weren't about Hollywood, but right then it seemed perfect for the job at hand; closed and quiet. It was raining outside, nighttime. Our only light was an open fire. Shadows moved around the walls like birds of prey.

Bella's donor must have been recovering without complications because she'd come home before dawn. Daddy, after a phone call from her, followed in the late afternoon. There had been arguments in Bella's suite through the rest of the day, the horrible sound of Powell begging for a physical comfort his daughter was no longer prepared to give.

Now he sat slumped in a large chair, gazing malevolently at the fire. He'd been gone from the house so long he looked out of place, a superfluous individual that nobody wanted around anymore. He knew something was coming. He'd been told who Ryan was and how he'd been augmenting his cop salary recently, and only a retard would have figured the evening's gathering to be without purpose.

Ryan and I had drinks. I listened to the fire and to the rain and waited for the beginning of Powell's end. Ryan stared silently at him for a long time, but the old junkie was too dosed to squirm like a clean man would. After a while my favorite policeman got pissed off with the game and prodded him with the toe of his shoe. Powell's head swiveled slowly around.

"I don't like being kicked."

"Something else you'd prefer?"

"Are you threatening me?"

"You bet. And I'm good at it, ask Jackie here."

"You're a thug."

"Tell me about Karen."

Powell looked uncertain and flicked his eyes at Bella, but her helpful switch was off.

"She was a donor."

"And?"

"And she was my daughter's lover for a time."

"What exactly was it made that time end?"

"These things run their own course. I assume they tired of each other. What are you driving at?"

"I'm driving at her turning up dead after she sold her kidney to you, you old fuck."

Ryan's voice got louder, he leaned forward in his chair like he was having trouble not jumping on Powell. I figured it must have been an interrogation technique, it seemed out of place otherwise. Powell looked a little frightened.

"She was healthy enough and the operation was performed successfully. It would not have resulted in her death."

"I know losing her kidney didn't kill her, fuckhole. I'm talking about what happened later, that second operation where you took out everything that was left then dumped her in the park."

Powell started to get out of his chair. Ryan pushed him back down.

"Uh-uh, Pops, we got a way to go yet."

"Bella...."

Bella's voice corroded the air about her. "He knows what you did. I know what you did. You couldn't bear to see me with someone else, so you killed her."

"Bella, darling, what are you saying? You know I didn't kill anyone."

"Karen and my mother. You killed them both, you sick bastard. Now tell him what he wants to know."

"I was jealous of the girl, I admit that, but I didn't kill her. And your mother.... Haven't you forgiven me for that?"

"Never. And I'll never forgive you for Karen. You cut her up like one of your dogs and threw her away as though she was so much garbage."

"Bella, no!" Powell was fast becoming distraught. "You know about the dogs, they don't mean anything. Tell him. They don't mean anything."

When Bella spoke next her face was cast in steel, like she was daring him to defy her.

"If it wasn't you, who was it?"

Powell worked his mouth, but closed it without saying anything and Ryan took the reins again.

"I've got proof."

"That's impossible."

Ryan lurched out of his chair and stood over Powell, breathing heavily, his fists balled.

"Why? Because you did such a good job? You figure with all her guts gone nobody'd know she'd had an operation? And if nobody knew that, they wouldn't be able to trace it back to you? Is that what you're telling me, motherfucker? Is that what you're telling me?"

Powell swallowed his fear and spoke calmly and clearly, making an effort to appeal to Ryan's rational side. Too bad no one had told him Ryan didn't have one.

"I'm telling you it's impossible you have proof, because I didn't do it."

"Really. Let's talk about home movies. One in particular – Karen doing a turn with a dildo. Nice angle on her ass. Taken, coincidentally, in your apartment."

"I know the one."

"You oughta. You fucking made it."

"I copied it from one of Bella's. She'll tell you."

"What Bella tells me is she never had a tape like that."

Powell looked past him at Bella.

"Bella, please.... The man is trying to crucify me. Tell him it was your tape."

"It wasn't my tape."

"Oh my God, I see what's happening. Please, he can't have any proof either of us is involved. It's a bluff. Don't say anything. I promise you, we'll be all right."

Bella stood and left the room. When Powell called after her his voice broke, but she didn't stop or even look over her shoulder. The door closed behind her and I felt vaguely frightened. Everything now seemed irrevocable, a string of events charging like a locomotive toward some unknown, but unalterable destination. And I had set it in motion.

Ryan chuckled.

"It don't look good for you, Pops. But you got one last chance. Roll your sleeve up. You got any usable veins left?"

"What are you going to do?"

Ryan took a syringe out of his jacket pocket, twisted the cap off.

"I want some blood to DNA against what we found in the body."

"You found something in the body?"

"Are you going to cooperate or not?"

"Of course I will. The test will prove I'm innocent."

"Yeah, yeah."

He sucked blood out of Powell's right arm, then capped the syringe and put it back in his pocket. Powell rolled down his sleeve and made a move to stand, but before he could get upright Ryan produced a pair of handcuffs and locked his arms behind his back.

"Until I get the word on your blood, Daddio, I want you where I can find you."

Ryan and I half walked, half dragged him down to a storage room in the basement. The door didn't look particularly strong so Ryan took the cuffs off, looped them behind an exposed pipe and put them back on again. Powell seemed to have retreated inside himself. When we left he didn't look up from where he was crouched at the base of the pipe, and he didn't say anything.

Back on the ground floor, I walked with Ryan to the front door.

"That was pretty brutal."

"If a thing's worth doing...."

"Handcuffing him and locking him up isn't going to look good when you get him to court."

"You let me worry about that side of things."

"Are we just going to leave him down there?"

"What do you want to do, suck him off?"

"He's a junkie."

"A few days ago fucking him up was your mission in life, don't start acting like a pussy now the shit's coming down. If you're that worried, give him a shot."

Ryan split to give the blood sample to whatever police lab technician he had leverage with. I went upstairs and fucked Bella, we didn't mention her father. When she fell asleep I sat in front of a TV and watched cop shows until I passed out myself.

Around three in the morning I woke and went to check on Powell. The storage room was puke free, he hadn't reached that stage yet, but the place smelt bad with his sweat and it looked like leg cramps weren't far off. He told me where his stash was. I got it from his suite and cooked him up a shot. After the smack had taken hold he tried to talk to me, but I didn't stick around to listen. I didn't want to know anything more than I already did.

Upstairs again I looked in on Bella, but Ryan had come back and was grunting away with his head between her legs. I found a bed somewhere else in the house and lay awake wishing I could take something. But I was shooting in the morning and I couldn't afford to oversleep.

Chapter 35

Lorn had a friend in Hawaii who sent her ice sometimes — totally cool that morning as my fucked-up sleep the night before had left me less than chirpy. We smoked it in a glass pipe that looked like something out of a chemistry set. An amphetamine variant that lasts and lasts. Enhanced brain speed, pumped up physical performance, improved concentration. An excellent drug that hadn't spread well because it was too cheap for dealers to make anything like they would on crack.

They say you start to hear voices if you do too much, but then they'll say anything.

James moaned that we were rushing when we got in front of the camera so we had to balance things out a little with a lude or two. By lunchtime we were faking normality pretty well — on an open-air bus that took tourists around various Hollywood death spots. We asked the driver questions and generally fucked about in the style demanded of presenters on that type of show.

At the end of the day Lorn wanted me to go with her to some Korean bathhouse she'd discovered. The thought of floating around naked and pretending nothing existed but her body and the heat and the water was enticing, but I couldn't do it. Things at Malibu were approaching critical mass and I couldn't risk being away too long. Also, I felt kind of responsible for Powell and I knew if I didn't give him his shot no one else would.

Driving back I thought about Rex. Right then, sitting stoned in a dark room with the TV on twenty-four hours a day seemed like a reasonable response when you compared it with the anxiety generated by most other ways of living.

Of course, you'd have to be careful which shows you picked to watch. Documentaries, nature programs, shows about poor people – they'd be okay, you wouldn't be confronted by any great difference between your lifestyle and theirs. But you'd have to stop yourself thinking about what great lives the producers had, and the directors, cameramen, presenters.... And you'd have to be majorly careful not to flip onto anything from Spelling or Starr.

I called him on my mobile but it sounded like he'd been disconnected. Not much of a surprise, considering.

Back at Malibu I got Powell's dose together and went straight to the basement. He had a strip of duct tape across his mouth now, but apart from that nobody seemed to have done much for him. Parts of his suit jacket were dark with sweat and there was a pool of piss over by one wall, as far away as he'd been able to squirt it from where he was cuffed. I thought about giving him some water, but I didn't want to take the tape off, so I just fixed him and went upstairs.

They were waiting for me, sitting at a round walnut table in a room that had a view of forest going vague in the twilight. It looked like they'd been there some time.

"Jackie, we were just talking about you. You were right all along. DNA makes Powell our man."

"You got the results?"

"A half hour ago, he matches the spunk. Me and Beauty here been deciding on an appropriate course of action."

"Arrest him, of course."

"That's not our favorite option."

"What are you talking about? You have to."

Bella cut in.

"Jack, things are complicated. For all of us. I admit, having him arrested was my first thought, too, but it's not something we can do. He's too closely connected to me."

"But you didn't have anything to do with the murder."

"Of course I didn't. But some of my interests would not be looked on favorably by the police. I'm sure you understand what I mean."

"What she means, Jackie, is she'd end up getting busted as well. Karen's death is linked to the kidney operations too tight for them not to come out, and they aren't something anybody's going to turn a blind eye to. Plus you can never really figure which way an investigation's going to go. Even if it starts off everyone's for Powell on the murder, things could get twisted around. Maybe Beauty being rich pisses some cop off, maybe a piece of evidence gets interpreted different from how I see it. Who knows?

"What's for sure is if we go with the law, all of us'll get fucked one way or another. Beauty'll do time for her operations alone, and the best you can hope for is withholding evidence – and they won't have much trouble upscaling that to accessory-after-the-fact. Not to mention that with Bella gone you could hardly expect to maintain your current lifestyle."

"Not to mention that any investigation would turn up your blackmailing."

"Good, Jackie, you got a handle on things – we're all in it together."

Bella put her hand on mine and spoke gently.

"It sounds ghastly, but there really is only one thing we can do."

She paused and shook back her hair as though she was trying to be very brave. "We have to kill him."

"Yeah, right."

"I'm serious. There's no other way."

"You honestly want to kill him?"

"You've seen what he does to dogs. I'm sure Ryan can describe what he did to Karen if you want. He's unstable. What do you think he's going to do if we don't deal with him? He won't have a choice, he'll have to kill us all."

"I thought you didn't want to go to jail."

"I'm sure Ryan has the necessary expertise to avoid anything like that."

"He's going to do it?"

Ryan put his elbows on the table and leaned toward me.

"Sure I am, Jackie. For another million bucks who wouldn't? Besides, I got my own reasons."

"You're getting another million dollars?"

"Beauty's promised it for services shortly to be rendered, and I don't have a problem trusting her. But what we really need to discuss, Jackie-boy, is your part in the action. See, I'm gonna need a little help."

"No fucking way."

Ryan put a surprised expression on his face.

"Why, Jackie, don't be churlish."

"You don't need me. You could do it better by yourself."

"That's where you're wrong. I do need you. See, I don't want you walking away from this thinking you're all uninvolved, and maybe a few years down the line getting an uncontrollable urge to talk. Nope, I'll feel a whole lot more comfortable with you nice and tied in. And it ain't only that. You're sucking up rewards left, right and center – a house here, a car there, you're own little TV show – and I'm fucked if I'm gonna carry the load for your life as well as my own. It's time to make a contribution."

"No."

"You don't have to pull the trigger, just be there to help, hold him down if he gets feisty, that kinda thing. It ain't exactly difficult."

"Ted, perhaps you'd give us a minute alone."

When I heard Bella use his first name I knew I was fucked. Ryan left the room and she moved closer to me.

"You have to think this through, Jack. We can't have Powell running around now we've gone this far. Sooner or later he'd destroy me. Doesn't that worry you?"

"Of course it does."

"And you do agree he has to be punished for what he did to Karen?"

"Well, yeah, but murder.... Look, you cut kidneys out and wank with them, and Ryan thinks killing is one of the perks of his job. But I'm just a guy. I've never done this kind of thing. You can't ask me to waste someone, for Christsake."

"But I am, Jack. Like Ryan said, you need to make a contribution. Just go along with him. He only wants you to watch."

"But being there will be just as bad if we're caught."

"Jack, I'm asking for some evidence of your love. I've given you a lot, but that can't continue if it doesn't work both ways."

"What about Ryan? He'll never go away after this."

"He'll go away and things will be better for us than they've ever been."

"I don't think he will. I think he'll stay forever, fucking you and taking your money."

"He'll go away."

The second time she said it I started to believe her. There was something in her voice that would have been frightening if she had been talking about me.

Bail on watching someone get whacked and say goodbye to my piece of paradise, or tough it out and get even more – that was the message. Not really a choice. So I said yes. I guess I'd been moving toward something like it ever since Karen's death – from hustling, to wanking over pictures of dead people, to doing it with a dead chick in the morgue. Taking a ride with Ryan wasn't really such a leap. Not when you considered what was at stake.

Ryan came back into the room and the rest of the evening went into fast-forward. I felt ill and cold.

We set off in the Jaguar around eleven. Ryan and I wore plastic spray jackets and over-trousers he'd bought earlier in the sporting section of a department store. We had the hoods over our heads. Powell sat uncomfortably in the passenger seat, hands cuffed behind his back, a few extra strips of tape on his mouth. Ryan drove, I was in the back. The black glass shielded us from the eyes of the world, which was just as well because two guys dressed for a monsoon on a mild Californian night and another one with his mouth taped shut might have attracted attention.

Ryan wanted it to look like a queer trick gone wrong, and he wanted a place where cooperation with the authorities wouldn't be overly forthcoming. So we made for the Drag. I could see the side of Powell's head, he looked drained of self-will and immensely tired. Twenty-four hours chained to a pipe and much less heroin than he'd ordinarily take couldn't have done him much good.

But it was more than that. He knew what was going to happen and he knew there wasn't anything he could do about it. I turned my head away and counted palm trees.

We cruised. Past the whores and on into faggot territory. We did it a couple of times so that if anyone remembered the car it'd look like a john out for trade. I knew each pass along the street was bringing us closer to going active and I had an almost uncontrollable urge to piss. I pressed my thighs together and held my knees.

My hands sweated inside the dishwashing gloves Ryan and I had accessorized our plastic ensembles with. I'd expected surgical latex, but that ripped too easily. Apparently. The knowledge Ryan had was chilling, but his obvious experience gave me a bizarre kind of reassurance. I guessed if anyone could get away with murder, he could.

We turned off the Drag about the middle of where the boys hung out and worked our way into the warren of vagrant hostels and warehouses that made up the southern flank of the area. Most of the streetlights didn't work and there wasn't anyone walking around. Ryan guided the car off the road, into the loading bay of some abandoned Mexican food company. Plenty of shadow, no windows overlooking.

Ignition off, park-brake set. Time to deal. Time to deal and hope to fuck I could maintain afterwards.

Ryan twisted in his seat like he was about to engage Powell in conversation, but he wasn't wearing his conversation face. In fact the fat white circle in the center of his tightly drawn hood looked like something made from putty.

"Guess you can figure the result of your blood test."

Powell made a high-pitched noise through his nose.

"What's that, Pops? You didn't do it? It wasn't you who cut open my little girl and jerked into the hole? Gee, could I have made a mistake?" Ryan screwed up his face like he was thinking, then shook his head. "Nope. No mistake, you fuck. You cut her guts out and you got off while you did it. Now it's my turn to get unglued."

Ryan took a knife out of the door pocket, something that looked like it was designed to skin animals – a short wide blade, sharp on both sides.

Powell started shaking his head around and making more noise, it sounded very loud in the car. My fear and his combined into a hideous tension that gave me a hardon. It surprised me a little, but I put it down to stress.

Ryan pushed the sides of Powell's jacket apart, unbuttoned his shirt and unzipped the top of his trousers, exposing him from his throat to the start of his pubic hair. White skin like Bella's, but not as tight.

"The man who sold me this knife said it was sharp enough to perform an operation with. Let's if he was telling the truth."

Powell tossed in his seat. He wasn't very strong because he was on the edge of withdrawal again, but it made things awkward for Ryan. This was where I came in. I reached over and wrapped my arms around his upper chest and held him still.

When the point of the knife got close to his sternum I heard him fart, not just air, but a long wet stuttering noise like he was letting go of everything in his colon. The air in the Jag funked up pretty bad, but we kept the windows closed all the same.

"Oh, deary me. Eat something that didn't agree? Maybe I can find it for you."

Ryan stroked the edge of his knife down in a single straight line – not deep, only about a quarter inch. There were a few small folds of skin around Powell's navel and he had to go back over them. For a couple of seconds the wound was just this weird track with white edges and a fine red center, more like a split than a cut. Then blood started running out of it.

Powell really shifted then, and I had to hang on tight. To get the best position I leaned forward with my chest against the back of the seat. This put my head next to his, my chin almost on his shoulder. The squealing he made hurt my ear. I could see blood collecting between his legs. I felt bad about what we were doing, and all I wanted was for it to be over. But my hardon didn't go away.

Ryan made another cut, following the same line, deeper now, beyond skin and fat into the first layers of abdominal muscle. Powell arced himself out of the seat and Ryan shouted at me to keep him down. I did what I could but it was difficult, blood kept splashing up and getting in my eyes and I had to let go with one hand to wipe it off. Ryan waited for Powell to slump back, then started cutting again. He paid a great deal of attention to what he was doing.

When the belly finally opened it happened in a kind of visceral explosion. The edges pulled apart like they were spring-loaded and guts and shit flew everywhere. Powell screamed and jerked in my arms and I came so hard it felt like someone had turned a hose on in my pants. If I had had the time I might have felt ashamed, but Ryan was busy pulling organs out of Powell and I had to work at keeping him upright.

"Greasy old fuck." Ryan flicked a gob of something off his glove and sat back breathing heavy and looking exhausted. "Should have made it last longer. Whaddya think, I went too fast? Shit, I wish Karen could see this."

Powell felt way too heavy to hold onto now so I let go of him. His head fell forward, but otherwise he didn't move.

"You know, Jackie, you see those cops on TV sniveling about how bad they feel when they shoot someone – just shows what bullshit it is. I felt good every time I ever did it. Especially now. How about you? You feel good? Won't be something you forget in a hurry, I bet."

I looked around the interior of the car. There was an awful lot of blood. It ran down the insides of the windows and dripped off the dash, the nice English carpet was swimming in it. No, it wasn't something I was likely to forget.

"You look pale, Jackie."

"I feel pale."

"Just keep telling yourself the fucker killed your wife, you'll be fine. Take the tape off him and let's get the fuck outta here."

Ryan climbed out of the car and started stripping off his plastic gear. I pulled Powell's head back and peeled away his gag. He made a raspy breathing noise like it was a big relief and opened his eyes. I jumped and was about to yell for Ryan, but Powell started to whisper something. His voice sounded like it was coming from the bottom of a drain.

"In the freezer...."

Then he vomited a bucketful of blood into his own open guts and died properly.

Out of the car, between its glossy black finish and the greasy concrete where trucks backed up to get loaded. I removed my wet-weather gear and wiped my face with handfuls of tissue. Ryan bundled all the blood-covered stuff into a holdall and told me he'd dump it some place away from the scene.

We walked casually back to the Drag, then up to Hollywood Boulevard and took separate cabs to the junction of Sunset and PCH where Ryan had his Plymouth parked.

On the drive to Malibu there wasn't much other traffic and I stared at the line in the middle of the road and thought about how Karen, who'd started everything, didn't really figure in anything, anymore. The reality of the bloodletting had shocked me into some kind of motivational clarity, and I could see now that revenge for her death had never really been the issue. She was just a name for the game. For a while I wondered how a person I'd lived with for two years could have become so ultimately insignificant. Then I thought of something else.

"How come you said 'my little girl'?"

"Huh?"

"Before you started cutting Powell, you called Karen your little girl."

"I said this, I said that. What the fuck?"

"You never called her anything like that before."

"Like I said, what the fuck?"

"Some things don't add up."

"Ain't that just like life?"

"I can't figure you killing someone, taking that kind of a risk, just for a hooker you used to know. It isn't you. And the way you did it.... Powell could have been made to lay out a stack of bucks, but as soon as you got proof, you whacked him. Seems like you moved so fast you didn't even think about money. It would have been more your style to bleed him for everything he was worth first."

"Maybe I was thinking about Bella. Maybe I'm more human than you think."

"Jesus, give me a break. You might like fucking her, but you wouldn't kill someone just to help her out."

"How about the million bucks?"

"You could have got that easily enough blackmailing her again about her operations. Shit, even Powell could have raised that much to stop himself getting killed."

Ryan didn't say anything, just looked through the windshield and made a show of concentrating on the road.

"And you basically tortured him to death. Why not just shoot him in the head? It would have been a whole lot safer than sitting in the car all that time. You got too much out of it for a straight execution. It meant something more."

"All right, Jack! Enough."

"I helped you do it, I've got a right to know."

Ryan glanced angrily at me, then his face changed and he sighed.

"No one has rights, Jackie. Not when it comes down to it. Food, shelter, love, life.... You ain't got a right to any of it. All you can do is grab as much as you can and hope you get hold of a decent chunk before you check out. But I guess it's over now, and you and me shared a few things, so I'll tell you. One thing though, Beauty don't get to hear about it. Ever."

"Okay."

Ryan shifted his ass onto one cheek and took out a wallet. He flipped it open and thumbed out a beat-up photograph – a girl in her early teens, colt-ish and pretty, blond hair cut short even then, shorts and a tank top, smooth limbed against the fence of a tract house, the kind they have in the shittier parts of the Valley. Unmistakably Karen.

"I don't understand."

"She was my kid."

Ryan's voice was flat, like he was frightened that if he allowed emotion to creep in it would overwhelm him.

"I had her with a whore I was fucking when I joined the force. We split up before she was born, but I stayed in touch. With Karen. I didn't have much else and I figured it was the right thing to do. It worked for a while, we had some good times together, but she got wild when she hit her teens and told me to stop coming around. I tried to keep it going, but I guess she was pissed off with me for not being there and all.

"When she was fifteen she ran away from home. I didn't see her for five years after that. Then, one night, I was working Santa Monica and I came across her selling her ass. I didn't hassle her, shit, all I wanted was some contact – you have a kid, that kinda feeling never goes away. But she didn't feel the same. She told me if I wanted to spend time with her I'd have to buy her. She only said it to get back at me, I know, but it pissed me off so much I did it – paid to fuck my own kid. It bothered me at first, but she was a great fuck and what was I gonna do? You hit fifty without family, the world's a cold place. We did it regular for a long time, but about four months before she was killed she got sick of it and told me to fuck off. The next time I saw her she was in the morgue."

Ryan put his photo away and cleared his throat.

"That's why I killed Powell. And that's why I did it the way I did. After the DNA there was no reason to wait. Million dollar joke on Beauty, huh? I woulda done it for free."

"You were never going to arrest anyone, were you? Whether it was me or Bella or whoever."

"Karen deserved more than the system. Who was gonna give a fuck about her? Shit, a dead whore comes in, they have to hold a lottery to see who gets the file 'cause no one wants it. Everyone's too busy trying to solve cases that can do them some good. And even if some cop has his ass in gear enough to get it to court, it could be the killer only gets ten years, out in less. If it's some crackhead or junkie they plead diminished responsibility. If it's someone with money they plea bargain. I wasn't going to let that happen. I wanted to make sure the punishment fit the crime."

I couldn't think of anything to say. I had a momentary urge to laugh at the ridiculousness of Karen being Ryan's daughter, but I didn't, because at the same time it seemed so disgustingly sad.

Ryan took a heart pill and I lit a cigarette. Our headlights cut a hole in the night. On our left the ocean gathered itself like a beast waiting to spring. I suggested tossing the holdall into it. Ryan said to stop worrying, he'd deal with it later.

At Malibu we spent the rest of the night in an extended fuck session – I guess Bella thought we deserved some kind of reward. I would rather have swallowed something and slept for a long time, but I felt shaky after the murder and got paranoid that maybe they'd start plotting against me if I left them alone together.

When the humping eventually stopped I curled up and thought about what Powell had whispered back in the car of blood. *In the freezer.* What did it mean? Could have been he was just so far gone with pain and fear it didn't mean anything. On the other hand, if a dying man tells you something it's pretty hard not to figure it might be important, one way or another.

Next day, Ryan moved out; took his cash and his Bentley and had me follow him in the Plymouth to a bungalow he'd rented in Westwood. It was a nice house in a nice area, not flashy, but easily middle-class – the kind of place where nobody was going to bother asking where your money came from as long as you looked okay. I took a cab back to Malibu and collected my clothes and the Mustang. Ryan had instructed me to disappear before the cops came calling to tell Bella they'd found her father – a lover hanging around the place would not look good, he said.

Bella stood with her hand on the car door as I was about to leave.

"You were very brave, Jack."

"Yeah."

"You can't know what it means to me to be free of him."

"There's still Ryan. He'll be back as soon as this blows over."

"Our future doesn't include him."

"I hope not."

We kissed, then I started the car. Before I pulled away, Bella stroked the side of my face.

"Being apart will be awful. I'll think of you every minute."

"Me too."

CHAPTER 36

Eight weeks was what Ryan figured to be a safe time. It only took the police four to determine that Powell had been murdered by assailants unknown, probably while trying to buy sex, and to dump the case with a million other unsolveds. But Ryan wasn't taking any chances.

The time dragged by in an agony of potential catastrophe. First I packed shit that I was going to get busted, then I packed it that being away from Bella for so long would spell the end of our relationship and its associated benefits.

While I was working, things weren't too bad, but downtime quickly became unbearable and in an effort to find some antidote to my anxiety I began to invite Lorn to Willow Glen. The only thing that made it less stupid now than the time she suggested it herself was that I figured Bella wouldn't risk visiting me during the separation period.

Lorn ended up staying about four nights out of seven and seemed to enjoy the continuity of our time together. I think she wanted to upscale whatever it was we had between us, to move to a place where we'd feel it necessary to start revealing ourselves to each other. I, of course, had no intention of playing that game. Sometimes, though, when I was holding her before sleep, I caught myself wishing that she could have been the one providing houses and cars and TV time. Then I'd have had everything.

On the nights I was alone, and sometimes in the day too when I wasn't working, I drove aimlessly through L.A. – I figured if I kept moving my fears wouldn't be able to take hold of me. But it didn't work. On one occasion things got so bad I had to stop at a pay phone and call Bella for reassurance. It helped because she told me she loved me and how good things were going to be when we got back together.

She even said she'd started watching *28 FPS* she missed me so much. I watched it too, but it was depressing. I timed how long my face appeared on the screen each half-hour show. Usually it wasn't longer than four minutes.

Lorn and I only went out together once during this time – to a club Dan Aykroyd owned. While we were there I had her take Polaroid photos of me standing at the bar with movie people in the background.

At home that night I shut myself in the toilet and stared at the pictures, looking for whatever it was that made this golden breed so much better than me. But it was a secret I couldn't learn. So I shuffled the prints up with the ones Ryan had given me and flicked through them – me a few feet away from Woody Harrelson – the dead chick with the crowbar up her ass – my face emerging from shadow behind Oliver Stone and some director from New Zealand in close conversation – an angle on the dead couple fucking, bags over their heads.... Flash cards that reflected something about me. But what? Probably everything there was to know, but I couldn't figure it out.

Toward the end of the eight weeks, with Bella reentry looming, I stopped asking Lorn over. Unfortunately that didn't end her visits. She started turning up uninvited, and to drive the message home I had to make it obvious my enthusiasm for our increased contact was not what it had been. I didn't want to sever things completely, but neither did I want the level of danger her presence in my house represented vis-à-vis Bella.

It was a fine line to tread and I guess I pretty much failed at it. The last time she came around she left well before dawn, not in floods of tears or anything, but I could tell by the expression on her face that things hadn't panned out the way she'd hoped. It made me feel bad for a while, but what could I do? Even if I'd loved her it couldn't have been any different.

Chapter 37

Back at Malibu. It was a relief to be close to Bella and her money again. We fucked a lot and generally did the reunited thing. Ryan had terminated his live-in stint, but a couple of times a week he swooped in from Westwood like a corpulent specter to exercise his humping rights and be taken out to places where the wealthy gathered – an additional payment for doing Powell that hadn't really been made clear to me before. He'd quit the police force and had some half-assed idea that mixing with the right people might lead to a technical advisor's spot on a cop show.

He gave me another set of photos, he said they were the last I'd get – without cop-access things of that nature weren't quite as easy to come by. These were lifted from the evidence folder of a recent bust – a couple of paramedics making extra bucks catering to a more extreme taste. When they got a dead body in the back of their truck they'd hang up a sheet so you couldn't tell where it was and bring out the camera.

I scored three glossies – a blonde girl in her twenties with her legs held open, the electrical flex with which she'd hanged herself still embedded in the flesh of her neck, the same girl flipped over, a head-and-tits shot of a dark-haired woman, unmarked but unmistakably dead, her eyes open and her lips slightly parted.

Work with Lorn on *28 FPS* carried on much the same as before. She was a little cold sometimes, but other than that we maintained a serviceable relationship, we even still snatched a fuck now and then. The only professional gripe I had was the continued non-expansion of my screen time. I figured getting Bella to do something about it would be easier while the flush of our reunion was still running hot. So one night, shortly after my return to Malibu, I looked pissed off long enough for her to notice.

"Aren't you happy, Jack?"

"Oh, sure...."

"But?"

"Ryan still being around frightens me."

"It won't be forever."

"You sound pretty certain."

"Would you expect me to be anything else? But we've talked about him before, so it's something else."

"Just hassles on the show."

"You don't you enjoy it anymore?"

"Of course I enjoy it. It's a dream come true. But I'm not getting anywhere. I hardly have any more screen time now than when I started."

Bella was silent for a while, like she was considering granting me an enormous favor.

"Perhaps I could ask Howard to have a word with Burns. It might be a little tricky, they'd have to take time away from the girl and it was originally her show. But I don't see why a few extra minutes should be a problem. I'll have to ask you for something in return, though."

"Anything."

"As wonderful as it is to have him gone, Powell's absence creates a difficulty."

"I thought everything with the police was cool."

"I'm talking about my operations."

"You're going to keep doing them?"

"Of course."

"Isn't that a bit dangerous? They've only just finished investigating."

"No more than it ever was. But that's beside the point, it isn't something I can give up."

"Don't tell me, you want me to get the donors."

"Yes."

"Jesus, I just helped kill your father. I thought that was going to be the end of it. Ask Ryan to do it."

"Don't be absurd. All you have to do is drive around, find the right sort of person and offer them money. They jump at the chance, believe me."

"Unless I pick the wrong one and get busted. Can't you get therapy instead?"

"The risk is minimal. And I don't think it's much to ask from someone who loves you."

"I do love you."

"Good. I need one soon, Jack. It's been two months."

Next day, after I finished some studio work on the lot, Burns called me into the production office and told me they were going to increase my participation in the show. I was to take over the new-release review slot, a high profile segment which had been exclusively Lorn's until then.

The air of resignation with which he relayed the news didn't spoil the elation I felt at the prospect of pumping up my public visibility and for a while, as I walked past the soundstages to the parking area, I kidded myself that I was no longer a faker in this place of genuine movie stars.

But the buzz didn't last long. By the time I'd pulled off the Hollywood Freeway onto Highland, the consequences of my promotion had thudded home. Lorn was going to be well and truly pissed off at the theft of her screen time, especially following so close on the downscaling of our affair. And worse than that, I was now so indebted to Bella that it would be impossible to drag my feet on the issue of finding kidney donors for her.

CHAPTER 38

Night. Bella was in her basement clinic at Apricot Lane. Waiting. I'd agreed to find a victim, but at least for this first one I had a softer option than trawling the Drag.

Over to Benedict Canyon with the top up on the Mustang. I turned the radio up loud and tried not to think about what I was doing. It worked for a while but when I parked outside Rex's place there wasn't much chance of escaping the kind of person I'd become. Or maybe always had been. But, shit, if it was easy to get to the top everybody would be there.

It had been a long time since my last visit and his place looked deserted. The small patch of grass between the house and the sidewalk needed cutting and was littered with newspapers and empty cans. Tendrils of bougainvillea hung down over the top of the front door. I'd tried to call him earlier, but his phone was still down and I wasn't sure if he even lived there anymore.

But he did. And things had gotten worse since my last visit. Only the TV for light, carpet sticky underfoot, wallpaper hanging in coiled sheets where it had been partly ripped from the walls, the stink of vomit.

And in the middle of it all, Rex, sprawled on the floor, back propped against the remains of the couch, looking like something out of Belsen. He'd lost a lot of weight and sometime in the last week or two he'd shaved his head. Under the stubble his scalp looked gray and too tight. The needle sites at the crook of each arm were over-used and weeping.

"Come to save me?"

His voice was nasal and when he leered up at me his teeth didn't look good.

"In a way. Do you want to earn some money?"

"How much?"

"Thirty thousand."

He didn't scoff. From the way we'd left things last time he must have known I wouldn't come around for an idle bullshitting session. I watched him translate that amount of money into smack. Enough to last him to the end of his life. More than enough from the look of him.

"Wasting that cop friend of yours might be a little beyond me right now. Anything else, fire away."

I laid out the kidney thing and it was cool by him. I made a call to Bella, then we got in the car.

On the way to Apricot Lane he stared out the window like L.A. was a new city to him, some vast tract of urban boredom he simply couldn't recognize anymore. I took Benedict Canyon Drive up to Mulholland to give him a better view. I told myself that it might rekindle some feeling of friendship on his part – we'd driven the same stretch the night he'd taken me to my first paid sex gig.

But maybe all I was doing was trying to connect again with a time when I wasn't responsible for murder, when I didn't get hard over pictures of dead people, and when I didn't have to serve up a one-time friend as fodder for a mad millionairess so I could stay on TV.

He hardly spoke during the drive. Once, though, he turned away from the window and looked at me so tenderly I thought I'd start crying.

"I'm sorry."

But when I smiled at his words, about to tell him everything was okay, he threw up the screens again and went back to the meaningless lights.

Bella met us at the bottom of the steps that led down from the garage, already in surgical green. Her eyes were dark and bright. She didn't try to make conversation with Rex or put him at ease. He was there for the money, she was there to get off. That's all there was to it.

She had him strip and take a shower. His scrawny ass, as he walked into the bathroom that adjoined the pre-op area, made her frown.

"Is he a close friend?"

"Why?"

"Will you miss him?"

"You're only taking his kidney out."

"He's in very poor condition. Without Powell I'm going to have to use intravenous anesthetic. I'll try to minimize the time he's under, but there is a risk of respiratory failure with that type of drug for someone so debilitated. And if he does make it through the operation his remaining kidney may not be strong enough to cope."

"He might die?"

"It's possible he'll suffer renal failure some days after the operation. The combination of the anesthetic and the heroin in his system may also prove dangerous."

"But he could be okay?"

"I can't promise anything one way or the other."

"Jesus, what do you want me to do?"

"I don't care what you do as long as I have a donor. If you want to go out again and find me someone else, fine. If you want to warn him of the dangers and he chooses to pull out.... Well, that's up to you."

She left the sentence hanging and it was obvious that delaying the night's proceedings was not going to win me any points. Even so, I could have gone out and found someone else – there wouldn't have been any shortage of trash down on the Drag just waiting to jump at thirty thousand dollars. But it was a risk and a hassle, and Rex would have been pissed off if I took away his chance at the money.

What swung it in the end, though, was that I realized the outcome of the operation didn't matter. He was going to die soon anyhow and I figured his death might as well do someone some good as not.

I helped her get him ready – shaved off a patch of fine hair on the left side of his abdomen and painted on some sticky brown antiseptic liquid. His eyes met mine as Bella fitted a lance into the back of his hand and fed in the pre-op. I didn't see much there, just abandonment to circumstance, a flicker of uncertainty, and maybe a little relief. I could have said something reassuring, but that kind of thing is meaningless when the person you're saying it to is chasing death. So I kept my mouth closed and watched him black out.

Bella wanted me to gown up and stay with her while she worked. But enticing Rex into a situation where he might sustain terminal physical damage was one thing, being there to see it happen was another altogether. So after I'd helped her wheel him through the swing doors into the green brilliance of the operating room and position him under the light cluster I went upstairs and watched TV. I fell asleep during some documentary about whales and didn't wake up until Bella shook me.

She had a lazy smile on her face and her eyes had gone soft. She looked like a sated vampire.

"How's Rex?"

"It went well. He's stable, but I don't know how long that will last."

"I want to see him."

He looked bad, his skin was gray and didn't have much life behind it. He was still groggy from the anesthetic but awake enough to ask when he'd get his money. He wanted to go home straight away but Bella refused. We left him with a drip in his arm and a machine on a stand that gave him a dose of morphine every five minutes if he pressed a button. Bella locked the door behind us.

That night we slept in one of the bedrooms upstairs from the basement clinic. Bella didn't make a move on me once, which suited me fine because right then I didn't feel like being close to her at all.

Chapter 39

Early evening sun, palms against the sky, a gritty wind that felt soft all the same. L.A. As good as the life you lead in it. Blacks killing each other over in Watts, movie stars fucking each other in B.H. Being one place or the other is just a matter of luck. But if luck happens to you here it happens big – beach bum to screen hero, cocksucker to supermodel, crack dealer to rap star...one extreme to another.

And I was in there somewhere, riding the tides of the city, playing a small part in what the place was famous for – journeys out of obscurity.

Bella had been strange toward me the last few days. When I spoke to her she answered in a tone of poorly disguised anger. She wouldn't allow me into her bedroom and she wouldn't fuck me. Such an abrupt reversal of attitude was frightening. All I could think was that she regretted allowing me to see the part of her that found it necessary to squander other people's kidneys. Maybe she was angry at making herself vulnerable.

Despite this fresh source of insecurity, though, I was feeling pretty good. I'd spent the afternoon with my Century City agent being styled and made up, photographed and videoed. There was a men's grooming gig doing the rounds and they'd wanted test material to sell me for it. If it happened it would be unbelievable – nationwide TV, billboard and press coverage, roll-overs into next year and beyond. The face of a glossy product, a kind of male equivalent to Isabella Rossellini or Elizabeth Hurley.

I hadn't bothered to wash off the makeup and when I stopped at lights I looked slyly at the other cars to see if the people in them were staring at me. I caught a few faces turned my way and I figured they must have been scrolling through lists of famous names, trying to see where I fit in.

Santa Monica Boulevard straight through Beverly Hills, Doheny up to Sunset then Laurel Canyon Drive when it came up on my left. I called Bella, not to tell her what I'd done with the day – I figured it was smarter to keep quiet about any potential future success that didn't involve her – but to check on Rex.

The news wasn't great. After a week and a half he'd had his fill of recuperation and had insisted on going home that afternoon. Bella, freed from having to monitor him, was already back at Malibu. Ryan had just arrived and she wanted me there to share the burden. I didn't want to fuck up my mood any sooner than I had to, so I told her yeah but it would be a while because I had to swing by Willow Glen and pick up some clothes. Of course I had more than I needed at Malibu, but my agent had rush-printed a few stills for me and I wanted to spend some time alone with them.

At my place the machine had messages from Lorn – different schedules had kept us from connecting. She'd heard about the expansion of my screen time and I could tell she wasn't at all happy. I couldn't blame her, losing exposure is the same as losing part of your worth as a human being. I knew I should call her, but I didn't. Maybe if I had had some coke I could have mustered the energy, but I'd decided not to do so many drugs – it was important to keep my skin clear.

Instead I looked at the prints I'd brought home. I put them next to shots of various male stars to see how I compared. I wasn't discouraged. Then I got my collection of sexy dead people out, mixed all the pics up together and spread them out on the polished wooden floor. I ran the tape of the woman getting slaughtered in the jewelry store. I tried to take in everything at once – Hollywood faces, myself, dead bodies getting fucked, the expensive house around me....

I wanked and spurted over the TV screen. Then I had a shower, and when I came out the stuff on the floor seemed dangerous – incriminating evidence screaming out to be discovered. Bad enough if I was a nobody, but if I got the grooming contract the pictures could spell disaster. It would have been safer to burn the lot, but I couldn't make myself do it. I put everything away in a drawer for another time.

Ryan pumped out two loads, one over Bella's tits and face, the other, half an hour later, between the spread cheeks of her ass. I guess he'd been saving it up because she was drenched. It came out of him like a fountain and, watching from a chair in the corner of her Malibu bedroom room, I was surprised his heart could take it.

Later, the three of us did dinner in Santa Monica and a post-screening party in the Hollywood Hills. Bella ignored me the entire time. We stood in a corner of a room that looked like a temple and Ryan made his usual obscene conversation until Bella had had enough and wandered off to take a piss.

"How are the nightmares, Jackie?"

"What nightmares?"

"You don't see that old bastard kicking about on the front seat when you close your eyes?"

"I don't dream."

He grunted and glanced about the room, then pulled me around with him so our backs were toward the way Bella went. When he spoke again his voice was low.

"I got something here that'll fuck your sleep for sure. You ever do those things when you were a kid, where you have to find what's wrong with a drawing?"

"What's your point?"

"The cunt's lying."

He took a video cassette out of his jacket like we were in some kind of spy movie and handed it to me. It was one of the small ones you use in a camcorder.

"Copy of the tape we got at Powell's. I figured out why it bugged me. Take it home, see if you can pick it."

"Don't play games, Ryan, just tell me."

"Where's the fun in that? I'll give you till the day after tomorrow. Come around to my place then, we'll have a little chat."

I put the tape in my pocket and looked over my shoulder to check for Bella. She was six feet away. She made it look like she'd only just come back from the toilet, but I got the feeling she'd been close enough to hear for longer than that.

We hung out for a while longer, then Ryan said he wanted to take us to a fuck club he knew from his days on vice. Even though I wasn't really interested it still shook me when Bella said she'd only go if it was just him and her. I tried to say something about it, but it wasn't open to discussion.

After they split I went back to Willow Glen and found Lorn sitting in her car out front. Inside the house she tried to stay calm, but she was too angry to maintain her self-control for very long and switched to loud almost immediately.

"Why did you do it, Jack?"

"What did you expect, I was going to turn it down?"

"You don't just get offered something like that. It's one of the most important parts of the show. You know someone."

"I don't know anyone."

"You're lying."

"You've got nearly all the rest, don't you think you're over-reacting?"

I tried to make it sound like I was talking sense and she was being irrational, but it didn't come off. We both knew how important those extra minutes were.

"You know what kind of message something like this sends to the industry. It'll read like I'm being phased out."

"Bullshit. Nobody'll even notice."

"Do you think I'm stupid? You're fucked in the head if you think I'm not going to get that slot back. You aren't the only one with a friend at the channel, you know."

She slammed out into the night leaving me wondering what the fuck was going on – Bella wouldn't let me touch her, and now, quite obviously, neither would Lorn. I couldn't help feeling somewhat rejected.

To distract myself I watched the tape Ryan had given me. Same as before – Karen lying, back to camera, in front of a mirror, doing herself with a dildo.

What's wrong with this picture? I ran it again and again, it didn't say anything to me. The bracelet glinted on her wrist, but Ryan and I had both seen that the first time. What else could there be?

Outside the sky paled. My eyes got tired and I gave up. Ryan would have to explain it to me when I saw him.

The cunt's lying....

CHAPTER 40

Rex's place. With his phone out I couldn't ring to check on his recovery so I figured I'd swing by and do it in person. There was no answer when I knocked on his door. It wasn't locked, or even properly closed, so I wandered in and found him curled up on the floor of the lounge. Dead and naked.

I'd known it was coming, but even so it was difficult to process what I saw. Unlike the people in my photos or the girl at the morgue, I'd known Rex. I was used to him moving and breathing. I'd listened to him talk, sat in a car with him, shared a beer. And to see him now, so quiet, so empty of the spark that had made him Rex was something I found impossible to comprehend. He should have been monstrously transformed for so great a change to have taken place – but his body was still his body, his face was still his face.

My first impulse was to touch him. I ran my hand down one side of his torso, over the outside of his thigh. He felt cold and hard. The stitches under his ribs shone like a row of black thorns.

I looked around the room for the story of his death. The clothes he wore to Apricot Lane were piled on the springs of the couch. The TV was on, its light dappled the floor and walls. On top of the set there was a clear plastic bag with what looked to be about a quarter kilo of brown smack inside. Next to it, a paper sack full of Pepsi and pots of chocolate pudding.

Overdose, or failure of his remaining kidney? What did it matter? He'd gotten what he wanted, whatever way it came. But it wasn't as simple as that. Back when I put him up for the gig I thought it would be. But it wasn't.

I knew that if I hadn't offered him up to Bella he'd probably still be alive, and the knowledge of my part in his death wasn't pleasant. I should have laid out the risks for him. I shouldn't have involved him at all. Shit, he was once the closest thing I'd had to a friend – he'd shown me a way out of the mainstream, given me that push into making money with my cock, even set me on the path that eventually led to Bella.

For a long time I studied his face, trying to force some link with the golden boy he used to be, wondering if I was going to cry. But I couldn't and I didn't. All I got was a closeup of clogged pores and stubble that grew in odd directions. I stood in the middle of the room wondering if there was anything I should do. Nothing occurred to me. I didn't want the smack, it was too much weight to be walking around with anyhow. I headed for the door. I was set on going through it, I really was, out into the world, away from that stinking, destroyed room. But it didn't happen. I was halfway along the hall when I realized I might never get the chance again.

Back in the lounge I maneuvered him into position. His stiffness might have been a problem in a different situation, but with the way he was curled it actually helped – when I pulled him up onto his knees and elbows his ass was angled just right. I wedged him against one end of the couch with the TV and got him set pretty firm. Then I went into the kitchen and found a bottle of cooking oil.

At Malibu that night there was a guest for dinner. I walked into the dining room and found them sitting cozily together over fish and salad at one end of the table – Bella and Lorn. Lorn and her new best friend at the station.

For a while I just stood there with my head blank. Then things started working again with a jerk and I realized there was a very good chance I was fucked. Added to Bella's less than friendly interaction with me recently, this pairing tonight had to mean she'd found out about my affair with Lorn. I could only imagine what the consequences would be.

Bella didn't bother explaining my presence, just waved me to a chair and carried on with whatever conversation they had going. Lorn's first reaction at seeing me was one of surprise. But that didn't last long. She might not have been a rocket scientist, but she was smart enough when it came to the hidden currents that drove the media business, and I saw her eyes harden as it dawned on her that I was connected – that all my protestations the night before about just lucking into the review slot were bullshit.

I helped myself to wine from an almost untouched bottle that stood between them, then sat and watched Bella send lezzie looks across the table at her new pal. Lorn played them for all they were worth, figuring, no doubt, that sexual influence here would translate into bucks and screen time back at Channel 52. At any other time not such a wild assumption, but right then I had the feeling that Bella had arranged this little meeting more for my benefit than to woo Lorn.

On the surface, her motives were obvious – retaliation in kind for my infidelity. But there was also the possibility it was something a whole lot more dangerous than that. If she'd overheard any of Ryan's conversation at the post-screening party it could be a warning not to start poking around. Either way, it was a clear message that I was a long way from irreplaceable.

After the meal they went up to Bella's suite. I wasn't invited. So I got in my car and escaped to Willow Glen. It seemed about as good as any other move I could have made right then.

Chapter 41

Next morning I woke early for my meeting with Ryan. I didn't know what was going to happen between Bella and me – the Lorn thing might blow over, it might not – but if Ryan had found something that could be dangerous to her, as he'd hinted, I wanted to get hold of it as soon as possible.

Westwood was sleepy in a haze of morning sunshine, the trees along Ryan's street made pleasant shadows on the road. Kids, dogs, somebody mowing a lawn – a normal place for normal people. Strange that a guy like Ryan should choose it as a place to live.

His bell made a hollow noise somewhere inside the bungalow. I could tell from the way it sounded that all the rooms were empty, but I kept on ringing it anyhow. No one answered. So I wandered around the back – nice garden, bougainvillea, jacaranda, pepper trees, an oval pool. Maybe that was what clinched it for him – happy-family surroundings for a man who'd missed out on them and spent his life in the city's colon instead.

I looked through windows, but there was no movement. What furnishings I could see were expensive but without taste. The pictures on the walls were arty photos of chicks with big tits.

I couldn't get in, the back door was locked and the windows had security grilles. Separate from the house, though, pushed against the edge of the property, was a windowless garage – stucco painted white. The Roll-A-Door was down but a wooden access door at the side opened when I tried it. I closed it behind me and waited for my eyes to adjust.

Smells – dry cement, gasoline, oil. Two cars faded up out of the gloom – the gray Plymouth and the bloated silver Bentley with its top up. Ryan had been driving the Bentley the night he laid his riddle about Karen's videotape.

I found the light switches and pressed them, fluoros flickered and caught. And I found Ryan. The driver's seat in the Bentley was reclined, but his head was still visible through the windshield. I opened the car door and stuck my head in. Dead. Shirt open all the way, pants rucked about his knees, dried semen crusting his pubic hair and the skin just above.

I could see shit in a wet smear under his balls – the car stank of it. There was more on the seat either side of his ass, like he'd been sliding around in it. His face was swollen and bluish and his eyes were puffy. I felt surreal. Two bodies in twenty-four hours was pushing things.

All the soft fat on his guts looked hard now, like it had been molded from cold lard. His black hair was mussed and a lot more scalp showed than when it was combed. No sicked-out Bela Lugosi anymore, nothing to be scared of, nothing to chase you through nightmares and threaten you with a murder rap. Just a mound of flesh with a badly colored head on top.

The first thing I felt was relief. What can I say? The guy had been scaring the shit out of me for the last six months. Even after Powell had taken the fall for Karen, his continued connection with Bella had been a threat to my future. But now that was all over – no more blackmail threats, no more having to share Bella. His departure made things a lot simpler.

Until I saw the vial on the dash.

Clear glass with blue printing. A top you punctured with the needle of a syringe. Same as Bella had used in the motel with Rudy.

I pictured it happening. After the party Bella says let's go to your place instead of the fuck club, Ryan's only too happy to oblige. They park in the garage, the door comes down and one of them figures it'd be a kick to do it in Ryan's new car. Sitting on him, riding his cock, him all tangled up with the steering wheel and her arms and legs, it wouldn't have been hard to stick a needle in his neck, then just hang on while he turned into a jackhammer, until he started squirting shit and his heart exploded. Just like she knew it would.

I climbed into the passenger side of the car and went through Ryan's pockets, hoping for a note or something to point me toward what he'd found. No luck – change, a wallet, bits of paper, his pills, a small amount of coke, but nothing that helped me. I sat there for a while breathing his stink, staring at the vial on the dash, hoping closeness to his body would bring inspiration. I put my hand on his bare thigh to see if contact helped. It didn't. He felt like he looked – unpleasant. And that was all there was to it, no message, no flash of enlightenment, just a fat dead man sitting in his own shit.

But the time wasn't altogether wasted. There was something about the vial that bothered me. It didn't click for a while, and then it did. It was placed too obviously, too close to the edge of the dash. It couldn't have been there before Ryan died, his jerking around would have knocked it off. And besides, Bella must have had the syringe already charged before they got down to it – filling up in front of him would have been a sure way to get asked awkward questions.

Why was it there at all? She certainly wasn't dumb enough to leave a clue like that if she wanted to make it look like a heart attack. Only one answer – she knew I'd go there, she wanted me to find it. It was her way of letting me know what she'd done, of warning me against digging too deeply. Maybe she even expected me to take the evidence away, increasing my complicity, tying myself ever more tightly to her.

Ryan's carcass didn't hold the remotest sexual attraction for me, so I left without touching his cock or trying to put mine inside him. I wiped my prints, put the vial in my pocket and closed the car door. Then I turned off the garage lights and stepped out into a bright soft morning which I suppose was autumn in some other part of the world. The sun dazzled my eyes and I kept them shut as much as I could on the walk back to the Mustang. Same way I tried as much as I could not to think about what it meant that Bella was a killer.

Chapter 42

From Westwood I beelined to an art-house cinema near the university where something trendy was previewing. It was my first review assignment and Lorn was supposed to come along and hold my hand. But it didn't surprise me that she wasn't waiting where we'd arranged. I was glad to be alone, having to deal with the shit she'd certainly dish up would have been too much right then.

When the picture finished I hit a cafe and attempted to make some notes, but I couldn't remember anything about the film. I couldn't even concentrate long enough to make up something.

Instead, I smoked a lot and gazed out the window. On the other side of the glass kids walked by, all totally cool with beatnik beards and a lot of facial piercing. I couldn't help wondering what it would have been like to go to college, to get a good job and a wife and move in professional circles. The best I could imagine was that you felt clean. You didn't have to fuck men in cars. You didn't have to help kill someone simply because it was financially more advantageous than going to the police.

I thought about the things I'd done. I saw Rex playing doggy on the floor, Ryan's cock in his ass. I saw myself fucking him in the mouth. I saw him dead, like he was when I found him the day before, those black stitches knitted into his side....

And that was it. That was what made those brain switches complete the necessary circuit. I threw money on the table and pushed the Mustang back to Willow Glen as fast as I could through the traffic.

In front of the TV, holding the remote, running the tape. I was certain of what I'd find. And I did.

I moved frame by frame through Karen sliding the dildo into herself until I got to a part where the mirror in front of her gave a clear shot of her belly. I froze the tape. She was wearing the bracelet Bella had said she'd given her the day she left Malibu, after recovering from the removal of her kidney. But her abdomen was smooth, there were no stitches. She hadn't been operated on.

The scene wouldn't have meant much to anyone else, but it did to me. It made me feel that everything around me – the ground under my feet, the walls of my house, the fabric of my life in this city – had suddenly become unstable. Even my ability to think, to draw conclusions, to understand events and actions seemed now to be built on fault lines at least as treacherous as those that ran beneath L.A.

Ryan and I had figured the bracelet proved the tape had been shot after the operation. And because Bella said she'd never seen Karen again after she gave it to her, we'd convinced ourselves it must have been Powell who filmed the dildo performance. That led to his DNA check, and that led, a very short time later, to his death.

But what I realized now, and what Ryan had obviously seen too, was that Bella had been lying. The absence of stitches meant she had to have given Karen the bracelet sometime before the operation. So the tape could have been shot anytime. In fact, it now seemed likely to me that Bella had shot it herself – just as Powell had said during Ryan's interrogation.

It would have been simple enough for her to take Karen to his apartment some day while he was out, then add the tape to her collection and wait for him to sneak a copy like he did with all her others. After that, the only thing necessary to make it look like her father alone had had any postoperative contact with Karen, was to erase the original.

And the only reason she'd do that was if she'd been involved in the murder and wanted an out if things got sticky. She could have killed Karen by herself, or she could have done a double act with Daddy. Whatever, it didn't really matter. What mattered was that she'd manipulated Ryan and me into getting rid of an old man she hated, and at the same time diverted any threat to herself that might have arisen from Karen's murder.

Things that had seemed without importance now became significant – Bella's instruction that Ryan and I search Powell's apartment, the lack of camera equipment there, the fact that Powell, a sixty-year-old junkie, sexually fixated on his daughter, would probably not have had either the energy or the desire to pursue Karen.... Things which should have been obvious to us.

What it came down to was that neither Ryan nor I had wanted her to be involved. We'd had Powell's DNA and his thing with the dogs, and stacked against Bella's money and cunt, that had been enough for us. We didn't look any further because we didn't want to find anything else.

CHAPTER 43

I woke with a feeling of doom, certain that something bad was going to happen. Just after nine it did, nice and early. Two motorcycle messengers on my doorstep. I could hear them doing the fellow road-warrior thing as I walked along the hall. When I opened the door they gave me mock salutes and bits of paper to sign. Two guys in one-piece leather suits and alien helmets, logos every place you could stick them.

I got an envelope off one and a small package off the other. They said *dude* to each other a couple of times then climbed back on their bikes and tore off down the canyon, no doubt completely unaware of the severe fucking they'd just delivered.

I sat on my front steps and opened my presents. First the package. From Bella. A videotape, unused, still in its cellophane wrapper, and a small fold of paper containing blonde pubic hair. Clever messages that said I KNOW EVERYTHING. The hair was Lorn's, the tape a reference to Ryan's discovery. And next, the only thing that could follow such a statement – a letter from Burns informing me I'd been chucked from the show.

I couldn't hear the birds, I couldn't see the white houses with red roofs that made holes in the foliage of the hills. I sat very still and tried to assimilate. Tried to swallow the fact that this was the end of my time in dreamland, the end of my one, unheard-of chance at some sort of justification for living. No more screen time, no more parties and premieres, no possibility of ever becoming as good as everyone else. Desolation didn't cover it. And I'd brought it on myself.

For a long time I was incapable of movement, but eventually I got up and went inside to call Bella. The phone rang for a long time but no one answered.

Grasping at straws, I called my agent in Century City. If a miracle happened and I got the men's grooming gig I'd be independent and Bella could go fuck herself. The response was encouraging. My tests were with the agency running the campaign and they liked them a lot. I was riding high on the short-list. But those decisions had to be made cautiously and, beg as I might, I couldn't get anything firmer than supportive advice to be patient. Not much use on a day when it felt like I was sinking in a sea of shit.

I smoked and drank a bottle of Coke. I thought about Powell's last words. "The freezer...." If there was a freezer anywhere with something useful in it, it would be at Apricot Lane for sure. I could have driven over there and done a little checking. But I didn't.

I told myself that this might all be a test, that Bella might only want to see if she could trust me and that if I kept my head down and kept cool it was possible that everything could still be fixed. Silence and non-action might make her see she had nothing to fear from me.

I scanned a few mags – Brooke Shields had had a bridal shower in New York. Drew Carey had received a bid of four million for a proposed book about life. Gary Oldman was slated to suck up part of a ninety-million-dollar budget playing Dr. Smith in a big-screen *Lost in Space* and Brad Pitt now owned five houses on the same block.

But these reports from heaven couldn't kill the anxiety that twisted me. I needed a stronger distraction to shield me from images of a disintegrating future. I needed something that would tear me out of myself for a while.

So I went down to the Drag before dark and asked indiscreet questions about snuff movies. I spent a while looking, but the closest I came was a guy selling cassettes from the trunk of his car in a side street. I checked the product on a Watchman he'd got wired to a VCR, but I was disappointed. It was just road accident footage he'd spliced into straight hard-core.

I gave up and checked an ATM. The monthly payment from Bella had gone into my account. It gave me hope that things hadn't bottomed out yet. But I couldn't really be sure. She might just have not gotten around to canceling the auto payment.

In the early evening I sat in a cafe on Melrose drinking black coffee and reading the paper. The dead man found a couple of days ago in Westwood had been identified as an ex-cop. He'd died from a heart attack, possibly during sex. Police would like to interview the woman they assumed he was with.

A few lines on page five. It didn't seem much of a marker for someone as monstrous as Ryan. Tomorrow it'd be even less, screwed up in the bottom of a bin, or stuck to the sole of somebody's shoe. Death. Just like I'd always known it was. When you're gone, you're gone. Unless you get yourself on screen first.

And on the gossip pages, a snap that made me grind my teeth – Bella and Lorn, out the night before at the opening of a new boutique, chummy together, radiant smiles, cute little cocktail dresses. Prime exposure, their names under the photo.

I ate some salad-type thing that made me gag, but I figured with the men's grooming contract starting to look possible it'd be smart to be smart. Then I sat for half an hour smoking and thinking. Nothing of much use occurred to me, so I dragged my ass out of the cafe and into the Mustang.

I cruised. Movement through the streets was a lullaby. Neon under a burnt-lemon sky slid by in time-lapse streaks, tweaking peripheral vision and interrupting thought, keeping a loose lid on my anxiety. Down to Santa Monica to look at the sea. No answers there. No beauty either – the water lay heavily against the coast like a planet-wide oil slick. The tramps looked worse than ever.

I took PCH and spent half the night driving to Santa Barbara. I left the top down and my body got cold. The numbness was pleasant. When I got there I walked out into the ocean on a pier that was part of the marina and looked back inland at the mountains and the houses with their warm lights scattered through the foothills. Around me white boats rose on the swell.

Chapter 44

At Willow Glen there wasn't anything to do but wander through the rooms and look at my possessions – my furniture, my technology, my clothes. It wasn't a particularly comforting occupation as I was acutely aware that, like the house itself, everything was in Bella's name.

Out by the pool the palms rubbed their leaves together, as though they couldn't wait to see what was going to happen to me next. I watched them move in the breeze that came up the canyon in the afternoons and figured it might not be so bad to be like them, to just grow out of the ground and not have to deal with the endless disappointments that come with mobility and free will.

Blue sky and sunshine. I sat in the middle of the lawn, my ears plugged with toilet paper, and stared up at the sky until bright dots of light danced in front of my eyes. It was pointless, I knew. I couldn't escape the stigma of not being famous simply by pretending nothing existed, but without those brief moments of non-thinking I would have been crushed by the reality of what was happening to me.

Time passed slowly. I tried to tell myself that each minute was taking me closer to a point where Bella would forgive me and allow me back into the only world where real happiness was possible. But it wasn't easy maintaining that kind of belief when there was nothing to support it.

I stopped leaving the house. Someone on the street might have recognized me and tried to make conversation and it would have been painful maintaining the lie that I was still a presenter. Food came in by courier and a news stand delivered every magazine they carried on the lives of famous people. I had invites to parties and screenings that I'd gotten while I was on the show, but I didn't use them. They were for another person, after all.

I didn't make plans for the future, I didn't think about the past. Even when my Century City agent called to say it was down to me and one other guy for the men's grooming gig I couldn't get excited. With the way things had been going lately it seemed an utter waste of time to seriously think I might luck into something of that magnitude. All I did was consume media, burying myself under an avalanche of gossip in the hope that it would make me forget who I was and what had happened to me.

One afternoon I spent an hour running the Tri Star identity tag over and over on video – that flying horse coming at you through the sky. I wanted to be in there, in with the clouds and the golden light – that distillation of Californian movie dreams. Johnny Depp and Kate Moss must have been in there somewhere, along with all the others, all loved up and wrapped safely in their fame.

One of my magazines had an article on the house Johnny had bought that used to belong to Bela Lugosi. I would have liked to rig the place with a camera so I could see what he and Kate did when they weren't being photographed or filmed. I didn't want to see them fucking, although that would have been pretty cool. What I was interested in was what happened at breakfast and times like that, times when other people plowed the boredom of their lives with meaningless activity.

I wanted to think that even with their money and their celebrity Johnny and Kate still shared some of the same everyday banalities as the rest of us. But I bet they didn't. I bet everything in their lives was extraordinary, right down to toasting a slice of bread or taking a dump.

It occurred to me occasionally that it might be better to cut myself off from that kind of Hollywood speculation altogether. That way maybe I could drone along frying burgers and not want anything else. Narrow, but happy. Or, if not happy, at least not tortured every minute of every day by the desire to be someone I wasn't. But then, if you don't have a dream....

Three weeks passed without a word from Bella. I'd hoped she'd call long before this. Lorn was the same. I rang her apartment constantly but no one ever answered. I knew, I just knew, she was spending her time with Bella at Malibu.

One night the two of them actually turned up on TV together. Some fan show was running a clip of stars coming out of an opening and I caught them in the background. Holding hands, for fucksake. For a moment it looked like the camera was going to get interested in *28 FPS* presenter Lorn, but then someone more famous came out and the angle changed. I was taking the show in broadcast so I couldn't run it again, but even in the few seconds they were on screen it was impossible to mistake the absorption with which Bella regarded her partner.

I didn't like it. I didn't like it one bit. In fact, next evening, the image of them standing so cozily together combined with my accumulated isolation to push me out into the Mustang and down to Santa Monica.

I was lucky. The morgue was quiet and the Japanese guy was on duty. He looked anxious when he saw me, like maybe he thought I was going to make a habit of this and end up getting him busted. But I had a lot of money and his fat face smoothed out when I showed him the notes. He had some kind of food dried to a crust in the corner of his mouth, it fell off when he started speaking.

"Not good to take one out back now. You do it here. I lock the door, but you don't take too long, okay? What you want, something hairy like before? We have a selection."

He bolted the door to the outside world and pulled open drawers. I pointed to three young women. He didn't look happy when I said I wanted them all, but I threw money at him until he agreed.

On the floor. Three dead naked bodies pushed close together in a row. I stripped down, climbed onto the one in the middle and worked my way inside her. She was much colder than the one I'd done with Ryan because she was straight from the fridge. But that didn't spoil anything. All three of them were that way, a bed of cold gray flesh.

Fatso was itching to do sentry duty, but he had to earn his money first. I made him hump up the other two bodies and lay them facedown across my back. I felt the rough pubic hair of one against the crack of my ass, the tits and ribs of the other close to my shoulders. He left me to go stand by the door and I just lay there for a while, quiet and still under the pressure.

The woman I had my dick inside had broken teeth and her mouth smelt bad. I turned her head sideways and pressed my face into the base of her neck. I had my arms under hers, holding onto her shoulders. I felt protected and secure, but it was difficult to move and I had to grind rather than thrust so the others wouldn't roll off.

Toward the end, though, I couldn't help jerking about a bit more and the girl across my ass flipped over and rolled to the back of my knees. Her head hit the stone floor and made a thunking sound that was just so empty, just so...dead, that the reality of what I was doing drove home like a stake and I blew my guts into the lifeless gash beneath me.

I wanted to stay there with my dick going soft inside the meat, breathing in the scent of the bodies – clammy like the stale water that collects in the defrost section of a fridge. If someone had asked me right then how I was feeling I'd have had to say comforted. These women used to be people. They'd lived, they'd had chances, but now they couldn't do anything at all.

No threats.

Human form without danger.

But when the Japanese guy saw I wasn't pumping anymore he started hauling them off and putting them back in their trays.

Chapter 45

Lorn took a seat in a Zone-diet cafe on Olympic. I'd followed her from Burbank through late afternoon traffic and, what with freeway-generated road rage and all, I was feeling slightly fritzed. This unscheduled meeting was uncool. Totally. I knew it, but I couldn't help myself. I had to know what was going on. I had to know if there was ever going to be another chance for me.

I walked into the slick self-righteousness of the place and stood just inside the door. She looked up and saw me and her face went blank. It wasn't encouraging, it wasn't at all like the best-case scenario of happy surprise I'd hoped for. But my need was great enough to armor me against this initial knee-jerk unpleasantness.

I walked down an aisle of molded plastic and sat opposite her. She'd already ordered and a waitress swayed up as I was settling in and put a plate of correctly balanced protein and carbohydrate in front of her. Lorn waited until she was gone before she said anything.

"What do you want?"

"You didn't return my calls."

"And you expected...what?"

"You can't still be pissed off about the review slot."

"You didn't tell me about Bella. We were sleeping together and you didn't say shit."

"She told me not to."

"Mmm, such a good boy."

"Give me a break. I lost everything because of you."

"Because of me.... You lost it because you couldn't resist fucking someone famous. It could have been anyone, I just happened to be accessible. How could you think she wouldn't find out? She owns half the fucking studio."

"I don't know, it didn't seem to matter at the time."

"Don't you fucking dare pull that emotional manipulation shit with me. What do you want? She'd be pissed off if she knew I was talking to you."

"She told you not to?"

"You don't have to be Einstein."

"Sounds intimate."

"She's going to make them syndicate me next year."

When I heard this, I knew there was no point asking Lorn how long she was going to stay with Bella, and even less trying to persuade her to end the relationship so I could take my place again at Malibu. Syndication is the golden prize every presenter covets, and Lorn would hang on until doomsday for it.

She ate some of her food. When she spoke again her voice was a little softer than it had been.

"I know it must hurt, what happened to you, but it's between you and Bella. I can't do anything about it. It isn't fair to ask me."

"I didn't."

"But that's why you're here."

"I guess.... Look, Lorn, you should be careful with Bella. I know her a lot better than you and she's not what she seems. You think you're using her, but it's the other way around."

Lorn put her fork down and her face went flinty.

"How stupid do you think I am?"

"Believe me, she's going to ask for more than you'll ever want to give. She's dangerous."

"Jesus, try and maintain some dignity."

"I'm just telling you. She's involved in a lot of bad stuff. You could get hurt, and I don't mean emotionally. Take my word for it."

Lorn stared at me in disbelief then stood and slid out from behind the table.

"That's an all-time high in pathetic. Stay away from me, Jack."

She left the restaurant without looking back. After she'd gone I sat for a long time kicking myself and trying not to think about what would happen if she felt the need to share the afternoon's conversation with Bella.

Eventually the waitress drifted over and asked if I wished to nourish myself. I didn't have the energy to reply.

Chapter 46

Next day, what was bound to happen happened. An expression of Lorn's loyalties. A lawyer and a couple of large guys walked into Willow Glen while Baywatch was on and I was doing the best I could to imagine what it was like being Pamela. The lawyer showed me Bella's signature on some papers and told me I had half an hour to quit the premises. I made a token attempt at refusal but it didn't get me anywhere. She owned the place and everything in it and my property rights numbered exactly zero.

All three of them followed me around while I packed, making sure I didn't take anything that couldn't legitimately be classed as a personal gift. This amounted to some clothes, my photos, the video from Ryan, my watch and a wallet. And they went through that, too. The only plastic they let me keep was my ATM card – access to the cash in my account, but no credit beyond.

I moved in a stupor. I felt like the people you see being walked to the edge of a pit in Nazi archive footage. But even through the frozen-gut brain-fuck I felt the stab of what they saved for last.

Out front. I was about to dump my bags in the trunk of the Mustang but the lawyer shook his head and put his hand out for the key. Insult to injury. But how else would something like that have gone down? They let me call a cab, then they took my cell phone off me.

Waiting with them for the taxi was uncomfortable. The lawyer took a fresh set of papers from his briefcase and flipped through them, no doubt readying himself to dispossess someone else. The big guys just stared at me. When the cab came, one of them opened the door and the other one pushed me carefully through it.

The drive from Laurel Canyon to Hollywood was long enough for my head to start working again. But thinking didn't give me much comfort. With Rex dead and Lorn busy sucking Bella's cunt, the opportunities L.A. offered for some kind of emotional succor were limited to motel rooms and hookers. I needed a hole to crawl into, somewhere to autopsy what had happened and figure out if I could recover from it.

I had the cab trawl Sunset, along by the motels. Several blocks of two- and three-story courts, all of them so scarred with neon the place looked like some kind of accommodation Vegas. There was no way to tell one from another so I got out at the Palm Grove. Apart from the flashing outline of an oasis, the wall that fronted the street was blank – no windows, no balconies, just slab concrete up and down.

My room wasn't bad. It had twin beds, a TV and a big mirror on the wall. The bathroom was at the back and at the front by the door there was a window covered with a blind so people going by on the walkway couldn't see in. Two stories down, in the center of the court, the pool looked faded and unused. I was sure if I stayed there long enough I'd see trash accumulate under the water.

I had about ten grand left out of what I'd managed to hold onto from my snack-food ad and Bella's last monthly payment. I could survive for a while, but it wouldn't last forever.

I turned the TV on. I took a piss and unpacked my bags, then I walked up and down trying to think. Ever since the night I'd walked in on Bella and Lorn having dinner together at Malibu I'd held onto the hope that things would work out, that my relationship with Bella would eventually regenerate itself.

Now, it was significantly more than obvious that that wasn't going to happen. Getting fired from the show might have been reversible, but eviction from my house and repossession of my car, without even a phone call from her, smacked of finality.

I considered my position. Incurring more of her enmity was a daunting prospect, but what did I have to lose? She'd taken everything from me already. Public exposure and money are drugs which once tasted can never be washed from the body, and I had no intention of living without them if there was any way at all of reconnecting to a supply. It was time to get a little leverage on the situation. Time to see if what Powell had said while he was dying meant anything.

By the time I came to that decision, though, it was too late to go pick up the Prelude – getting tough would have to wait until tomorrow. Instead, I wandered around the Strip long enough to score a selection of pills and some fried chicken. A little while after that, things didn't seem so immediate.

Chapter 47

F our months in storage and the Prelude ran as smooth as ever. It didn't have the grunt of the Mustang and nobody turned to look, but it beat walking. The sledgehammer I'd bought that evening from a hardware store in Santa Monica thudded about in the trunk as I took corners.

The streets were quiet once I got through the flats of Beverly Hills and they got quieter still when I hit Peavine Canyon.

Apricot Avenue was as dead as the other times I'd been there, no people moving about, no cars on the road. I coasted slowly to the end and parked. No light in the house, but that didn't mean anything. The basement didn't have windows and if anyone was home tonight that was where they'd be.

I went carefully with the garage Roll-A-Door, levering it up an inch at a time with the long handle of my hammer until I could see through the gap that there were no cars inside. Bella might have been there, checking on her instruments, maybe even working on a donor. Without Powell or me to scout for her the possibility was slim, and I couldn't see Lorn taking over the role, but it had been something to consider nonetheless.

The absence of the 850ci meant I'd have free run of the place and I felt vindictively gleeful forcing the door up until the mechanism broke and the jointed metal rolled up the rest of the way nice and smooth.

The door into the house proper had been replaced since my last visit, it had a couple of locks on it and a thicker sheet of steel. But my hammer and I had expected something like that and we went to work confident that a little sweat would be rewarded. It was, but I felt light-headed by the end of it.

Powell had said a fridge, so at least I knew what I was looking for – kind of. There was one in the operating room, I'd seen it before and it seemed as good a place as any to start. I was planning on a quick professional search, but when I pushed through the swing doors from the pre-op area I couldn't help taking a few moments for myself. All the hard edges and the glittering steel gave me the start of a hardon.

It wasn't because I was remembering what Bella did to herself there. It was more to do with the alien starkness of the place, a place without the usual sympathies humans demand from their environments. I turned on the cluster light that hung like a great inquiring head on its swing arm. It didn't let anything hide. Under its harsh mercury limning the vinyl surface of the table shone almost silver.

The fridge was against one wall and looked like something you'd find in an undersized kitchen. The stuff in it didn't mean anything to me – just vials of drugs I didn't recognize waiting to be sucked into syringes. If Powell had been hinting at something in here, his dying breath had been wasted. But I knew his junkie condescension would have placed me somewhere close to the bottom of the brain-power league and I figured whatever it was I was searching for had to be at least halfway obvious. So I kept looking.

I checked every room in the basement, even those I was sure didn't have fridges. After a while I found a storeroom – shelves of disposables: gloves, gowns, scalpels, dressings, along with more reusable-looking equipment made from cream colored plastic and chrome steel. And, in one corner, a fridge humming away to itself. Only it wasn't your average cooling unit. It was round and orange and looked like a scaled-down version of something you'd go to the bottom of the ocean in. Pipes and warning stickers cluttered up the sides and instead of a door it had a kind of plug thing recessed into the top, about a foot across.

A long pair of heavily insulated gloves and a set of tongs hung from a hook on the wall next to it. It was pretty obvious what they were supposed to be used for, so I did.

Inside, once a cloud of vapor cleared, the first thing I saw was a stack of frozen blood in wrinkled plastic slabs. I used the tongs to lift them out one by one. They felt hard enough to shatter. Unless it was all Karen's, it didn't mean much. I couldn't see even fuck-ups like Powell and Bella draining someone. More likely it was just stock to be used in transfusions during the kidney operations.

But the fridge held one or two other things as well. At the bottom, under the last slab, I found a couple of small plastic packets with creamy liquid frozen inside. And something else, very flat and thin, wrapped in cling film. I put the blood back and closed up the fridge. I took the other things upstairs to the lounge and sat around waiting for them to thaw.

It didn't take long – I wasn't defrosting a chicken, after all. I squished the pale liquid around. It felt slimy under the plastic and it didn't take a major leap to figure it for semen. Or work out whose it was – somehow Bella had managed to stash a few spurts from her fuck sessions with Powell. I felt a thrill of elation. Finding it here removed Bella's best protection against being marked the killer – the impossibility of her spunking up into Karen's guts. Now it was obvious that all she had had to do was empty one of these little packets into the body.

Of course there might have been other explanations. Powell could have been storing the semen in the freezer himself, or it could have come from one of Bella's male donors. But I was pretty sure that wasn't the case. Powell hadn't struck me as a guy who'd had any great desire to preserve his genes for the benefit of mankind, and there was no reason at all why Bella would want to save bodily fluids from any of the losers they'd dragged in off the street.

I figured I had Bella pretty well fucked, what with the video and an explanation for the goo inside Karen. And when I unwrapped the thing in clingfilm I was certain of it – a square of skin with an Egyptian scarab tattooed onto it in black ink. The square of skin that had been missing from Karen's shoulder blade when they found her in the park. Not a thing Powell would want to hang onto, coming as it did from someone he loathed. But definitely something Bella might treasure.

I put the bags of semen and the tattoo on a coffee table in front of me and lit a cigarette. I thought about Powell. His last words had led me to this haul.

That he'd known it was in the fridge had to mean he'd known about the murder, about its incriminating specifics. And knowing these specifics he could not have avoided the conclusion that Bella had been planning to frame him for it. But the poor fuck had been so hung up on her he hadn't let on, even to save himself – until right at the end when his guts were in his lap.

Looking back on it, though, remembering the tone of his voice at the time, it occurred to me that even then he hadn't been trying to destroy his daughter, but to rob me of my self-righteousness, my self-generated certainty that he was guilty. He'd known I'd wanted it to be him, that I'd blinkered myself to anything that might have forced me to confront the possibility that Bella was a killer. And he hadn't been about to allow me the comfort of maintaining that illusion.

If Bella and Powell had been co-killers, everything was cool. Powell had deserved his death and I had something to threaten Bella with. On the other hand, if it had been Bella by herself – and, if I was truthful with myself, that was what I now believed – then the semen as evidence would still function, but Powell had died without reason. And that meant I'd helped kill an innocent man, or at least a man innocent of Karen's murder.

I forced myself to relive that night, to bring up again the image of the blood-soaked car interior, Powell's belly bursting open, the smell of his insides. I tried to feel bad about it. I tried to feel angry with myself for doing it, with Bella for manipulating me into it. But dredging up those kind of emotions right then was a nonstarter. I was too busy basking in the knowledge that before me on the coffee table I had the means to force a return to my preferred lifestyle.

Chapter 48

I connected with Bella through her machine. She hadn't returned any of the messages I'd left since she took *28 FPS* away from me, but I recorded a few lines about wanting to discuss something Ryan had told me the last time I saw him alive and she was on the line before midday.

We sat in her video suite, the obvious place. Bella had her hair tied back and was wearing a robe with nothing on underneath. As she shifted position in her chair the silky material slipped open to show her cunt. She didn't bother to cover herself and I caught the scent of fish.

I played my cassette and explained how there should have been stitches on Karen's belly. Bella spent more time watching me than the screen and the satisfied look on her face gave me a bad feeling that things weren't going to go quite as well as I'd hoped. For an absurd moment the whole purpose of the meeting seemed to have been reversed; that rather than accusing her of murder, I was there to admit my guilt at being in possession of something dangerous to her. I did my best to fight it down, but I knew my voice sounded weak.

"Ryan had it figured the night you killed him, it took me a little longer. What did you think, we weren't going to see it?"

"Oh, I thought you'd see it all right. But I was quite sure you'd be reluctant to recognize it."

"Because of your money?"

"You and Ryan were very similar. You see money as life's ultimate validation. It makes you easy to predict."

"Powell didn't kill Karen."

"No, he didn't."

"You made this tape. You knew he'd take a copy and that sooner or later we'd find it. And you knew how we'd read it."

"I knew how you'd want to read it."

"How long had you been planning it?"

"Killing Karen? I didn't really plan it at all."

"But the tape was made before you took her kidney out."

"The tape was just one I had, it wasn't part of any plan, at least not until later. I shot it in Powell's apartment to hurt him, to rub salt in the wound, so to speak. That's all. The planning only came after I realized what it could be used for. Erase my copy, make up a story about the bracelet.... Almost too easy."

"Why did you kill her?"

"Do you care?"

I didn't say anything. Bella shrugged, rewound the tape and started it playing again, this time in slow motion. She watched it as she spoke.

"Karen came back much sooner than I'd expected. We hadn't planned to meet again until a couple of weeks after she'd recovered from her operation, but she had some trouble at home. The man she was living with threw her out and she had nowhere to go. I let her stay, of course. But knowing she was accessible, that she was a woman who had no real prohibitions against selling parts of herself, was a constant temptation. The door had already been opened, you see, and I wanted to go back. After a week I offered to buy her appendix and she agreed."

"Only you didn't stop with her appendix."

"No. It's a much simpler operation to perform, so I was working without Powell. I hadn't planned to do anything other than what I'd paid for. But being there alone, with her laid out on the table so...available, it seemed cowardly to limit myself once I'd started. I took out almost everything she had."

"But why?"

"I've told you before the operations are a test, even with outcasts they require an effort of will. With Karen, when I took her kidney, I moved to another level. She wasn't anonymous. She was my lover, I felt a great deal for her. And to damage her, even surgically, required proportionally more from me. The second time the challenge was even greater."

"But you rose to it valiantly."

"We only achieve self-mastery by testing ourselves, Jack. It's the only way to become more than we are. But I don't expect you to understand."

"What about Powell, did he understand?"

Bella laughed.

"Hardly, he wanted to leave the country. He was so frightened he re-moved her kidney scar, he thought it could be used to trace us. I thought he was being ridiculous, but I suppose Ryan proved me wrong in that respect. I wouldn't have involved Powell at all, but I needed his help getting rid of the body."

"And his thanks was that you decided to frame him. To kill him."

"I couldn't allow him to have something like that to hold over me."

"He would never have told anyone."

"Perhaps not. But it changed the dynamic of our relationship. He came to feel that he could make demands of me. And that wasn't something I could tolerate. Besides, it would have been stupid not to take whatever steps I could to protect myself against the possibility of investigation."

"But he was innocent. He didn't do anything."

"Can you imagine what it feels like to wipe your father's come from be-tween your legs?"

Bella stopped the tape and turned toward me.

"If Powell means so much to you, perhaps you should think about this – he only died because Ryan came to Malibu. And Ryan only came to Malibu because you brought him here. Without you, Jack, Powell would still be alive."

"I'm not buying it. I want my life back."

"You still have your life."

"My house, the car, the show, all of it. I want it back."

"But you told Lorn I was dangerous. That was...indiscreet."

"Either make things the way they were, or this tape is going to the police."

"Oh, Jack, I really hoped you wouldn't do this. It was so much nicer when I could pretend you loved me."

"I'm serious."

"What does the tape really show? A girl masturbating. It shows I had contact with her, I suppose. But she was a prostitute and there's nothing to say I ever saw her again. It certainly won't support an accusation of murder. What's to say I didn't find it on the street even?"

"Your other tape, the one with the donors. She's on that too."

"Already erased. And you've forgotten the semen in her body. A little hard to lay that at my door, don't you think?"

I took the tattoo and one of the bags of come out of my jacket and dropped them on the console in front of her. She didn't move to touch them.

"Powell's last laugh, I presume."

"Right at the end your attraction for him lost some of its hold. I guess being set up to be killed does that to a guy."

"An event in which you played such an integral role."

"What's with the tattoo? Was she so disposable you thought you'd forget her if you didn't keep a piece of her?"

"I'm not going to forget her, Jack. We had them done together, at the same place, on the same day. It's an unusual design and there was a slim possibility it might have connected us. It had to be removed. I probably shouldn't have kept it, but I have a sentimental side."

I snorted and pointed to the packet of semen.

"Cute idea."

"Effective, at least."

"You must have been over the moon when you figured blackmail wasn't Ryan's only bag. He was ready-made. You were able to get rid of Powell without any of that nasty fuss an investigation would have involved."

"And something else as well. I got to link you to Powell's death. Funny how one thing leads to another."

"It was Ryan who forced me into helping, not you."

"Who do you think persuaded him it was so important you participate in the first place?"

"Bullshit."

"I'm not going to argue about it. The fact is, even if you can explain the semen, you won't go to the police. You're too heavily implicated yourself. Now that Ryan's not here they'd probably hold you solely responsible."

"There's nothing to prove I had anything to do with it."

"Actually there is."

Bella ejected the tape of Karen, chose another from the cupboard and ran it. The screen showed a pair of kitchen gloves covered with blood, lying on a sheet of newspaper.

"From Ryan. They have your fingerprints inside, I believe."

"I don't fucking believe this! You set me up!"

She ejected the tape and put it away.

"I bought some insurance. I hope I won't have to use it."

A high-speed about-face seemed the only possible course of action given this less than encouraging development. I put a lot of effort into it.

"Look, I wasn't really going to show that stuff to the police. I was just trying to get my life back. I mean, I can't take it, Bella. Don't you understand?"

"You shouldn't have said what you did to Lorn."

"I know. Jesus, isn't there anything I can do?"

I took the tape of Karen, put it in the machine and erased it.

"There, I was just bullshitting. I'd never have gone to the police. You know I'd never do anything like that. Don't you feel anything for me anymore?"

"This isn't about feeling, it's about safety."

"But you *are* safe. Keep the tattoo and the semen. I can't do anything without them."

"There was another packet."

"Yeah, sure, here."

I took the second wrap of semen out of my pocket and handed it to her.

"Now you've got everything. Please, Bella, I'm begging you. Will you give me the show back at least?"

Bella weighed the semen in her hand for a moment then reached out and killed the power to the video console.

"Give me your number. I'll consider it."

"Thank you!"

I passed her one of the Palm Grove's cards hoping to see her smile a little and let me know things were okay between us again. But she didn't. She just looked coolly at me and pulled her robe closed.

"I'm not promising I'll call, Jack."

Chapter 49

TV, TV, TV. It made me mad with wanting. I watched it nonstop. Days had
passed and Bella hadn't called and it was getting harder to keep a lid on the
feeling that it was never going to happen, that I was going to be left forever
in this nightmare world of cheap motels and non-identity.

Sometimes I went outside, mostly to look at the colors in the sky near
evening. I walked up and down the street in front of the motel trying to feel
connected to the city. But everything was foreign to me, as though I was lost
in some Asian city where I couldn't understand the language or recognize
even the most fundamental patterns of behavior.

I had the management hook up a VCR and I watched the jewelry shop
raiders fuck the young cleaner to death. I watched it over and over and
wanked endlessly, trying to expel my growing anxiety. I bought a second TV
set so *Melrose* and *Baywatch* and *90210* could run at the same time. But nothing
worked, and each time I shot my load over the carpet I was left in a state of
dissatisfaction that bordered on rage.

Brad Pitt and Gwyneth Paltrow, Johnny Depp and Kate Moss, Keanu
Reeves, Matthew McConaughey, Chris O'Donnell, Leonardo DiCaprio,
Drew Barrymore, Linda Hamilton, Winona, Sigourney, Woody, Pamela....
Jesus, I couldn't stand it. The collected media of the United States bombarded
me with these people. I closed my eyes and blocked my ears, but it was too
late. They were all already stuck inside my head and there was no way to ever
get them out.

I swallowed pills – Rohypnol, Valium, Lorazepam, anything to help me cope with the onslaught. But chemicals weren't enough. They slowed things down but they couldn't rid me of the feeling that I didn't exist. And eventually, as Bella still hadn't called, I was forced to go out and look for a more effective means of escape.

The evening was smogged and the sky looked like it was going to rain – dirty black clouds with bleeding bellies. A warm breeze came down off the hills smelling of eucalyptus and jasmine. I had all the windows open and the air stormed through the car. For a while the roaring it made blanketed the screaming inside my head. At red lights I turned the air conditioner on to keep up the noise.

The Drag hadn't changed in my absence. It still stank of fast food and cunt, its neon still rolled in waves of dusty color across the bare thighs and shoulders of tiredly strutting whores. I was too early for the high-density trade, but people seemed to be moving around pretty fast all the same. Maybe it was the pressure in the air, maybe they all wanted to do whatever they had to do before the rain came. I parked and went looking for Rosie, the hooker who'd let Ryan shit in her mouth.

She wasn't in her usual doorway. I checked a few of the surrounding streets without luck, then give up and went searching for a substitute back in the main flow. There were a lot of women to choose from, there always were, but I had difficulty picking one. I got close a couple of times, but there was always something that put me off. Maybe they looked too clever, maybe they looked too strong.

I told myself I should get back in the car and go home, take some pills and have a wank. But I was driven by a body hunger that wouldn't let go, a desire born at a cellular level, indefinable and uncontrollable.

I made circuit after circuit of the area. It got late and it started to rain. I walked until my legs ached and the heavy men outside the live sex shows started giving me suspicious looks. The uglier whores who'd been waiting for trade about as long as I'd been trawling began to call to me each time I passed. The night slid into a time-lapse blur of bright light and water until, around two in the morning, I passed Rosie's doorway on an off chance and she was there.

She was wearing a tight pink dress that didn't look too good on her un-toned body. But she had tits and a cunt and I knew she was fucked up enough to agree to just about anything.

In a taxi on the way to some rotting hot-sheet dump on Lexington she asked me about my diet and the size of my bowel movements. It was obvious she didn't remember me from before.

The motel had a main block and a few bungalows out back. A couple of junkers with bumper stickers that said something about guns were parked off the street in a lot strewn with weeds and empty cans. It looked like the kind of place that catered to fugitives.

At the desk I gave a fake name, paid in cash and avoided eye contact. The check-in guy stared at Rosie and licked his lips. His breath smelled of bour-bon. We got one of the bungalows. Not really secluded or quiet, but separate at least.

Inside, Rosie spread out her sheet of plastic, took off her clothes and lay on her back. Her body looked pale. She kept opening her mouth as wide as it would go then closing it again.

I took my clothes off slowly, allowing myself to recognize at last what I wanted from the night. It was kind of frightening knowing I wouldn't be able to make excuses to myself the next day. That I wouldn't be looking back on a body Ryan had supplied or one I happened across like Rex, somebody already dead. And that I wouldn't have been forced into it like I was with Powell.

Rosie started to mutter about wanting me to hurry up. I told her it would turn me on more if she was tied up. It was cool with her and I ripped up one of the sheets and bound her hands behind her back. I wanted to tie her feet to something as well, but there wasn't anything close enough.

All these arrangements felt like they were happening somewhere out-side my head. What I was more consciously occupied with was the sight of the woman on the floor – the bright fluoro light that fell so harshly against her, punching her into my retinas, making her super-real. That and a rabid impatience to put my dick inside her and feel whatever it was you felt when someone died underneath you.

I climbed on top and pushed inside her. She started complaining that the deal was she got to eat my shit first and that her hands were uncomfortable behind her back. I listened to every word she said, I looked at her as hard as I could, trying to absorb every detail of her appearance – the workings of her face, the feel of her body moving under mine, her heat. Her life.

I told her I was going to fuck first then shit, and eventually she shut up. After she'd been quiet for a while, after I'd breathed in the scent of her hair and her skin and her pussy, I put my hands around her neck.

She didn't realize what was happening at first because I'd never done it before and I wasn't sure how much pressure to use. Absurdly I had this notion that I didn't want to hurt her, that I should be trying to do it as painlessly as possible. But of course that wasn't going to get the job done, so I pressed down hard with both thumbs at the base of her throat. Maybe the middle would have been a better place, but I couldn't stand the feel of the cartilage there.

She got the idea then all right and started rolling from side to side, trying to throw me off. She couldn't scream because my hold was too tight, but she made some really quite alarming choking noises. They sounded so awful I almost stopped. But the way her hips bucked against me and the warmth of her piss as her bladder let go felt so good that I didn't.

At least not until someone started hammering on the door.

I froze, but the hammering continued and whoever was doing it started shouting.

"Hey, buddy, open up. I wanna ask you something."

The check-in guy. I let go of Rosie's throat. She'd passed out, but I jammed some sheet into her mouth just in case. Then I got off her and yelled to the guy outside, asking what he wanted.

"Let me in. I can't stand here shouting through the door, people are try- ing to sleep."

I looked at Rosie lying on the floor in her pool of piss. She wasn't too good, but she was alive. I could see her tits move as she breathed. The guy started banging again. It was obvious he wasn't going to fuck off. He sounded drunk.

I opened the door a couple of inches and peered around it. At that angle he couldn't see Rosie.

"What do you want?"

His skin was oily and he hadn't shaved in about three days. His hair was oily too, stuck down flat on his head with some kind of old-fashioned dressing. He grinned through the opening.

"Come on, buddy, you know what I want. I saw that piece you brought in here, I got eyes. That kinda thing could get you kicked out. Get you busted too, using the premises for immoral purposes."

"Fuck off."

"She's a hooker. Am I right or am I right?"

He giggled a bit at this and staggered out of my line of vision for a moment. When he lurched back he was holding up a quarter empty bottle of Jack Daniel's, waving it in front of my face.

"I thought maybe you and me and her could all have a drink together."

"I don't think so."

"Hey, don't be like that. Sitting on your ass all night gets a guy hot, you know? It won't hurt you none to share her around. I got money."

"Fuck off."

I tried to close the door but he stuck his foot in it.

"No need to be unfriendly, not when I'm offering my liquor. You shut this door, I'm just gonna to get my pass key out and open it up again."

I looked over my shoulder at Rosie. She was still out and it looked like she was going to stay that way for a while.

"Okay, you can throw one into her, but she's pretty out of it right now. She took a load of pills and shit."

"Buddy, I don't care if she's in a coma."

"Let me get some pants on."

He took his foot out of the door and I closed it. I went over to Rosie and shook her. She didn't respond but her breathing was nice and even. I took the gag out of her mouth, undid her hands, hid the ripped sheet under the bed and put my clothes on. I figured if I let the fuckwit get started I could be long gone by the time he realized anything was wrong. When I let him into the room his face lit up.

"Hey, out of it is right. What's with all the water? You trying to wake her up?"

"It's piss. She lets fly when she passes out."

"Wow, I wish I'd come around earlier. Lucky you put that plastic down, it could have fucked up the carpet. Who goes first?"

"I already fucked her."

"I'm the lucky guy, then."

He opened her legs and stuck a couple of fingers into her.

"Hey, this is great. I'm gonna get piss all over me, though."

"You don't have to fuck her."

"Are you kidding?"

He got his cock out and gave it a few strokes. I edged toward the door.

"Listen, man, I got to go out for cigarettes. I'll be back. If she wakes up don't listen to anything about money. I already paid her."

"Sure thing, buddy."

But he was too busy lifting her legs over his shoulders to pay any real attention.

I walked fast down the street until I could flag a cab. Five minutes later I got out halfway along the Drag and walked back to where I'd left the Prelude. A little while after that I was back at the Palm Grove, gulping pills and making sure the door was locked.

CHAPTER 50

The phone woke me about midday. Bella calling with an offer of resurrection.

"You can do something for me."

"Anything."

"I want your help with Lorn."

"What do you mean?"

"I haven't had a donor since Rex. I want her kidney."

"What does she say about it?"

"I haven't asked her. I know what her answer would be."

"Offer her more screen time, she'll do whatever you want."

"I'm using that to get her into bed. And money won't work, she's not desperate enough."

"So what do you want me to do?"

"Use your imagination."

"You want to do it by force?"

"Force sounds a little melodramatic."

"But that's what we're talking about, right?"

"There won't be any violence. I'll use a drug. I just need you to help me carry her."

"What's she going to say when she wakes up?"

"What can she say? It'll be too late by then."

"She'll be a bit pissed off, don't you think?"

"I'll take care of it."

"How are you going to take care of something like that? It's not like she won't notice the scar."

"I said I'll take care of it. If it's a problem, she needn't know you're involved. I'll knock her out before she sees you, and you can leave before she comes around."

"But Lorn's just a person. It's not like she's connected to Ryan or Karen or anything. Can't you use someone off the street?"

"I want her."

"What difference does it make? A kidney's a kidney, for God's sake."

"Doesn't she remind you of someone?"

"Who?"

"Karen. She looks like Karen, Jack. Same body, same hair, just a little less rough. I can't believe you've never noticed."

"No, I never noticed. And I don't like the idea of you trying to relive what you did to Karen."

"Jack, I only want her kidney, I'm not going to kill her. Helping me could be extremely advantageous to you."

"How advantageous?"

"Your house and car, and I'm sure Howard could be persuaded to find something for you on one of his shows."

"And if that's not enough?"

"I'm giving you a chance to get back what you lost. It's more than you deserve. Of course, if you're going to be difficult I could always take another approach, one you might find a lot less pleasant."

"The gloves."

"If you force me to. An evening's work, Jack. It isn't much of a sacrifice to avoid a murder charge."

She was silent for a moment, I listened to the faint hiss of static on the line. Then Bella's voice came again, confident and sexy.

"You aren't going to be difficult, are you, Jack?"

After Bella hung up I sat on the edge of the bed and thought about Lorn. She wasn't the love of my life, but helping her get mutilated was still something

I found difficult to come to terms with. At one point I called the studio and managed to get through to her. But when she came on the line I didn't say anything. I just held onto the phone and listened to her say hello a few times and ask who it was, wanting to warn her, wanting to tell her what Bella was planning, but unable to do it. I just couldn't find it in me to throw away my ticket back to the world.

Luckily, I didn't have to suffer my conscience too long.

CHAPTER 51

Bella reeled in her fish the very next day. She wanted me to meet her at Apricot Lane, early evening. Lorn would be with her.

I showered and changed my clothes, then sat staring out of the window at a square of wall and a door exactly like mine on the other side of the pool, figuring on not doing much else until it was time to head into the hills. I hadn't eaten anything all day except a couple of donuts and I felt hollow and thin. But I guessed that was the right way to feel, considering what I was about to have a hand in.

I was two cigarettes into a pack when my Century City agent rang and told me to get over to his office immediately. He wouldn't say anymore on the phone and I pretty much floored it all the way.

When I got out of the elevator all the staff were lined up to greet me. The agent himself fountained a bottle of champagne in my face and put an arm around my shoulders. Everyone started clapping. I'd scored the men's grooming gig. Locked in and irrevocable. I was going to be the guy on TV and billboards and magazine pages all across the country. High, high profile. Exposure to three hundred million people. They might not know my name for a while, but walking down the street would certainly be a different experience soon.

The gig would wipe out my entire previous existence. It would put what I had with *28 FPS* in the shade. I had a two-year contract to be the face of a product. I was an L.A. success story. I was what other people dreamed about.

I hung around for a while, signing papers and going through a schedule of upcoming photo and video shoots, soaking up the attention from these people who suddenly loved me. Then I got back in the car and drove into the hills.

I didn't need Bella for wealth or visibility anymore. The grooming campaign was going to put my face in front of more people than most TV stars, and the money from it would set me up for life. At a stroke, she'd become obsolete.

But that didn't mean I could avoid the evening's entertainment up at Apricot lane. Bella would find out about my windfall sooner or later and if I messed up her kidney fix she'd strike back for sure. Maybe she'd use some kind of financial leverage on the ad company, or maybe she'd go straight for the throat and send the gloves from Powell's murder to the police. Either way the result would be the same – I'd lose everything.

Santa Monica Boulevard, Beverly Drive, San Ysidro Drive – streets through a town I belonged to at last. The houses and cars I passed on the way were no longer the impossible possessions of people better than me, but things that would be mine as a matter of course.

I estimated prices, I planned purchases. I thought realistically for the first time about position, setting, design, about the convenience of a flatland property versus the seclusion of higher up. I considered whether I should go for a Mustang again or whether I should try a Corvette, maybe something European. It was a hard decision to make.

The sky was shaded at the edges by the time I drove through the open gates of the clinic and into the garage. Bella's 850ci was already there. She climbed out of it impatiently like I'd kept her waiting and opened the passenger door. Lorn sprawled unconscious across the leather upholstery. The only thing keeping her off the floor was her seat belt.

She looked pale and vulnerable and for a second I wondered if it was really me who was about to participate in this visceral rape, or whether some other desperate, driving, fame-obsessed soul had taken possession of me.

Then I got her under the arms and dragged her downstairs. It took a while because she had a tendency to flop about.

Bright light, sharp instruments on a tray. Lorn lay naked and uncovered on the table, a needle in the crook of her right arm fed anesthetic into her system from a drip-bag on a frame. Her face was so white it was hard to tell where her bleached hair started.

Bella was naked too under her gown. The opening at the back was only loosely tied and I could see the crack of her ass and sometimes a rear shot of her cunt as she bent over Lorn making her final preparations. She wore rubber gloves and a cap, but no mask.

"Things will be different after tonight, Jack."

"She won't like you so much, that's for sure."

"I never intended it to be long term."

"Just as a punishment to me."

"I wanted to set some boundaries."

"And now that I know them, what? You want me back?"

"Isn't that what you want?"

I shuffled about and avoided the question.

"Do you want me to turn her on her side?"

"No, I'm going to enter through the abdomen."

"Why?"

"Pass me a scalpel."

Bella was locked in. She didn't look at me. Her attention was focused on the smooth white belly in front of her. She ran her hands over Lorn's breasts, then on down to the outside of her hips, as though trying to commit the body on the table to some tactile portion of memory. I gave her the sharpest looking thing I could find on the tray of instruments, then moved to stand behind and a little to one side of her.

The scalpel blade caught light from the overhead cluster. I felt myself holding my breath. Bella leaned forward and kissed Lorn for a long time. She stroked the side of her face and it looked like she was whispering something. Then she straightened and stood absolutely still, and for a moment it was as though everything in the world was copying her. Even the air in the room seemed to stop moving.

But things didn't stay that way. Bella reached out with her scalpel. And even while her hand was moving through the air it was obvious to me that something was wrong. She was going for a point immediately below Lorn's sternum, a point that looked way too high up the body to be anywhere near the kidneys.

I took a step forward then hesitated. I mean, I wasn't a doctor and this could easily have been a bona fide technique. But then Bella made her incision. She held the scalpel like a pencil and drew it firmly down in a straight line to the top of Lorn's pubic hair – it was too much of a cut, and far too similar to what Karen had ended up with in the park.

I jerked her away from the table and spun her around.

"What the fuck are you doing?"

Bella's hand flicked out and the scalpel sliced the air in front of my face.

"Back off. You had your fun with her, now I'm having mine."

"You said just her kidney."

"I changed my mind. Wait upstairs if you don't want to watch."

Bella looked disgusted and turned back to the table. Blood ran from Lorn's wound, out over both sides of her stomach in bright red sheets. Her cunt hair was soaked with it and small rills were already spilling from the table and spattering against the floor. The cut was deep but her abdomen held together, Bella wasn't all the way through yet. She got ready for another stroke. I grabbed for her arm but she was fast and managed to bring her blade across the back of my hand before I could get a decent grip. It hurt like fuck and I jumped back expecting her to try for more damage. But she didn't come after me, she just stood there like an animal defending a carcass, her face stretched and ugly.

"Don't be stupid, Jack. You've got a lot to lose."

She stared hard at me, then, like she figured the gash on my hand had sufficiently impressed upon me the idea that I shouldn't interfere, she prepared to start work again. But all I was impressed with was the obvious fact that nothing short of force was going to stop her opening Lorn up all the way and scooping out her guts.

So, walk away and let her get on with her killing? Or do a little of my own? It wasn't a difficult choice to make. Any affection I'd felt for Bella had been choked out of existence the night Ryan and I killed Powell. And now, with my new ad contract, there was absolutely no reason to stay linked to her. On the other hand, I still kind of liked Lorn.

And there were two other reasons that made removing Bella an attractive proposition. One, it would get rid of that nagging glove problem – the only physical evidence connecting me to Powell's murder. And two, I could fuck her while I was doing it.

This last was the clincher and before she started cutting again I moved up close and hit her full force on the side of the head. She went down hard and slumped around one of the legs of the operating table, unconscious. I moved quickly about the room collecting a few things and stripping off my clothes. I took Bella's gown off too and tied her hands in front of her with a roll of bandage. Then I flipped her onto her stomach and waited for her to come around. She didn't take much more than a minute, which was good because I was worried about leaving Lorn too long without attention.

Bella made a few painful sounds before she opened her eyes, after that her noises got angry and I figured it was time to start. She was still groggy so it wasn't much trouble to pull her ass up, get her knees under her and slide my cock in from behind. I wrapped a length of yellow-brown surgical tubing around her neck while she was like that, then just stayed that way – my cock hard as a pipe inside her, the tubing in place but not tight enough to do anything. Until she got a little more active and tried to speak. Then I went to work.

I held the tubing like the reins of a horse and cut off her air. It surprised me how deep the rubber squeezed into her neck, it looked almost like a cartoon. She tried to move forward and started shaking her head. Her movements were jerky. I pulled back harder and pumped my dick into her.

She'd been silent since I tightened up, but now she started to make grunty choking noises which I figured were some kind of breathing reflex. Her cunt went a bit loose too, which I hadn't expected, and she lifted her tied hands off the floor to claw at her neck. I loosened my grip suddenly so she overbalanced and fell face-first against the floor. There was blood on the vinyl when I hauled her up again.

I felt the tension in her body, the locked muscles, the bones which seemed suddenly to protrude where before they had been so smoothly padded. She tried repeatedly to get her fingers under the tubing and pull it away from her neck, but her weight made it difficult and she went through this weird cycle of snatching her hands up to her throat then jamming them back down again before gravity could kick in and do its thing with her face and the floor.

It was hard to keep my eyes open. I wanted to close them and absorb the raft of sensation pouring from the woman beneath me – the straining of her back, the taste of sweat between her shoulder blades, the smell of the gas she farted out as she struggled to free herself. Her cunt vibrated loosely around my cock, like whatever usually held it tight and in place had already given up and let go. I felt a withdrawal of the life inside her, as though some emergency survival instinct was sucking it toward the center of her body, away from the edges, trying to save it.

She pissed against me. It felt hot and thick and it made my head swim because it meant I was actually doing it – I actually had my dick inside a body that was racing toward death. Sometimes when she moved around I could see her face. It wasn't a good color. Her tongue was so swollen it looked like the front half of a shoe.

She lurched around more and more desperately, kicking her legs out and trying to get to her feet. After one particularly violent effort she sagged for a moment and started to pump shit. It blasted out of her ass in a liquid brown fountain that went on so long I had to pull my cock out and watch. My stomach dripped with it, it made a pool around our knees.

And because I didn't have my weight against her anymore she was able to get her feet under her and jerk upright. The movement took me by surprise and I lost my hold on the tubing. For a second I thought I was in trouble, but then she slipped on the shit and fell heavily on her elbow. Something snapped, but she didn't scream. She was too busy trying to suck air past her tongue.

I jumped on her and we rolled around until I trapped her arms between our two bodies and got her on her back. It was awkward pushing inside her this way because I was using my hands to strangle her now and I had to keep tight against her so she couldn't free her arms. But with one of them broken and her being pretty badly fucked up already, she couldn't fight hard enough to stop me.

Face to face made everything so much more immediate. I wanted our mouths to be together so I could share her last breaths, taste her spit, be as intimately involved in her experience of dying as possible. Her tongue made it difficult, though, and she kept moving her head around. The best I could do was put my forehead against hers and catch what smell of her I could over the shit.

She made weak humping motions with her hips, trying to throw me off, but her strength was gone. I fucked her as hard as I could, expecting a gradual relaxing of her body as the life drained from it. But when it happened, it happened quickly, like a switch had been thrown, and the change was exquisite. I felt it around my cock, through my belly and arms, a profound stillness that was suddenly there, reaching out to me with a promise of endless tranquility.

I took my hands off her neck and looked closely at her open eyes, at the way her tits shuddered with each of my thrusts. And when some of the air trapped in her lungs worked its way out of her nose and made a hissing noise like a blow-up toy deflating I started to spurt. It went on forever and after it was over, after I'd pumped myself so dry it felt like I'd never be able to come again, I lay on top of her, listening to the thudding in my chest and the silence in hers.

A little later I checked on Lorn. Her breathing was very shallow and the amount of blood on the floor around the table was frightening. I thought about unhooking her from the anesthetic, but with a wound like that on her guts, getting conscious again without major pain relief might have been even more dangerous than the buildup of sedative in her system. So I left her as she was, there wasn't anything else I could do. I left Bella as she was, too.

On the way back to the Palm Grove I called the paramedics from a pay phone.

Epilogue

So, who says you can't have everything?

The men's grooming gig went as planned, a juggernaut of publicity for shaving gel, shampoo, deodorant and soap rolling across America with my face on the front. It made me a lot of money and it made me a celebrity. Not movie star level, not quite yet, but I'm starting to get offers.

I bought a bigger house than the one I had on Willow Glen and I got a faster car than the Mustang. Evenings I go out to places where household names pass the time between films. On weekends I go to their houses for dinner. When I have a shoot I travel by limo and if it's out of town I stay five-star. I can go to any state in the country and get recognized, interviewed and laid. My agent tells me in a couple of years I'll be the new Brad Pitt.

The paramedics got to Lorn, but they weren't quick enough. She was dead before they could load her into the ambulance – a combination of blood loss and respiratory failure brought on by the anesthetic. If she'd made it through I guess I would have tried to start up a proper relationship, and I have to say I felt pretty bad about what happened to her for a long time.

But it all worked out in the end. On a shoot in Marina del Ray I connected with a Hawaiian Tropic girl. We live together now. She's the perfect partner for me – a blond Californian with good tits who shows up on TV and in magazines. We're close, we have similar goals and interests, and if it isn't exactly love, who gives a shit? We only have to step outside for that.

The police never decided exactly what happened to Bella. They couldn't figure if the same guy who killed her cut Lorn open as well, or if Bella did it herself for some reason before she got offed. Even the function and ownership of the Apricot Lane clinic couldn't be satisfactorily determined because the paper trail on it dead-ended with a sugar company in Mauritius that went out of business six years ago.

I guess, after all, I got some kind of revenge for Karen. But even back when she died it wasn't something that really mattered, and I care even less now. In fact I find it pretty difficult to care much about anything that happened before Bella checked out. There was Rex I suppose, a guy whose death I indirectly caused. And Powell, a semi-innocent man I helped murder. But Rex would have died eventually anyhow, and Powell wasn't someone I could dredge up much emotion for.

The only person from that time I even halfway miss is Ryan. I'm not about to wish he was alive again, but at least he lives in my memory as someone of significance. He tried to frame me, he beat me up and he fucked things between me and Bella, but he also forced me to recognize things about myself.

Some people might say those kind of things shouldn't be recognized. I don't know, maybe they shouldn't. But I figure if they're in there, ignoring them won't change the person you are. And, shit, I'm a pretty normal guy, I'm not that different from a lot of people. Maybe only a few men ever actually get to fuck someone who's dead, but I bet a whole lot of others think about it.

And Bella? She's already started to fade. I guess she did a lot for me before she turned nasty, and I know I should remember the good times. But I can't. All I remember about her is the sight of shit pouring out of her ass, and the way she went still around my cock.

The End.

About the Author

Matthew Stokoe is a novelist whose work has been translated into French, Spanish, Russian and German. In 2014 his third novel, *Empty Mile*, was nominated for the *Grand Prix de Littérature Policière* – France's most prestigious award for crime and mystery writing. He lives with his wife in Sydney, Australia. His books are available through Amazon.com.

Made in the USA
Las Vegas, NV
22 February 2024